MW01126917

The Wrong Kind of LOVE

The Wrong Kind of LOVE

New York Times Bestselling Author

LEXI RYAN

The Wrong Kind of Love © 2018 by Lexi Ryan

All rights reserved. This copy is intended for the original purchaser of this book. No part of this book may be reproduced, scanned, or distributed in any printed or electronic form without prior written permission from the author except by reviewers, who may quote brief excerpts in connection with a review. Please do not participate in or encourage piracy of copyrighted materials in violation of the author's rights. Purchase only authorized editions.

This book is a work of fiction. Any resemblance to institutions or persons, living or dead, is used fictitiously or purely coincidental.

Cover and cover image © 2018 by Sara Eirew

Interior designed and formatted by

emtippettsbookdesigns.com

Other Books by
LEXI RYAN

The Boys of Jackson Harbor

The Wrong Kind of Love (Ethan's story)

Straight Up Love (Jake's story – coming May 2018)

Dirty, Reckless Love (Levi's story – coming August 2018)

The Blackhawk Boys

Spinning Out (Arrow's story)

Rushing In (Chris's story)

Going Under (Sebastian's story)

Falling Hard (Keegan's story)

In Too Deep (Mason's story)

LOVE UNBOUND: Four series, one small town, lots of happy endings

Splintered Hearts (A Love Unbound Series)

Unbreak Me (Maggie's story)

Stolen Wishes: A Wish I May Prequel Novella (Will and Cally's prequel)

Wish I May (Will and Cally's novel)

Or read them together in the omnibus edition, *Splintered Hearts: The New Hope Trilogy*

Here and Now (A Love Unbound Series)

Lost in Me (Hanna's story begins)

Fall to You (Hanna's story continues)

All for This (Hanna's story concludes)

Or read them together in the omnibus edition, *Here and Now: The Complete Series*

Reckless and Real (A Love Unbound Series)

Something Wild (Liz and Sam's story begins)

Something Reckless (Liz and Sam's story continues)

Something Real (Liz and Sam's story concludes)

Or read them together in the omnibus edition, *Reckless and Real: The Complete Series*

Mended Hearts (A Love Unbound Series)

Playing with Fire (Nix's story)

Holding Her Close (Janelle and Cade's story)

Other Works by
LEXI RYAN

Hot Contemporary Romance

Text Appeal

Accidental Sex Goddess

Decadence Creek Stories and Novellas

Just One Night

Just the Way You Are

ABOUT
The Wrong Kind of LOVE

From *New York Times* bestseller Lexi Ryan comes a sexy new standalone romance novel about a runaway bride, a single dad who's sworn off love, and the kind of family secrets that can threaten to break even the deepest bonds.

You never forget your wedding day. Or the moment your twin sister pukes on your bouquet and confesses she's pregnant . . . with your fiancé's baby.

I wanted to get away, to hide until my heart mended. I found myself in a strange town with a mysterious stranger whose talented mouth and hands almost made me forget it was supposed to be my wedding night.

Afraid to go home to face my broken life, I pretend to be my twin so I can take her job in Jackson Harbor caring for a six-year-old girl. Imagine my surprise when I find out my new boss is my mysterious stranger—Dr. Ethan Jackson.

I never meant for Ethan to discover my secrets. I never meant for them to matter. But the longer I work with him and his sweet daughter, the harder I fall, and the clearer it becomes that I'm not the only one carrying a secret that could tear us apart.

Get ready to fall for the boys of Jackson Harbor in Lexi Ryan's sexy new contemporary romance series. These books can all be read as standalones, but you'll enjoy reading them as a series!

The Wrong Kind of Love (Ethan's story)
Straight Up Love (Jake's story)
Dirty, Reckless Love (Levi's story)
Wrapped in Love (Brayden's story)

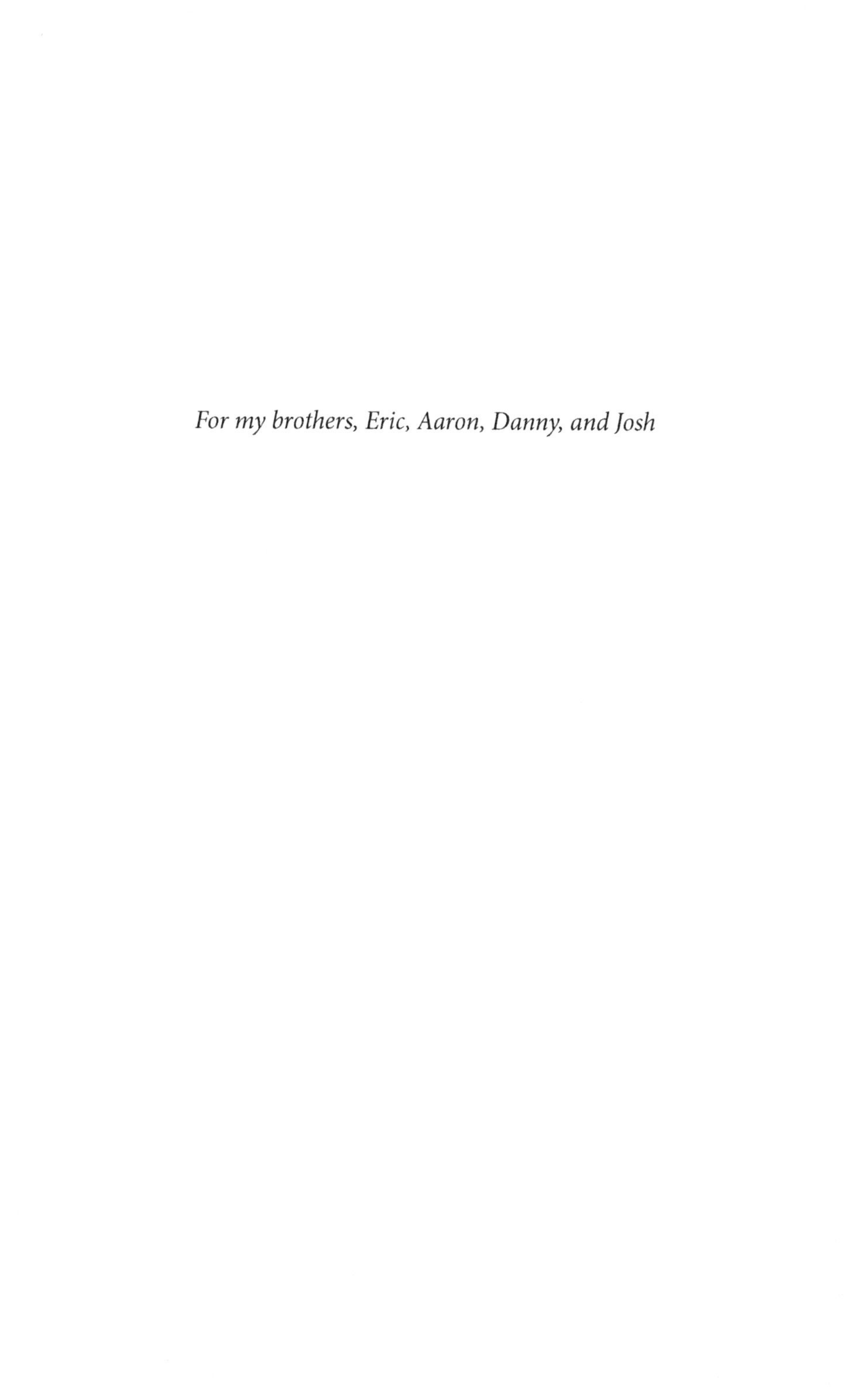

For my brothers, Eric, Aaron, Danny, and Josh

Chapter ONE

NICOLE

I've never been a runner—not marathons or 5Ks or those "fun runs" the kids at the preschool like to do. I don't even have lofty goals of becoming a runner someday. Yet last night I dreamed of running longer, farther, and faster than I ever have before. Last night, I dreamed of running so hard my lungs burned. Today's my wedding day.

A coincidence, I'm sure.

My future brother-in-law croons at the head of the aisle, his fingers dancing over the strings of his acoustic guitar, and my husband-to-be bobs his head to the beat. My groom, who's maybe, most likely, not cheating on me. My groom, who wouldn't do that to me. Probably.

I gulp in air, but it's thick with humidity and too many people. The wedding coordinator set up this tent at the far end of my outdoor ceremony so no one would see me before my big moment. At the time, it seemed like a great idea. Right now, it feels like a torture chamber.

"Are you up for one last swap?" I ask my twin sister in a whisper.

Veronica's eyes go wide. She looks gorgeous in the cranberry lace maid-of-honor gown, her long hair piled into a cascade of curls at the back of her head. "A swap? Are you serious?"

"No. Of course not." *Kind of.*

We spent the entirety of seventh grade pretending to be each other just to see if we could, and we pulled it off. Why not for my wedding ceremony? Why not for . . . forever?

Okay, *now* I'm being melodramatic. But it's my wedding day, and I'm supposed to be memorizing every detail, savoring every moment. Instead, I'm obsessing over two sentences I heard Marcus whisper into his phone yesterday morning. I stopped by to surprise him with my famous bacon cinnamon rolls—because everything's better with bacon. His kitchen window was open, so I could see him holding his phone to his ear and could *almost* hear him. "Just one more time, baby. Please? I can't stop thinking about you."

At least, I think that's what he said. But maybe it was "Just one more time, maybe Jesus. I can't stop thinking that's how too." Sure, the second option doesn't make any sense, but neither does what I think I heard. He's about to marry me. Why would he be telling some woman he can't stop thinking about her? And what would he be asking her to do *one more time*?

All questions you should have asked before you were ready to walk down the aisle, you big coward.

"You shouldn't joke about that," my twin says, disapproval twisting her lips. "You're really lucky to marry Marcus. He's . . . amazing."

"I know that." I force a smile. Because I do know that. Assuming he's not screwing around on me. But I've spent the last twenty-four hours listening to women tell me how lucky I am to marry this man, as if I won the lottery or something. Are people telling him how lucky he is to marry *me*? Probably not. They're probably warning him away. *"This is your last chance to run, Marcus. You can do better than some foster kid nobody wanted."*

I suppose from the outside looking in, Marcus is brave for marrying me, and I'm lucky to marry him. Unless he's a backstabbing, no-good, lying, cheating asshole.

"I didn't mean I wanted *you* to marry him," I tell Veronica, and my voice is doing that nasal thing that happens when I get defensive. "Just that I don't want everyone staring at me."

Veronica presses her lips together in a thin line. I wish we had that twin telepathy everyone always talks about in books and movies. I want to know what she's thinking. I wish we were close like we used to be so I could tell her about what I heard—or thought I heard—and get her feedback. I guess I could have run it by a friend, but there are the friends you laugh with and then there are the friends you cry with. I've always struggled to open up enough to make the second kind.

It's stuffy and crowded in here. Maybe there *isn't* enough oxygen for all of us. I have seven bridesmaids—Veronica and all of Marcus's female cousins, ages thirteen to twenty-eight—because every respectable Southern girl knows the bigger your bridal party, the happier the marriage.

I stick my hand between the flaps of the tent I've been peeking through and gulp in the fresh air.

Marcus's mother, Martha, tugs my arm, pulling me away from the fresh air and my view of my maybe-cheating groom. "Someone's going to see you!"

"It's just so hot in here." The lace on my wedding gown is itchy, and it feels like there are four thousand people sitting out there—though I know it's only one hundred and ten. Martha was really embarrassed about that. *"When my niece Kristen got married, she had one hundred and ninety people. Now I'm going to have to listen to my sister gloat."*

"This is the happiest day of your life," Martha says. Her cool hand cups my bare shoulder. "Don't ruin it by having one of your freak-out moments."

I force a smile. Martha isn't just another woman who thinks I'm lucky to be marrying Marcus—she's the founding member of the club. If I want any hope of a decent relationship with my mother-in-law, I need to stop acting like I'm terrified of what's about to happen. "I'm fine." *I'm lying.*

Everything is just as we planned it. I wanted an autumn wedding so I could say my vows against the backdrop of technicolor leaves. I wanted an outdoor ceremony and reception, so I chose a date after the Alabama summer humidity was supposed to have spared us for the season, but before the leaves fell and left the trees looking barren.

Choosing to hold the ceremony and reception outside was a gamble, and I've spent the last month and a half with nightmares about rain and thunderstorms. But today, we have soft blue skies and white clouds so fluffy they look like you could take a bite and they'd melt on your tongue like cotton candy. And instead of nightmares about thunderstorms, I had dreams about running.

I've been blaming my nerves on worries about wedding logistics—the weather, the caterer, the flowers. But now that it's here and everything's in order, I can't blame this hitch in my belly on anything but the words Marcus may or may not have whispered into the phone.

Why didn't I tell him what I heard? Why didn't I demand an explanation?

"You okay?" Martha asks. "You look a little green around the gills."

I loosen my grip on my bouquet. I'm going to crush the stems if I hold them any tighter. "I'm fine, Martha." Too late, I realize she's talking to Veronica, not me. And she's right. My sister looks ill. Come to think of it, she wasn't feeling well earlier this week either. I've been so preoccupied with my own anxieties that I didn't consider she might be coming down with something.

"Must've eaten some bad catfish last night," Veronica says.

I frown as I study her face. It's like staring in the mirror. She has the same light brown hair, pert nose, and heart-shaped face. But today she's pale under the blush Marcus's cousin Raina applied. "Did you go out drinking with the boys?"

Marcus and his cousins hit the bars last night, and I know they invited the bridesmaids who are of legal age—and those close enough to pass. I didn't get any such invitation, though, being Marcus's "good girl" and all that. Who else did Marcus spend last night with?

"I can't stop thinking about you."

The pinch in my stomach grows tighter.

Everyone says, *Trust your intuition*, but I think maybe I was born without one of those. There's no other explanation for my romantic history.

"I stayed in," Veronica said.

"If she'd been drinking with us, she would have puked up the catfish by now," Kate, the oldest cousin, says. "Jesus protects those who protect themselves." She pops a couple of Tylenol into her mouth and takes a big slug from her water bottle. "Does anyone know how many shots of tequila I took?"

Martha tsks.

Marcus's brother ends his song, and his aunt begins to play "Canon in D," which everyone told me was quintessential wedding music. For some reason, it's always made me think of funerals, but I agreed to include it in the processional because I didn't want Marcus's family to think I was a diva.

"Ready or not," Kate says, smirking at me.

"Course she's ready," Martha says. "She's marrying my Marcus. Half the girls in town would cut out their own eyes for this chance."

That's a disturbing image. The pinch in my stomach has morphed into a gnawing ache. Maybe I'm not nervous at all. Veronica's sick. Maybe I'm coming down with whatever she has.

The girls pull mirrors from their purses and reapply their lipstick.

I thought my wedding day would be different. I thought I'd be more excited than scared. Maybe we should've waited. Maybe what Veronica said is true, and eight months isn't enough to go from dating to married.

But Marcus said, "When you know, you know," and I've been

dreaming of this day since I was five. More, I've been dreaming of what comes after—making a home, making a family—and I've never been good at waiting for what I want.

"Are you sure you're okay?" Martha asks my sister.

"I'm fine," Veronica says. She doesn't sound fine.

"It's probably nerves about that new job," Kate says. "Who moves to a new state the day of her sister's wedding?"

"Today?" I stare at my sister, who's studying the ground as if she's seriously contemplating lying down. "You're leaving right after the reception?" I knew Veronica took a job in Michigan, but I assumed she'd be leaving sometime next week.

She lifts her eyes to meet mine and shakes her head. "I'll have to leave the reception early to catch my flight."

I stare at her. "It's my wedding day," I whisper helplessly. How could she have plans to leave in the middle of everything and not even tell me?

"Why aren't you driving if you're moving there?" Kate asks. "Don't you need your car?"

Raina snorts. "You think that pile of junk would make it to Michigan? Anyway, they're giving her a car at that fancy new job."

I scowl at my bridesmaids. I don't care how she's getting there. I care that she's leaving in the middle of my wedding day.

"I'm sorry." Veronica covers her mouth, closes her eyes, and lets out a long, slow stream of air.

"She's already anxious, Nicole," Martha says. She always did like my twin more than me—her and everyone else. "Don't make her feel worse."

"Do you need to lie down?" I ask Veronica. We might not have that psychic twin link, but I'm not some bridezilla who's going to make a sick girl walk down the aisle. Even if said sick girl is my twin and should be by my side on the most important day of my life.

Martha pulls a handkerchief from her purse, pours water onto it, and blots the back of Veronica's neck. "You'll feel better once we get out there. Just need fresh air, is all."

Veronica steps away from Martha's blotting. "I'm fine. It's fine." She looks at me. "I'm so sorry."

I shake my head. "It's not your fault."

The music changes.

"That's my cue," Martha says. She kisses me on the cheek. "You look beautiful."

"Thanks," I say. But I don't feel beautiful. I feel like every doubt and insecurity is written on my face. Like I'm going to walk down the aisle and everyone's going to see Marcus's *"I can't stop thinking about you"* scrolling across my forehead like a teleprompter.

His mother slips through the front of the tent and starts her graceful trek down the aisle to take her seat in the front row. The bridesmaids follow, one by one, and I peek through the flaps and spot Marcus at the altar, handsome as ever. He's tall and slim, with rough hands and a secret romantic side. His best friend whispers something to him, and his dimple makes an appearance as his chest shakes with a repressed chuckle. His brown eyes crinkle in the corners. Sweet Lord, he's gorgeous.

And maybe a cheater. Possibly. Probably.

The flower girls take their turn down the aisle to a chorus of "aww," and then it's my turn, and Marcus's father, Dean, appears to escort me down the aisle. I take his arm and meet Marcus's eyes. His chest rises and falls, and he shakes his head in awe.

Now I feel beautiful.

Was I really worried? Did I really believe that Marcus, *my Marcus,* could do something so terrible?

I pull my shoulders back and smile at him—my strong, capable fiancé, my soon-to-be-husband, the father of my future children. The anxiety in my gut fizzles away. Later, I'll tell him what I thought I heard, and we'll laugh together over how my shit luck with men has made me think the worst.

Everything is going to be fine.

Dean squeezes my arm when we reach the end of the aisle.

"Who gives this woman to this man?" Pastor Rickman asks.

"In honor of her mother, I do," Dean says, and my eyes well with tears, but I don't know if it's because of the reminder that my mom isn't here or because I'm so grateful for Marcus's family, and I'm literally minutes away from being one of them.

"Thank you," the pastor says.

Dean takes his seat, and I turn to Veronica and hand off my bouquet, just like we practiced.

Veronica looks at me, her eyes pleading and desperate. She grimaces, and in the next breath, she vomits all over my flowers and down the front of her dress.

The flower girls screech.

"Ew!"

"Disgusting!"

"Oh my God," Veronica says, staring at the watery flowers. "I'm sorry."

"That's some mighty bad catfish," Kate says.

"Is that what they're calling it these days?" Raina says, too loud. "That girl is knocked up."

The guests gasp, and I step back. Away from the smell of stomach acid. Away from my sister with the worry and helpless grief all over her face.

Knocked up? Have we drifted so far apart that she wouldn't even tell me something that important?

"V?"

She nods in answer to my unspoken question.

This is good news, right? A baby is always good news.

So why do I feel like the earth is falling away beneath my feet?

"I'm sorry," Veronica repeats, still looking at me. "I'm so sorry."

"Veronica?" Marcus pales. My gaze ping-pongs between him and my sister. His eyes are fixed on my twin and hers on him as she slowly nods again. "Why didn't you tell me?"

Chapter TWO

NICOLE

"You have to listen to me!" Veronica sobs.

I climb out of the car and slam the door behind me before running up the stairs and into my apartment.

I walked so slowly up that aisle, but even with all my doubts, I never imagined how fast I could run back down it.

I grabbed Veronica's purse from the tent because she's the one who drove me here. I climbed into her car and started for home. She chased after me and jumped into the passenger seat of the moving car. I should have shoved her right back out the door, but I had to think of my unborn niece or nephew.

Marcus's baby.

The drive between the park and my apartment is less than five minutes, but it felt more like an hour, and as we sat next to each other in silence, I felt like my whole life was washing away under my feet.

"Nicole!" She chases up the stairs after me, and I think about slamming the door shut, but I'm too busy trying to unzip this damn dress. I just want out of this lace. It itches, and I can't breathe.

How long have I known and not let myself know? How long have I suspected and not let myself suspect?

Every time he left the room for a phone call. Every time he pulled away from my touch. Every time he insisted that our wedding night would be better if we waited.

But with my sister? No, even with all my shit luck in love, even with all my insecurities and anxieties, *that* I couldn't have imagined.

"I can't get the stupid zipper!" I spin in a circle as if the momentum might give my hand a better grip on its target.

"Will you please quit flailing around like a crazy woman and listen to me?"

"Unzip my dress!" Maybe it's a ridiculous request. Maybe I shouldn't speak to her at all. But she unzips my dress, and when it falls from my shoulders, it's the sweetest kind of relief.

"I didn't mean for it to happen," she says, her voice cracking. "It was an accident."

"An accident?" My words are slower now. Calmer. I'm too tired for this fight—or maybe I just know this is one I can't win. "Do you expect me to believe that?"

"You know what I mean."

"Actually, I don't. I don't understand how you *accidentally* sleep with your sister's fiancé."

"He hasn't always been your fiancé."

What's that supposed to mean? Marcus and I have been engaged for six months. We'd been dating for two when he proposed. We wanted to be married by now, but the pastor insisted we have at least a six-month engagement, given how short our courtship was. I look at my sister's still-flat stomach before meeting her eyes again. "How long have you been sleeping with Marcus?"

She puts her hand over her mouth. "I'm gonna be sick again."

I laugh, but the sound comes out crazed. "*I* haven't even slept with him. Is that why you encouraged me to wait? So you'd have him in your bed longer?" I step out of the dress that's pooled around my feet, sweep it off the floor, and throw it at her, but it's so heavy that it barely brushes her chest before slinking back to the floor. "Take it!" I scream. *Oh, look. My crazy's back.* "It's yours. He's yours. You want my life? You think it's so perfect? Take it!" It's like I'm out of myself, watching this crazy woman in my body lose her mind.

"I didn't mean to," Veronica says. "I'm in love with him!"

"You think I'm not?"

"I know." She sobs. "I know." She shakes her head. "That's why I got the job in Michigan. That's why I'm leaving. I never meant to ruin your marriage."

"Well, it's too late for that." *She's having his baby.* I *was supposed to have his baby.*

"I'll go." Her face is wet with tears, and I vaguely wonder what's wrong with me that she's the one who's crying and I can't feel . . . *anything.* "I'll get out of your life. You'll never have to see me again. Just let me fix this. Let me leave. It's the best and only solution."

"Don't." My moment of crazy has slipped away. I sound so calm. Now that my dress isn't trying to eat me, I *feel* calm. "Leaving won't fix this."

She puts a hand on her stomach. "Then tell me what will."

"Veronica!" Marcus roars from the front door. "Veronica!"

I close my eyes. If any part of me believed we could salvage this, the fact that he came here looking for her and not me has killed it. "Nothing. You can't make something like this better." *She's having his baby.*

I peel off my pristine white bridal underwear—I was supposed to spend my wedding night wearing this, and now I want nothing to do with it. I dress quickly, pulling on a black bra and panty set to replace the virginal white that seems to taunt me. I top it with a flannel shirt, a jean skirt, and a pair of cowboy boots.

"Where are you going?" she asks.

"I don't know." My eyes fix on the duffel bag in the corner, packed for our honeymoon in the Bahamas. A week at the beach with my new husband. It was going to be so romantic.

I need to get out of here, but my car is at my mother-in-law's.

She isn't going to be your mother-in-law anymore.

"I need to borrow your car," I blurt.

"What? Sure, okay. Anything you want."

"Don't call me." I throw the duffel bag over my shoulder and run down the stairs right past Marcus.

I'm pulling out of the parking lot when Marcus returns to the front of the building. He doesn't come after me. He lifts a hand in a helpless wave. *Asshole.*

Where am I going?

The only thing that sounds more depressing than going on my honeymoon alone is staying here, so I drive to the airport. Screw Marcus. Screw Veronica. I'm going to the beach.

When I get to the airline counter, I clutch my purse with shaking hands and paste on a smile for the attendant. "I need to see about changing my flight."

"Sure. May I see your ID?"

I stare at the purse in my hands and freeze. Because I don't have my purse. I have Veronica's. And Veronica's ID.

"Ma'am? Your ID, please?" The chipper attendant cocks her head as she waits for me to hand over my identification.

I have *Veronica's* purse. *My* purse is back at the ceremony site. With all those decorations I spent months preparing, and all those people who have talked about me behind my back most of my life.

"Ma'am, you'll need a photo ID to fly today," the attendant says.

Didn't Veronica say she was supposed to fly to Michigan tonight? I pull her wallet from her purse and slide over her identification. "I don't remember when my flight leaves."

The woman taps something into the computer. She looks at Veronica's picture then at me and nods, satisfied. "It leaves in two hours. Would you like to upgrade to business class for your flight to Grand Rapids?"

Grand Rapids, Michigan. I don't even know what they have in Grand Rapids. I've never left Alabama. But anything is better than staying here.

I pull Veronica's credit card from her wallet and pass it over to the attendant. "I'd love to."

SIX HOURS LATER...

"God, you're hot."

"God, I am." I wave my hand in front of my face. "They sure do have the heat cranked up, don't they?"

The guy smiles and steps closer to my stool. He's good-looking by conventional standards—a strong jaw, a big smile, and thick blond hair parted to the side. He leans in so close that I can smell the whiskey on his breath. "Can I confess something?"

I tilt my head to the side, and the whole bar spins. *Tequila is so fun. Why don't I drink it all the time?* "Confess what? I'm not a priest."

"It's not that kind of confession." John—I *think* he said his name was John, but maybe it's Judas. My sister's name should be Judas. How could she betray me like that? How could she walk down the aisle at my wedding carrying my fiancé's baby?

"I can't stop thinking about getting inside you," John says, snapping me out of my thoughts. He lowers his head so his lips sweep my ear. "It's going to feel so good."

That escalated quickly.

I giggle because his mouth on my ear tickles, then I giggle again because this is so ridiculous. Look at me, sitting here on my wedding night in a strange bar, in a town I've never heard of, and a guy I met less than ten minutes ago just whispered something dirtier than anything Marcus has ever said to me. Then I giggle more, because it feels good and if I stop laughing . . .

I'm afraid of what happens if I stop laughing.

"You like the sound of that?" He pulls back enough for me to see his smile.

My giggle turns to a snort. "Nope." I wave to the bartender for another drink. Since I started drinking, I stopped caring so much about where I'm supposed to be right now, and I really, really don't want to care right now. About anything, but especially not the things I can't let myself think about.

My wedding night. The Plaza Hotel. Marcus.

I need more tequila.

"No?" John frowns at me, as if I'm a complex puzzle.

I reach for my drink but frown when I find it empty. I wave to the bartender again before turning to face John. "You're awfully nice, John, but I don't think we're on the same page."

He takes my hand in his and squeezes. "Then let me read to you."

I look around to see if anyone else heard what he just said—because *gag*—and catch the eye of a tall, dark-haired man standing a few feet behind John. I flash him a smile, but he doesn't seem to share my amusement.

I pull my hand out of John's. "No thanks."

John looks baffled. As if I just turned down eighty grand in cash and not a ride on his disco stick.

I snort again. "*Disco stick.* Does anyone actually call it that?"

He blinks at me. "Are you asking me what I call my dick?"

"No!" I shudder, then think again. "Marcus called his Henry. That should have been a sign, shouldn't it? He talked about his penis like it was separate from him and had a mind of its own. *Henry can't stop thinking about you.*" I giggle. "Oh my God, how did I not expect this?"

John looks into my eyes and brushes my hair behind my ear. "Did he break your heart? Let me prove that men can be good."

"I'm not convinced that's true." Maybe men can be good, just not with me. There's something fundamentally wrong with me that makes formerly good men change when they try to love me.

I perk up when I see the bartender slide a drink in front of me, and then frown when I realize it's a glass of ice water. "Tequila?"

She nudges the glass closer to my hand and arches a brow. "This first. Pace yourself, okay?"

"Right. Sure. Water's a great idea." I try to sound extra sober so she'll bring me more tequila next time I ask. Tonight, the drinks are on Veronica, so I'm ordering top-shelf booze. I take a sip of water, then cringe when it hits my stomach. Have I eaten today? There was the toast Martha made me before we went to the hair salon. I think I took one bite to appease her, but I was too nervous and eating felt like swallowing sawdust.

John watches the bartender retreat. "Ava has a stick up her ass, but I have plenty of tequila at my place. I'll take good care of you."

I shake my head, then realize it's kind of fun to roll it from side to side, and do it again. "I don't want to go to your house," I tell John. "I want to stay here and forget that today was the worst day of my life."

"I'll make it better."

The tall man behind John narrows his eyes at my overly aggressive suitor before turning his gaze on me. This time, I really look at him. He's like a Greek god—tall, with shoulders so broad they probably have their own zip code. His lips quirk, and his eyes—oh God, his eyes are amazing. They're this deep brown and turn down a little at the corners, as if he smiles so rarely that his eyes have forgotten how. He could play a tortured movie hero with those eyes.

"We both feel this thing between us," John says, and I tear my gaze away from the tortured hero. "Let's get out of here. I promise we won't do anything you don't want to do."

"All I *want* to do is drink more tequila." But not with him. No, that doesn't actually sound like a good time at all.

"Then let's get out of here."

"*No*." Suddenly, I'm out of patience with John and his inability to take no for an answer. I push on his shoulder to urge him away from me. "Give me some space, okay?"

John doesn't budge. His hand wraps around my upper arm, and his thumb rubs tiny circles on my shoulder. "I think you *like* me in your space."

I do my best to conjure psychic abilities and telepathically beg the guy behind John to help. When he continues to stare with those sad eyes rather than intervene, I mentally chastise myself. I'm a grown woman. I don't need some tall, dark stranger to scare away unwanted suitors. I can save myself. "I don't, actually," I tell John. It's crowded in here, but if I slide off the barstool and squeeze behind the group of guys by the pool table, it'll put distance between me and this guy, and maybe he won't try to follow. *God, what a buzzkill.*

Before I can decide the best way to escape, the Greek god steps around John to stand by my side. In the next breath, he sweeps John's hand away from my arm. "Johnny boy," he says. "I see you met my girlfriend. I think you're making her uncomfortable."

John's eyes narrow, and his lips twist. "You don't have a girlfriend."

The tall guy slings an arm over my shoulder and smiles, but it's not sincere, and definitely not kind. "Sure I do. And even if I didn't, I'm pretty sure she asked you to give her some space."

John backs up a full three feet and holds up both hands. "Listen, sorry if your girl was making eyes at me. I guess it was a misunderstanding."

The tall guy arches a brow, and I don't have to be a mind reader to know what he thinks of John. His expression says, *You're a fucking douche, and if you don't back off, I'm going to see how it feels to bury my fist in your face.* Or maybe that's just wishful thinking on my part. I've never had one guy punch another for me, and right now, that sounds fun. *Sorry, John.*

"Fuck this. She's not worth it," John says. He swipes his beer off the counter and stumbles to the other side of the bar to a group of guys standing around a pool table.

When John's gone, my Greek god turns to me. "You okay?"

I really like him. I wish I'd let *him* buy me a drink and not John. Then again, John *wanted* to buy me a drink, and this guy seems more irritated at having to help than interested in making small talk with a random drunk girl. "I'm fine." *I'm not fine. I'm so far from fine that I don't even know what fine looks like anymore.*

"John doesn't take a hint very well."

"I've gotten more foreplay from my gynecologist."

He chokes on his beer. "Is that so?"

"I suppose this is my fault. I smiled at him and let him buy me a drink."

"John or your gynecologist?"

I shake my head. "John. My OBGYN doesn't drink, and anyway, she's not my type."

The guy bites his lip, and I think there might be a smile trapped under those perfect white teeth. "I'm still not convinced it's your fault. Anything else you did to give John the wrong idea?"

"Asked him questions."

He folds his arms. "What kind of questions?"

"I asked his name. Is that, like, a mating ritual here? *What's your name?* means we'll be screwing like bunnies in fifteen minutes?"

He chuckles then shakes his head. "Are you just drunk, or are you always this adorable?"

I frown. Did he just flirt with me? I'm pretty sure he doesn't even like me, so why would he flirt? "Can't it be both?"

He turns his head and cuts his gaze to John before bringing it back to me. His eyes scan my face as if he's still trying to determine if I'm okay. "Listen, I've got a meeting."

"Isn't it Saturday night?" I tap my phone to wake it, and the screen reads 11:05. If I were still in Jeffe—if Veronica weren't pregnant, if Marcus hadn't betrayed me—I'd be in the bridal suite at the Plaza right now. Instead, I took my sister's plane ticket to Grand Rapids. While I was on the plane, I used her phone to open her email account, where I found a reservation for a rental car and a night in a hotel in a town called Jackson Harbor. Fast forward a few hours, a few shots of tequila, and a whole lot of trying not to think, and here I am.

And somehow, my story is still more believable than this man having a business meeting at eleven o'clock on a Saturday night.

"You don't have to make up some meeting just because you don't want to talk to me," I say.

He holds my gaze for a long beat, and I feel something. It's not that desperate need to forget Marcus that I felt when John offered to buy me a drink. It's something else—a long, slow tug that's unraveling the knots in my belly and turning them into something better.

When he breaks the connection and drops his gaze to my glass of water, the feeling disappears, as if it was never there to begin with. "If he bugs you again, don't hesitate to come over, okay?"

Don't go. "Okay." I extend a hand. "Nic. My name's Nic. What's yours?"

He shakes his head. "Sorry. I've got plans in fifteen minutes."

I frown as he walks away. Just when I might have felt foolish, he looks at me over his shoulder and winks, and I get it. *The mating ritual.* "You're funny!" I call after him.

"And you're drunk." He grins, and holy hell, the Greek god with the sad eyes and the broad shoulders has a *dimple.* I'm such a sucker for a dimple.

My smile falls away. Marcus has a dimple too. I thought I'd see that dimple tonight. I imagined stripping out of my wedding gown and watching him smile in appreciation of my body. I've been dieting and exercising for months so I could look my best on our special night. All the while, he was fucking my sister.

I'm gonna need more tequila.

Chapter THREE

ETHAN

I cannot take my eyes off the woman at the bar.

She's not my type—more cuteness than sex appeal with that pert nose and innocent brown eyes. She has an air of innocence. Sweetness. Even her name is cute. Nic. Not *Nicole* or *Nicki-with-an-i.* Nic.

She's probably the kind of woman who's had the same boyfriend since she was sixteen and has already named her future children. Girls like that should be handled with care. Wooed, sweet-talked, seduced.

Definitely not my fucking type.

But there's something off about her. She's dressed casually enough in a jean skirt and a flannel, but her light brown hair is stiff with hairspray and pinned to the back of her head in one of those 'dos girls get for proms or weddings. At the beginning of the night, her pink lips puckered into a pout and there was misery in her eyes, but her sadness fell away more and more with every drink.

Maybe that's why I can't keep my eyes off her. Despite all signs pointing to her being too sweet for me, I'm a miserable son of a bitch who's drawn to the sadness beneath her smile.

"Are you going to chime in with your opinion, or should I leave you alone so you can eye-fuck the new chick in private?" my brother Brayden asks.

"Shut the fuck up," Jake tells Brayden. "Eye-fucking is the most action he's gotten in years."

"Did you see him with her?" Carter asks. "He was smiling. *Ethan* was smiling."

Reluctantly, I tear my gaze off the woman in question and find every pair of eyes at the table on me. Brayden is irritated, but Carter and Jake are wearing identical smirks. If Shay and Levi were here, they'd be smirking too, but luckily, I only have to deal with three of my five siblings tonight.

"It's not healthy," Carter says. "That shit gets backed up and starts messing with a man's mind. Let the boy look."

I shoot my brothers a warning glance. They respect that my love life is off-limits as a topic of conversation, but they view my *sex life* as something else entirely. Which is fair, I suppose, since I have no intention of having a love life ever again.

"She keeps looking over here," Jake says.

Brayden groans and drags a hand through his hair. "Why do I even bother?"

"You're the one who suggested we have the meeting in my bar on the busiest night of the week," Jake says. "Did you think we were going to have the privacy of the boardroom?"

"Maybe I chose this location because I knew it was one that would make your ass show up," Brayden shoots back.

Jake just shrugs. He's not offended—probably because it's true.

I shift my eyes back to the stack of papers in front of Brayden. When Dad died, he left his business to all six of us in equal parts, so even though Brayden's the one who runs the business side of the family brewery, he insists we be part of the decisions and the quarterly P and L review. He set this meeting months ago, but Shay and Levi had last-minute excuses and couldn't make it. *Lucky schmucks.*

Nic turns away from the bar and catches my eye again—not hard for her to do, since I can't stop looking in her direction. Her cheeks turn a pretty pink before she looks back to her drink.

"Is she from around here?" Carter asks, following my gaze.

I shrug because I have no idea, but if I had to guess, based on her heavy vowels and sexy Southern drawl, I'd say no.

"I haven't ever seen her before," Jake says. Since he runs Jackson Brews—the face of the family business—and spends his fair share of time behind that bar, he has a better grasp of the population of Jackson Harbor than the rest of us.

I rake my gaze over Nic, searching for something that seems familiar. I'm sure I've never seen her before tonight, and maybe that's part of the appeal. In Jackson Harbor, the only faces that aren't familiar belong to the tourists. They fill our streets and beaches in the warmer months of the year, but once November rolls around and the wind off Lake Michigan turns unforgiving, everyone here is too familiar. Day in and day out, it's the same pitying glances and judgmental stares.

I should have left years ago, but instead, I endure their whispers as if I don't have to live with my own doubts every fucking day of my life.

Maybe it's freeing to meet someone new with winter creeping over the town and the tourists gone. Maybe I like having a woman who isn't thinking about my past notice me.

"Would you just go talk to her?" Jake asks. "I'm getting a case of secondhand blue balls just watching you two look at each other."

"Jesus." Brayden gives up on us and jams his stack of papers back into a manila folder. "Clearly, we're not going to talk business tonight, so look over the reports I sent you and let me know if you have any questions."

"See what I mean? This could have been an email," Carter says. "Every fucking meeting—could have been an email."

"I don't know why you think we need to look over the books every quarter," Jake says. "It's not like we don't trust you. And hell, if you ran this company into the ground, you'd be fucking yourself over more than us."

Brayden grunts in response, and I don't chime in, but Jake's right. The family business has become Brayden's whole life. Between distribution contracts, packaging, and marketing, he's constantly trying to grow and expand what our father started. He works more and harder than anyone else I know, and I work a fucking lot.

A few of us offered to sell our shares to Brayden, but Mom wouldn't hear of it. She says the business will hold us together when everything else falls apart. I'm pretty sure there are a thousand family-business-gone-bad cautionary tales out there that would argue otherwise, but it doesn't matter. Everyone wants to make Mom happy. Present company included.

Brayden looks at me. "Your hornball brother is right. If you're interested in the hot chick, you should go talk to her." He takes a breath, and when he speaks again, his tone is uncharacteristically gentle. "It's been almost three years."

"I'm not talking to anybody." But I want to. My stomach tightens with guilt and shame at that. "She's not my type anyway."

And yet I'm sitting here wondering if those smiling pink lips taste as sweet as they look, wondering how it would feel to have them wrapped around my cock while my hands are buried in her hair. In other words, I'm being a fucking creep.

She's too sweet. Stay. Away.

Brayden smacks a hand on the manila folder in front of him and nods. "Shall we call this meeting to a close, boys?"

"Let's," Jake says. "This place is packed tonight, and Ava's gonna kill me if I don't get back there to help real soon."

They all stand, but when I keep my ass in the booth and my gaze on Nic, Jake nods at me. "Life's too short, brother. Eat the steak, drink the beer, fuck the girl."

"You should have that embroidered on a pillow," Brayden mutters.

"Ethan doesn't know how to fuck anymore," Carter says. "It's been so long, his dick's probably fallen off."

"Have you seen the way he looks at her?" Jake points a thumb at me. "That's not the face of a dickless man checking out a woman."

"Fuck off, all of you," I say, but there's no conviction in my voice.

My brothers are the types who can spot a girl in a bar, decide she's theirs, and make it happen. I've never been like that. When they were living out their glory years picking up chicks and probably playing fast and loose with some STDs, I was madly in love with Elena and proposing marriage. My wife was the only one for me. She was my high school sweetheart, my first love, and my rock through med school. We lost our virginity to each other. We shared all the most important firsts.

My brothers are wrong about how long it's been for me. I haven't been celibate, but the sex I have had has been rare, secret, and too often disappointing. I'm not interested in a relationship—*fuck no, never again*—but the feel of a woman's body under mine, greedy hands, skin on skin . . . It's been too long. In the three years since Elena died, I've only seen women who wanted what I wanted—sex, companionship, no strings, no expectations. Contrary to stereotypes, there are plenty of women who aren't looking for love or picket fences, but I can't imagine the sweet thing at the bar would be down for such an arrangement.

I wave to Cindy, our waitress, and tap my coffee cup, signaling that I'd like a refill. She winks at me and heads to the bar. I lean back in my booth, trying to decide what the fuck I'm doing and why I'm still sitting here.

Nic watches as Brayden and Carter go out the door and Jake returns to his post behind the bar. Then her gaze settles on me and she bites her lip. I don't know if she's *trying* to be sexy or if she's just accidentally irresistible. Either way, it's working. Her teeth sink into her plump bottom lip, and the sight makes something shift in my chest. My mind flashes with an image of her doing that in a very different context—more pleasure, less uncertainty.

She might not be my type, but the chemistry between us is so potent that I can feel it across the crowded bar.

"No bourbon tonight?" Cindy asks, refilling my mug.

"I'm on call."

She nods, familiar with my crazy schedule. "Well, it's too bad you can't have a little liquid courage because Jake told me to tell you that if you don't go talk to her, he's going to slip her a note like he did with Teresa Remington in the seventh grade."

Huffing, I shake my head. I remember that. I was so hung up on the tiny blond cheerleader that I got tongue-tied every time I tried to talk to her. Eventually, Jake took pity on me and slipped a note in her locker. *Do you like Ethan Jackson? Y / N Circle one.*

Teresa gave me the note back in earth science, her cheeks bright red, the *Y* circled with a little smiley face above it. It turned out that Teresa and I didn't have much in common, but the skills she taught me under the bleachers served me well into my high school years.

Our note-writing days might be behind us, but I wouldn't put it past Jake to do something to hook Nic and me up. I grab my coffee and make my way to the new girl before Jake can play matchmaker and give her the wrong idea of what I'm after. A sweet thing like her is going to have expectations, and nothing can happen between us if we're not on the same page.

The stools on either side of Nic are occupied, so I slide between her and the girl beside her and lean against the bar.

Nic's eyes widen, as if she's surprised I came over here despite the fact that I've spent the better part of the last fifteen minutes staring at her. "Um, hi?" she says.

I rub the back of my neck. Hell, I guess I am rusty. I could have sworn she was just waiting for me to make my move. "You doing okay?" I clear my throat—full-throttle awkward now—and catch Jake watching me with a smirk on the opposite side of the bar. He turns away, but not before I see his chest shaking with laughter. He busies himself filling orders and cleaning up behind the bar, all while staying within earshot. That fucker is witnessing my complete and utter lack of game.

"I thought you were having a meeting over there," Nic says. "What happened? The guy with all the papers looked pretty serious."

I shrug. "Family business. Nothing exciting." I look at her water and the empty shot glass beside it. "What are you drinking? Can I get you another?"

"Tequila. But . . ." She shakes her head and lowers her voice. "I don't think the bartender chick likes me."

"Ava," I call, waving to Jake's bartender and best friend. I point to Nic's empty shot glass. "Thanks."

Ava rolls her eyes but reaches for a clean shot glass.

"Do you know everyone around here?" Nic asks as Ava turns away.

"Pretty much. That's how a town like this functions. Everyone knows everyone. And their business."

She draws in a shaky breath. "Sounds familiar. They know your business and talk about it like it's their own personal soap opera." She wrinkles her nose. "That sounded bitter and dramatic."

I chuckle. "You said you're new to town. Are you visiting or moving in?"

"Visiting. I think." She worries her bottom lip between her teeth. "I thought it was temporary, but now that I'm here, I'm thinking why not stay forever? I'm certainly not in any rush to go back where I came from."

I take a sip of my coffee. "Why's that?"

She flashes a grin that's so wide it should take over her whole face, but it doesn't. That sadness is back at the corners of her eyes. "I need a fresh start."

"A fresh start? How old are you?" *Please be older than I think.*

"Twenty-four."

I'm simultaneously relieved and disappointed. At least at twenty-four she's not some college kid, but she's still nine years younger than me. I suppose she's old enough, but I've lived a lifetime in the nine years between us—all the best and worst years that made me who I am today. But instead of finding a way to politely excuse myself, I study her and sip my coffee. "What makes a twenty-four-year-old think she needs a fresh start?"

She shrugs. "I like the idea of living somewhere where people don't know my business, and why not here? Big water, nice people—what's not to like?"

"Nice people, huh?" Cynicism colors my words.

"Y'all seem nice." She lifts her eyes to meet mine. "Aren't you?"

"It's just like any other place. Some people are genuine and kind. Some are assholes."

"Sounds about right." She tilts her head to the side. "Which are you?"

"Oh, I'm definitely an asshole."

"Yeah, right." She laughs as if this is the funniest joke she's ever heard, but I was being absolutely serious. "Thanks for what you did earlier. With John. That conversation was getting all kinds of awkward."

"It was nothing. John's a prick. He doesn't understand that women don't exist to get him off."

"Yeah." Something flashes over her face that tells me guys like John are a fact of life she's uncomfortably familiar with. "Still embarrassing to find myself in that position."

"Give yourself some credit. John's pretty slimy, and a lot of girls don't realize that until, well, later than they'd like."

"Unless you're there to save the day." She smiles. "I don't normally do the damsel-in-distress thing. I don't want you thinking I'm helpless or anything."

"I knew you could handle him. Actually, it was more a favor to John's balls than it was to you."

Her laugh comes out so sharply that she sort of giggle-snorts. It's pretty fucking adorable. Just like the rest of her. "Yeah, that's definitely the direction we were headed. A knee to the balls usually gets the message across."

"You have to do that a lot?"

"No!" She shakes her head and laughs. "Not at all! I'm a pacifist."

Ava comes back with Nic's tequila. She plops it in front of Nic and scowls at me. "If she pukes on your shoes, don't come crying to me."

I frown and reassess Nic. "How drunk are you?"

"I'm working on *forget everything* drunk. Not there yet, unfortunately." She reaches into her purse. "Let me settle up."

I look at Ava and shake my head. "I'll take care of her tab."

"Not tonight," Ava says. "The boss said she's drinking for free."

Jake winks at us, and Nic's brow wrinkles in confusion.

"That's Jake. He's my brother and he runs this place," I explain. Damn Jake. Now it just feels weird, as if we're working together to get the girl drunk. "Perks of hanging out with me, I guess."

"Oh." Nic gives Ava a bright smile. "Well then, tell your boss I said thank you." Ava walks away, and Nic lifts her shot glass and looks at me. "To friends in high places." She drains her shot and puckers her lips. "Yikes!" She shudders delicately. "It burns a little less each time, but it never tastes better."

"If you don't like tequila, why do you drink it?"

"Oh, I usually don't drink. At least not very often, but when I do drink, I like beer because it slows me down and it's fun to taste all the different varieties. There are a couple of breweries where I grew up that—" She winces. "Sorry. I'm rambling."

But I like it. I like the way she waves her hands around when she talks and the way she seems to communicate with her whole body, swaying into her sentences. Of course, that might have more to do with the amount of alcohol she's consumed than with her personality. "Don't apologize. It's great. Half the folks in Jackson Harbor fancy themselves beer artisans, so there are plenty of craft breweries around here. It'll be good for someone like you."

She wrinkles her nose as if my words smell bad. "Someone like me? What's that supposed to mean?" She doesn't sound offended, just baffled.

"Young, carefree, the type of girl who . . ." My eyes drop to the swell of her cleavage at the top button on her flannel. I'm trying not to look at the black lace of her bra that's peeking out there, but it's taking more self-control than I'm interested in commanding tonight. "No responsibilities. The world is your oyster."

"Unlike you, then, huh? What are you, seventy? Did you just age spectacularly well?"

I swallow hard. "I feel ancient some days, but my wild and crazy days are behind me."

She shakes her head. "I don't think I've ever been wild and crazy. Maybe that's what's wrong with me. Coming here was the most impulsive thing I've ever done in my life."

"Coming to the bar?"

"No, to Jackson Harbor. I just . . ." The pink in her cheeks blooms and morphs into a flush that creeps all the way down her neck. Her skin reminds me of the petals on the white roses in front of Mom's house—soft, perfect, and calling for my touch. "I want to start over."

"What's stopping you?"

The flush from her cheeks races down her neck. If I followed the color with my fingertips, it would lead me to the swell of her breasts.

The persistent direction of my thoughts surprises me. I appreciate looking at a beautiful woman, but I don't typically gawk and let my imagination get away from me. Maybe my brothers are right and my virtually nonexistent sex life is starting to affect my brain. I'm overdue to scratch an itch, but I already know I can't do that with this girl. She's too sweet and doesn't strike me as the one-night-stand type. Hell, her admission that she's never done anything wild or crazy is practically an admission that she's not. But even as I think it, I'm in no hurry to leave her side.

Ava returns and drops a plate of deep-fried appetizers on the bar in front of Nic and me. She gives me the stink-eye as she says, "Don't you dare think about leaving this bar with her until she's eaten something."

I meet Ava's eyes and nod. Regardless of what she might think of me, I understand what she's saying and respect her for wanting Nic to sober up before making decisions she might regret.

Nic's eyes go wide as she looks at the food. "Do you have any idea how long it's been since I've had fried food?" She bites her knuckle then looks at me. "Am I drooling? It smells so good that I'm afraid I might be."

I chuckle. "Well, if you're going to indulge, Jake's cheese balls are where you should start. That's goat cheese rolled in a homemade batter, deep-fried, and then drizzled with honey."

"Seriously?" She's so captivated by the food in front of her that I feel actual jealousy toward a fucking fried ball of cheese.

I wave to the plate. "After you, then." I wait as she pops a cheese ball in her mouth, and then I'm enthralled by the sight of her chewing and swallowing. Her eyes close, and I think she might have moaned.

"I'm never dieting again if this is what I've been missing." She shakes her head. "Never again."

I love that she's not afraid to eat in front of me. I love that she *enjoys* food. Suddenly, I want to feed her. Not just Jake's notoriously greasy fare, but lobster from the wharf, crab legs dipped in butter, the tiramisu from Jordan's Inn.

There's a spot of honey on her bottom lip, and her tongue darts out to catch it. She stops with a second cheese ball halfway to her mouth. "Do you always look at girls the way you're looking at me?"

"How am I looking at you?"

Her pink cheeks flare brighter. *Christ.* "Like . . . like I'm your dinner."

Behind the bar, Jake freezes in the middle of pouring a beer, then he puts the glass down and folds over in a full-on belly laugh. *Asshole.*

I'm saved from answering when her phone buzzes. She digs it out of her purse and fumbles with the screen, entering her passcode twice before it unlocks. As she reads whatever message was waiting for her, it's almost like watching her transform into a different person. Her smile falls away, and all that bubbly energy dissipates.

She puts the phone back into her purse and avoids my gaze. "Excuse me," she whispers. Then she slides off her stool and disappears into the crowd.

Chapter FOUR

ETHAN

Am I supposed to go after her? Jesus. I don't even know her, but she's been drinking and I think she was here alone. It's not really my business if she left, but I can't help but worry.

If I could just stop thinking about the sadness behind her smile . . .

It's the sadness that gets me. It's what draws me in, what makes me curious, and what makes me want to stay the fuck away. I turn my back to the bar so I can ignore Jake watching me. The crowd is thinning a bit, but there's still no sign of Nic. If she was just using the restroom, she'd be back by now.

She's not coming back, and I need to accept that and get my ass home.

When I turn to set my glass down, I find Ava standing in front of me with folded arms and a disappointed scowl. "What did you say to the new girl?"

I frown. "Nothing. She got a text message and left."

"You didn't ask where she was going?"

"She didn't really give me the chance."

"Men," she mutters. She shakes her head before meeting my eyes again. "She's in the bathroom. Pretty upset." She shrugs. "But I guess it's only your job to hand the drunk girl more tequila, not to check on her when shit goes down."

I flinch. Ava's known for being a ballbuster, but only when guys deserve it. I've never had the pleasure of having her disapproval directed at me. "What's wrong with her?"

I get another classic Ava eye-roll. She reaches under the counter and hands me a magnetic sign. "Just go check on her."

Fuck. I have to do something. I push away from the bar and weave my way through the crowd to the women's restroom. There's a line, but I step to the front of it and stick my head inside the men's room. "Anybody in here?" When there's no response, I close the door and cover the *Men's* sign with the magnet that reads *Women's.* "There you go, ladies! This is now the women's restroom. The other one's closed."

There are a few grumbles, but the line shifts to the other door. My sister, Shay, thinks the need for the sign is hilarious. She's never hesitated to use the men's room before waiting in line for the women's, but most women aren't like my sister.

I weave my way around the line to step into the women's room. There are two women washing their hands at the sink who frown at my intrusion, but I smile as if I visit the women's room all the time. When they finish, I close the door behind them and lock it. I go to the last stall—the only one still closed—and put my hand on the door. "Nic?"

She sniffles. "Yeah?"

Jesus. I never intended to spend my night in the bathroom talking a strange woman down from some sort of emotional breakdown. What the fuck do I think I'm doing? "Are you okay?"

"Yeah. I'm fine. Just . . ." She draws in a shaky breath. "I'm just having a bad day." The lock slides open, and I move to the side as she steps out of the stall, her mascara smeared down her face, her eyes so damn sad.

And fuck, it's not my problem, I don't know her, and I'm probably the world's biggest fool for thinking I can fix this, but I know there's no way I can walk away from her tonight without trying.

"Oh, hell," she mutters. She sweeps past me and puts her purse on the counter while she runs the water hot. She grabs paper towels from the dispenser on the wall, wets them, and washes her face. When the worst of the makeup streaks are gone, she looks at me in the mirror.

Helplessly, I tuck my hands into my pockets, because I don't know what else to do with them. I lean against the bathroom stall. "You want to talk about it?"

With a slow exhale, she turns, then hoists herself up on the counter. "I do. But I don't."

"Did somebody hurt you?" My gut knots with the question. *You can't save her, Ethan.*

"You could say that."

I step forward. Maybe that's why she's here on this impulsive visit to Jackson Harbor. Maybe she's running from someone, escaping a home that's not safe. "Do you have somewhere safe to go?"

"It's not that kind of hurt," she whispers. She swallows, and her gaze dips to my mouth. "Why are *you* so sad?"

Because you remind me of Elena. Because I couldn't walk away from her either. "I'm just worried about you." I don't know if I step closer or if gravity pulls me that way, but in a breath, she's at my fingertips and my thighs brush her knees.

"Will you do me a favor?" she asks, her attention still on my lips.

"What?"

"Will you kiss me?"

"Nic . . ." I wait for the excuses to find their way onto my tongue, but they don't, and I realize I don't want an excuse to walk away from her. My whole body is warm and my fingers itch to touch her. The only thing I want is my mouth on hers. I want to taste her joy and sadness. I want to know how it feels to have that body pressed against mine.

I'm silent a beat too long, and she winces. "Sorry."

"Don't be. It's not that I don't want to, but you're vulnerable."

"Are you always so noble?"

"If you think my thoughts are noble right now, you're even more naïve than I feared." I lean my forehead against hers. *Christ.* Who am I kidding? She's asking me to do something I've been thinking about since I first laid eyes on her. I couldn't deny her if I wanted to, and I don't want to. Not even a little.

I cup her face in my hand and run my thumb along her jaw.

She slides a hand behind my neck. "I like the way you look at me. You make me feel sexy. Wanted."

"Who made you feel like you weren't?"

"A mistake."

"Then he didn't deserve you." I lower my mouth to hers, telling myself the kiss will be brief, that I won't get carried away. But then her other hand joins the first behind my neck, and her breasts press against my chest. Her thighs part, and I step between them in my instinctive need to be closer. A soft moan slips from her lips as our mouths connect.

This girl kisses like she does everything else—with unabashed emotion. She doesn't hide a thing she's feeling, and I'm hard even before her mouth opens under mine and our tongues sweep across each other.

I thread one hand into her hair and slide the other up her bare leg, my fingers curling into the flesh of her hip while my thumb strokes her inner thigh. Her skirt is bunched around her waist, and it would be so easy to follow this soft skin up and find her panties. She's making the sexiest sounds, and I'm dying to touch her, to find out if she's as turned on as she sounds, but I keep my hand where it is and give her the kiss she asked for. I offer the evidence that she's sexy and desirable, no matter what some asshole made her think.

She's the one who breaks the kiss. Eyes closed, she leans her forehead against my shoulder, her body rocking as her breathing slows.

Still too tempted to explore the soft skin at the apex of her thighs, I pull my hand away and place it on the counter by her hip. She lifts her head, and her gaze follows my hand. Is she looking at my bare ring finger? I came here straight from the hospital and I don't wear it at work—I wash my hands all day long and it gets in the way. For the first time since Elena slid that band on my finger,

I have a moment when I'm glad to not have it. That moment is immediately followed by a sharp pang of guilt.

I don't want to forget my wife or pretend she never existed. If I thought touching this woman would make me forget Elena or my grief on any level, I'd walk away. I don't want to forget. I don't deserve to. "It's late. Can I get you a cab?"

She shakes her head. "I walked. My hotel is close."

There's no way I'm letting her walk there alone. Her encounter with John proves she's a creep magnet. Add the tequila and emotional vulnerability to that equation—and the way she just kissed me like her life depended on it—and I know I won't rest unless I see with my own eyes that she's safely locked in her room.

"Let me walk you." I tilt her face up until she meets my eyes.

"It's not far," she says. "I'll be okay."

"It's late and you're . . ."

"Drunk?" She laughs, then shakes her head.

"I wasn't going to say that."

"What were you going to say, then?"

You're too fucking beautiful for your own good. "You're new here. But yeah, you have been drinking."

"There's nothing like a good cry to kill a girl's buzz."

"Either let me walk you or get you a cab."

She meets my eyes, and I see the indecision on her face. That's good. I'd be worried if she immediately agreed to walk in the dark with a complete stranger. "Okay," she says. "A couple of questions?"

"Shoot."

"Your name might be a nice place to start—if there's a way

you can give it to me without the mating ritual."

Jesus. I was two seconds away from having my hand between her legs, and she doesn't know my name. I forgot I didn't give it to her earlier. "I feel like the 'mysterious stranger' thing is working for me. I'd hate to lose that advantage so early in the night." She laughs, and I smile. I like her laugh. A lot. "I'm joking."

She shakes her head and holds her hand to my lips before I can say more. "You're right. I only need a mysterious stranger tonight. No names."

"But I already know yours."

She shrugs. "*Call me but love and I'll be new baptized.*"

The line from Elena's favorite play is like a punch to the gut. "Do you always walk around quoting Shakespeare?"

"Only *Romeo and Juliet.*" Jesus. She has layers beneath her layers, and I want to learn about each one.

"What else do you need to know about me before I walk you home?"

"Have you ever been convicted of a felony?" she asks, but the question comes with a smile that makes her eyes crinkle at the corners.

I shake my head. "Can't say that I have."

"And are you just hanging out with me tonight because you're trying to hide the fact that you're gay?"

I laugh—something I've done so rarely in the last three years that it feels foreign coming from my lips. "I'm a little offended that you feel the need to ask after that kiss." She only shrugs. "I promise you I'm not gay, but if I were, I'd still want to make sure you got home okay."

"I have a bad track record with men. The fact that you kissed me means you're either gay, married, or have irredeemable character flaws."

"Oh, I definitely do. I'm an asshole, remember?"

"That's what you said, but I haven't seen any evidence to support that claim yet." She sighs and rolls back her shoulders as if bracing herself for something. "A cab is unnecessary. It's only a couple of blocks. You can walk me."

I take her hand to help her off the counter, and the front of her body brushes mine as she stands.

"Thanks," she whispers. She looks up at me through dark lashes, and I freeze for a beat, fighting the temptation to dip my head and taste those sweet lips again. But I'm not sure I could stop there, and it would take me no time at all to have her against the counter again, my hand up her skirt while I discovered her sweet spots. I resist and release her hand.

When we exit the bathroom, curious eyes follow us to the front door, where I grab my trench coat off a hook. "Which one's yours?"

She shakes her head. "I don't have one."

I blink at her. "It's thirty degrees outside."

She shrugs. "I'll be fine."

I hold mine open. "Here. Wear this."

"No, you don't have to do that."

"My mother taught me to be a gentleman. Don't make me disappoint her."

She smiles and lets me help her into the coat. The wool trench hits her mid-shin and is almost big enough to wrap around her twice, but she looks adorable. "Thank you," she says softly.

"Where are you staying?" I ask when we reach the sidewalk.

"The Tiffany Hotel on Fourth and White Bank. I think it's . . ." She spins in a full circle before stopping and pointing in the direction of Second. "That way."

I take her by the shoulders and turn her a one-eighty to face in the direction of Fourth. "I think you mean that way."

She worries her bottom lip between her teeth, then nods. "I guess I'm glad you're walking me."

There's a bite in the air, and her nose turns pink as we walk. "I take it you're not from Michigan if you didn't think to bring a coat," I say, as if her Southern accent didn't give it away.

"I'm from a little town in Alabama called Jeffe." She wraps her arms around herself and shivers. "I don't think I'm cut out for Michigan. The cold cuts right through me."

"With the right clothes and some time, you'll adjust. It gets pretty nasty come February, but a couple of winters here, and thirty degrees feels balmy."

At the corner, we wait for the light and cross Third, and we're at her hotel far too quickly for my liking. The front lights of the old Victorian glow, illuminating the porch that stretches the length of the front of the house. It appears this is one of the many homes in this area of town that have been restored and converted into a small hotel. Places like this usually have half a dozen rooms and no night staff or kitchen—more like a B&B than a hotel. A lot of the old neighborhood near downtown is like this—catering to tourists who visit Jackson Harbor for its small-town charm and don't want to stay in a chain hotel.

On the front porch, Nic fishes her keys from her purse. She only fumbles a bit as she unlocks and opens the door and steps inside before turning back to me. "My room's on the second floor."

"I'll walk you up." I pull the door shut behind us and shove my hands into my pockets, as if that might be enough to help me resist temptation.

On the stairs, I almost regret giving her my coat. If I hadn't, I'd have a great view of her ass and the soft skin of her thighs between the tops of her boots and the hem of her skirt. Maybe it's better that I can't see what I know is under my coat. I don't need any more temptation. She quotes Shakespeare, has skin like porcelain, and kisses like she was born to do it. *Whoever hurt her is an idiot.*

She rounds the corner on the second floor and uses the same key to unlock the door to her room. "Thank you."

"For what?"

"For tonight. For lending me your coat and walking me." Her gaze drops to my mouth and stays there. She lowers her voice and adds, "For kissing me when I needed to be kissed."

"It's been my pleasure." The corner of my mouth quirks into a smile. "All of it."

She nudges the door, and it swings open, revealing a large bedroom with a king-size bed against one wall and a couch against another. She takes my hand from my pocket and backs into the room.

"What are you doing?"

"I'm bringing you in. I don't want you to go yet."

I swallow hard. "I don't want to go."

She loops her arms behind my neck and kisses me again. It's just as good as it was in the bathroom, but faster, greedier. This is a kiss that knows what it wants and where to find it.

I pull away with a groan and lean my forehead against hers. "This is such a bad idea."

Chapter FIVE

NICOLE

This kiss doesn't feel like a bad idea. It feels like the best idea I've had in months. His mouth is warm, and his big hands make me feel safe.

His coat slips off my shoulders and falls to the floor around our feet.

"Tell me to leave." His breath is hot on my neck, his hands skimming up my sides even as he says the words.

"Why?"

"Because you're too sweet. Because you've had a shit day and someone's hurt you." His eyes search mine, even as his hand slides under my shirt and his knuckles graze my belly. "Because I'm not what you're looking for."

"How do you know what I'm looking for?"

He groans and nips at my neck. "You're telling me you'd be

okay with this?" He's breathless, as if these kisses are doing as much to him as they are to me. I know the question he's asking is important, but all I want right now is more. More of him. His heat. His touch. His mouth. "You'd be okay with me touching you tonight and just being another guy you see at the bar tomorrow?" He flattens his palm against my stomach and his fingertips brush under the waistband of my skirt, getting him closer to where I want him, closer to where I'm aching.

I want this, and so much more. I can hardly breathe. The tequila helped me forget, but this—his hands, the quickening of my pulse, and the dangerous ache between my legs—*this* washes the whole day away.

"Tell me to leave," he repeats.

I pull away and look into his eyes. I take his hand off my stomach, step back, and hold his gaze as I unbutton my shirt. It slides from my shoulders as I unzip my skirt and let it fall from my hips. Then I'm standing before him in nothing but my cowboy boots, a black lace bra, and panties.

His eyes darken as they skim over me.

"I'm not asking you to leave," I tell him. "I'm asking you to stay." This is the craziest thing I've ever done, but I'm desperate to cling to this feeling. I love the way he looks at me. I'm so sick of falling short in everything, of trying and trying and never being enough. I want wild. I want crazy. I want pleasure without promises.

Maybe he's right. Maybe tomorrow I'll regret this and count it as a reckless mistake. But right now, I don't care about tomorrow. The only thing I want is exactly what he's offering: his touch, his attention, and this thrill that vibrates from low in my belly and out through my fingertips. I feel alive when he touches me. I feel daring and bold. Have I ever felt this way?

I back up to the couch and sit before crooking a finger at him. As surely as if I pulled a leash, he comes, his gaze never straying from my face. His lips are parted and his hands fisted at his sides, as if he can't trust himself to touch. When he stands in front of me, our eyes lock as he unbuttons his shirt, pulls it off his arms, and throws it to the side. He peels his undershirt off, and then his chest is bare and he's standing before me in his jeans, that raw hunger in his eyes. I break eye contact to take him in—to appreciate the hard planes of his stomach and the breadth of his chest. There's a dark smattering of hair across his pecs that tapers into a soft line over his navel and disappears into the waistband of his jeans. His arms and chest are roped with lean muscle and covered in ink. The tattoos take me by surprise. He seems so put-together—he's the clean-cut boy next door with his shirt on and the dangerous bad boy without it. I like both sides of him. I like that he has both sides—that he wants to be noble and walk away, but he also wants to take what I'm offering.

Reaching forward, I hook two fingers through a belt loop and tug him toward me.

He closes his eyes and groans, but instead of joining me on the couch, he drops to his knees in front of me. He takes my wrists in his hands and guides my arms to rest behind my head. He trails rough fingertips down my arms, over my shoulders, across my collarbone, and down between my breasts. I arch toward him instinctively, and he cups a breast in each hand and skims a thumb over each nipple. "You have no idea how beautiful you are, do you?" Then he brings his mouth to my breast and sucks at the nipple through the lace, pulling so hard the pleasure is just this side of pain.

I cry out and grip handfuls of his hair. He pulls back to look into my eyes while he drags one hand slowly up my leg to part my thighs.

He swallows thickly. "Take off your bra." I obey with shaking hands. I keep my eyes on his as I unhook it and slide it off. He exhales slowly. "Fuck, you're gorgeous."

"So are you."

He slides a hand between my legs, and I moan as he scrapes his knuckles across my center. The light contact is exactly where I need it and has me coming off the couch and toward his hand, adding friction to the touch. "Shh, baby. Be patient. Let me play."

My body is shaking—trembling at the slightest touch and begging for more. When he peels my panties from my hips, I practically whimper in gratitude, but before I can be embarrassed by the desperate sounds slipping from my lips, his eyes go hot and he watches his fingers toy with me.

I'm shaking. God, it feels good to be wanted. To be desired. To be *touched.* Marcus wanted to marry a virgin—just another way I fell short of the mark. Since I wasn't the virginal bride he'd imagined for himself, he insisted we go through the process of becoming "born-again virgins" through his church. It was so important to him that we wait until our wedding night, and he hadn't touched me intimately in any way in months. He said abstinence would make our wedding night special, so our contact was limited to chaste kisses and hand-holding.

I squeeze my eyes shut at those thoughts. I don't want to think about Marcus or his bullshit or his lies.

My mysterious stranger circles my clit with his thumb and returns his mouth to my breast. The combined pleasure is too much, and I squeeze my legs closed, trapping his hand there.

"Are you okay?" He softens his touch then pulls away entirely. "Did I hurt you?"

"No. I . . ." I part my thighs again. "Please, don't stop." I meet his smoky gaze. "I need this. I need you to touch me."

His nostrils flare. "You can't say things like that to me, sweetness. Not if you don't mean them."

"I mean it," I whisper.

"You don't even know me."

I shake my head. "Does it matter?" I thought I knew my fiancé. I thought I knew my sister. They both betrayed me. I just want to feel beautiful and desirable for one night. *Just one night.*

"You're sure?" he asks.

I nod, slide a hand behind his neck, and bring his mouth down to mine so he can't see in my eyes how scared I am that he might say no, that he might walk away and leave me alone in this hotel room with my thoughts and my regrets. With my doubts and the loneliness that has dogged my heels my entire life.

I nip at his lips, tug at his hair, and kiss him with all the desperation I feel as his hand plays between my legs. He slips and slides over every inch of me, circling my opening before he finally slides a finger inside me and I gasp against his mouth.

"Holy shit, you're wet," he whispers. "So wet and tight."

I'm worried for a minute that he might realize how long it's been for me. I don't know this man, but tonight I've seen enough about who he is to believe that any signs of vulnerability might make him back off. But he doesn't. He kisses his way down my neck. He slides his finger out and back in, making my hips lift off the couch and a moan slip from my lips.

He adds a second finger with the first and groans against my neck. The stretch of two fingers is almost painful at first, but then it's good, and then it's better. His thumb teases my clit as he works his fingers inside me. "How can you be so fucking beautiful? You're even sexier when you're turned on, and I wanted you from the second I saw you."

I like his words against my neck, the husky timbre vibrating through both our bodies as he strokes me.

"Do you know how hard it's going to be for me to walk away without fucking you?" He nips at my neck, bites and sucks.

"Then don't," I whisper. It's the craziest thing I've ever wanted, but right now it seems perfect. I don't want to be alone tonight. Can I really say I wish I was with Marcus right now? Would I have wanted to be ignorant and have learned only after our wedding what kind of man Marcus really is?

When I open my eyes, my sexy stranger is looking at me like I'm a broken piece of fine china. He must have felt me tense as my thoughts went to Marcus.

He runs his gaze over me slowly—over my face and down my body. In this moment, his inspection isn't sexual, more an assessment of my injuries, and I can't decide if I'm grateful that my hurt doesn't show on my skin or if I wish it did. I don't want pity, but for just one moment it would be nice for someone to see me as I am, not as I present myself. Someone to see the fault lines hiding under my dutiful smile. Someone to see the darkness that claws at me when I'm alone.

I don't know what it is about this stranger that makes me

want that someone to be him.

When I reach for the button on his jeans, I don't have any idea what tomorrow holds, but I know exactly what I want tonight. I want to give myself to this man, a stranger who can make me warm from the inside out just from the way he looks at me, a tattooed mystery with sad eyes.

He places a hand over mine, stopping me before I can unzip his jeans. "We aren't going there tonight, sweetness."

"Don't you want to?"

He stills and squeezes his eyes shut. He shakes his head as he opens his eyes and studies me. "I don't want to be something you regret."

"You won't be."

He sweeps his mouth over mine. "Just let me touch you." He dips his head and nuzzles the crook of my neck. He pulls his hand from between my legs, and I whimper at the loss. "You smell good. You feel good." He meets my eyes and his go darker. "Do you taste good too?"

I gasp—at his words, at the idea of this man putting his mouth where his hand is, and at the promise in his voice.

He slides his hands under my ass and pulls my hips to the edge of the couch, parting my thighs wider and exposing me to his greedy eyes. Every nerve ending lights on fire as I watch him lower his mouth to my breasts. He rakes his teeth over my nipples and kisses down the center of my belly.

He grazes his nose from one hipbone to the other, then places a chaste kiss right above my clit. "Can I kiss you here?"

I answer with a ragged inhale, a nod, and the jerk of my hips. I'm trembling. Shaking with a need I'm not sure I've felt before.

His mouth trails to my inner thighs, one side, then the other, first closed lips, then a hot, open mouth. First teeth, then tongue, and suction as he works his way to my center.

His tongue slides over me, finding my clit, circling my entrance. I've had this done a few times before and it was never particularly memorable, but this is different. Better. Crazy. Wild.

My hands go in his hair and I fight to still my hips, but I can't resist arching into the silky stroke of his tongue.

He groans against me and lifts me up to his mouth, his fingers curling into my flesh as he devours me. It's raw and it's hot, and it's crazier than anything I've ever done, but it's so good.

I hear myself whimpering, "Please." I don't mean to say anything, but I'm lost to this tightening inside me, this aching squeeze, this need for *more.*

He slides two fingers inside me and then I'm slipping. My entire day has had me at the edge of an awful precipice, and half the hurt has come from trying to hold on.

Finally.

Finally.

I let go.

ETHAN

When I climb onto the couch with her and pull her into my arms, I'm sure of two things: one, Nic falling apart from my mouth is one of the most beautiful things I've seen in my life, and two, if I'm even a fraction as noble as she thinks I am, I'll make sure our wild night ends here.

My heart is racing and my cock is rock-hard, but something about the way she reacted to my touch reinforced the impression of innocence I got from her earlier. Whatever happened to her today has left her vulnerable, and I can't take advantage of that more than I already have.

She nuzzles my bare chest and releases a low, throaty moan that sounds like a purr and sends an electric shock of pleasure up my spine. She lazily follows the outline of the phoenix on my left pec, then dips her hand down to trace the line of hair beneath my navel to my waistband.

When she palms my cock through my jeans, I groan. "Jesus, Nic . . ." I press my head into the cushions, and my hips buck into her touch. "You don't have to."

"I want to."

"But tomorrow . . ."

"Tomorrow, I'll remember this as the hottest night of my life." She licks her lips and shifts over me, slowly unzipping my fly, and despite all my better judgment, I'm helpless to stop her. When she tugs my jeans and boxer briefs down my hips, my dick springs free, and she wraps her hand around me.

I hiss at the contact. The pressure. "Fuck, that feels good."

She strokes and squeezes, and I close my eyes, trying not to blow this like a teenager getting his first hand-job.

She puts her mouth to mine, her hand working between our bodies. "We need a condom."

I pull in a shaky breath, and before I can decide whether a condom is a good idea or a bad one, my phone rings.

Ring one, I ignore, my mind on the condom I don't have and shouldn't want. But at the second ring, I come to my senses. "I have to get that." I cup her face in my hands and kiss her hard before reaching into my pocket to take the call. I don't want her thinking I'm blowing her off, so when she tilts her head and deepens the kiss, I slide my tongue against hers and thread my hands into her hair.

She clings to me. "Ignore it."

Fuck. I wish I could, but I already know by the ringtone that it's the answering service, which means it's about a patient and I need to take it. "I can't," I whisper against her mouth. "It's work. I'm sorry."

She climbs off me. My jeans have fallen to the floor, and I pull them back on as I answer the call. "Hello?" I stand. I have to step away from Nic if I want to have any chance of hearing what the answering service has to tell me.

"Dr. Jackson, Penny Gibson was just admitted. She's already at eight centimeters and feels like she wants to push."

After three babies, she'll go from eight to ten in no time. "Thank you. I'll be there in five minutes." I end the call, slide the phone into my pocket, and turn to Nic. "I have to go."

She flinches and pulls her knees to her chest, covering her naked body. "Okay. Sure."

I shake my head. "It's not like that. I swear to you." I pull on my tee, then shove my arms into my dress shirt. "You have no idea how much I want to stay here, but it's work."

"I understand," she says. "You don't owe me an explanation."

I find a piece of the hotel stationery on the desk and scribble down my name and number. "If you need anything at all while you're in Jackson Harbor . . ." God, that sounds like I'm writing her off. I take a breath. "I'd like to see you again. Maybe we could do it right next time. Dinner, a movie, something like that?" Maybe I'll regret those words tomorrow. I don't do dates. But with this woman . . .

She takes the paper from my fingers and swallows as she looks down at it. "Maybe." She studies me for a beat, then climbs off the couch and loops her arms behind my neck. She lifts onto her toes and presses a kiss to my mouth. "Goodnight."

"Call me," I say against her mouth. I don't remember the last time I said that and meant it. I'm not done with her.

"No regrets," she says, and I don't like the finality in those words.

Chapter SIX

NICOLE

The shrill ring by my head makes my jaw snap shut and my eyes fly open. The sound repeats two more times before I realize it's coming from the phone next to my bed. The *hotel phone*. In Michigan. Where I came after I ran from my wedding. Where I messed around with a sexy stranger without ever getting his name.

Right.

I reach for the receiver. "Hello?"

"Ms. Maddox, there's a Teagan Chopra downstairs for you. Would you like me to put her on?"

I blink and straighten in bed. *Teagan?* I haven't seen her since college. She attended the small state school in Jeffe on a track scholarship, but I thought she moved back home to Virginia after she got her nursing degree. What's she doing in Michigan? "Yes.

Please do."

There's a muffled voice and the sound of the phone moving.

"Teagan?"

"Veronica? What's wrong? Are you okay?"

"I'm not Veronica. I'm Nicole."

She grunts. "I'm not falling for that bullshit again."

I shake my head then wince when that just makes my pounding head ache more. One issue at a time. "What's going on? What are you doing here?"

"Well, you didn't show up to breakfast and I was worried. Your phone must be dead because it's going straight to voicemail."

"I turned it off." I didn't want Veronica or anyone else calling. I just wanted to sleep for as long as possible.

"Did you forget about me? Oh my God, this woman is giving me the stink-eye. Give me your room number so we can have this conversation in person."

"Um . . ." I shake my head. I don't really understand what's happening, but that seems to be the theme of my life lately. So, why not? "I'm in 218."

"Up in a flash."

I hang up, then pull myself out of bed and rub my eyes, but they don't want to stay open.

Now what? Yesterday was all about running away, both physically and emotionally. But today, the sun is shining, and I'm in my sister's hotel room in *Michigan.*

"Veronica?" There's a knock on the door. "Veronica? Are you okay?"

I stumble out of bed and open the door to see Teagan standing on the other side. She looks just like she did in college—long, dark hair, and the flawless olive skin she gets from her Indian father. Today she's showcasing her usual impeccable style with boots, jeans, a sweater, and a pair of chunky earrings. I remember her always looking put-together, no matter the occasion. "Teagan?"

"Eeep!" She rushes at me with open arms and wraps me in a hug.

"God, it's been so long. I don't think I've seen you since college."

She frowns and pulls back, rolling her eyes. "Except for last month? Don't worry. I won't take it personally. I just got you a *job* and a whole new life, but whatever, I'm not important enough to remember. I get it." She looks me over. "You're not even dressed yet? I thought we were doing breakfast, you ho."

I wander to the couch and sink into it. The enormity of the last twenty-four hours is suddenly so heavy that standing feels like too much. Right now, even the task of convincing an old friend that I'm me—and not my sister pretending to be me—sounds like far too much effort. "I don't think I'm up for food."

"Oh, hell no. You're not getting out of this." She looks around the room. "My sister told me about pregnancy brain, but I always thought she was exaggerating. She'd stop in the middle of a sentence and have no idea what she'd been saying."

I blink at her, momentarily tempted to pretend I'm my sister just to find out details. "You knew about the pregnancy?" *Does she know about Veronica and Marcus too? Did everyone know but me?*

She props her hands on her hips. "I'm trying not to be insulted, but you're not making it easy. You can really be self-centered, girl. Where's all your stuff? I'll dress you myself if I have to."

I point to my duffel. "That is all I have. And most of it isn't appropriate for the cold. *Why* is it so freaking cold here? I feel like my bones are growing icicles."

Her eyes go wide as she stares at my duffel. "Since when does Veronica Maddox pack light?"

Since I'm not Veronica. I take a deep breath, but instead of helping me relax, queasiness washes over me.

"You look like you haven't slept a wink. Are you feeling okay?"

I shake my head. "I'm a little nauseated." I should have eaten something before going to bed. Or had some water. Now I need an aspirin and an industrial-size bottle of Gatorade.

Turning away from my duffel, she looks down at my stomach and then back to my face. "Morning sickness?"

"Hangover."

Her jaw unhinges, and she stares at me. "Girl."

"I'm not pregnant," I say softly.

"Oh my God. I'm so sorry. No wonder you're such a mess this morning. When did you lose it?"

I shake my head. "I've never been pregnant. I'm not Veronica."

I don't know if it's from sheer repetition or something in my tone that finally gets through to her, but Teagan lifts a hand to cover her mouth. She sinks onto the couch beside me and proceeds to stare into my eyes for a period of time that could only be described as *awkward*. "*Nicole?* Nicole Maddox?"

"In the flesh."

She tilts her head to one side, then the other, as if searching for the sign that I am who I say, which would make sense if

Veronica and I weren't completely identical. "It's really you," she says. "Aren't you supposed to be on your honeymoon? Why are you here?"

"Veronica is pregnant."

"I know." Her brow wrinkles in confusion. "That's why I got her the job up here with the Jacksons. People aren't as judgy about single moms here as they are where you two come from."

"She's pregnant with my fiancé's baby."

"*No.*"

"Yes."

"*No.*"

"Yes."

"Well, she left out that little detail when she was here last month." She scowls and mutters, "What a cunt."

My stomach rolls and I squeeze my eyes shut. "I wouldn't use that word."

She snorts. "Of course you wouldn't. You're the good twin. But I swear to you, if you slept with *her* fiancé, she'd call you a cunt so many times you'd think it was the name your mama gave you."

"I'm sorry I stood you up for breakfast, but I'm not her, so if you want to leave now, I'll get back to sleeping off the worst day of my life." *And the hottest night.* Did that really happen? Or did I dream it?

"Wait, so when did you find out about them? Before or after you married the dude? And did he know he was sleeping with the wrong twin, or was Veronica pretending to be you like she used to do in college? Did you suspect anything?"

I rub my temples. "That's too many questions at once." I lean back on the couch—the same couch where a sexy stranger gave me the most intense orgasm of my life just last night—and press my hand to my head. "I don't know if I'm hungover because of the tequila or because of *life*."

"You need food. I'm taking you to Sunny Side Up. Best breakfast in town."

"Okay, start at the beginning," she says when we're seated in a booth at the back of a bustling diner.

I give her the abbreviated version of what happened. The phone call I overheard, the wedding, Veronica puking on my ivory roses, finding myself at the airport with her purse, the panicked flight to Grand Rapids, and the drive in the rental car to Veronica's hotel in Jackson Harbor.

I leave out meeting the stranger at the bar, but jump to the text from Marcus that sent me into the women's bathroom. I hand over Veronica's phone so she can read it, though I read it so many times last night I could probably recite it from memory.

Teagan takes the phone and reads aloud. "*Nicole, Veronica told me you took her purse, so I'm texting you on her phone in case you have it. I'm sorry. I misled you. I lied to myself. I don't think I ever loved you the way a man should love his wife. I'm fond of you, but you don't light my soul on fire. I think this pregnancy was God's way of stopping you and I from making a terrible mistake. You'll never be the one I need, no matter how much I wanted you to be.*"

Teagan drops the phone to the table with a clatter. "Oh my

God, has he always been this big of a douche, or is he just letting the douche flag fly because he was found out?"

I shrug. "I thought I was lucky. I thought we were meant to be. He's . . ." My eyes fill with tears. "I *thought* he was a good guy."

I was so angry when I got that text, and then that beautiful stranger was there, looking at me like he didn't want to be anywhere else, even though I had mascara running down my face and probably seemed like the biggest drama queen in town.

Then he kissed me, and I let him walk me to my hotel, and . . .

I drag a hand over my face.

My phone's ringing—no, *Veronica's* phone. I stare at it.

"You should answer that," Teagan says.

The call is coming from my cell, which means there's a good chance it's my sister. Or some other random relative person in Jeffe who got their hands on my purse. I swallow hard and shake my head. "I can't. I'm not ready."

After a few rings, it goes to voicemail, and I exhale. I've never been good at telling my sister no, even for the smallest thing, like taking a call.

"Nobody can blame you," Teagan says. "But you two are going to have to work something out eventually, right?"

"But not today."

The phone beeps, alerting me that I have a voicemail.

"Do you want me to listen to it for you?" Teagan asks.

I shake my head, swipe the phone to unlock it, and tap the voicemail notification. I put it on speaker because knowing Teagan can hear it makes me feel a little less alone.

"Hey, Nic. It's Veronica." Just the sound of my sister's voice makes the backs of my eyes sting. It sounds like she's been crying, and that tugs at my heart and pisses me off at the same time. I cling to the anger. I'm the one who should be upset. I'm the one who should get to cry.

She's the one who's pregnant.

"I know you took my flight to Michigan," Veronica says. "I don't blame you, but I need to call the Jacksons and tell them I can't come, and all the information is on the phone. I was going to get it from you so I could call them, but you're not answering my calls."

Teagan rolls her eyes and reaches over to punch pause on my voicemail. "What bullshit. Has she ever heard of Google? Ethan's a doctor. She could find his office number with minimal effort."

I curl my hands into fists. How many times have I stepped in for Veronica when there was a tough call or meeting she didn't want to take? I thought it was my job to get through the hard parts of life for her. No one else was around to do it.

I take a breath and un-pause the message.

"I understand if you don't want to talk to me, but I was thinking about it, and if you want to stay in Jackson Harbor for a while . . . I know I don't have the right to ask you any favors, but the little girl I'm supposed to be working with is such a sweetheart. The position is only for three months. Would you think about stepping in for me?" She pauses a beat. "The money is yours, of course. I just don't want to leave the family in the lurch."

"How thoughtful of her," Teagan grumbles.

"Talk it over with Kathleen—that's the woman who arranged this. She's the little girl's grandma, and I was supposed to meet with her at noon today. The information's in the calendar on my phone." I hear a noise in the background that sounds like someone speaking over an intercom. "Listen, I've gotta go. Our flight leaves—" She cuts herself off, and I can practically hear the wheels turning in her head as she carefully restructures that sentence. "Marcus and I are going to go ahead and go on the honeymoon. It's not what it seems. We just need to get away so we can work some things out. It's not like I'm taking your place, it's just . . ."

That's exactly what it is. I close my eyes. I just want to go back to bed and stay there for as long as possible.

"This is hard for me, too," Veronica says. "I hope you can understand that someday. I don't expect you to understand it now. I love you. Bye."

Teagan gapes at the phone. "So, you took her plane ticket to Michigan, and she's taking yours to the Bahamas?"

I nod, my stomach rolling. "It appears that way."

"And she took your fiancé and you're taking . . . her job?"

I make a face. "Why would I want her job?"

She shrugs. "I don't know. What else are you going to do? Go back to Jeffe?"

That sounds terrible. "No. I'm not going back there. Not for a while, at least." I meet Teagan's eyes. We were friends in college, but I lost touch with her while I focused on one toxic relationship after another. I would have been better off focusing on my friends. "It was so terrible. Everyone was staring as I ran away. I'm just not ready to face that yet."

"Then stay here. Take Veronica's job with the doctor, and have free room and board for a few months."

"Easier said than done, Teag. I'm not sure this doctor is going to think one sister is as good as the other. He hired Veronica. Why would he want me?"

She frowns. "Why do you make it sound like you're the generic, store-brand version of your twin?"

"You know what I mean. This isn't just any job. People are peculiar about who they let near their children."

"You have experience, and this isn't just any nanny gig. It's a totally cushy one. Lilly is six years old. No dirty diapers or terrible twos. And the little girl's in kindergarten so your days are practically your own."

I frown. "Then why does he need a nanny?"

"He's an OBGYN—delivers babies at all hours of the day. He needs someone at the house so he can leave without notice in the middle of the night."

"How do you know all this?"

Teagan shrugs. "I know Dr. Jackson from the hospital where I work. I'm the one who told Veronica about the job. She'd found out she was pregnant and called me, asking if I wanted a roommate. No offense to your sister, but I wasn't interested in that arrangement. It worked out, though, because I'd just heard that Dr. Jackson was looking for a nanny."

I look at my watch. "I guess I have to go to the meeting. It's not this family's fault that Veronica is heading to the Bahamas instead of moving in with them." In fact, it's my fault. If I hadn't taken her flight, she could have done the right thing by the Jacksons.

"If Kathleen needs someone to vouch for you, tell her to call me."

I shake my head. "Don't get your hopes up, Teagan. I'm going to this meeting to break the news that Veronica isn't coming. That's it."

"And what are you going to do after that?"

I turn up my palms. "Book a few more nights at the Tiffany Hotel and lick my wounds?" I think about the piece of paper with my mysterious stranger's number on it. I left it unread on my bedside table. I should throw it away as soon as possible. I have a long track record of throwing myself headlong into the nearest possible romance, from heartbreak to new love again and again. Last night was fun and amazing and possibly exactly what I needed, but anything resembling a relationship is exactly what I *don't* need.

When I get back to the hotel, I'll throw it away. Otherwise, my mysterious stranger might prove to be too much temptation.

Chapter SEVEN

ETHAN

"Nana and I made cinnamon rolls!" Lilly announces, racing into the kitchen of my childhood home.

We started Jackson Sunday brunches when my oldest brother, Brayden, went to college. The tradition continues even now, when Dad is gone and we're all out on our own. The house is still technically Mom's, but Brayden's been living here since Mom moved into my in-law suite to help with Lilly.

"Oh, look, more carbs and fat to tempt me," my sister, Shay, says, inspecting the cinnamon rolls with a disapproving frown.

My mom slides the pan onto the counter and shakes her head. "One cinnamon roll won't hurt you, Shayleigh."

"Tell that to my hips," Shay mutters.

"She's already mad at Brayden for the bacon," Jake says.

"He made three pounds of it!" she says. "Even you have to

admit that's excessive."

"One, there's no such thing as excessive bacon," Brayden says. "Two, there are a lot of us." He helps Lilly put the cinnamon rolls onto the breakfast bar with the other fixings of this morning's meal—bacon, biscuits, gravy, egg casserole, and fruit salad.

Jake shrugs and swivels his gaze to me. "Look what the cat dragged in." He makes no attempt to hide his amusement. "Late night?"

Carter's eyebrows shoot up into his hairline. "No shit?" He takes a sip of his coffee. "The girl?"

"Late night *at the hospital*," I say, avoiding their eyes.

"You're no fun," Carter mutters.

"He left with her," Jake says.

I glare at him. "Seriously? How about some discretion?"

"Ethan went home with someone?" Shay asks. "Who?"

"New girl," Jake says. "Hot as hell, with a sexy Southern accent."

"Language," Mom says, glaring at Jake.

"I walked her home," I say. "That's it."

"She made him *smile*," Carter says, as if this is some grand accomplishment.

"I smile all the time," I growl.

"Whatever you say, big brother." Shay shoves a cup of coffee in my direction. "No matter what kept you up last night, it looks like you need this."

I take a long pull from the steaming cup and sigh. Shay takes coffee very seriously, and the rest of us benefit. No one makes a cup of joe as good as hers.

"Daddy." Lilly tugs on my jeans and tilts her face up to me.

My heart swells at the sight of those big brown eyes, her perfect face framed by her mother's thick, dark hair. "Can I have a cinnamon roll?"

I look around. "Is everyone here?"

"Levi isn't going to make it. He got held up in Florida," Brayden says. He drops to his haunches and scoops up Lilly. "Let's get you some breakfast."

I shake my head. I've tried to tell my brothers that now that Lilly is six, she's too big to be carried around, but they don't listen to me. She has them all wrapped around her little finger, so I'm pretty sure that if she wants piggyback rides when she's fifteen, she'll still get them.

Brayden grabs a plate from the far end of the bar and fills it for his niece.

Jake leans against the wall next to me. "Are you going to see her again?"

"I don't know." I shrug and try to act like *I don't know* means *I don't care*, but I'm sure he sees right through me. I can't stop thinking about her, and if Jake knew how many times I've checked my phone since I rolled out of bed this morning, he'd give me no small amount of hell.

"You want to," he says, his voice low for once. "Don't be a chicken shit. If you want to see her again, make it happen."

"Nana is taking a long flight tomorrow," Lilly announces as Brayden settles her into a kitchen chair.

I exhale, relieved Lilly is providing an exit from the conversation about Nic. "She can't stop talking about the plane," I tell my mom.

Mom already has a plate of food and takes the seat next to

Lilly. "She's excited for her nana."

"I don't want you to leave." Lilly wraps her arms around Mom's arm and nuzzles her face into her sweater. "I love you *so much*, and I'll miss you to the moon!"

Mom kisses my daughter's head. "I'll send you postcards every day, and I'll buy you special trinkets and mail them to you."

Lilly turns her head and flashes a victorious grin at me, and she looks so much like her mother in that moment that I feel like the floor is falling away beneath my feet.

See what you're missing, Elena?

"Nana's been waiting most of her life for the opportunity to travel to Europe," I tell Lilly. I get a plate for myself and start filling it. "She'll miss you, but this has been a dream of hers for a long time."

"Bucket list," Shay says with a grin.

"I know." Lilly frowns and studies her food. Mom strokes her hair. We've had this conversation more times than I can count since Mom announced her trip last month.

By the time I get my food and make it to the table, Lilly has finished her cinnamon roll.

"All done," she says. "May I be excused?"

I nod. "Clear your plate."

"Why do I always have to clear my plate?" she whines.

"Because I want you to grow up to be a responsible adult who has a sense of—"

"*Personal responsibility*," she says, mimicking the words she's heard me say so many times.

"See?" I say as she slides her plate into the dishwasher. "You already know."

Shay puts her coffee down. "Want to dance?" she asks Lilly.

"Shayleigh," Mom says. "Eat something."

My sister shakes her head. "Had a protein shake when I got here."

"That hardly counts as food," Mom mutters, but Shay and Lilly are already rushing to the basement. Brayden has a PlayStation down there, and a dance game that Shay and Lilly love playing together. I'm not sure who's more competitive—my sister or my daughter.

The rest of us finish our meals, and Jake teases Mom about what he's sure is her secret plan to find a handsome retiree while in Rome or Paris. When we've finished, everyone heads downstairs but Mom. It's my turn for cleanup, so I stay behind in the kitchen. Mom stays with me, watching me like a hawk. I say a silent prayer that she's not going to ask me about last night. I'm a grown man, but I'm no more interested in talking to my mom about hookups than I was as a teenager.

"Don't forget, the nanny starts tonight."

Oh, my other least favorite subject. "I haven't forgotten." Even though I try to make my words kind, they come out hard and cold.

"I really wish you would have met her when she came to town."

"I've already apologized for missing your meeting, but I can't control when babies are born."

Mom holds my gaze for a beat. We both know I'm dreading meeting the nanny—I was then and I am now. I can't stomach the idea of someone stepping in where Elena should be, and I took the coward's route and let Mom make the tough choices.

Mom sighs. "Regardless, when you meet her and see her with Lilly, I think you'll agree Veronica is perfect."

"No one is perfect, but I trust your judgment." Mom and I have had this conversation. I know that a nanny is the best choice for Lilly while Mom travels, but I can't shake this fear that my daughter's going to get attached and struggle when it's time to say goodbye. And with anyone who isn't family, goodbye is inevitable.

You don't know sadness until you try to explain to a little girl that her mommy isn't coming back, and I'd do about anything to protect Lilly from feeling that kind of sadness again.

For three years, I've been leaning on my mother, and she's helped me raise my daughter. While Mom was happy to step in, and loves Lilly more than anything, I also know she's dreamed of traveling her whole life. She couldn't do it when her kids were small, and then when we were grown, Dad was too sick to go with her. Now, Dad's gone, and she's getting older. When her old friend from college invited her on this three-month trip to Europe, I knew I had to help make it happen.

I never expected Mom to put her life on hold after Elena died. But one year turned into the next, and it was as if I'd barely blinked and Lilly was starting kindergarten. When Mom gently suggested a temporary live-in nanny so she could take this trip, I agreed. When she suggested that I might ask the temp nanny to stay on long-term if she seemed like a good fit, I didn't argue.

It's better this way. I'm called to the hospital at all hours of the day. I need someone who's always there. I just can't think about it too much, because that someone was supposed to be Elena. I wanted her to be the one I knew would be home with my child when I delivered a baby in the middle of the night. I wanted her to be the one I'd come home to when I was exhausted after too many hours stuck at the hospital.

"I know it's hard," Mom says. She reaches into the dishwasher to rearrange the dishes I've already loaded. "And I'm telling you now, Ethan, if you try this and it doesn't work, we'll figure something out."

I squeeze my eyes shut for a moment and shake my head. "You've done enough, Mom. I've let you do too much."

She presses a hand to her chest and her eyes fill with tears. "It wasn't a hardship. Lilly is the light of my life." She smiles. "Next to all my children, of course."

I grunt. "Sure, Mom." We all know that Lilly, her first and only grandchild, ranks far above all of us, but we wouldn't have it any other way.

"You don't have to decide right away whether or not you want to offer Veronica the position permanently. Give yourself a couple of months to see if you're a good fit. I just hope you like her as much as I do."

I shake my head. "How do you pick someone to raise your child?"

"She's not raising her, she's *helping*."

We both know that's not true. When you're a single parent working sixty or more hours a week, the person you hire for childcare is as responsible for raising your child as you are, if not more.

"So, I'll see you tonight, then," Mom says.

I nod. "Thanks for taking care of this."

"I know how hard it is for you. And I know how much you

miss her."

My throat is thick, and it's a familiar feeling. I've endured three years of grief and a guilt that never loosens its hold. The thickness in my throat and the knots in my stomach are my new normal. Some days are better than others, but today's going to be hard because today I meet the new nanny—the woman who will have so many experiences with Lilly that Elena never will.

NICOLE

How on earth is my sister on my honeymoon on a sunny beach and I'm in freezing-cold Michigan, cleaning up her mess?

My stomach squeezes.

I found the note in Veronica's calendar about meeting Kathleen Jackson at the Ooh La La! coffee shop at noon. Teagan insisted I borrow her coat and a couple of outfits, and that I "keep an open mind" about working with the Jacksons.

So, here I am, dressed in Teagan's black leggings and oversized red sweater, sipping on a latte and trying to decide what to do next. Do I run out the door or do the right thing and let these people know the woman they hired won't be coming?

The coffee shop is adorable. The barista greeted me with a cheerful smile and asked me half a dozen questions about what brought me to Jackson Harbor. When she found out I have a meeting with Mrs. Jackson, she acted like I was meeting local royalty. Apparently, the Jackson ancestors founded Jackson

Harbor in the early 1800s and are responsible for a lot of the city's longstanding traditions. After giving me that history lesson, she offered me some handcrafted chocolates, which looked amazing, but my stomach isn't up for anything like that yet, so I passed.

I stare out the window as I wait, marveling at how winter has already settled over this town, when back at home in Alabama, the leaves have just hit peak autumn color. Maybe I'll stay here for more than a few days. Maybe I'll stay the whole winter. I'll hibernate—cocoon and be reborn. *Figure out who I am.*

"Veronica!" The woman approaching me has long, perfectly straight gray hair that's parted in the middle and reaches just past her shoulder blades. On anyone else, that hairstyle might say *hippy*, but this woman manages to pull it off and make it look regal. Maybe it's the pearls in her ears, the slight upward tilt of her chin, or the air of authority about her. "Thank you for agreeing to meet me before going to the house tonight. I just want to go over a few things I'd rather not discuss in front of my son." She reaches for my hand and squeezes it between both of hers. "It is such a pleasure to see you again, Veronica."

"Nic," I say.

She blinks. "I didn't realize you went by a nickname. My apologies."

I shake my head. I'm used to correcting people when they think I'm my sister, but this moment makes me ashamed. Ashamed Veronica didn't do better, ashamed I have to deliver the news that we'll be letting this family down. "No, ma'am. I'm sorry, but I'm not Veronica. I'm her sister, Nicole."

The smile falls from her face. "Is this a joke?"

"I'm afraid not."

"You look just like her."

"We're identical twins." I pull my shoulders back and take a breath. "I don't want to go into why, but Veronica isn't going to be coming."

"And you're here to take her place?" She shakes her head. "I'm not sure how I feel about that."

"That's not what I'm saying." *Oh, God. Could this be more awkward?* "I don't know who will take her place. That's not my choice to make, obviously. I just . . ." *Oh, damn you, Veronica.* My words come out in a rush. "My sister's not coming to Michigan, and through a series of events I'd rather not go into, I'm here instead, but not to take her place. I'd never be so presumptuous as to . . . I'm sorry if that causes a problem."

She nods. "Your sister sent *you* to clean up her mess?"

"No . . . yes . . ." I wince when I realize her words echo my thoughts moments ago. Did Veronica send me to clean this up? She has so many times, but I can't help but feel partially responsible this time. I took her ticket to Michigan.

Of course, I wouldn't have had to do that if she hadn't gotten pregnant with Marcus's baby.

"It's complicated," I say.

"How do I know you aren't really Veronica and pretending to be a twin to get out of the job?"

"If she would do that, would you really want to hire her?"

"No," she says. "But I want the truth, regardless."

"I have no way of proving to you that I'm not Veronica." I release a huff that might've been a laugh if I could find anything about this situation funny at all. "I'm not the one who let you down, and *I* feel awful. I'd be too embarrassed to face you if I were her."

She nods thoughtfully. "Fair enough."

"I didn't want to come either, but I couldn't not."

The barista comes out behind the counter and hands Kathleen a cup. "Here you go, Mrs. Jackson."

"Thank you, dear." Kathleen beams at her before turning back to me. "Veronica mentioned she had a sister. In fact, I wanted her to start last week, but she said she couldn't come up until after her sister's wedding?" She arches a brow.

"Yeah, that's me."

"And the wedding?"

"It was canceled."

"Well, I'm sorry to hear that. And is there any chance Veronica will change her mind and join you in Jackson Harbor later this week?"

I fold my arms. I was trying to be classy and not air my dirty laundry, but since I'm in no mood to defend my sister or explain her choices, I abandon that plan. "Since she just boarded a plane to the Bahamas with my ex-fiancé, I'm guessing not."

Kathleen's jaw works, then she snaps her mouth shut. "Well, I'm terribly sorry to hear that." She lifts her chin farther, and I can't tell, but I think her eyes are watering. "Do you happen to have experience caring for children?"

"I—" I shake my head. "I'm sorry, I don't understand what's happening here."

"Well, I'm trying to decide if you'd be suitable for the position, of course."

"Really?" It's tempting to grab this opportunity. To beg her, even, to give me a job so I don't have to go home. "I worked as a nanny for some local families during the summer while I was in college, and I've been working at a daycare up until recently." *Until recently, when I quit because Marcus didn't like the idea of his wife working. When I said goodbye to the job I loved and the kids I adored because he didn't think my minimum-wage job warranted taking my attention away from our home.*

"Do you have a degree in early childhood education? Like your sister?"

I look away and swallow. "I didn't make it through school. Too many distractions." How many times have I let my entire life be derailed on account of love? In college, it was Corbin, who needed me to work full-time because he was having financial troubles. When I returned to school after Corbin dumped me, it was Eddie, who owned a bike shop and needed a secretary. When the hours didn't work with my class schedule, I didn't even hesitate. *Love above all else.* "Veronica is the good student. I only have a couple of semesters' worth of general education under my belt."

"The education was just a bonus, not a requirement." She narrows her eyes and studies me. "You look just like her."

I hate for her to feel cornered into giving me this job. "Listen, I don't want to leave you hanging because of my sister's decisions, so if I can stand in for a few days while you find a replacement . . ."

She folds her arms. "Find a suitable nanny with childcare experience who's willing to relocate to Jackson Harbor for the coldest months of the year in a *few days*? Do you know what a rare find Veronica was? Do you know how hard it was to convince my son that Lilly would be safe with her?"

"I really am sorry." I look at my hands. "I'm sure this is a nightmare for you."

"When are you going home?"

I shake my head. "I haven't gotten that far yet. My life was turned upside down yesterday, and I need some time before I go back there."

She nods sharply. "Good. You can take Veronica's position on a trial basis. I'll need a couple of references and will have to have my lawyer run a quick background check, of course, but assuming that comes out okay, you can move in with my son and care for my granddaughter."

"You don't know anything about me." I don't have any children of my own, but if I did, I struggle to imagine trusting a stranger with them. There has to be something else going on here.

She arches a brow. "I know you showed up to this meeting, while your sister—a girl I was convinced I could rely on—didn't. I know you're here even though this is embarrassing for you, and I know my gut says more about a person than their résumé ever could."

"Would you really be willing to give me a chance?" I want to throw my arms around her and thank her. I didn't realize just how desperately I wanted an excuse to stay.

"I would." She clasps her hands on the table and turns to study the display case of chocolates.

"Thank you," I whisper. "I don't really have anything to go home to right now."

"*I* would," she repeats, her gaze not meeting mine. "But my son isn't me. It took Ethan a while to come around to the idea of Veronica. Changing to *Veronica's twin* at the last minute . . ." She shakes her head. "Ethan won't like it. He won't respect her because she didn't show, and you'll be guilty by association."

My shoulders sag. "Oh." Then why all the fuss about the references and background check?

"It'd be easier for everyone if you pretended to be your sister."

I laugh. "Yeah, right."

"I mean it." Her expression is stoic, and my stomach aches.

"I can't. I won't. I'm sorry."

She looks me dead in the eyes for so long that I want to look away, but something makes me hold her gaze. "I need the favor. If I have to tell Ethan the truth about you, I'll have to tell him the truth about my trip, and I've gone to a great deal of trouble to keep that from my family."

I frown at that. What's she hiding from them? A secret lover? I shake my head. "I can't just lie about who I am." The idea of taking this job was crazy, but there's no way I'm taking it and pretending to be Veronica. I don't play those twin-swap games anymore.

"Then don't. Nic could be short for Veronica, couldn't it?"

I swallow. "With all due respect, ma'am, I'm not comfortable with the lie."

"Nic?" She reaches across the table and takes my hand in hers. Her skin is cold, but her grip is firm. "I'm going to tell you something no one else in my family knows. I don't know you, but I'm trusting you to keep this between us."

The intensity in her gaze makes me want to run from this conversation, but I stay put. "Okay."

"I'm very sick."

My stomach drops. "I'm so sorry. I didn't realize."

"I have cancer. The kind of cancer where one must get much sicker if one wants any hope of getting better."

I draw in a shaky breath. "I'm so, so sorry." My apologies mean nothing—I know that—but I offer them anyway. "This must be a very stressful time for you."

"My family has been through too much. My kids all watched my husband die slowly. By the time he passed away, he wasn't their father anymore. He was a shell—a body living with pain. I don't even remember how many times they all rushed to his side to say goodbye. Then when Lilly lost her mother . . ." She looks away. "Well, Elena had her own kind of slow death."

I didn't think about the child's mother. I thought maybe she'd left, not that she'd died. "I'm so sorry. That must have been horrible."

"It was devastating to the whole family. Ethan still hasn't recovered." She lifts her gaze to meet mine, and I see the stubborn steel in her eyes and the set of her jaw. "I won't do that to them again."

I look around the coffee shop to make sure no one is close enough to hear me. "You're not going to tell them that you're dying?"

"I'm not dying until I decide I'm dying," she snaps. She takes a breath. "I'm going to fight this. I'm going to Germany for treatments. If I get better, I'll come home, and it won't be goodbye. But if I don't . . ." She shifts her gaze to the windows, and I wonder if she sees the street beyond or if all she can see in this moment is an image of herself living the last days of her life alone in some foreign country. "I won't make my children watch me die a little every day, like they did with their father. I won't put my sweet granddaughter through that."

"They're your family. They'd want to know the truth."

She brings her attention back to me and pulls her hand away from mine. "I don't need you to agree with my decision, and I don't need your approval. But I hope you have enough compassion in your heart that you hear my plea. I know my family. I know what they've been through and what they can handle. Believe me when I say that everything I do for them I do because I want them to have the best lives they can. And that includes asking you to do this little favor."

"To pretend I'm Veronica?"

She nods. "To pretend that nothing's wrong. To take this job. You pretend to be Veronica because my son has agreed to take her into his home. Everything else, you can be you. We know so little about your sister, honestly. You don't have to lie about anything other than your full name. And that lie isn't so much a lie as a favor to a sick old woman who loves her family more than her own life and desperately wants to protect them."

I draw in a ragged breath. I don't want to go home. There's nothing there for me but failure, judgment, and a history of mistakes. But I don't want to pretend to be my sister, either. In fact, right now I'd rather forget her altogether.

"Please," Kathleen says. "I had to pull so many strings to get in with the specialist I'm seeing in Germany, and I don't know what'll happen if I have to put this off. I'm desperate."

I find myself nodding. This is temporary. There's nothing waiting for me in Jeffe. I've spent my entire life trying to find my place there and failing. I can pretend to be Veronica for three months as a favor to this sweet woman. I'll use the time to heal, to figure out what *I* want for the first time in my life. And at the end of it all, I'll find somewhere to start a new life.

Chapter EIGHT

NICOLE

Teagan's screech of excitement is so loud that I have to pull the phone away from my ear. "This is awesome!" she says. "You always were my favorite twin."

I roll my eyes. "Shut up. You didn't have a favorite. And you'd still think I was Veronica if I hadn't told you the truth."

"Just because your looks are identical doesn't mean your personalities are. You're the good twin; she's the evil one. This is not news to me."

I bite my bottom lip, fighting the instinct to defend Veronica. I know Teagan doesn't mean it, but she's not the first person to suggest that I'm the "good" one. "If she's so evil, why did you get her a job in your town? And as a nanny, no less?"

"She's not *evil* evil. Just a little evil. Kind of like me, but with less remorse. I'm selfish in preferring you. You're the yin to my yang."

Truth be told, Veronica isn't evil at all. She's self-assured and unapologetic, and when we were children, she was a bit of a troublemaker. But other than sleeping with my fiancé, she's never done anything I could classify as outright *evil.* What Teagan means is Veronica's more adventurous than I am. She goes after what she wants, while I've always been happy to hang out in the shadows. Okay, maybe not *happy*, but more comfortable. I've never been the brave one, never been willing to take risks or make choices for myself alone. I've always admired those characteristics in my twin.

"While I enjoy hanging out with your evil twin from time to time," Teagan says, "I'm much more excited about having *you* live in Jackson Harbor."

"You don't think the lie is a big deal?" I couldn't tell Teagan why Kathleen asked me to do this special favor, but since she seems to know the Jacksons, I figured it was important that she know the rest of the family will believe I'm Veronica.

"Who cares? It's a name, and you're still going by *Nic.* It's hardly a lie at all."

"I'm not sure I agree with that, but it's just temporary." *And Kathleen needs this favor.*

"Exactly. So, you're on your way there now?"

"Yeah. I forwarded my references to Kathleen so she can make sure I'm not a psycho, and I start tonight. Wish me luck."

"You don't need it. You were the kiddie whisperer in college. They always loved you, and I'm sure that hasn't changed. Call me when you get settled so we can make plans for later in the week."

"Thanks, Teagan. I appreciate it."

"Anytime, girl."

I end the call and toss the phone into the passenger seat. On one hand, it's weird not having my own phone. I've lost count of the number of times I've reached for the phone, forgetting it wasn't mine. But on the other hand, I might be tempted to check social media if I had all my accounts at my fingertips. I don't know what people are saying about me and my wedding, and I don't want to know. In that sense, I'm glad to have Veronica's phone. She uninstalled her social media apps months ago. I probably should have taken that as a sign that something weird was going on with her.

Dr. Jackson's home is a ten-minute drive from my hotel in downtown Jackson Harbor. It's an old two-story house with a big front porch and cheery yellow siding. There's a big oak tree in the front yard with a tire swing tied to it. If someone wanted to put the American dream in a snapshot, I'm pretty sure they'd use this house, with its wooded backyard and big bay windows.

I park on the street, unsure if pulling into the driveway might block someone in, and walk up to the door with my hands fisted in my pockets.

You're perfectly qualified to do this job. The lie isn't important—the favor is.

I climb onto the porch and stop in front of the door. Squeezing my eyes shut, I pull in a deep breath and force myself to think positive thoughts. Maybe I'm making a bigger deal out of this than it is. I do that all the time—get myself in knots over little details that don't matter in the long run.

I find the doorbell and press it once, firmly. Seconds later, heavy steps boom toward me, and I hold my breath as I await my fate. But the man who opens the door isn't a stranger. It's the guy who was behind the counter at the bar last night. The one who wouldn't let me pay for my drinks—the mysterious stranger's brother.

The bartender recognizes me immediately, and his lips curl into a smile. "Hey, I wasn't sure I'd get to see you again." He seems really pleased. "My brother's in the backyard with his daughter."

"What's he doing here?"

"Isn't that why you're here? Want me to get him?"

"Um . . ." I turn to the house number then look down at the information that's typed into my—*Veronica's*—phone. "I'm looking for Dr. Jackson?" I swallow. "Maybe I have the wrong house. I'm supposed to be the new nanny for a little girl named Lilly?"

"Dr. Jackson?" He cocks his head and studies me like I might have a few screws loose. "My brother did tell you his name last night, right?"

I blink at him. What the hell is going on here? Is Jake the bartender also Jake the doctor? That's . . . ridiculous. Maybe I'm on the wrong street. "No, but that's not important. Listen, I don't want to be late, and I'm supposed to be meeting—"

"Dr. Jackson?" He brings his fist to his mouth and bites his knuckle as if he's trying not to smile. "Because you're *Dr. Jackson's* new nanny?"

I nod. "Yeah. Do you know where he lives?"

His eyebrows shoot up into his hairline and his jaw works as he stares at me. "Oh, he lives here. Ethan Jackson is my brother."

"Is he one of the guys from that meeting last night?" I frown. *Jackson Brews.* Shit, I thought the "Jackson" in Jackson Brews was for *Jackson Harbor.* Of course, now that I know the "Jackson" in Jackson Harbor is from this family, I really should have put it all together.

Jake's face splits into a big grin. "Holy shit, this is beautiful. Let me just take a moment and soak it in."

My mysterious stranger appears behind Jake. He's wearing a black leather jacket and gloves, and his eyes darken when they take me in. There's already a swarm of nervous butterflies occupying my belly, and the sight of him makes them do the cha-cha. He narrows his eyes at me. "Nic? What are you doing here?"

Jake straightens and presses a hand to his belly, taking a deep breath before turning to face his brother. "Nic is here because she's the new nanny." He turns back to me and points to my mysterious stranger. "Nic, this is Dr. Jackson, but you can call him Ethan."

I can feel the blood draining from my face even as I watch the same happen to Ethan. Last night, he put his name and phone number on a piece of paper. And I was so proud of myself for throwing it away. If I'd read it, I could have avoided this. Or at least been prepared.

Jake chuckles and smacks Ethan on the back. "The good news is you already know you enjoy her company, am I right?" He holds his side and tries to breathe around his laughter. "I'll leave you two alone."

Please don't. I stare at Jake's retreating form, but he's gone, and I'm standing here clutching my purse, staring at Dr. Ethan Jackson. The sexy stranger who gave me the hottest night of my life.

My new boss.

How did this happen?

All the heat in his eyes turns cold. Even though it sucks to have his anger directed at me, I think I prefer it to his completely blank expression. “You told me your name was Nic.”

“It is.”

“My nanny’s name is *Veronica*.”

I nod stupidly. “That’s right.”

He folds his arms. “Which is it? Veronica, or Nic?”

I’m speechless. It was one thing to plan to lie to a complete stranger, but lying to a man who touched me the way this man did last night feels unforgivable. “I’m sorry.” I shake my head. “I didn’t know. Maybe I should leave?”

“You’ve met!” someone chirps behind me.

I swing around to see Kathleen Jackson climbing the front steps. She’s in a long black peacoat and has a Burberry scarf wrapped around her neck. She’s smiling so brightly that I almost don’t recognize her as the woman who confessed she was ill and begged me to lie as a favor to her.

Her gaze bounces between me and Ethan. “Everything okay?”

“Yeah,” Ethan says. “Everything’s fine.”

Guilt ripples through me. I haven’t even started yet, and I feel like I’ve already let this woman down.

ETHAN

Since I walked away from her last night, I've done little but think about Nic. Her taste, the feel of her skin under mine, the sound of her moan when I slid my hand between her legs and parted her thighs.

I spent half my day trying to convince myself that I didn't need to see her again. When that didn't work, I proceeded to spend the next half trying to imagine a scenario in which I could taste her again. I was distracted with thoughts of showing up at her hotel room and kissing her before she could speak. I went to the gym and worked out hard, trying to shake the memory of her, and when that failed, I spent my shower with my dick in my hand and the memory of her taste on my tongue.

But nowhere in my grand scheming and daydreaming did I imagine her moving into my home. In none of the scenarios I cobbled together did I want her to get close to Lilly.

"Why are you two out here in the cold?" Mom asks. "It's freezing. Get inside."

I tear my eyes off Nic for the first time since I spotted her on my porch. Mom is beaming at Nic.

"I'm sorry I was late. Those ladies on the Friends of the Library Committee wouldn't stop chattering about stuff that has nothing to do with the library. Those women, I swear they only do it for the gossip." Mom waves a hand. "Anyway, I'm here now."

"Good to see you, Mom." I lean forward to hug her and kiss her cheek. I need to buy time. I need to think. If I send Nic away right now, it'll mean Mom has to cancel her trip. It would also mean . . . sending Nic away.

Nic's cheeks are bright pink. Is that embarrassment? Last night, I'd have confidently interpreted her expression as embarrassment, but now I'm questioning everything I think I know about her. Was her bullshit about not wanting my name all part of a game? Did she already know who I was? That's the only explanation for how *convenient* this all feels.

"Come on." Mom puts a hand on each of our backs. "Into the house, you two."

Suddenly, I'm sixteen again and called into the kitchen after my mom found condoms in my bedroom. That day she sat me and Elena down and gave us the most straightforward sex-and-consequences talk any parent has ever given.

Nic shoots me a helpless glance before following Mom into the house. I go in after them and pull the door shut behind me.

In the kitchen, Lilly is sitting at the counter drinking a mug of hot chocolate that's piled with marshmallows—because she has Uncle Jake whooped.

"You've met Lilly before," Mom says to Nic.

Nic blinks at her. She's still reeling, too. Good. I don't want to be the only one here without my bearings.

Lilly hops off the stool and stands in front of Nic with wide arms and a hot chocolate mustache. "My new nanny!"

Nic drops to one knee and gives Lilly the hug she's waiting for. The gesture seems so instinctive that it makes my throat thick.

"Nic and I met in town earlier so I could give her the rundown on Lilly's routine," Mom says. She pulls a set of keys from her purse and puts them on the counter with a pile of paperwork. "You'll use my car while I'm away, and your house keys are here as well. And there's also a family credit card for you to use for groceries and gas, that kind of thing." She turns to Jake. "Have you met Nic?"

"I thought her name was Veronica," I snap. I sound like a sullen asshole, but that's in line with how I feel, so I'm going to roll with it.

"Nic can be short for Veronica," Mom scolds me. "Seriously, Ethan. You have no imagination."

"We met last night at Jackson Brews," Jake says, his eyes all but twinkling. *Bastard.* "But I can't stress enough how good it is to see you again, Nic."

"You're different," Lilly says softly, scanning Nic's face. She touches her temple. "Why are you sad now?"

Nic shakes her head. "I'm not sad, but today's a big day for me. I'm nervous."

"No need for that," Mom says. "Lilly, you'll take care of Nic, won't you?"

Lilly giggles. "She's supposed to take care of *me.*"

"But we all need friends," Nic says. "I'd love it if you'd be mine."

Lilly puts a finger to her lips as if she has to pretend to think about it. "Do you like Shopkins?"

Nic nods solemnly. "Kooky Cookie is my favorite."

Lilly's eyes go wide, and I know for a fact that Nic just earned cool points for knowing a Shopkin by name. "Mine too!"

Nic wrinkles her nose. "Do you have any Shopkins I can play with?"

Lilly nods. "I'll go get them!" She rushes to the stairs.

Nic stands and looks at me. "Can we speak privately?"

"Oh, I'll get out of your hair," Mom says. "Jake, would you help me get my luggage down? I still need to finish packing."

"Sure thing." He follows Mom down the hall, and I watch their retreat, not turning back to Nic until I hear the click of the door that leads to the apartment behind the garage.

Nic has her arms wrapped around her waist and is looking around the kitchen like she's just stepped into Narnia.

I clear my throat. "Nic?"

She walks over to the stack of papers Mom left and fingers through them without looking at me. "Do you want me to leave?"

I drag a hand through my hair. "Yes."

Her gaze snaps to meet mine, but she looks away just as fast. "Okay. I understand."

"But you can't. Not without ruining my mother's plans or putting me in an impossible situation." I step forward until I'm standing in front of her. My jaw aches, and I unclench my teeth. "Nic? Look at me."

Slowly, she lifts her eyes to meet mine, and lust zips hot and fast through my blood. For a beat, I'm tempted to forget the mess we're in and focus on her and her alone, tempted to make those soft honey eyes hazy with pleasure one more time.

I lock those instincts away and focus on what matters here. "I need a nanny. Not a wife. Not even a girlfriend."

She winces and draws in a breath. "I didn't know you were my new boss."

"I didn't know you were my new nanny."

I'm aware of every thundering beat of my heart as we stare at each other. The longer I look into her eyes, the more the frustration and anger knotting my gut morphs into desire. The tension between us is palpable, and it's thicker than anger. This push and pull is full of sex and longing. I shouldn't want her now. This whole situation feels off. Too convenient. Too coincidental. But I want her anyway. I didn't get enough of her last night. All the anger in the world couldn't make me forget the way she tasted or the sounds she made when I put my mouth on her. Even as I stand here and think of what a mess last night has made of my future, I want to push her against the counter and finish what we started in her hotel room.

Instead, I take a step back. "What you and I did was a mistake. I need a nanny more than I needed an easy screw."

She shakes her head and looks me over, disgust curling her lips. "I guess you were telling me the truth after all. You really are an asshole."

"You can stay until I find a suitable replacement." My voice is crisp, and my words snap.

She lifts her chin. "Good. Start your search as soon as possible."

Chapter NINE

NICOLE

Me: What would you say if I told you I hooked up with a guy last night?

I stare at my phone and wait for Teagan to text me back. I'm alone in my new—temporary—bedroom. After Lilly came downstairs and introduced me to each of her forty Shopkins, I got my bag from the car and Ethan showed me the upstairs bedroom where I'll be staying.

Ethan and I didn't talk much. In fact, since the moment we agreed that he should find my replacement sooner rather than later, he's said as few words to me as possible and barely looked in my direction.

My phone buzzes in my hand, and Teagan's name and number pop up on the screen. "Hello?"

"Okay," Teagan says, "one, when you text me from your sister's number, it confuses the shit out of me."

"Sorry."

"Two," she says, "you haven't even been in town twenty-four hours, and you've officially seen more action in this place than I have in the two years I've lived here."

Twenty-four hours? So much has happened since yesterday morning that I feel like I left Jeffe weeks ago, not a day.

"And three," she says, "I'm jealous as fuck right now, which is pretty pathetic, given the current state of your love life."

"Teagan, trust me when I say there's no reason to be jealous."

"Don't pull that 'Mr. Right is waiting for you' crap on me. We're getting to a 'desperate times, desperate measures' situation over here."

I'm grateful that she can somehow make me smile despite the mess around me. "That's not what I mean." I take a deep breath. "I met a guy at the bar last night, and he took me back to my hotel."

"And I shouldn't be jealous *why*? Did you do the dirty? Did he make up for the months of chastity Marcus was inflicting on you?" She makes a gagging sound. "Seriously, the born-again virgin thing should have been a red flag."

"I know." I shake my head. "And no, we didn't have sex, but we did . . . *a lot*."

"Tell me about your dirty night. Go ahead. Spare no details."

My cheeks are so hot they could fry bacon, and I'm glad no one's in the room to see it. "It was a rough day, and he was sweet, and I had tequila." Maybe I should be grateful that things worked out the way they did. Kathleen made it sound like Ethan was having a hard time accepting anyone to care for his daughter, and our situation will encourage him to find my replacement faster than he might have otherwise. Since I only agreed to carry on with this ruse because she didn't have anyone else, it might all work out for the best.

Except that now I'm even more uncomfortable about lying. Even if it's only for a couple of days.

"I never got his name," I say.

"Dirty. I like it."

"And I met him again tonight."

"You were supposed to move into Dr. Jackson's place."

"Exactly." I stand because I'm too antsy to be still. "I hooked up with Ethan Jackson last night."

"You hooked up with Dr. Jackson?" She pauses a beat, almost as if she wants her question to sink in. "Your new boss?"

"Yeah."

"He didn't recognize you? I mean . . ." She lets out a low grumble of frustration. "Didn't he know Veronica?"

"Apparently his mom arranged the whole thing, and when Veronica came into town for her in-person interview, Ethan got called to work and he didn't have a chance to meet her. He was just as shocked as I was when I showed up at his house."

"Oh, Nic . . . At least you didn't have sex, right?"

"Small blessings, I guess." The things I did with Ethan were so intimate that I'm not sure the distinction really matters. "But he's pissed about it, so I'm only here until he can find a replacement."

"If that asshole fires you, you can come live with me. We'll get bunk beds."

I laugh, but my eyes are burning with unshed tears. *What*

a fucking crazy twenty-four hours. "Thanks. That's the sweetest thing anyone's offered all weekend."

"Except for what Dr. Jackson offered last night, *am I right?*"

I roll my eyes. "Shut it."

"I'm just teasing. I really am sorry. You deserve a break."

"I'll call you tomorrow, okay?"

"I'm working three twelves starting tomorrow, but let's get together on Thursday. We'll do lunch while the kid's at school."

If I haven't been replaced by then. "Deal."

We hang up, and I stare at my duffel bag. I don't know how long I'll be here, but whether it's for a day or a week, I should unpack what I have with me. In addition to my honeymoon attire, I have a couple of outfits from Teagan, but regardless of how quickly I'm dismissed, I'll definitely need to buy some clothes that are appropriate for Michigan winter. My sundresses and bikinis aren't gonna cut it.

When I'm done hanging my clothes in the closet, I set to the task of filling the drawers. Of course, I have my hands full of panties when Ethan walks into the room.

Because that's my life.

"Hey, do you—" He stops, his eyes frozen on the pile of lace and cotton in my hands. Is it my imagination, or do his eyes darken? Do his lips part incrementally?

Don't do this to yourself. He's only looking at your underwear because you're holding it in front of him like some sort of peace offering. You don't want him to want you anyway. He called you an easy screw!

I force my feet to move and go to the drawer to put away the underwear, angry about the "easy screw" thing all over again. I'm just gonna hold on to that for all the moments that his ridiculous hotness makes me want to fantasize about him.

Ethan clears his throat. "Have you eaten dinner? Lilly and I were just about to have some tacos."

We can't have a simple conversation without my skin blazing from the *awkward.* I'm sure dinner at the same table will be a total blast. "I'm actually not hungry, but I'll be down in a bit to hang out with Lilly. I'd like to spend time with her this evening so she can get comfortable with me while you're around."

"That makes sense." His gaze shifts from me to my bag on the bed—still half full of the sexy lingerie I packed for my honeymoon. I'm not sure how useful a dozen negligées and four bathing suits are going to prove for a nanny gig in winter-stricken Jackson Harbor, but thankfully, Ethan doesn't seem to process what's in the bag—or the giant box of condoms sitting next to it. Those were for my honeymoon too. Marcus wanted to have kids right away, but I wasn't sure *I* was ready, so I packed them just in case, and never stopped taking my birth control.

In retrospect, there were a lot of signs that I shouldn't have married him.

Ethan runs a hand through his hair, and the light catches on his wedding band. *His wedding band.* "Listen, I'm sorry about how I reacted when you came to the door tonight. Seeing you here definitely took me by surprise."

I tear my gaze off the wedding ring. It shouldn't matter that he wears it or that he wasn't wearing it last night, but it feels like it matters. It makes me feel like the other woman, even when I know his wife is gone. "It was unexpected for me too."

He takes another breath. "And I'm sorry about last night. I

should never have done more than walk you home."

My heart sinks—which is absurd, since he called me an easy screw, but my heart doesn't seem to care about cruel words and unfair judgments. It never bothered discriminating before, so why start now?

I didn't expect anything to come of my night with Ethan, and now that he's my boss, that hasn't changed. Honestly, the best-case scenario is that we forget about last night, so I shouldn't care that he's apologizing. But if I had the choice to undo it, I don't think I'd want to. He made me feel precious and special exactly when I needed it the most.

"I promise I'll rein in those behaviors while you're living here," he says.

I burst into laughter. "Oh my God, you make it sound like you're some sort of sexual deviant who can't control his impulses."

He arches a brow. "I didn't control my impulses very well last night."

I shake my head. "Last night wouldn't have happened if you'd known who I was." *Or who I'm pretending to be.* "Give yourself some credit. Let's just . . ." I want to say forget it ever happened, but my mouth won't obey. I think he might beat me to it, but then his gaze shifts from my eyes to my lips, and I hold my breath.

"I'll see you downstairs." He leaves the room, and I rush to the door.

"Ethan," I say, stopping him when his back is to me and he's two steps into the hall.

He turns. "Yeah?"

I've spent my whole life letting people think what they want about me because I hate confrontation. Hell, I almost married

Marcus when I was sure he was cheating on me just because I was scared to confront him about the phone call I overheard. I can't be that girl anymore. I won't. If I'm going to be here pretending to be my sister, I might as well channel her self-confidence.

"I'm not an easy screw. Don't talk about me like that again." I close the door before he can reply.

ETHAN

I'm an asshole.

This isn't news to me. God knows Elena made sure to tell me repeatedly before she died, and I've worn the fucking label as a badge of honor since. It's my own personal scarlet letter, except instead of punishment, it's protection. It's the wall I keep around me—around Lilly. I'd carry a sign if I could. *Asshole. Stay away.*

I've met too many women who want to step in and replace my wife. They think marrying a doctor would be great. I mean, nobody with money has real problems, right? It's a fucking joke, but it doesn't mean people don't believe it. But Elena can't be replaced, and Lilly doesn't need a new mommy. I've been diligent to avoid women who don't understand that. Sure, I had that misstep with Kyrstie—she said she was looking for the same thing I was but decided she wanted more and tried to strong-arm me into giving it to her. Otherwise, my scarlet letter A has served me fucking well.

Tonight, for the first time I can remember in so long, I don't want to be an ass. I just want to take it back.

"I'm not an easy screw. Don't talk about me like that again."

Was it the look on Nic's face or the way her words trembled as she spoke them? Or maybe it's that I knew calling her *easy* was unfair the moment I said it. Hell, she probably skipped dinner tonight just so she didn't have to be near me. The asshole.

I walk halfway down the basement stairs and stop to watch the girls. Lilly's been dragging Nic around the house all night, and now they're in the basement playing with Lilly's kitchen set. Nic is sitting on the floor with her legs crossed under her as Lilly pretends to be her waitress and brings her plates full of toy food.

"How did you know lemon and hot dog sandwiches were my favorite?" Nic asks. She dips her head down to the plate and inhales deeply. "It smells *so good.*"

I'm not sure what I expected, but Nic is amazing with Lilly. She's not just a competent caregiver—she *clicks* with my daughter. A lot of people talk down to kids or ask them questions to pretend to make conversation, but never listen to the child's answer. Not Nic. She listens when Lilly talks. She treats Lilly like the most important person in the room.

Nic pretends to take a bite of the plastic hot dog and moans in appreciation. The sound zips through me, carrying with it a memory of my face between her legs, and goes straight to my cock.

Lilly giggles. "You don't *really* like that, do you? You just mean pretend, right?"

"What? You don't like hot dog and lemon sandwiches?" Nic asks.

Lilly throws her head back to laugh and then spots me on the stairs. "Daddy, come play with us. Nic is so funny."

The smile falls from Nic's face as she follows Lilly's gaze and meets my eyes.

I tear my gaze from hers and smile at my daughter. "I need to make some calls. Are you two okay?"

"That means he's going into his office and we can't bother him," Lilly says to Nic. "He has to do that sometimes because he's a baby doctor."

Nic studies her plate and toys with the plastic lemon. "We're fine."

I swallow hard. *Asshole.* "You can come get me if you need me, Lil."

I head back upstairs and to my office at the front of the house, where I've already pulled up the website for a nanny service. I feel like such a dick for making my mom go through the whole nanny search only to replace her choice the moment she arrives.

Even then, I knew I should do it, but it was easier to let my mom take on that responsibility. I couldn't think about bringing in a nanny because it meant thinking about Elena. But now I see my mistake.

The problem isn't just what Nic and I did last night. I never would have hired her if I'd met her during the interview process. I'm too attracted to her, and even if we hadn't already messed around, that attraction would have been a problem. And fuck, since I saw her underwear when I walked in on her unpacking, I'm never going to be able to look at her without thinking about anything but the lace beneath her clothes.

"You're really a next-level creep when it comes to this girl, Jackson," I mutter.

I sink into my chair, wake up the computer, and stare at my partially completed request form on the screen. Guilt rips through me. Lilly has already connected with Nic, and I'm going to send her away.

We'll come up with an excuse. Lilly will understand. If anything, I should think of their connection as a reason to find Nic's replacement sooner rather than later. I don't want Lilly getting too attached to anyone.

Do you have an age preference for your nanny?

I scroll through the choices and click fifty-plus.

Chapter TEN

NICOLE

There's a soft knock on my door. When I open my eyes, I expect to see my apartment in Jeffe—the buttery yellow on the walls, the sun slanting in across my beaten wooden dresser. Instead, I'm disoriented, unsure where I am for a few sleepy moments.

I'm in a big, soft bed, weighed down by a fluffy comforter, and the gray-blue walls around me aren't familiar. It takes me a beat or two to click everything into place. *Lilly. My new job. The most awkward first day ever. The sexy asshole.*

The lie.

I blink at the clock. It's 3:49 a.m.

"Nic?" Ethan calls from the other side of the door.

I sit up in bed. "Come in."

The door opens slowly, and Ethan takes a single step into my room. He's dressed nicely in a shirt and tie and crisp black pants.

"I just got called to the hospital. I'm sorry. I wanted to be here to help you with Lilly on your first day, but I doubt I'll be back before you have to leave to get her to school."

"It's fine." I clutch the blanket in my lap and resist the instinct to cover my sleep clothes. When I changed for bed last night, I chose the least slutty of my honeymoon attire, but the lacy cami and shorts are hardly appropriate. Can he see? God, am I hoping he can or can't?

He called you an easy screw. It's like my new mantra. If don't-be-attracted-to-the-asshole mantras are a thing.

I force myself to keep my eyes on him. "That's why I'm here, right?"

"Right." His voice sounds rusty, like he just rolled out of bed too, though if I had to judge by his appearance alone, I'd guess he'd been up for hours. "You have the itinerary Mom gave you?"

I nod. "And the directions to the school and her emergency contacts. There's nothing to worry about."

"Mom's still here, so she can help too, but I know she has some meetings today. If you have questions, you can get me on my cell. Leave a voicemail, and I'll call you back as soon as I can."

I nod. He doesn't need to apologize. Honestly, I'm way less nervous about tackling my first morning with Lilly now that her father won't be looking over my shoulder. I can care for children. I can follow a simple itinerary for her day and get through the items on the household to-do list. This is what I did for three different summers in Alabama. I'd even say I'm good at it. Though, to be fair, I've never found it particularly difficult. "Got it." I mentally urge him out of the room. What is it about him seeing me in bed that feels so intimate?

He stays rooted to his spot. "Are you sleeping okay?" His gaze dips from my face and down to the bed, as if it might reveal the answer to his question.

"Just fine." It's almost true. I don't know how long I lay here last night thinking of Ethan downstairs and replaying our front-porch introduction, remembering his hands on me. Getting my brain to shut off is always the hardest part, but once it did, I was out like a light.

"The bed's okay?"

"It's great."

He doesn't look convinced. "I'll see you later, then?"

"Sure. Have a good day." *Awkward.*

He backs out the door and pulls it shut as he goes.

Only when the door clicks closed do I let myself look down and see what Ethan just saw. Under my lacy cami, my nipples are at full attention. They, apparently, don't care that he's an asshole.

"We're turning over a new leaf, you little hussies," I whisper. "No more assholes."

I slink down into my bed, pulling the comforter to my chin. At some point this week, I need to buy myself new pajamas. I'll replace the skimpy lace negligees that scream "fuck me" with flannel neck-high full-length nightgowns that'll get me a jumpstart on my life as an aspiring cat lady.

I squeeze my eyes shut—*sleep first*—but it's too late. I'm way too wired to fall back asleep now.

I might as well get up and get a start on this day. I climb out of bed, grab my things, and head to the bathroom across the hall. The Little Mermaid smiles at me from the shower curtain, and my heart squeezes. I have seriously mixed emotions regarding

Ethan Jackson. How can the jerk who sneered at me yesterday also be the doting father who decorated his daughter's bathroom in a Disney theme? Then again, maybe his mother put this together for her. Or maybe his wife before she died?

I finish my shower, pull my wet hair back into a braid, and dress in jeans and a sweater—the other outfit Teagan let me borrow. Teagan's bustier than me, so the sweater is a little baggy, but it beats running around in a sundress when it's thirty degrees outside.

After taking my things back to my room, I head downstairs. I didn't get a formal tour last night—that would have required Ethan to speak to me, and I don't think he was interested in exchanging any more words with the "easy screw" than necessary. But Lilly showed me around after she finished her dinner. Ethan's house is a large country-style home with three bedrooms upstairs. Ethan's room is on the main floor, and there's an apartment behind the garage, where his mother lives. Lilly didn't show me her father's room, but she insisted on showing me every toy in her room as well as the basement, where there's a big-screen TV, a comfy-looking sectional sofa, and a play kitchen set.

This house definitely has what most people would call "a woman's touch." There's a cute little sign above the coffee pot that says, "But first, coffee!" There are words painted onto the wall in the breakfast nook that say, "Eat Well, Live Fully, Love Completely." I'm sure Ethan's capable of doing this kind of decorating, but my instincts tell me these are touches his wife left behind.

I have a couple more hours before I need to wake up Lilly, and since no one's watching, I take my time as I walk through the living room. I pause at the pictures of Ethan's wife on the mantel, taking in her dark hair and smiling face. I don't know how long she's been gone, but Lilly doesn't look older than two or three in any of the pictures.

I brush my fingers over an image of Ethan and his wife kissing baby Lilly's forehead. They look so happy, and my heart aches for them. What did Kathleen say about Lilly's mother? *Elena had her own kind of slow death.*

I wonder if she had cancer like Kathleen. That would explain why Ethan's mother is so set on keeping her disease a secret. I bet Ethan was a happier man before he lost his wife, and knowing about that loss helps me understand the sadness that never leaves his eyes. No one can blame him for grieving. I can't imagine what it's like to lose your spouse, the mother of your child.

I study another picture of the happy family from when Lilly was a toddler. Ethan's smiling, but I see the same sadness in his eyes I noted that first night I met him. As surprised as I was to find out he was the doctor I'm supposed to be working for, I somehow wasn't surprised to learn he was a widower. It just made sense. It explains the hurt he seems to hide behind his quiet demeanor.

But in this picture, that hurt is already there. The sadness is already creeping into his features. And his wife is standing right by his side.

"Every one of your references had nothing but praise for you," Kathleen says. She's sitting at Ethan's kitchen table with a cup of coffee, the newspaper spread out in front of her. I just got back from running Lilly to school.

"I'm glad you were able to reach them so quickly." I pour myself a cup of coffee—my third for the day, but who's counting?

"I think they're all quite jealous we stole you away."

I smile. "I've always been lucky to be placed with kind people." *Until now,* I think, but I have no interest in telling Kathleen my opinion of her son.

"Your background check won't be back until tomorrow," Kathleen says. "But I don't have any concerns."

"Oh." I'd forgotten she was going to do that. "Good."

"How'd the morning go?"

"It was smooth." Since Ethan woke me up so early, I used my extra time to work on a menu for the week and check the kitchen's inventory. I thought I'd need to go to the grocery store today, but the kitchen is well stocked, so a trip was unnecessary.

I woke up Lilly at the time Kathleen suggested in her notes. Lilly had picked her clothes out for school the night before, and she dressed herself and brushed her teeth without a hassle.

Kathleen didn't come out of her apartment, and I suspect it was because she wants me to have a chance to go through the morning routine on my own before I really am on my own.

"Lilly is really easy to work with," I tell the girl's grandmother. "She's very independent for a six-year-old."

"She's like her father," Kathleen says. "I always said he was born a self-starter. He never needed me to remind him to do his homework or study for a test, and he always held himself to high standards in everything he did. Lilly takes after her daddy like that."

"What about her mother?" I ask before I can stop myself.

Kathleen looks down at her newspaper.

My cheeks heat when I realize how personal that question is. "Lilly's very compassionate. I bet she gets that from her mom."

"Yes, Elena was compassionate," Kathleen says softly. "She felt very deeply about all those she cared for."

"When did she die?" Another personal question, and I hope I'm not overstepping into rudeness, but I feel like I should know more than I do.

"Three years ago this Christmas."

My breath escapes me in a rush. *They lost her at Christmas.* "That's awful." I shake my head. I can't imagine what that must have been like for them. I had a tough childhood, and there's something about the way Christmas is idealized that makes all the tough things hurt even more on what's supposed to be a magical day. There were always good people who tried to make the day as special for Veronica and me as for other children, but there's no protecting a child from the heartache of a lost parent.

"It was awful." Kathleen lifts her head and meets my eyes. I wait for her to tell me more—about Elena or the cause of her death—but she doesn't.

After the silence grows too intense, I take a breath. "Are you all packed?"

"I think so, but I keep remembering little things I'll need." She pushes back from the table, stands, and walks over to me. "I wanted to thank you again before I go. For everything." She tries to smile, but it wavers, and her eyes fill with tears. "If it weren't for you . . ."

"You don't have to do this," I say softly. "You can tell them the truth. You can stay."

She wraps her hand around my wrist and squeezes. Her jaw hardens and she pastes on the smile she was struggling to find a moment before. "And miss my chance to see Europe? No thank you."

I'm not sure what to say, so I just nod. I may not agree with her decision, but it's not mine to make. Obviously, I don't know the details of all her family has been through, and all I can do is trust her judgment. "It's never too late to come home. Just remember that."

Her smile stiffens, and she releases my wrist. "I have to run some errands and then I'm having lunch with my daughter. Will you be okay without the car until this afternoon?"

"I still have Lilly's car seat, and I don't have to return my rental car until tonight, so I'm fine."

"Did Ethan tell you we're having family dinner at my house tonight?" She shakes her head. "Well, my son Brayden's been living there for a couple of years now, but I still think of it as my own, I suppose. All of my children will be there."

"I didn't know that." I make a mental note to adjust the week's meals. The chicken and rice dish I had planned can wait until tomorrow. "I'm glad you're getting together with them before you leave."

"Me too." The tears return to her eyes. "I hope you'll come too. You know Ethan and Jake, but I'd like you to meet my other children. You'll see them a lot while you're here."

"I—" Should I tell her about me and Ethan? Tell her that there's no need for me to meet everyone since he's already looking for my replacement? Is that really what she needs to be thinking about as she begins the battle for her life? No. I can't bring myself to add another worry to her list. "It's family time. I don't want to intrude."

"You know my secrets," she says. "You're officially family."

If I had a family for every time someone promised that, I'd never be alone, but despite a past that should probably leave me jaded, I relish her words. I like this woman. "If Ethan's okay with it, I'll come along."

She shakes her head and squeezes my wrist again. "For one more day, I'm the boss of this family, and I say you come."

Chapter ELEVEN

NICOLE

The dryer buzzes, and I pull out the laundry and pile it into a basket. I've been flitting around the house all day, doing this and that. My first real day on the job and I didn't need to go grocery shopping or prepare dinner, so I felt a little lost while Lilly was at school. Despite the fact that I know I'm temporary and shouldn't feel like I have anything to prove, I hate to sit around or even run errands for myself on my very first day, so I cleaned showers that didn't need cleaning, scrubbed toilets that didn't need to be scrubbed, and mopped floors that were already sparkling.

Kathleen went with me to get Lilly from school so we could drop off my rental car. When we got home, I was ready to put on my childcare cap, but Lilly wanted to hang out with her nana and I was left to feel unneeded again. I decided to wash the little bit of laundry I'd seen in Ethan's laundry room and practically paced until I could pull them from the dryer and busy myself again.

I iron Ethan's dress shirts, fold his T-shirts and athletic shorts, and carry the basket to his bedroom to put away his clothes. In the doorway to his room, I hesitate. This was never on my list of chores. Lilly's laundry, sure, but not Ethan's.

At the last house I stayed at, I did everyone's laundry, so I didn't even think before tossing his in with the rest. But suddenly it feels like an invasion of privacy to walk into his bedroom and put away his clothes.

I take a breath. I've made it this far. Acting weird about it is just going to make it more awkward. I brace myself and flip on the lights.

The bedroom is large, with floor-to-ceiling windows on the far wall. The drapes have been opened—or maybe they always are—and dappled sunlight pours into the space from the big backyard. I take in the walnut bedside tables and the dresser across from the foot of the bed.

I can tell which side of the bed Ethan sleeps on—the covers are turned down from where he got out of bed this morning. A crime novel sits on his bedside table with a little notepad and pencil, as if he makes notes to himself while he's in bed. On the opposite side of the bed, there's a self-help book that was popular with the daytime TV hosts when I started college. I walk over and skim my fingers over it. A pencil marks a place inside, and I open it out of curiosity. A feminine scrawl covers the margins. The notes are a seemingly unconnected series of thoughts.

Happiness is a journey.

Tell Ethan you love him every time you see him!!!

We believe the lies we tell ourselves.

Marriages take work.

Love born in a lie is THE WRONG KIND OF LOVE!

I snap the book shut and put it back on the bedside table, feeling like I've just eavesdropped on a very personal conversation. I do my best not to analyze her notes—the state of her marriage when she died isn't my business, and, frankly, it's irrelevant.

But the book itself is telling—not just its subject or her notes inside, but the fact that Elena's been gone three years, and the book she was reading when she died is still sitting on the bedside table.

Has he opened it? Does he know what she wrote inside?

I swallow hard and back away. Kathleen didn't hire my sister to fix her son or help him let go of his wife. I need to mind my own business until Ethan finds my replacement, but the more I learn about this family, the more questions I have.

I put his casual clothes in his dresser, then flip on the lights to the walk-in closet to put away his dress shirts and pants. The lights flicker, and my breath catches when they illuminate the walk-in closet. It's filled with women's clothes. I look over to the other side of the dresser and realize there's another door that must be his, but I can't look away from all the contents of this closet.

These must be Elena's. Has Ethan gotten rid of anything of hers? Does he carry on as if his dead wife still lives here?

"What are you doing in here?"

I jump at the sound of Ethan's voice and drop the pile of his clothes as I spin around. "I'm just putting away clothes."

He looks from the slacks on the floor to the lit-up closet

behind me. “You’re putting my clothes away in my wife’s closet?”

I swallow. Is it any use to pretend I wasn’t snooping? I squat down and scoop up his dress pants. “I’m sorry. I went into the wrong closet at first and then my curiosity got the best of me.” I take a breath. “If you need any help moving that stuff out . . .” I flinch, realizing how callous that sounds. “I just mean if you need any help sorting through it. I’m sure it must be hard to decide what to keep and what to donate. And you’re really busy. You have an important job and a big family, and you probably want to spend as much time as you can with Lilly.” *Dear God. I’m rambling.* I take a deep breath. “I’m here all day while Lilly’s at school. All I mean is that I’d be happy to help.”

He lifts his chin. “Why don’t you just worry about yourself?”

“Ethan . . .” I step forward, wanting to say sorry but biting back the words. I apologize too frequently. I need to stop apologizing when I haven’t done anything wrong.

He folds his arms. He seemed more accepting of me when he woke me this morning, but now I feel like we’ve taken two steps back. “Why did you really take this job?”

I carry the stack of clothes back to the basket and avoid his gaze while I try to imagine what Veronica would say. “Because it pays well, and it’s a great opportunity to live in a new place.”

“I looked at your résumé. You’re so overqualified it’s ridiculous.”

Veronica is overqualified. I’m just your regular, run-of-the-mill babysitter. I grab the basket and turn back to Ethan. He’s staring at me. “Maybe I’m running away.” I look away as soon as the words come out of my mouth, embarrassed to have confessed something so raw.

"From the *mistake*," he says dryly.

"Yes, from the mistake. From a town that thinks it knows me when I don't even know myself." I look down at his clothes. I feel too vulnerable when I look in his eyes. What is it about this man that makes me say too much? Maybe I just want him to see me the way I thought he did that first night. But when I lift my gaze back to those sad eyes that seem to have lived a hundred lifetimes, it's like he doesn't see me at all. "Surely after all you've been through, you understand what it's like to hurt so much you'd do anything to escape it."

He grunts. "Life doesn't work like that. You can't escape without stomping on the people you're so desperate to leave."

I open my mouth to defend myself and then close it. He doesn't see me, and nothing I say will make him. "I don't know how to do this."

He takes the basket from my hands and puts it back on his bed. "I never asked you to do my laundry."

"That's not what I mean. I don't know how to pretend that nothing happened between us."

For a second, I think he softens. His eyes dip to my mouth and down my body. His jaw relaxes and his hands release from fists at his sides. "You're going to have to try. Nothing can happen between us. I told you that night would become something you'd regret. I told you that I don't make promises."

I flinch again. "I never asked for your promises."

ETHAN

The asshole strikes again.

I swallow, and my gaze returns to her lips. I can't help it—I can't stop thinking about those lips and can't stop wishing to have them on me. When I woke her this morning to tell her I had to go, she looked so fucking sexy that I was ready to crawl into bed with her and make a whole new set of rules for how our arrangement was going to work.

Her hair was tousled from sleep and her face scrubbed clean, and she should have looked sweet and innocent, but her nipples were hard through her silky sleep shirt, and it was all I could do to keep my eyes off her body. I spent my day thinking about her, wondering if I overreacted to our situation and considering calling off the new nanny search in favor of having her close. After all, it's only for three months, and Lilly already adores her.

Then I came home and found her looking in my wife's closet like she was trying to take inventory. The suggestion that I should be sorting through Elena's things just rubs me the wrong way. The last woman who tried to remove Elena's things from my house went so far as to go behind my back and hire a service to come in and do it for me. Just like Nic and her offer to "help," Kyrstie thought I should be grateful.

Fuck no. I don't need to make room for anyone in my life but my daughter, and Lilly has everything she needs—including evidence that her father misses her mother every single day.

I drag my gaze off Nic—off her too-fucking-tempting mouth and away from the sweetness in her eyes—and turn to Elena's closet to flip off the lights and close the door. "Where's Lilly, anyway?" I demand, turning back to Nic. "Maybe you should be more concerned about her than about getting rid of Elena's things."

She cocks her head to the side and frowns at me. "Lilly who?"

"My *daughter*, the whole reason—" I snap my mouth shut when I realize she's being sarcastic. "You're hilarious."

"She's with your mom. They wanted to spend some time together before Kathleen leaves, and I thought it was a good idea."

My chest feels heavy at the thought of my mom's imminent departure. I know it's just temporary and is exactly the kind of trip she deserves, but I also know how hard it's going to be on Lilly.

"I already checked, and she doesn't have any homework," Nic says.

"Thank you." I need to remember that Nic is a professional. Not only does she have experience, she has the perfect educational background for dealing with children. Just because I can't keep my thoughts professional every time she's around, it doesn't mean she's having the same problem. "I applied for a new nanny through an agency today. They're going to get back with potential matches within the next five days, and then I'll have to go through the interview process. So, I'll need you to plan on staying at least a couple of weeks."

I'll need to keep my asshole mouth in check so she's willing to. And my dick in check so I don't decide to keep her here longer for all the wrong reasons.

She tucks her hands into her pockets. "Sure. I should be able to do that. If you're okay with it."

I'm not sure I trust my thoughts on anything regarding

her right now. "I have a conference this week, so I'll be gone Wednesday and Thursday." The timing is crappy, since Nic just got here. I work so much that Lilly doesn't usually get upset when I have to leave for a couple of days, but I'm not sure how it'll go when she's staying with someone new instead of her grandmother. "My sister Shay offered to come stay here if you want help."

Nic shakes her head. "That's not necessary at all. Lilly and I will be just fine. Leave me Shay's number and tell her I'll call her if I need anything."

"I can do that. This week is going to be hard on Lilly with her grandmother leaving, so she might need to be distracted, and I won't be around to help cheer her up."

"I promise I'll call Shay if she needs family." She tilts her head to the side, studying me. "I know you don't think much of me, but I wouldn't have taken this job if I didn't know how to work with children."

"Right." I grab a stack of my pre-hung shirts from the basket. They're carefully ironed and look like I just picked them up from the dry cleaner. "We're going to Brayden's tonight, so you'll be on your own for dinner."

She twists her hands in front of her. "Your mom actually asked me to go to dinner with you."

Of course she did. "Fine. We'll need to leave in fifteen minutes."

She heads out of my room but stops a few steps into the hallway. "Let me know if I can do anything to help with the nanny search," she says without looking at me. "I'd really hate for you to have to endure my presence for any longer than necessary."

A is for asshole.

Chapter TWELVE

NICOLE

Teagan: How's it going? Any development in your Grey's Anatomy-style drama? Any middle-of-the-night sexy times?

Me: Grey's Anatomy? How do you figure?

Teagan: Come on. You hooked up with the hot doctor the night before you started working for him. It's TOTAL Grey's. So, is he Dr. McSteamy or Dr. McDreamy?

Me: Neither.

Teagan: Liar.

Me: He's Dr. McBroody Pants.

Teagan: You're killing me. I was counting on you for some vicarious orgasms.

Me: He's a jerk who wants me out of his house as soon

as possible. There will be no middle-of-the-night sexy times. You're just going to have to get your vicarious orgasms elsewhere.

The energy in Kathleen's house is completely unexpected. Sadness and grief seem to be hiding around every corner at Ethan's, but his childhood home is full of happiness and laughter. I can't help but smile as I watch the family bustle about the kitchen. The space is huge, but these boys—no, *men*—are bigger. Kathleen introduces them to me as they arrive one by one, and the oxygen in the air is slowly replaced with testosterone.

I have myself tucked into the back corner with my minor dinner-prep task of chopping up a fruit salad—an assignment Kathleen was reluctant to give me at all.

On the other side of the kitchen, there's an informal dining area with a TV mounted over a small fireplace. The guys gather around it, pointing to the screen and arguing about the football game that's supposed to start later tonight. I already knew Jake from the bar and that first day at Ethan's, but there are three other brothers, all varying degrees of tall, dark, and handsome—it might be tough to keep them straight—and a sister who hasn't made it into the kitchen for introductions yet.

I watch her in the dining room with her mother. She's raven-haired and curvy. If her brothers are Greek gods, she's Aphrodite. When she comes my way, I quickly avert my gaze and pretend I wasn't staring.

She squeezes past the guys and extends a hand in my direction. "Thank God! It's so nice to have some more estrogen around here. I'm Shayleigh, but everybody calls me Shay."

I take her hand. "I'm Nic. I work for Ethan." My cheeks heat, and I realize I sound like an idiot. "But obviously you already know that."

"You bet. Lilly told me all about you the second I walked in the door. It seems you've won over the family princess."

"She's precious."

She purses her lips, but I can tell she's biting back a smile. "She's not the only one who's told me about you."

I stop chopping and meet her eyes. "What?"

She lowers her voice and leans toward me. "Word on the street is that you're good for my grumpy brother, so I apologize in advance if he fires your ass just because he thinks he's allergic to happiness."

I bite my tongue and direct my eyes back to the salad, a little too delighted to discover Ethan is grumpy in general and not just with me. I was right to dub him *Dr. McBroody Pants*, but it's probably best not to share that with his sister.

Jake saunters over and grabs a strawberry from my bowl. "What are you two scheming over here?" he asks before popping it into his mouth.

"World domination, mostly," Shay says.

"So, the usual." He nods then turns his attention on me. "Are you having trouble keeping everyone straight?"

"Well, I've got Shay down," I say, and she snorts in response.

Jake starts pointing out his brothers. "That's Levi in the Colts jersey, fucking traitor. Carter's the one in black, and Brayden's the one who always looks like he just got off work at the bank."

"Cool. So, if y'all could wear the same outfits every time I see you, I'll be all set."

"I run the bar," Jake says. "And I'm the best-looking, so I'm easy to remember."

Shay rolls her eyes. "You wish." I can't help but chuckle at their good-natured ribbing. "Jake is easy to remember because he's the biggest *nerd* of them all. The girls all think he's such a stud because he runs a bar, works out, and has tattoos. What they don't realize is he wastes *hours* of his life playing video games, and has strong opinions on Marvel versus DC." She holds up both hands and looks me in the eye. "I shit you not—he still plays Dungeons & Dragons with his buddies from high school."

Smiling, I turn to Jake. "I had a boyfriend who played D&D once. It's kind of fun."

Jake shrugs, obviously confident enough to have his sister boil his entire personality down to "nerd." "It keeps me young."

"So, Jake's the nerd," I say to Shay. "What about the others?"

"Levi rides bikes for a living," Shay says.

"You can do that for a living? Like, Tour de France?"

"No." She giggles. "God no. That isn't nearly cool enough for Levi. He rides motocross." I'm not sure I even know what motocross is, but I don't get to ask before she's pointing to Carter. "Carter's a firefighter. Brayden's the one who runs the family business." She lowers her voice and meets my gaze. "He's very serious all the time."

"What about you?" I ask. "What do you do?"

She smiles sweetly. "Whatever I want."

"Shay's a professional student," Jake says. "She's trying to see how long she can go without getting a real job."

"Academia *is* a real job." She smacks him on the chest before turning back to me. "I'm working on my PhD in American women's literature. I'm actually finishing up my dissertation now."

"Impressive," I say. "I can't imagine staying in school that long. I was never any good at it."

Jake tries to steal another strawberry from the bowl. Shay smacks his hand away and turns to me. "Mom said you were working on a master's degree, so you can't be *that* bad at it."

I give a shaky smile. It's Veronica who's started on her master's in early childhood education. Kathleen must have shared that before she knew Veronica wasn't coming. Before we hatched our plan for me to be a big fat liar.

"A master's, and you're working as a babysitter?" Jake says.

"Jesus, Jake," Shay growls. "Don't be a fucking dickhead!"

"Language!" Kathleen shouts from the dining room.

Shay lowers her voice. "Don't be *rude*."

"Sorry," Jake says, wrinkling his nose. "I'm just surprised."

"It's okay," I say, but then he reaches into my fruit bowl again, and I point to his hand with my knife. "But it's not going to be okay if you keep stealing my fruit. That's for dinner."

He chuckles. "Now I see why Mom hired you."

I turn the subject back to Shay. "What do you want to do when you finish your dissertation?"

"That's the million-dollar question," her brother says.

"I'll prepare future students to get their PhDs in literature so they can then prepare additional future students. It's the circle of academic futility." She grins. "And I'll write shit occasionally and try to get it published."

"You write novels?"

She pulls back, as if I just shoved a dead rodent in her face. "Hell no. I write papers *critiquing* books. And right now, I'm writing a book that's essentially a compilation of papers critiquing books."

"That sounds . . . intense." It sounds like she's way smarter than me. "If you could do that, I bet you could write anything."

"Nah," Shay says. "I just know myself, and this is the side of the creative dynamic I need to stay on."

I scrape the last of the apples into the bowl just as Kathleen calls us for dinner. I grab my bowl of fruit salad and carry it to the table, where everyone's already taking their seats.

"Nic, you can sit on that side by Ethan," Kathleen says, pointing to two empty chairs across from her.

"I want to sit by Nana!" Lilly announces, wrapping Kathleen in a hug.

"Of course," her grandmother says. "Do you think I'd want to sit by anyone else?"

ETHAN

I'm sure my mother put Nic by me at dinner to make her more comfortable, but Nic's body language says she'd much rather be somewhere else—under a rock in a dark cave, for instance.

"Is the turkey too dry?" Mom asks Nic.

"It's delicious," she says. "I think I've just had too much coffee today and it's killed my appetite."

Mom tsks. "You and Shay both need to eat more food and drink less coffee."

"I eat plenty," Nic reassures her. If that's true, I'm not sure when it's happening. She's barely eaten more than a few bites in my presence, and I'm sure that's once again because I'm making her uncomfortable. At this rate, I need to find a new nanny ASAP, or there's going to be nothing left of Nic by the time I find her replacement.

"Me too, but Mom worries. It's her MO," Shay says with a sympathetic smile in Nic's direction.

"What do you think of the new nanny?" Brayden asks Lilly.

"I think she's hot," Levi says. He winks at Nic, who blushes so hard that her ears turn red.

"Smack him for me?" Mom asks Shay, who's sitting by Levi.

"Nic is the *best*," Lilly says, oblivious to Levi's inappropriate come-on. "We're gonna have so much fun together. Aren't we, Nic?"

Nic nods and grins at Lilly. "Absolutely."

"Why does the kid get to have all the fun?" Levi asks. Shay smacks our youngest brother upside the head, and he winces. "Ouch!"

Nic fixes her gaze on her plate.

"What does Uncle Levi mean?" Lilly asks.

Shay shoots a glare in Levi's direction. "He's just jealous because we never got to have a nanny when we were kids."

"So jealous," Levi says, then ducks before Shay can hit him again.

"Daddy?" Lilly asks, turning her attention to me. "I have a question about this whole nanny thing."

"Sure, kiddo." I'm used to Lilly's questions. She's full of them, and I've always tried to be as open and up-front with her as possible. "What's that?"

"Why is Nic sleeping in the guest room?"

Nic and I exchange a look. "She's going to be staying with us," I say carefully. "Remember what we talked about? Nic is our new friend, and she's going to take care of you while Daddy is on call." *Until I find you another nanny and shake up your life yet again.* Shit. This whole thing is a mess.

Lilly rolls her eyes. "I know that, but why is she sleeping upstairs?"

"That's where her room is," Mom says.

"She's not staying in Nana's apartment because Nana needs a place to stay when she comes home," Shay adds.

"Of course she wouldn't stay in Nana's apartment." My child looks seriously irritated with all the adults at the table. Because we're morons, apparently. "I didn't say that."

"I guess I don't understand the question, sweetie," I say softly.

Lilly's nose wrinkles, and she folds her arms as she stares me down. "I thought she was going to be sleeping in *your* room."

There's a collective inhale at the table, followed by a few coughs as my brothers try not to laugh.

I try to play it cool. "If Nic slept in my room, where would *I* sleep?"

"In your room," she huffs. "In your bed. With Nic."

Carter, Levi, and Jake give up on holding back their laughter, and their chests shake. Shay bites her lip, and Brayden, ever the dignified one, takes a big gulp of his wine to hide his smile.

Next to me, Nic's eyes are wide as saucers. "Lilly, no, honey. Your daddy and I are just friends. I won't be sleeping in his bed or his room."

Lilly frowns. I don't know where she thought this conversation would go, but she clearly doesn't care for the direction it's taken. "But my mommy slept in his bed."

Well, shit.

My mom and I look at each other, and she gives me a sympathetic smile. In all of our careful preparation to get Lilly ready for the new nanny, it never occurred to any of us that it might sound like we were getting her ready for a new mommy.

Nic reaches across the table and takes Lilly's hand. "Your daddy and mommy were married, sweetie. They were *more* than friends. They were husband and wife. Your daddy and I, though, we're just friends."

Nic shifts her gaze to mine, and a shot of lust surges through me. There's something in me that rejects "just friends" with Nic on a very chemical level, but Nic sounds so convincing that I can only assume this arrangement hasn't been as difficult for her as if has for me.

"Daddy will sleep in his room," she continues. "And you'll sleep in your room like you always do."

"Oh." Lilly looks thoughtful. "I just thought you were a *special* friend."

"I am, I guess," Nic says cautiously.

"But Ripley's daddy's special friend sleeps in Ripley's daddy's bed."

"Good for Ripley's daddy," Levi says.

Shay jabs her elbow into his side, but even she seems to be struggling to hold it together.

Nic bites back a smile. I think about jumping in, but I decide she's doing such a good job that I'll let her finish this up herself. "Well, that's between Ripley's daddy and his friend, I guess, but your daddy and I aren't that kind of friends."

Lilly looks like she's considering this very carefully. "Could you be someday?"

"That's not the plan, sweetie," Nic says. Something like hurt sweeps across her face, and I'm so busy trying to imagine what that could mean that I almost miss the rest of her reply. "But families come in all different shapes. Your daddy doesn't need someone sharing his room for you to be a family."

"I know, I know. Okay." Lilly pushes her plate away. "Well, at least you'll be closer to me this way. Sometimes I have nightmares."

"Really?" Nic asks. "Me too. What are yours about?"

"Bears and stuff." Lilly turns to her aunt Shay, bored with the conversation now. "Dance battle?"

"You bet." Shay pushes back from the table.

Lilly beams. "May I be excused?" Even as she asks, she's leaving the table. She rushes out of the dining room before I can answer, and Shay follows behind.

"Well done," Mom says to Nic.

Nic's cheeks flame, and I'm not sure if it's from the praise or if she was simply able to hide her embarrassment until Lilly walked away. "I wasn't prepared for that."

"I don't think anyone expected it," Jake says, winking at Nic as he starts to clear plates.

"Let me help," Nic says.

Mom tuts. "You're a guest tonight, Nic. Have a seat and relax." She looks at Brayden and says, "She didn't sit down all day. Ran around Ethan's house scrubbing everything to a shine."

Carter picks up the bottle of wine and gestures it toward Nic's glass. "Are you sure you don't want any wine?"

Nic holds up a hand. "None for me, thanks."

"Ethan, tell her she's allowed to drink," Jake says.

"You like beer, right?" I say. "There's beer in the fridge."

"This is a Jackson house," Mom says. "One thing you can always count on at a Jackson house is beer in the fridge." She grabs the turkey platter and salad bowl and heads to the kitchen.

Nic shakes her head. Her cheeks are still pink, and she's more adorable than ever. If anything, my brothers' attention is making her blush more. "I don't drink much."

"That's a little sacrilegious around here. You know we brew beer, right?" Levi says. "Malt and barley are the very foundations of this family."

Brayden grabs a handful of plates and heads to the kitchen with Mom. "Leave the girl alone," he calls as he goes.

Nic slides her gaze to me then back to Levi. "I have poor judgment when I drink."

Ouch. I'm pretty sure that was a jab directed right at me.

Jake grunts and shakes his head. "I'm staying out of this." He exits the dining room and my remaining brothers follow, leaving me and Nic alone. She pushes her food around her plate.

"If you don't like the turkey, I can find you something else."

Her head snaps up. "What? No. I'm fine. Really."

"I'm sorry about that with Lilly. I'm sure she didn't realize that conversation would embarrass you, but Mom's right. You handled it like a pro." I swallow hard. *She* is *a fucking professional.*

"It's okay." She pushes her plate away. "I'm sure she's used to your friends sleeping in your room, but we can make it clear that I'm different."

"Whoa, hold up. Where are you getting that idea?"

She arches a brow. "You're a grown man, Ethan. No one would judge you."

"Veronica—"

Her jaw hardens. "*Nic.*"

"*Nic,* I haven't brought a woman into my house since my wife died for precisely this reason. I don't want to confuse Lilly. The only women who come into my home are family." The one exception was Kyrstie, who I thought understood that her time in my home as my *friend* was unrelated to her time in my bed as my lover. And we all know how badly that ended. I lower my voice in case curious ears are trying to eavesdrop from the kitchen. "That's why I was so upset to realize you were the new nanny—because the women I sleep with *aren't* in my daughter's life. I don't blur those lines, and I don't intend to."

"Oh, so it's sex and never anything more. Got it."

Jesus. "I'm not some asshole who goes around using women for sex, but my daughter . . ." I push my plate away. My appetite is gone. I can never eat when I have Elena on my mind, and I've been thinking about my wife a lot since Nic walked in my door. "She lost her mother. It's a wound I'll never be able to fix, and I don't intend to parade women around her so she can be hurt again and again."

"Understood," she says, her eyes on her plate.

"Would you look at me?"

"Sure." She lifts her gaze to meet mine, and her eyes look less like smoked honey and more like hard amber. "You don't have to continue reminding me where I stand. If you'd have bothered to ask, you'd know I'm not interested in having a relationship at all. But I'm especially not interested in one with Dr. McBroody Pants."

I frown. "Dr. who?"

She shakes her head and averts her gaze. "I'm not an easy screw and I'm not looking for love. I'm here to do a job, so please stop assuming I have any other intentions." She pushes away from the table and leaves the room.

I watch her go, feeling duly chastised but also *rejected.*

Just because you want more from her, that doesn't mean it goes both ways.

Chapter THIRTEEN

NICOLE

"But Nana, I don't want you to go."

"I'll be back," her grandmother says.

Lilly's bottom lip trembles, but I can tell by the firm line of her shoulders and the tilt of her chin that she's determined not to cry. That alone tugs at my heart. I know what it's like to be a little girl who has to be braver than she wants to be.

Dinner's been cleaned up and the leftovers have been put away. Carter and Levi already said their goodbyes and headed home, and now Jake is supposed to take Kathleen to a hotel by the Grand Rapids airport so she can catch an early flight to New York. There, she's meeting the friend who's going to accompany her to Europe—or, at least, that's what she's told them. I'm not sure which parts of her story are true and which are fabricated, but I think it's easier if it stays that way.

"You'll miss Thanksgiving and *Christmas*." Lilly's hushed voice suggests she's saying something shameful.

"How about we do one of those video chats? I'll make sure I'm somewhere with the best internet connection so I can see my girl's face on Thanksgiving Day. And on Christmas . . ." Kathleen looks at me and her chin quivers. "We'll have to see about that."

Because she'll be further along with her treatments then and might not want Lilly to see her at all. Because she wouldn't want Lilly or Ethan to see her ill on Christmas when they lost Elena at Christmas.

Jesus. This whole situation is awful.

"But we'll video-chat on Thanksgiving?" Lilly asks.

"Yes. Because you . . ." Kathleen touches the tip of the girl's nose. "You are what I'm most grateful for."

Oh hell. My eyes burn. I've only known these people for a day, and I'm getting choked up.

Lilly wraps her arms around her grandmother's neck and squeezes her hard. "I'm grateful for you too, Nana."

"Draw me a picture while I'm gone."

"I'll draw you one hundred."

"Then I'll put them all together and have Mr. Vanguilder at the paper shop bind them into a book for me. I'll put it on my shelf and keep it forever. Something you can be proud of."

Lilly looks over her shoulder at me and then back to her grandmother. "I'll be okay," she says with a nod. "Nic will take care of me."

"Yes, she will. I know it."

Guilt knots in my stomach. I hate misleading these people. I have every faith in my ability to care for Lilly, and with the exception of my name, everything I told Ethan from the moment I came to his door has been true. But the guilt remains anyway.

"My plane leaves very early," Kathleen says, looking at me. "I need to head over to my hotel so I can try to get some sleep. Ethan, you make sure to help Nic settle in."

"You enjoy your trip," Ethan says to his mother. "When you get back, we'll have a second Christmas." He looks at his daughter. "With the cabin decorated and presents under the tree."

"Yay! Double Christmas!" Lilly shouts.

Kathleen wraps me in a hug, and in a whisper so low I can barely hear it, she says, "Thank you. Without you, this would all fall apart."

On my second full day at Ethan's, I'm not sure what to do with myself after I drop Lilly off at school. I used all my nervous energy to clean the house yesterday, so I'm without even the excuse of chores to keep me busy.

Maybe I should use the time to get weather-appropriate clothes. There are only so many ways I can cycle through the outfits Teagan let me borrow. Today I'm wearing her black leggings with one of my sundresses, my boots, and the flannel I wore on my first night in town, and I can't decide if the look is hobo-chic or just *hobo*.

On the drive to Kathleen's last night, I saw a sign for Walmart, so I'll go there first. As tempting as it is to run my sister's credit card up with debt for designer clothes, I know myself well enough to realize that I'll inevitably decide to pay her back. When that day comes, I'd prefer to have as few regrets as possible.

My first stop is for nanny-appropriate PJs. In other words, the kind of PJs I'd typically wear at home anyway. The last thing I want to do is find myself tucking a restless kid back into bed while wearing a see-through negligee. I'm not used to this cold, so I choose all the flannel and fleece I can find.

In the women's section, I grab a few pairs of jeans, yoga pants for housework, and some long-sleeved shirts along with a coat so I can return Teagan's. I'm contemplating a new bathrobe when I catch a woman watching me. I turn and offer a smile. "Hello?"

The woman has dark hair and hard blue eyes, and when I smile at her, her nose crinkles like she smells something bad.

I look down at myself to make sure I don't have an unzipped fly or toilet paper hanging off one of my shoes.

"Are you making yourself at home?"

I frown. "Excuse me?"

"I wouldn't get too comfortable if I were you. You're as disposable as any of his other women." She shakes her head and mutters an insult before turning on her heel and disappearing into another aisle.

Did she just call me a tramp?

The encounter leaves a bad feeling in my stomach, and I hurry to finish the rest of my shopping. On my way to the register, I pass an endcap with crafts. Precut pieces of felt are supposed to be glued together to make a turkey. I throw one in the cart for Lilly and make my way to the checkout.

I have to stop thinking about the cold-eyed woman. She probably thought I was someone else. Anyway, it's not like she said anything meaningful. I try to let it go, but the cashier seems to be staring at me too.

"You're Dr. Jackson's new nanny, right?"

"Is that a problem?" I flinch at my tone. Just because some stranger made me uncomfortable, it doesn't mean I should take it out this poor girl.

She shakes her head. "Not at all. Between you and me, I'm just glad he has some help." She reaches for my things as I add them to the belt.

I turn toward the door and realize the woman I spoke with by the bathrobes is leaving. "Did she say something to you about me?"

"Kyrstie was just running her mouth. I wouldn't give it a second thought if I were you."

I gape. "But I don't even *know* her."

The cashier shrugs. "I know you're not from around here, so I'll tell you this: don't mind these other women. They're just jealous because you're where they want to be."

"Where's that?"

She smirks like I just said something clever, but when I hold her gaze, waiting for an answer, she says, "Well, in his bed, of course."

I shake my head. Is this what everyone thinks? First Lilly and now this woman? Kyrstie? I mentally tuck the name away. "I'm just the nanny."

"Mmm-hmm." She winks at me, as if we're sharing some sort of secret. "Robin Gastonez saw you two cuddling up the other night at Jake's bar. She said she didn't need to be in that bathroom to know what was happening in there. Were you *just the nanny* then?" She chuckles and shakes her head.

Oh, crap. Does everyone in this town know what happened on Saturday night? Do they know he walked me back to my hotel? That he stayed for a while? If they know that, I'm sure everyone assumes we had sex. Heck, we probably would've if he hadn't been called to work.

"That was nothing. I was having a bad day and he was being a friend. That's all." I hope my smile is more convincing than it feels, but I think I could be an Academy Award-winning actress and nothing I said would change the mind of this woman.

After I pay, I hurry out of the store and load the car with my purchases. I was going to explore Jackson Harbor today, but the last thirty minutes have made me feel exposed and cheap. I want to hide at Ethan's house until it's time to pick up Lilly. It's a small town. Word spreads fast in small towns, and maybe people seeing us at the bar together on Saturday night got the gossip machine rolling. I'm sure it'll fade in a day or two, but in the meantime, it's all too familiar.

I try to stop thinking about it, but I hate the idea of anyone not liking me. I can't help it. It's in my nature. When I was growing up, my quality of life depended on my ability to make people like me. You can't just outgrow something like that.

I tell myself it doesn't matter. I tell myself my stay here is temporary. I tell myself that only I get to judge my actions—not some random woman at the local Walmart.

But when the doorbell rings, I'm feeling so anxious, torn down, and vulnerable that I don't want to answer it, and I have to give myself a lecture about how *it's my job* to greet whoever's at the door.

"Can I help you?" I ask as I pull the door open.

"Surprise!" Teagan throws her arms out wide and grins at me. "Guess who got called off today?"

"How did you know where the house was?"

She shrugs. "Small town. I know stuff."

I wrap her up in a hug before she can even get inside. "You have no idea how much I needed to see a friendly face."

"Aww!" She strokes my hair. "What's wrong?"

"Come inside," I say. "I need a cup of coffee, and then I'll tell you about my awesome day."

In the kitchen, I make a fresh pot of coffee and give Teagan the rundown of everything she's missed since we saw each other last—Ethan finding me in his wife's closet, dinner last night, and, finally, the women at the store today.

"I wonder who the bitch was," she says, making a face.

I shrug. "I don't know. I'm sure I've never seen her before, but she was awful. And then the cashier all but admitted they were gossiping about me." I take a long swallow of my coffee. I know caffeine isn't a good idea when my anxiety is flaring up, but coffee is liquid comfort to me, so I'll just try to stick with a half-cup and hope for the best. "Wait. Kyrstie? I think the cashier said that was the lady's name."

"Dr. Weir," Teagan says with wide eyes. "Blue eyes and total resting bitch face?"

"Sounds about right."

"Oh, yeah. That makes sense. She and Doc Jackson were messing around last summer, and she didn't take it well when he wasn't interested in turning their fling into something more serious."

"How crazy do you have to be to take it out on the new nanny?"

"Bitches be jealous," she says with a shrug.

I grunt. "Jealous because I get to live with Dr. McBroody Pants? *Seriously*? I mean, he's hot, but no amount of sexy can make up for the guy being an asshole."

"Come on, Dr. Jackson isn't that bad," Teagan says. When I gape at her, she holds up her hands. "Okay, okay. He's been terrible to *you*. But he's nice to the nurses at the hospital, which is more than I can say for a lot of doctors. It's more like he's closed off. Mostly, I think the women are just disappointed that he's so hard to get close to. Otherwise, he'd be eligible bachelor material."

I grimace. "Well, they can have him. I mean, what kind of man doesn't want to be involved in selecting the person who's going to care for his child? Don't you think that's weird? His mother did everything to hire Veronica."

"It is a little weird," she says. "I bet the whole thing's hard on him because he still hasn't gotten over his wife's death. He doesn't like the idea of another woman moving in here—even as an employee."

The reminder takes the snark out of me, and I sigh. "Kathleen told me Elena died at Christmas."

Teagan flinches. "That's rough."

"Brutal," I agree. My heart aches for Lilly. I'm sure that day left a mark on her. "Do you know what happened to Elena?"

Teagan shakes her head. "I don't know. Dr. Jackson was a widower when I moved here."

"It's weird, Teagan. I'm sure losing her had to be hard on him, but when I walk around this house, it's like she never left. Her clothes are all still hanging in the closet, her jackets are on the rack in the mudroom, and there's even a book on her bedside table and a pair of her shoes by the back door—as if she might show up and pick up where she left off at any minute."

"Wow." She blinks and rocks back on her heels. "How long has she been gone?"

"Three years this Christmas. And if he wasn't ready to pack up her things, you'd think his mom or one of his siblings would have come in here and done it for him."

"Maybe he wouldn't let them."

"I'm sure he wouldn't, but what exactly is he going to accomplish by keeping all of her things in place?" I shake my head. "I guess I've never lost someone like that, so maybe I don't have any idea of what's normal. When I see him holding on to her like that, I almost can't hate him for being an ass."

She tucks her hands into her pockets and studies me. "Is he still looking for your replacement?"

"Yeah, but he said he'll need me here at least a couple of weeks. They'll send him a list of candidates and then he'll have to go through the interview process and all that." I take a deep breath. "I'm anxious to get away from Ethan, but I hate to leave Lilly. That child is amazing. She's a super-smart, happy kid. She deserves better than a revolving door of nannies, you know what I mean?"

Teagan reaches out and squeezes my arm. "I know you're worried about her best interests, but don't get yourself too worked up, okay? Look at this place, and look at her with Ethan."

"I know," I say quickly, hoping she won't finish her thought.

She does anyway. "Lilly's mom might be gone, but she's gonna be just fine. Her situation isn't like yours and Veronica's."

Chapter FOURTEEN

NICOLE

I'm up early because I couldn't sleep. I keep thinking about Ethan's wife.

Last night, when I was cleaning up the kitchen after dinner, I found a note taped inside a kitchen cabinet. It was written in the same loopy script I saw in the book by Ethan's bed.

E,
You give me the courage to face another day. Again. And again.
—Elena

I told myself it was romantic, but I kept thinking about the things my mom would say to us when we were kids—about how she kept going for us, about how she didn't see the point if we weren't with her. Sometimes people disguise their crutches as love, but pretty words don't change the fact that it's not healthy to put your whole purpose for being on someone else.

I feel like I'm spying on their marriage, but it's hard not to when he refuses to let her go.

I pour myself a big mug of coffee and then grab my prescription from the medicine cabinet as Ethan walks into the kitchen. Lust knots in my belly at the sight of him in a dark suit and tie. I don't want to be affected by him, but I am. He's supposed to head to his conference this morning, and I know he's nervous about leaving me here.

"You ready to head out?" I ask.

He nods. "Yeah. I think so. I . . ." He frowns as he spots the bottle of pills in my hand and marches over to me. "What is this?" he asks, taking them from my hand.

"It's my medicine." I snatch it back. I'm grateful I packed my meds in my honeymoon bag. If they had been in my purse, I'd be without them.

He turns it in my hand to look at the label before bringing his eyes back to mine. "We specifically asked if you were on any medication when you interviewed for this job."

Shit. Veronica isn't, but had I been the one who interviewed, I would never have lied about my need for meds. That would be like a diabetic lying about needing insulin. "Why does it matter?"

"Why does it *matter*? That's a medication for depression, and you're caring for my daughter."

"Are you really that big of an asshole? Because I thought you were a doctor, and a doctor should understand that somebody who suffers from this is better off with the medication than trying to pretend she doesn't need it."

"That doesn't forgive you for lying about it."

A knot forms in my stomach, and I search for the best way to speak the truth and only the truth. "I don't know what your mother asked everyone she interviewed, but I know I wouldn't have lied about this." *Damn it, Kathleen. Why didn't you ask me about this?*

"Fuck." He spins away from me and drags a hand through his hair. He puts his hands against the wall and leans forward. "Are you okay? Should I cancel my trip?"

"I'm *fine*, Ethan. I've been stable for years. I just want to stay that way."

He pushes off the wall. "I wish I'd known about this."

"Now you know." I lift my chin. I refuse to be shamed for taking the medication I need.

"Call Shay if you need anything, okay? I'll call tonight after my meetings." Then he stomps out of the house as if he's going off to war.

"And then Madison D—not my best friend, the other Madison—she said she thought Mrs. Cooper was a meanie head, and Mrs. Cooper made her apologize and miss recess."

I can't hear the other end of the conversation, but I have to smile as I watch Lilly chatter on about her day with her grandmother. Kathleen called last night before her plane left New

York, and again this afternoon after Lilly got home from school.

"Okay," Lilly says. "Love you too. Call again tomorrow?" She nods. "Okay, here's Nic."

I take the phone, and Lilly hurries back to the table to work on her drawing. "How was your flight?"

"It was very long," Kathleen says, "but I was able to sleep some. Caroline and I are in Berlin, and we'll go meet the specialist at the treatment center tomorrow."

I exhale heavily and walk out of the room so Lilly won't overhear. "You really do have someone with you. I'm glad to know that."

"Caroline is a dear friend. You don't need to worry about me."

"No one should have to go through that alone," I say softly.

"Put it out of your mind. Did Ethan leave for his conference this morning?"

"He did. He'll be back late tomorrow night."

"That's great. I was worried he'd cancel with you being so new there. The timing just couldn't be helped."

I'm honestly surprised he didn't cancel, but I don't say that. Instead, I take a breath and tell her what I can only imagine Ethan will bring up next time they talk. "Mrs. Jackson, I take a prescription for depression. Ethan saw me with it this morning, and he was really upset."

She's silent a beat, and I can hear her long exhale before she speaks. "Oh, dear."

"I wish you'd have asked me. I'd have told you about it."

"What did he say when he saw? Did he ask you to leave?"

He's already asked me to leave, so he didn't have to ask again.

"He was upset. He thinks I lied to you."

"I'll call him tonight and smooth his feathers. I'll tell him I forgot to ask. Something. I don't want him angry with you."

"Well, thank you. I think that might help." I pause a beat. "You don't have to worry about me. I'm perfectly capable of caring for Lilly."

"Of course you are," she says. "I wasn't worried at all."

But Ethan is. "Call when you can, but focus on resting."

"I will. Give Lilly kisses for me and tell her I miss her. I'm not sure how often I'll be able to call once I start these treatments."

I want to tell her to come home, to remind her that she doesn't have to leave her family while she fights this, but I've already told her what I think, so I bite my tongue. "Okay. I understand. We'll talk soon."

We say our goodbyes, and I end the call then return to the kitchen to find Lilly frowning at the drawing in front of her, a tear rolling down her cheek.

"What's wrong, sweetie?" I walk over to the table and look at the picture. There's a little girl holding hands with a taller figure with long silver hair—Lilly and her grandmother, I assume. "That's a beautiful picture."

Lilly shakes her head. "I messed it up." She scribbles over the hands. "I can't do hands. They're too hard, and it looks bad."

My heart aches. "Oh, honey. I thought the hands were nice, but if you want to do it again, that's okay too."

"I just want it to be perfect so Nana knows how much I miss her."

"I have an idea." Lilly's sad face is tugging on my heart. "After dinner, what do you say we go to the store and each pick out our own candy, then we come home and make a big batch of popcorn and watch *My Little Pony: The Movie* on the big screen in the basement."

Lilly's eyes light up, and she wipes a tear from her cheek. "Candy?"

I grin. "You can choose anything, but just one thing. And no king-size because we're not kings, we're *princesses.*"

She laughs. "What if I want Sour Patch Kids?"

"Then you should choose Sour Patch Kids."

She cocks her head and narrows her eyes at me, then props her hands on her hips. "Does Daddy know you're filling me up with sugar while he's away?"

I bite back a smile. "I promise we'll brush our teeth really well before we go to bed."

"That sounds nice," she says softly.

After dinner, we bundle up and go out to the car, because it's getting dark and too cold to walk. At the drugstore, Lilly is far too excited about the prospect of Sour Patch Kids to beg me for additional candy, and we're in and out of the store in no time.

Back at home, we put our PJs on—Shopkins for her, penguins riding inner tubes for me. I make the popcorn and put it in a big bowl for us to share. I start the movie and sit down on the couch next to her, and she spreads out her favorite blanket so it covers my legs and hers.

I wrap an arm around her and kiss the top of her head.

"You're my favorite nanny," she says.

I laugh. "Have you had a lot of nannies?" I ask, even though I know I'm the first. She probably means *babysitter.*

"No." She shakes her head. "You're the only one. But even

between you and all the others I haven't had, you're still my favorite."

My heart squeezes and expands all in one painful moment. I don't know how long I'll be here, because I don't know how long it'll take for Ethan to find my replacement, but even after only a few days, the idea of leaving this little girl kills me. She's so smart and sweet. Even when she's sad about her grandmother leaving, she still manages to fill the room with joy.

"And you're my favorite kid," I say. "No contest."

She leans her head against my arm. "I love my Nicky."

Oh, kid. You're killing me here. "I love you too, Lil." And I mean every word.

"Nic, I think I ate too much candy." The small voice comes from my bedroom doorway.

I pull back the covers and climb out of bed, and I'm halfway to Lilly before she vomits all over the carpet. *Oh, crap.*

"You poor sweetie." I lead her to the bathroom across the hall and pull her hair back into a tie. As she loses the remaining contents of her stomach into the toilet, I wet a washcloth with cold water and wipe the back of her neck. She's burning up.

"Clara eats Sour Patch Kids at lunch and she never pukes," she says, still gripping the sides of the toilet bowl.

"Oh, honey, I think you caught a tummy bug. This isn't because of the candy." She didn't even finish her little package, and it's not like she's never had candy before, but I hate that she's blaming herself. When her stomach stops heaving, I hand her a cup of water. "Rinse your mouth out. It'll help you feel better."

"I am better, I think."

I get her some Tylenol and say a prayer it'll stay down long enough to lower her fever. When she's tucked into bed, I put a plastic washbasin next to her in case she can't make it to the bathroom next time. Then I get busy cleaning up the vomit on my bedroom floor and scrubbing the toilet in the bathroom.

Just when I'm done washing everything and am ready to head back to bed, I hear her retching again, and her pathetic cry for me. I help her to the bathroom, where we wipe her face and she rinses her mouth before I guide her back to bed.

"Will you stay with me?" she asks as she pulls her blankets tightly around her.

I sit in the chair by the head of her bed. "I'm not going anywhere, baby. I'll be right here when you wake up."

Chapter FIFTEEN

ETHAN

Home.

The conference was good, but I can't wait to get home. I'm anxious to see Lilly, as always, but more so because it felt odd to leave her with someone new. Even though I know Nic is completely capable of doing the job, when I called this morning and found out Lilly was sick with a stomach bug, I had to fight every instinct to rush home right away.

I park the car in the garage and throw my keys in the mudroom, sorting through the mail I missed while I was gone. The lights are on in the kitchen. I head that way, expecting to see Nic at the sink or over some dish she's prepping for tomorrow.

Instead, I see my sister Shay with a big glass of wine in her hand, circles under her eyes and shoulders that sag with exhaustion. I tense immediately, memories rearing their head and dragging my thoughts down the path of worst-case scenario without my permission. "What are you doing here? Is everything okay?"

"I've been taking care of Lilly. The stomach bug's been sweeping through this house."

"Where's Nic?" Did she leave? She wouldn't do that, would she? I just spoke with her this morning, but I have been a bit of an asshole to her.

"Your rock-star nanny got it too. She called me this afternoon. Lilly was finally feeling better when Nic came down with it." She shakes her head. "She didn't want Princess Lil to have to see her nanny worshipping the porcelain god, if you know what I mean. Lilly's all better, just a little run-down. She's sleeping now. Has been for a few hours. Wish I could say as much for poor Nic. I swear, I love you and I love my niece, but if I get this shit . . ." She shudders. She lifts the can of Lysol and shakes it. "You're out of Lysol. I sprayed down everything. Nic was in the middle of washing all the sheets when it hit her, so I finished that and started another load. Now I'm gonna go home, turn the shower as hot as I can stand it, and scour myself with bleach." She drains the rest of her wine. "Do you need me to be back early to take Lilly duty so you can make your rounds?"

I shake my head. "No. I'll get Henderson to cover for me."

"Okay, well, if you change your mind, you know where to find me."

"Thanks, Shay. I really appreciate it."

"Nothing I wouldn't do for that kid. Or for you." She studies me for a beat. "You know that, right?"

I nod. I see her out the front then pad up the stairs to check on

Lilly. Her room smells like clean sheets and linen-fresh-scented Lysol. As Shay promised, Lilly's tucked in and sleeping deeply. I tiptoe quietly into her room, smooth her hair back, and press a kiss to her forehead. *No fever.* Aunt Shay's got it under control.

I head for Nic's room next but stop in the hallway in front of the bathroom. The light's on. I knock on the door. "Nic?"

"Yeah?" Her voice is weak, and I barely hear her reply.

"Can I come in?"

"Yeah."

I open the door and find her curled up on the bathroom floor in front of the toilet. Her shirt is damp with sweat, but she's shivering and her face is pale, and I feel like a dick for not getting to her faster.

"I'm sorry I had to call Shay." She doesn't open her eyes, as if looking at me would take too much effort. "Didn't want Lilly to be alone. I couldn't . . ." Grimacing, she holds her stomach. "Sorry."

I grab a washcloth from the cabinet and run it under cold water. I sink to my haunches and wipe it across her forehead. "It's okay. Have you had anything for this fever?"

She waves limply toward the counter, where a bottle of Advil sits next to a liter of untouched Gatorade. "Don't think it stayed down."

"Let's get you back into bed."

"No, it's easier if I stay here."

I slide an arm under her. "Come on. Bed." I help her off the floor and guide her out of the bathroom, but instead of going to her bedroom, I take her downstairs to mine—the only bedroom with an attached bathroom. She doesn't protest; she doesn't seem to have the energy to care.

I pull back the sheets and tuck her into bed. I put the trashcan by the side of the bed, just in case, and go to the kitchen to get her some water, but when I return, she's sleeping.

NICOLE

My mouth tastes like rotten-egg-flavored sawdust, but for the first time in I don't know how long, I'm thinking of opening my eyes for a reason other than finding the nearest toilet. I stretch in bed, my arms overhead, my toes pointed, and hum in appreciation of the warmth from the sunlight coming in the window.

It feels good to feel healthy, but I'm in no hurry to get up. I open my eyes and bolt upright when I realize I'm not in my bed. I'm in Ethan's bed, and I'm not alone in the room. Ethan's sitting in the recliner in the room's little alcove, a book in his lap. His eyes are on me, and there's a gentle smile on his face.

I look down to make sure I'm still decent. I have no memory of coming in here. I'm in the dirty gray T-shirt I wore to disinfect the house yesterday and some fleece sleep pants. I shift my gaze to him. "How did I get here?"

"I got home after midnight," he says. "You were sleeping on the floor in the upstairs bathroom. I moved you."

I frown. "Why'd you put me in here?"

He nods to his bathroom door. "Closer to the toilet?" He

shrugs. "And it was more comfortable for me to keep an eye on you in here. The only place to sit in your room is the floor."

I drag a hand over my face, trying to wipe the grogginess away. I have too many questions and I'm not sure where to start, so I begin with the most important. "Where's Lilly?"

"At school."

"Is she up for that?" I grimace as soon as the question comes out of my mouth. Her father would know, wouldn't he? Between being her father and, you know, a *doctor*?

He's unfazed. "She's fine. Shay said Lilly was fine all evening, and she was her usual Energizer Bunny self this morning, so I took her to school. She made me promise to tell you she said goodbye. I wouldn't let her wake you."

I feel like I'm failing at this nanny gig. My first week on the job and I've had to call in the sister to help and Ethan had to let me sleep in his bed. "And why aren't you at work?"

"A friend is covering my rounds. I stayed home to take care of you."

"I could have taken care of myself."

"I have no doubt about that." He stands and puts his book in the chair before coming toward me. "But just because you could doesn't mean you should have to."

My stomach flip-flops happily, not just at his words but at the warmth in his eyes. It appears I've finally won the approval of Dr. McBroody Pants. All I had to do was puke for twelve hours straight.

I'm suddenly all too aware that Ethan's eyes are on me and I'm sitting in his bed. Even though he's here tending to me in a totally platonic way, my overactive imagination is trying really hard to make it into something more. I scooch out of bed and straighten my sleep clothes.

"I'm gonna get a shower." I wave to the bed. "Then I'll change these sheets."

"I've got it, Nic. I know how to do laundry."

"What are you paying me for if you're going to do your own laundry, run your daughter to school, and miss work?"

He smirks. "Don't even the broodiest employers give their employees sick days?"

"I'm sorry I said that."

He shrugs. "I suppose it's true. I've never been known for my sparkling personality." He steps forward and presses the back of his hand to my forehead. When he pulls it away, his gaze snags on my lips for a long moment.

My heart pounds. "No fever," I say, though I'm sure he already figured that out himself.

"I could have come home from the conference to help you out. Shay said you were a total rock star."

"There was no reason for you to come home. I was fine until . . ." *Until I wasn't.* He stares at me for a long time, and I nervously tuck my hair behind my ears. "I'm going to get that shower and get dressed."

"Don't push it, okay?" He reaches around me and grabs a bottle of water off the nightstand. "Drink this and about five more. You're dehydrated."

"How do you know that?"

He grunts. "Logic? And"—he sweeps his index finger across my bottom lip—"I can see it here."

See, Nic? He's not looking at you in a sexual way. He's looking at you because he's a doctor and that's what he does.

I feel myself deflate but try not to show it. I'm being ridiculous.

"Hydrate and your energy will come back faster."

"Yes, doctor." I back out of the room, and once I hit the hallway, I hustle to the stairs to the bathroom, where I strip out of my grimy clothes and turn the shower to hot.

While it warms, I brush my teeth for five minutes, because vomit is disgusting, and that's how long it takes for my mouth to feel clean again. After I'm done flossing and using mouthwash, the mirror is completely steamed over.

I step under the hot spray, all too aware that Ethan and I are alone in the house together until Lilly gets home. What is it about a surly man turning into a nurturer that's so damn sexy?

I distract myself from thoughts of Ethan and his sad eyes by making a list of the things I want to disinfect today and the supplies I'll need to give the house a good scrubbing.

When I finish the longest shower of my adult life, I pull on a pair of gray sweats and a long-sleeved black shirt. The energy I woke up with is fading fast, and I feel a little weak, but I ignore it and get to work.

I start with the bathroom I share with Lilly. I deep-cleaned it yesterday, but it needs it again now. I'm scrubbing the base of the toilet with bleach water when I hear someone clear his throat behind me.

I turn to see Ethan, his big arms folded over his chest.

"What are you doing?" he asks.

"Cleaning."

He shakes his head and grabs the scouring pad from my hand. "Go read a book or watch TV or do something that doesn't involve manual labor. I'll clean the bathroom. And before you think about making some fancy dinner with your extra time, it's already been taken care of."

Standing, I smooth down my pants and bite my lip. "Thanks. I'm just . . . I'm not very good at doing nothing."

"I noticed." His eyes sweep over me. "Go rest, Nic. I need you to rest now so you can get well again. If you push it, you'll just catch something else or have a rebound of the stomach flu."

I nod. His logic is sound. I can't laze around in bed, though, so I head to the living room to pick a book from his bookshelves.

I pull out a romance novel. I've gotten so used to Elena's notes that I'm not surprised to discover a piece of paper folded inside, but it's not the kind of note I was expecting.

> Elena,
> I can't stop thinking about you. Come to me tomorrow after he leaves. You deserve happiness.
> –M

With shaking hands, I put the note back and pick another book, trying not to think about what I read. Who's *M,* and why was he writing notes to Ethan's wife? And why did she leave the note in her book instead of throwing it away? Did she want Ethan to see it? *Has* he seen it?

Maybe Ethan and I have more in common than I ever realized.

"Did you find something?" Ethan asks behind me.

I turn away from the bookshelf and give him a tentative smile. "I did."

I found more than I wanted to.

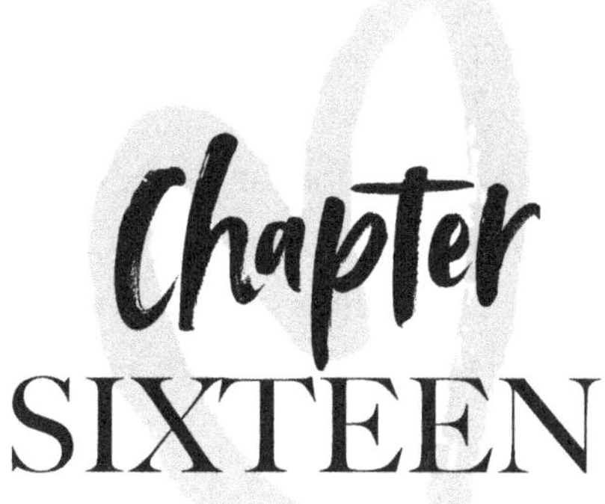

Chapter SIXTEEN

ETHAN

"These candidates aren't what I asked for." I grip my phone tighter and glare at my computer. What's the point in paying a company to help you find an employee if they can't even follow simple directions?

"Your highest priority was that the candidate be available to start within the month," the woman from the agency says. "That limited our field drastically. Many candidates don't want to move right before Christmas, especially for such short-term employment."

I bite back a growl. It's not fair to take my frustration out on this woman, but the entire list of candidates is unacceptable. Too young, too uneducated, one who doesn't speak English—*how* is she supposed to talk to my daughter?—and another who doesn't drive. I suppose that one could teleport with Lilly to all of her activities.

I hear clicking on her end of the line and tap my pen impatiently. Nic's been here for almost a week, and I'm losing my mind. She's so on top of everything, so easy with Lilly. *So completely perfect for this job.*

Except she's also really fucking sexy and sweet, and she makes me think I want things I can't have.

Last night, after I put Lilly to bed, I found Nic in the living room. She was curled up in the chair with a blanket and the novel she started after I caught her cleaning. She had a steaming cup of tea by her side and looked like she belonged there. *I fucking miss that,* I thought as I stared at her. I didn't think I would. When things were their worst with Elena at the end, I thought I'd take any level of loneliness to simply escape my marriage. I didn't think I'd miss it at all. But last night, looking at Nic like that woke some dark, long-dormant corner of my heart. I found myself aching for this thing I told myself I didn't want again. *Company. Companionship. Love.*

"Did you need me?" she asked when she caught my eye. She got to her feet before I could stop her. "I'll get out of your way."

"Don't leave." I shook my head. "I mean, you're not in my way, and I don't need anything." *Except you. Except that mouth.*

Then I grabbed a beer from the fridge and opened the email the agency had sent me earlier that day. I was sure it would be as simple as picking the best of the best and arranging some interviews. Instead, there's not a single candidate on the list who's remotely acceptable.

Now, Nic's taken Lilly to her Saturday-morning swim lesson. I wanted to get this call out of the way while they were gone.

Since we're essentially going back to the drawing board, I'll be lucky to arrange interviews before Thanksgiving, let alone get someone new in here. I wanted Lilly to have a chance to adjust to the new nanny before Christmas. It's bad enough that her nana won't be here, but I'm afraid she's becoming attached to Nic so quickly that she'll melt down when she finds out Nic is leaving before Christmas too.

Am I fucking this up? Should I just keep Nic on until February, like we planned? It'd be one thing if she wasn't a good fit, but she's better than I could have imagined. *Except for the part where you like the way she looks sleeping in your bed and you woke up this morning with a raging hard-on after dreaming about her.*

"Sir?" the woman at the agency says. "Are you still there?"

I push away my thoughts. "I'm here."

"Sorry about that. Perhaps you'd be willing to consider extending the term to a year? It's the relocation that makes the short-term contract difficult, and since I don't have any nannies in your area who fit your requirements, a longer contract would certainly open up the field."

Sighing, I lean back in my chair and drag a hand over my face. The plan was always to find someone we could transition into a long-term position if it worked out, but the idea of committing to a year without spending any significant time with the person is brutal. "I don't want to commit to room and board for a year in case it's not a good match, but what if the year's salary is guaranteed even if we part ways before that?"

More tapping. "That'll help," the woman says. "I'll be in touch when I have more candidates."

"Thank you." I end the call and blow out a breath. If they

don't come up with anything good this time, I'll ask Nic if she'd be willing to stay on. I can find a new nanny who can start when Mom gets back in town. Hell, maybe I could just scrap the search and have Mom head it up again when she returns. She was spot-on with Nic. She keeps the house clean, and if the dinners she made Tuesday and the leftovers in the fridge are any indication, she's a phenomenal cook. But most importantly, she's great with Lilly. She manages that difficult balance between playful and still being in charge. She's the perfect choice for us.

Except for the part where I can't stop thinking about getting her in my bed.

It's a pity my dick's ruining this for everyone involved.

"Daddy!" Lilly shouts from the kitchen. I was so lost in my thoughts that I didn't even hear them come in. "I got a postcard from Nana!"

I head to the kitchen and find Lilly dancing around with her postcard and Nic at the coffee pot. "You're worse than Shay with that stuff," I say.

She grins and pours herself a cup. "Want some?"

I shake my head. I'm about to say *no thank you*, but Nic takes a sip and moans, and the words get caught in my throat. Her hands are wrapped around the cup and her eyes are closed, and *fuck*. I did this to myself that first night. When I walked away from her, I thought we'd see each other again. I promised myself we'd get to finish what we started, and now my body wants me to make good on that promise.

"Daddy, why are you looking at Nic like that?"

Nic's eyes fly open and meet mine. My thoughts must be written all over my face because her cheeks bloom red.

I tear my eyes off her and turn to Lilly. "Like what, sweetie?"

"Like you're thinking *really hard* about something," she says. She skips over to me and hands me the postcard, apparently not interested enough in my ogling to wait for an answer. "It's from New York City!"

I look at the postcard that shows the Statue of Liberty and flip it over to read the back.

> Lilly, my big adventure begins here. I hope you are having a great week! I miss you already!
>
> Love, Nana

"Where are you going to put it?" I ask, handing it back to Lilly.

"Nic said we could buy a photo album and put all of Nana's postcards in it so they're safe and don't get lost. Isn't that a great idea?"

I turn to Nic, whose cheeks are a shade lighter than the last time I allowed my eyes to roam in her direction. "It is. Really great. Thank you."

"How long until Thanksgiving?" Lilly asks, pulling my attention back to her. "That's when Nana and I get to video-chat!"

"Twelve days," I say. "Are you excited to go to the cabin?"

Lilly nods enthusiastically, then turns to Nic. "You're going to love the cabin! It has tons of bedrooms and a pool table and the best sledding hills, and everyone is there!"

"Lil, Nic gets Thanksgiving off. She might want to spend it with her family."

Nic flinches—is that at the mention of her family, or the

time off? Maybe she thought she'd be replaced by Thanksgiving. Maybe she's already lined up a new job . . .

Shit. I practically fired her on her first day, so she's probably already looking. She's so overqualified that she won't have any trouble at all finding something.

"No," Lilly says, tugging on Nic's arm. "You don't have plans, do you, Nic?"

Nic's face softens as she looks down at Lilly. "I don't have plans yet, sweetie, but your Thanksgiving plans are for family."

"They're not just for family." Lilly shakes her head. "Uncle Jake brings Ava all the time, and sometimes Uncle Levi's friends come too. Nana says there's room for everyone." She turns her sweet, pleading eyes on me. "Doesn't she, Daddy?"

"There *is* room for everyone," I say dutifully. It's practically our family creed. "But like I said, Nic has Thanksgiving off."

"Please come to the cabin," Lilly says. "It can still be your day off. Everyone else will do the cooking, and I promise I'll let you sleep in. I want to show you the kids' room. I'm the only grandkid right now, so I get it to myself, but it's full of bunk beds, and when I'm bigger, Daddy says I can have a sleepover there with my friends."

"We'll see," Nic says gently.

Lilly's shoulders sag. "That means *no.*"

"It means I need to think about it and see how my friends are spending the holiday." She smiles and chucks Lilly under the chin. "It means I need to talk to your dad and look at my calendar before I make any decisions."

"Okay." Lilly folds her arms. She's at that age when she doesn't like ending any conversation without getting the answer she wants, but she's also old enough that she knows throwing a fit won't help.

"Have you drawn a picture for your nana yet today?" Nic asks.

"Eeep!" Lilly rushes to the pantry where we keep her box of craft stuff. "I almost forgot."

"You can work on it while I make lunch," Nic calls after her.

"Okay," Lilly says. She's already on her way to the living room with a notebook and a box of crayons, and just like that, Nic and I are alone together.

Nic meets my eyes for a beat, and just when I think she's going to say something more, she turns around and starts gathering items from the fridge. "Do you want to join us for grilled cheese sandwiches and tomato soup?"

"Sounds good." I expect her to pull out cans of soup, but instead, she grabs a big container from the fridge. "Is that *homemade* tomato soup?" I ask.

She grins at me as she carries it to the stove and transfers the contents to a pan. "I made it early this morning. It's tomato *bisque*, actually, but don't tell Lilly. She insisted that soup is good and *bisque* is gross, so we're just going to call it soup." She stirs the soup and turns on the gas to warm it.

"No wonder Mom was so insistent on hiring you." I shake my head in wonder. "You're the whole package, Nic."

"It's not a big deal," she says softly. "I like to cook."

"But you barely eat," I say.

She shrugs and drops her gaze down her body. "I eat plenty. I'm not in any danger of wasting away."

"You're perfect," I say before I can stop myself. She meets my eyes and blinks, and I drag a hand over my mouth. "I'm sorry. It's just . . . you are. You're gorgeous. I hope you don't feel like you need to lose weight. Your body is . . ." I swallow hard. "You know."

She makes me tongue-tied and fumbling when I've always found it easy to flirt with women. Maybe that's the difference. I'm not trying to flirt. I sincerely want her to know how gorgeous she is.

She avoids my gaze and stays silent, further evidence that I'm more awkward than charming when it comes to her.

"And now I'm the asshole boss who says inappropriate things to his employee."

She laughs and pulls a loaf of bread from the bin. "You're fine, and thank you. That's nice, especially coming from someone whose body is also . . . *you know.*" Her pink cheeks grow darker and she avoids my eyes. She's so fucking cute when she's embarrassed.

"I'm sorry about that Thanksgiving conversation. I really didn't mean to put you in an awkward situation. You have four days off while we're at the cabin, and you can spend that time however you want." She told Lilly that she needed to see what her *friends* were doing, but made no mention of family. I take another breath as she slices cheddar cheese from the block. "You won't go home and spend it with your parents?"

She stills her knife mid-slice, hesitating a beat before finishing. "No."

I wait a beat, hoping she might fill the silence with some detail about herself, but she doesn't. "I guess you probably want to use the time to look for a new job."

Her careful expression falters. She puts down the knife and

turns to me. “You want me gone that soon?”

“No. Not at all. Actually . . .” I shove my hands into my pockets. “I had to call the agency this morning because none of the candidates they sent me were acceptable. I was hoping you could hold off your search until we find someone.”

“I wasn’t planning to leave you in the lurch.”

“I couldn’t blame you if you did.” I take a step forward. I shouldn’t, but I do. One step, then two more. I take another step so I’m standing right in front of her and she’s looking up at me through her lashes. “You don’t owe me anything. I was a jerk to you the second you walked in my door, and you responded by throwing yourself into this job. I don’t deserve all you’re doing for me.”

“I made a promise,” she says. “I’m just trying to follow through.”

“I screwed this up, Nic. I take responsibility for that.” I fist my hands at my sides because I want to touch her and she’s right here. So close, so warm, so sweet. “I’m the one who missed the meeting when you came to visit last month. I’m the one who isn’t comfortable having any personal history with my daughter’s caregiver.” I swallow and release my fists so I can tilt her face up to mine. Once my hand is on her jaw, I instinctively slide it into her hair. “I’m the one who can’t stop wanting things from you that you’re not here to give me.”

Her gaze drops to my mouth. “I didn’t think you wanted anything from me anymore.”

“I’m trying not to, but I keep thinking about . . .” *Don’t finish that sentence.* I flick my thumb over her earlobe and down the column of her neck.

She closes her eyes and releases a shaky breath. "About what we left unfinished," she says for me.

"Daddy!" Lilly calls from the living room. "How do you spell *forever*?"

It's Nic who moves first. She takes my hand from her neck and steps back. "I won't look for another job until you find a replacement."

Relief sweeps through me—too much relief—followed by dread at the thought of searching for someone suitable. Or is that dread at the thought of her inevitable departure?

"Daddy!" Lilly calls again, and Nic bites back a grin.

"F-O-R-E-V-E-R," I call back slowly, eyes still on Nic.

"Thank you!" Lilly says, exasperated.

"And what about this thing between us?" I ask Nic quietly. "Do we just pretend we don't feel it?"

She turns back to the counter. "That's what I'm trying to do right now," she murmurs.

"Is it working?" My heart is racing. As if we're standing here doing more than talking. As if I touched more than just her jaw and neck.

"Not with you standing that close," she whispers, her eyes on the ingredients in front of her. "If you could go back to being a cold jerk now, it would be very helpful."

"I'll see what I can do." I walk away, and every step is like pulling against a magnetic force.

Chapter SEVENTEEN

NICOLE

Teagan: How's everything at Casa Jackson?

Me: Great. Except there's all this sexual tension in the air and I DON'T KNOW WHAT TO DO WITH IT.

Teagan: Does this mean that Dr. McBroody Pants is getting you all hot and bothered?

Me: Kind of. I don't know what to think about him. One second, he's pushing me away as hard and fast as he can, and the next, he's telling me that he can't stop thinking inappropriate thoughts about me.

*Teagan: I mean, you could fuck him? *shrug emoji**

Me: I can't even with you.

Teagan: If fucking is off the table, there's always masturbation.

Me: You have no boundaries.

Teagan: You brought it up.

Me: Fine. True confession time? I can't get myself off without a vibrator.

Teagan: For real? Have you even tried? It's not rocket science.

Me: For real.

Teagan: Need me to draw you a picture and label the parts?

Me: Shut up! It's not like I don't know where things are. It's too hard to stop thinking about what I'm doing, so I can't disconnect and just fantasize. Know what I mean?

Teagan: I guess. But still, I think you could figure it out if you had to.

Me: I'd rather have a battery-powered friend help.

Teagan: Oh. Damn. I know! Why don't you tell HIM about your little problem? I bet he'd help a girl out. If you recall, he's quite capable even without fucking.

Me: You're crazy. He's my boss.

Teagan: And that's not hotter, how?

Me: I've made terrible decisions regarding men my whole life.

Teagan: You really, really have. What was the name of the guy you dropped out of school for?

Me: The first or second time?

Teagan: Point made. I just remember the one who looked at my tits every time I talked. I started to think they did choreography to my words.

Me: See? Terrible decisions. NO MORE ASSHOLES.

Even assholes who are sometimes not assholes at all. Even assholes who keep forgetting to be assholes and who look at me like I'm melted chocolate he wants to lick up.

Teagan: Maybe just a one-time exception for Ethan. JUST FOR SEX. (It's the other shit that always screwed with your life anyway.)

Me: No. More. Assholes.

Teagan: Okay, okay. I get you. The shop I use is on Pine and Twenty-Fifth. Great selection, discreet staff.

Me: I can't bring a vibrator into a house where I'm looking after a kid!

Teagan: So lock it up.

Me: I feel like a creep. No. I'm just going to have to suffer.

Teagan: Or . . . you know, figure out how to deal with it the old-fashioned way. Desperate times, desperate measures.

I made myself a promise that I'd use at least one day this week to explore Jackson Harbor.

Last week's unpleasant encounter at the Walmart made me afraid to venture out any more than necessary. Yesterday morning, when Lilly and Ethan went to brunch with the rest of the Jacksons, I thought about exploring town, but I was too afraid of running into the bitchy doctor again, so I stayed in and finished the book I started on Friday. But my fear of Jackson Harbor ends now.

After I finish my errands, I head downtown.

I park on the street before heading into Jackson Brews. First things first: lunch. I've been fantasizing about those little balls of goat cheese since I tried them my first night here. I want to replicate them, but since I was a bit intoxicated when I sampled them, I need to try them again first.

"Look who's here," Jake says when I walk in the door. He's behind the counter in jeans and a fitted white T-shirt that shows off his broad chest and tattooed arms. Maybe Ethan's father was actually a divine force who came down to give Kathleen perfect children. It doesn't seem reasonable that two mortals could produce such gorgeous offspring.

Jake is good-looking in a more obvious way than Ethan, but he doesn't make my insides do that shimmy-shake-and-melt thing that Ethan does. *Thank God.*

"It's always good to see you." He throws his towel over his shoulder. "What can I get you?"

"I had something the last time I was here. I think it was fried goat cheese."

Jake grins. "Everybody's after my goat balls."

I snort. "That's a lovely description. Why haven't they written up the recipe in *Epicurean Magazine* yet?"

"They wish," he says with a wink. "But it's a secret. What else can I get you?"

"I think a plate of fried cheese will suffice."

"And to drink? I just tapped an amazing ivory stout—not a Jackson brew, but local. From a place I like in Grand Rapids."

"Just water. I have to pick Lilly up from school in a couple of hours."

"So how is it, working for my sullen brother?" he asks.

My cheeks heat, because it would probably be fine if I hadn't hooked up with said sullen brother. I was starting to get over that before our little—*so hot*—conversation in the kitchen on Saturday. "It's fine."

"Real convincing," he says, sliding a glass of ice water across the bar. I stiffen, but he chuckles and shakes his head as he walks away, and I realize he's not going to push me on it.

A few minutes later, he brings me my plate of fried cheese.

I take a bite and whimper, holding my hand to my mouth. "Oh. My. Gosh. Even better than I remember."

Jake smirks. "If I had a nickel for every time a woman told me that . . ."

I ignore his innuendo and finish my goat ball, taking careful mental notes. I'm determined to replicate these little bites of heaven. There's something in the batter that gives it a subtle crunch.

"What are you up to today?" he asks.

"I kind of want to get a feel for Jackson Harbor. I've been here over a week and don't know much about it. Where should I go?"

"Well, you've already found the most important place."

"Obviously," I say around a bite.

He folds his arms. "Though you haven't really experienced Jackson Brews until you have a draft beer."

"I'll add it to my list for a day I'm not driving around a small child."

"Fair enough." He taps his finger to the side of his jaw. "Hmm.

Do you mind walking?"

"I've got a coat," I say proudly. "It has a fleece lining and everything."

"If you don't mind the cold, keep your car parked and walk a block north to Lakeshore Drive. Most of the shops along the boardwalk are closed for the season, but it's a beautiful view of the beach if you can handle the wind off the water. And there's a lighthouse."

"That sounds perfect. Thank you."

"You know, I'd be happy to babysit my niece if you want Ethan to show you around. There are a bunch of nice restaurants around here, and the walk out to the lighthouse is really romantic at sunset."

"I think you have the wrong idea about my relationship with Ethan."

He arches a brow. "Do I?"

"He's my boss. I'm his employee. That's it."

He stares at me for a long beat before nodding. "You made him smile when you barely knew him. And when you two are in the same room, he can't take his eyes off you."

"You've hardly seen us together," I say, but I feel warm from his words. I like the idea of Ethan watching me, of being special because I can make him smile. I don't *want* to like it, but I do.

He shrugs. "I guess I just liked the idea of him finding someone who could make him happy again."

"No one can make someone happy. That's something we can only do for ourselves." I frown the second the words leave my lips. I've often repeated the advice a social worker gave me when I was sixteen, but I've never been good at believing it. I've been looking for someone who could give me the happiness I've found so elusive, from one bad relationship to the next. Happiness is like sand. It's easy to grab a handful, but it slips away before you want it to, and the only times you can hold on for long are when it's rocky and a little painful.

"Where were you with that wisdom three years ago?" Jake asks. He stares into space as he shakes his head.

"You mean when Elena died?"

"Yeah." He takes a deep breath and swings his gaze back to me. "And before, I guess." The sadness in his dark eyes is at odds with the goofy personality he's always presented to me. It seems like Elena's death took a toll of the whole family.

"Jake . . ." I should hold my tongue, mind my place in this family. But it feels important, so I ask, "What happened to her?"

"Heart attack?" Jake says, and the way his voice cracks makes it sound almost like a question.

I press my hand to my mouth. I'm not sure what a woman who's likely to have a heart attack at her age *should* look like, but I certainly wouldn't have guessed that answer from Elena's pictures. "She was so young."

He wipes at an imaginary spot on the bar, his brows knitted together. "Yeah. She was."

"Ethan must have been madly in love with her. She left a hole."

He squeezes the back of his neck. "They were high school sweethearts. She was the love of his life, and he would have done anything for her."

I think of the contradictory notes I saw in the book by his bed, then about the note I found inside the novel. I push the thoughts away. Their marriage isn't for me to analyze or understand. Relationships are complicated. I, of all people, know that. "I imagine she felt the same about him."

"Maybe once." He says the words so softly that I'm not sure he intended to let them out. He shakes his head, then his whole body—as if ghosts are holding him in the past and he has to break free. "Don't tell Ethan we had this conversation, okay? He doesn't like anyone talking about her unless it's the good memories." He forces a smile. "You know, for Lilly."

"Right. Of course. I'm sorry if I overstepped by asking. I just . . ." *Sometimes it's like she never existed, and other times it's as if he expects her back at any moment.* "I'm sorry."

"You didn't," Jake says. "Anyone in your position would be curious. He just doesn't want to let himself move on."

I nod, my heart twisting for Ethan. It aches for Lilly too, but she speaks about her mother in such vague terms that I don't think she remembers her much anymore. Although I'm sure those first months without her mother were tough, Ethan's the one who's still grieving. Lilly's grief will come later, in the moments when a girl is supposed to have a mother and she finds herself without. When she has questions about her body or is getting ready for prom. When she's choosing a major or thinks she might be pregnant. *When she's planning a wedding . . .*

Those were the tough moments for me, and my mom's still alive. *Or at least I think she is.* I give myself a little shake, much like Jake just did. Everyone has ghosts that pull them down sometimes. "Thanks for telling me. I promise I won't say anything."

"Are you coming to Thanksgiving?" He surveys my empty

plate. Grinning Jake is back now, as if the specter of his sister-in-law was swept from the room. "Because I'm doing a lot of the cooking, and it's fun cooking for people who enjoy it."

"I don't know." I sigh heavily. "Lilly really wants me to, but I think I'd feel like I was intruding."

"It's our family cabin," Jake explains. "We stay there every holiday—well, as many of us as we can manage. Ethan is on call a lot of holidays, but he got Thanksgiving off so he'll be there all weekend, and I think everyone else will be too."

"Maybe I'll just drive up for dinner and then back to Ethan's Thursday night." I finish my water and reach for my wallet. "What do I owe you?"

"Nothing. Family members eat free."

I laugh. "I'm not family, Jake."

"You take care of my Lilly. That's family enough for me."

I thank him—I've probably given Veronica's credit card enough of a workout this week anyway—and then head out in the direction he indicated.

This town is adorable. Jackson Brews is in the middle of an area filled with bars and restaurants, including the coffee shop and chocolatier, Ooh La La!, where I first met Kathleen.

I head toward the beach, admiring the finely trimmed houses and imagining what they'll look like decorated for Christmas. When I turn onto Lakeshore Drive, the wind off the water nips at my skin, and I have to loop my scarf around my neck. There's a pier and a lighthouse in the distance. Another day, when I have more time, I'll walk out there and investigate. I've always loved lighthouses. They're beautiful, but I'm also drawn to the idea of them—the metaphor of a constant light in the darkness helping you find your way home.

I'm standing there, staring at the lighthouse, when—like a visit from some magical fairy—it starts to snow.

My fingers are frozen and my cheeks go numb, but I close my eyes and let the magic of snowfall wash over me. This little town is stealing my heart with every detail.

The problem is, so is Ethan.

Chapter EIGHTEEN

ETHAN

My Thursday started with a patient in pre-term labor at three a.m., and I didn't get a chance to slow down all day. My rounds at the hospital were followed by a day of office visits and my twice-weekly volunteer shift at the local clinic for expectant moms who can't afford prenatal care.

I'm exhausted and anxious for this time next week, when Dr. Henderson will take calls and I'll enjoy a short vacation. When I first finished my residency after medical school, I couldn't wait to have my own practice, but Elena and I quickly found that constantly being on call with only the very rare day off was too hard on our marriage. So, I joined a bigger practice. There are definitely downsides, but I think I'd be burned out if I hadn't made that change. I definitely get more time with Lilly this way.

When I walk out of the clinic at seven, it's dark, and the lights in the parking lot reflect off the freshly fallen snow. I look around and guess we got about six inches—a lot for this early in the season. Lilly will be thrilled. The first snow of the year is always the most exciting.

When I pull into the drive, there's only a fine sheen on the driveway and the rest has been shoveled to the side. My lawn service guys plow my drive during the winter; they must have been here already. Looks like some good came of my word with the owner about their negligence last year.

When I get into the house, there's Christmas music playing. I freeze. I haven't heard Christmas music in my house in years. I don't ever put it on, and the holidays themselves are spent at the family cabin, where there's always someone else to play DJ. Surrounded by family, I can handle the songs that make my heart ache.

It's good to hear it in my home again, and that surprises me. I associate Christmas and everything that goes with it so closely with Elena's death, and though I've tried to overcome that for Lilly's sake, it hasn't been easy.

I find Lilly and Nic in the kitchen cutting shapes into rolled-out dough.

"Daddy!" Lilly says. "You're home!" She runs to me, unconcerned about the flour coating her hands, and throws her arms around my waist, getting little handprints all over my dress pants.

"Hi, baby." I kiss the top of her head and breathe in the smell of her strawberry shampoo. This is the way it should be—Lilly getting excited about Christmas and dancing around the kitchen to "Rudolph the Red-Nosed Reindeer." I can't let my own holiday demons destroy the day for my daughter.

"Did you have a good day, Daddy?"

I smile. Sometimes she sounds so grown-up. "I did. I delivered two babies and helped one baby stay in her mama's belly."

She frowns. "Why would you do that?"

"She wasn't ready yet. It's safer for her in her mommy's tummy for now."

"Any girl babies?"

I have to grin. As far as Lilly is concerned, the only babies that count are the girls. "One girl, one boy. How was your day?"

"It was *perfect*! Nicky picked me up from school and then we drove to the lighthouse. Did you know Nic loves lighthouses?" I didn't, but Lilly doesn't slow down to let me respond. "She said ours is the prettiest she's ever seen, and I told her my great-great-grandpa built it. That's right, isn't it?"

I nod. "That's right."

Lilly prattles on. "When we got home, we did homework and had hot chocolate, then built a snowman, and Nic let me make snow angels while she shoveled the driveway."

I look to Nic, curious to see what she thinks of Lilly calling her *Nicky*, but it doesn't seem to faze her. "You shoveled that whole driveway by yourself?"

"Lilly and I sang Christmas carols the whole time, so it went fast," Nic says.

"I hire a company to do it, and I have a four-wheel drive, so I can always make it in and out of the garage even if they don't get here in a timely manner." *Which happens too often.*

She shrugs. "It was fun and a good workout." She rubs her right shoulder. "Maybe too good. I'm already getting sore."

"You do enough," I say softly. "You don't have to add lawn work to your list, okay?"

She nods. "Got it."

"Are you ladies about done with the cookies?"

"This is the last batch for the oven," Nic says. "They need to cool, and then Lilly and I will decorate them tomorrow after she gets home from school."

I get the impression the review of the timeline is more for Lilly's benefit than mine. Not that I'm surprised. I'm sure waiting a full day between baking the cookies and decorating them is killing my little princess. I nod and look at my daughter. "Sounds fun."

"She's going to let me put the food coloring in the frosting!" Lilly says, bouncing on her toes. "And then we get to take them to family brunch on Sunday."

"That's awesome." I turn to Nic, and my breath catches. She has a little bit of flour on her nose, her hair is pulled up into a sloppy bun on her head, and her cheeks are pink, as if she came in from the snow seconds ago, not hours. Again, I'm struck by how perfectly she fits here and how foolish I'd be to try to replace her.

I'm not supposed to *like* seeing any woman other than my mother and sister with my daughter. I'm not supposed to imagine the woman could find a role here as something more than temporary help. I decided a long time ago that Lilly and I were good with the family we had. A serious relationship with a new woman would mean introducing Lilly to someone who might leave her. I won't do that to her again. Losing one mother was bad enough. *So why do I feel like I'm standing at the edge of a cliff, confident the life I want is waiting in the water below? Why do I suddenly want to take a risk I was never willing to consider before?*

"Look what Nana sent me," Lilly says. She rushes to the counter opposite where Nic's been working and grabs a postcard. "It's from *Paris*!" she says as she brings it to me.

The picture on the front is of the Eiffel Tower lit up against a dark sky. I flip it over and read the note from Mom.

> Isn't it beautiful, Lilly? The lights twinkle at dusk. I hope you get to see this someday.
>
> Love, Nana.

I frown and show it to Nic. "That's weird. It's postmarked from Berlin."

She glances at it and shrugs. "I bet that's where she was when she mailed it."

Shrugging too, I hand it back to Lilly. "This is awesome. You can add it to your others." I'm grateful Mom's taking the time to send these. It's such a small gesture, but it means the world to my daughter.

"Can Nic take me to bed tonight?" Lilly asks. "I love the voice she does when she reads *Pete the Cat.*"

"*I'm* taking you to bed tonight, goofball," I say, pinching her nose lightly between two fingers. "I always take you to bed when I'm home to do it."

"Fine, but you have to read me *two* stories."

"We'll see how well you brush your teeth, and then we'll enter into story negotiations."

She giggles. "I'm the best brusher!"

Nic places the last of the cookies on the tray and slides them into the oven. There are already a couple dozen laid across cooling racks on the counter. She punches the buttons to set the timer. "Well, it's that time, Lillypad. Why don't you head up and see if you can get your PJs on before your daddy makes it up there?"

Always one for a challenge, Lilly squeaks and runs out of the kitchen, scrambling when her socked feet make her slip on the hardwood floor.

Nic turns to me. "I hope it's okay that I let her play in the snow. She was so excited, and I knew you wouldn't be home until after dark."

"It's great. I'm glad she got to play." I shove my hands into my pockets. I want to touch Nic. I want to wipe the flour from the tip of her nose, then cup her face and thread my hands into her hair until I've made a mess of it. But I want to do all that without fucking up anything else, and life just doesn't work like that.

She rubs her shoulder and winces. "I'm starting to think I should have worked my way up to the whole driveway."

"Here." Just like that, my hands are out of my pockets and touching her. I sweep her hands away and nudge her to turn around so I can dig my thumbs into her shoulders. I can tell she's sore because she tenses against the pressure. "Try to relax."

She tilts her head forward and takes slow, steady breaths. "Do you need any help getting Lilly to bed? You have to be exhausted after such a long day."

"No, I like to do bedtime when I can. I miss it all too often, and she's growing up fast."

"You're a good dad, Ethan."

I swallow hard. I don't want to care what she thinks of me as a father, but those words mean so damn much. "Have you thought any more about next week?"

"Thanksgiving Day?"

I nod. "And the weekend. I wasn't just being polite when I said you'd be welcome."

"I think I'll come to the cabin for dinner if I wouldn't be intruding."

I find the knot in her shoulder and dig into it with my thumb. "You won't be intruding, and you'll make Lilly's day when she finds out you'll be there." I want to tell her she should stay the whole weekend. I love the idea of her hanging out with my family. I could see her sitting in front of the big stone fireplace sipping coffee with Shay, her smile warming the whole place.

"I've never been to a big family Thanksgiving," she says. "I can't decide if I'm excited or terrified."

I still. "Never? What about your family?"

She tenses under my hands. "I don't have a big family. Always dreamed about one, though."

The stereo flips to "Baby, It's Cold Outside." I want to spin her around and pull her against my chest, to feel what it's like to dance again, to have a woman curl into me again. Not just any woman. *This woman.*

"The nanny search is still a bust," I say softly. I don't want to stop talking, because as long as we talk, I can stand here. I have an excuse to touch her.

"I'm sure you'll find someone." She rolls her head to the left, and I dig a little deeper into her right shoulder, and she moans.

I want you to stay. The words are right there on my tongue, but I can't ask until I'm sure that's what I want. Would I be asking her to stay until Mom returned? To stay indefinitely? I'm so conflicted—my fears about the long-term are at odds with what would be best for Lilly in the short-term, and what I want for my daughter is at odds with my own desire.

"You should take a bath," I say, my voice rough.

"No, I don't want to disturb Lilly. I'll be fine."

I drop my hands and step back. The bathroom she shares with Lilly is right across from Lilly's room, so I can understand why she wouldn't want to run a bath while my daughter is supposed to be falling asleep. "Use mine. You can throw some Epsom salts in there and run the jets. You'll feel so much better."

She turns to meet my eyes. "Are you sure you don't mind?"

I shrug. "I'm not using it. Please, help yourself."

She beams at me. "Not gonna lie, I've had full-blown fantasies about that tub, so I'm struggling to dismiss the idea."

"Then don't." Everything in me—including my voice—has gone weak at the sight of that smile. The first night I met her, I thought she was beautiful, but seeing her with Lilly transforms that beauty into something that leaves me in awe on a daily basis. Now having that smile directed at me, I look at her, and for the first time, I understand the word *stunning*.

And that scares the shit out of me.

NICOLE

When Ethan walks away from me, my body is still humming from his touch. I liked his hands on my shoulders and the heat of him standing so close. I liked it so much that I let myself close my eyes and commit the moment to memory.

His footsteps fade into his bedroom, and I imagine him changing out of his work clothes, stripping down to his briefs, and pulling on the type of lounge pants and T-shirt he favors for his evenings at home. Not long after, I hear the sound of his feet on the stairs, then the landing as he heads to Lilly's room.

I take a deep breath. Intellectually, I know our interaction was about my sore shoulder. But the less intellectual parts of me—the parts that have replayed our conversation from Saturday *ad nauseam*—want to believe he enjoyed touching me. The wicked parts of me want to believe that when he's alone later, he'll think about an alternate reality where that touch could have become something more.

I wonder if his kiss was as good as I remember or if the tequila made it seem better than it was.

Sighing, I shake my head and try to snap out of my fantasies.

I wipe down the counters and wash the sink full of baking dishes, then put the cookies from the cooling rack into Tupperware. When the timer on the oven beeps, I remove the last tray of cookies and put them on the stove to cool. I'll wrap those later.

I head upstairs and pass Lilly's room on the way to mine. She and Ethan are sitting on the chair at the head of her bed, and she's snuggled in his lap as he reads her *Pete the Cat*. I poke my head into the room. "Night, Lil. See you in the morning, sweetheart."

"Night, Nicky!" she says, snuggling into her daddy's chest and smiling.

I get my robe and pajamas from my room before going back down to Ethan's, grabbing my phone and wireless headphones from the kitchen counter on my way.

The light in his bedroom is on, and his bed is still unmade from this morning. I feel weird using his bathroom. It's an oddly intimate space to share, but my desire to sit in that big tub with all the jets on my sore muscles outweighs any awkwardness I feel.

I run the bath and let the tub fill while I strip off my clothes and fold them into a neat pile in the corner.

On the counter, there's a container of Epsom salts that I didn't notice when I cleaned the sinks in here this morning. He must have pulled them out for me. I bite back a smile and dump a scoop into the tub before I climb in. The water feels amazing—hot and fizzy against my skin.

I cue up my favorite relaxing playlist, turn on the jets, sink into the water, close my eyes, and indulge in a *Grey's Anatomy*-style fantasy starring Dr. McBroody Pants and his daughter's dutiful nanny.

Chapter NINETEEN

ETHAN

Lilly is such a chatterbox when I'm getting her to bed that I think it might be hard for her to settle down. But once her head hits the pillow, her eyes close, and her whole body goes limp. It's going to be one of those blessed nights when she doesn't fight sleep.

"Goodnight, Daddy," she murmurs as I tuck her in.

I kiss her head. "Goodnight, princess." I turn on the closet light and close the door behind me as I leave.

Nic must have really worn her out in the snow. My mom did a lot with her when I couldn't be here, but Mom's getting older and has been getting tired really easily lately. She can only do so much snowman-building and cookie-baking before her various aches and pains start to get to her.

After heading downstairs, I pour myself a couple of fingers

of bourbon and head to my bedroom with it. I settle into my recliner in the alcove and try not to think about the fact that Nic is naked on the other side of my bathroom door.

I fail.

In fact, that's all I can think about. Nic naked and wet and . . . *thinking about me.*

I close my eyes and let myself imagine going in there, seeing her in the water. She'd hold my gaze as I strip, her eyes as hot and greedy on me as they were that first night. I palm my dick through my pants as I imagine climbing in the tub with her. I'd sit behind her and pull her between my legs so I could cup her breasts and toy with her sensitive nipples. I apply more pressure to my cock as I imagine the sounds she'd make, imagine her tight ass grinding against my dick as she writhes in pleasure. I'd kiss her neck and put a hand between her legs to give her the release she craves. She'd be slick and tight, and when I slid a finger into her, she'd beg me for more.

My breathing is shallow now, and the pressure of my palm through my pants isn't enough. I eye the door. Still closed. The jets are still running. "Fuck." I'm too turned on thinking about Nic to stop and exercise good judgment, so I pull my cock from my pants and take it in my fist in long, hard strokes.

The fantasy changes. Instead of being in the tub with her, I'm right here in this chair. She walks out of the bathroom—nude and wet and heading straight to me. She drops in front of me and gets on her knees. When I imagine her perfect lips sliding over the head of my cock, I come hard all over my hand, squeezing and pumping as I imagine her mouth still on me.

Seconds later, my fantasy is snatched away when the message

alert on my phone beeps and brings me to my senses. *Shit.*

I'm sitting outside the bathroom jacking off to the image of the woman inside. I'm not sure if this is a new low or a sign that Nic and I need to do something about our unfinished business as soon as possible.

I grab some tissues from the bedside table and clean myself up, still listening for the jets to turn off or the tub to drain so I'll know if she's coming. The door remains closed while I clean up, and when I pour myself another drink.

I haven't heard a sound from the bathroom since I came in here. I can hear the whirring jets, but nothing else. No splashing water. No music to entertain her. Just . . . silence.

I don't trust myself not to get lost in another fantasy. Jacking off like a creep once in a night is enough for me, so I try to distract myself by grabbing my phone. The text message is from Brayden, letting me know he emailed details about a new distribution deal. My mind is in no place for business, so I put a pin in that and scroll through email. But this time it's not a fantasy that has me distracted. I'm *worried.* I can't stop thinking about Nic and the lack of noise coming from the bathroom.

With a sigh, I drain my bourbon and rise from my chair to go to the bathroom door. I hesitate before knocking, not sure exactly what to say. The most appropriate thing would be: *"Hey, I'm a little neurotic after finding my wife dead in my living room, and my imagination runs away with me. Tell me you're still breathing, and I'll leave you alone."*

I knock on the door. "Nic, did you find everything you needed in there?"

She doesn't answer. *Fuck.*

I look at the ceiling and close my eyes, trying to muster patience I don't feel. Then I rap on the door again. "Nic? Are you okay?"

No answer. *Shit.*

I try the handle. It's unlocked. I crack open the door. "Nic?" I say softly. After giving her hell on day one for being in my private space, it would be dickish for me to invade hers right now. But when she still doesn't answer, I'm too worried to give a shit about privacy, and I burst into the bathroom.

She's in the tub, the jets whirring, headphones covering her ears. Obviously, she couldn't hear me. Obviously, she still can't. But that's not what has me frozen in my tracks.

I can't take my eyes off where her hands are. One between her thighs. One cupping her breast and toying with her nipple. Those soft thighs. Those fucking perfect breasts.

She's stroking herself between her legs, her fingers dancing over her clit. Her eyes are closed. Her neck is arched. Her lips are parted. And my cock is so damn hard it aches. I fist my hands at my sides, because *fuck*, I want to touch her more than I want anything else.

This is the moment when it would be good for me to remember her right to some privacy. It would be a great time for me to back the fuck out of this room and pretend I was never here. But I'm hypnotized by the rhythm of her hand moving between her legs, her thumb brushing her nipple.

"Nic," I whisper softly. And though I'm sure there's no way she could have heard me whisper her name, she must sense my presence, because her eyes open, and when they meet mine, she draws in a breath. She gasps, but not in shock. *Pleasure.*

She shuts her eyes again as she arches her back and moans, and holy shit . . . I get to watch her come apart.

NICOLE

"Oh my God. First of all, I *knew* you could do it if you just believed in yourself," Teagan says. "And *second,* you're, like, a seduction genius!" Her grin stretches from ear to ear, and I'm pretty sure that my confession about last night's bathroom discovery is the best thing she's heard all day.

"Except I'm not trying to seduce anyone!"

She lifts her palms as if to say, *That's relevant how?*

We're at a table at the back of Jackson Brews, where Teagan agreed to meet me for lunch and where I've spilled my mortifying tale from last night. Because apparently even stories that end in amazing orgasms can be mortifying.

"So tell me," Teagan says, "on a scale of *one* to *shouting your ex's name during sex*, how awkward was talking to him after? Was he in his room, or did he just stand there and watch you get out of the tub?"

I scowl at her, too embarrassed by this whole conversation to merit her questions with a response.

"Was it, like, tit for tat? Did he whip it out and jack off in front of you?"

Apparently, the longer I sit here and scowl at her, the more cringe-worthy questions she's going to recite. We're all better off if I stop her now. "He was in the living room drinking when I got out of the tub," I say. "And I don't know exactly how awkward it'll be to speak with him again, because I haven't done it yet. I wasn't going to sit around and wait for the awkward to blossom last night, and he was gone when I woke up this morning."

"But you don't know if it would've been. It could have just been zero to *sexy*. He could have finally sealed the deal. That's the problem, you know. If you two would have just finished the business between you the night you met, you wouldn't be walking around like giant throbbing balls of sexual tension."

"Are you two talking about giant throbbing balls?" Jake asks, sliding our water glasses onto the table.

I point to Teagan. "She is. *I* am not."

"Do you need advice?" He looks her over with a grin. "About giant throbbing balls?"

She rolls her eyes. "You wish. What's on special today, Jake?"

"I've got a pastrami on rye or a fried chicken club."

"Do you have anything that isn't loaded with fat and sodium?"

Jake folds his arms. "Yeah. Beer. I've got lots of beer. It's an American pub—what do you expect?"

She sighs and looks at me. "Want to share the *fried* chicken club?"

"Sounds perfect to me," I tell Jake, because, come on, I grew up in Alabama. It wasn't until high school that I learned there was a way to cook chicken that didn't involve batter and a pan of hot oil.

Jake glares at Teagan and points a thumb at me. "Why can't you be more like her?"

"Because she's an angel and I'm just a *little bit* evil." She thrums her fingers on the table. "That's why I like her so much more than her evil twin. Need me some yin for my yang."

Jake swivels his gaze back to me. "You have a twin? For real?"

I nod and swallow hard, shooting a glare in Teagan's direction for bringing it up. Seriously, what am I supposed to say if he asks her name? "For real," I say softly.

He drags his gaze down my body—or as much as he can with me seated in a booth. "Please tell me you're identical. Lie if you have to."

"We are," I admit. Every piece of truth I give this family alleviates my guilt incrementally.

"And you kiss sometimes?" he asks. "On the lips? With a little tongue?"

I fold my arms. "No."

"You're disgusting," Teagan says, but she doesn't hold back her snicker. "Go make our food, pervert. We're hungry."

Jake winks at me and heads back to the bar.

"Don't do that," I tell Teagan when Jake's gone.

"Do what? Flirt with Jake?" She shakes her head. "It's harmless fun. Trust me, if we were going to hook up, we would have done it a long time ago."

"I mean, don't bring up Veronica."

Her big brown eyes go wide. "Oh, shit, Nic. I didn't even think about it. I'm so sorry."

I draw in a shaky breath. "It's okay. I just don't want to be put in a position where I have to tell more lies."

"I'll be more careful. I promise." She reaches out to squeeze my hand. "Please don't be mad at me."

"Of course I'm not mad at you. I just panicked a little."

She tugs her bottom lip between her teeth, and in that flash, she looks uncharacteristically vulnerable. "Well, good. Because I've been so much happier since you've been here. I have friends, but it gets lonely in this tundra." Her smile widens and all the vulnerability vanishes from her eyes, replaced by her usual playfulness. She laughs. "I guess I'm trying to say, I think I'm falling in love with you."

I laugh too, but I squeeze her hand. "I love you too, Teag." I wish I'd been more focused on friendship in college and less focused on finding my happily-ever-after. If I hadn't been so obsessed with making myself a family, I would have avoided so much heartache and maybe even had *friends* I could call family. "What made you move to Jackson Harbor, anyway?"

She shrugs and toys with her straw. "I got a job here."

I narrow my eyes. "You're a nurse. There are jobs everywhere. I thought you went back to Virginia after college."

"I did. Briefly." She drags her bottom lip between her teeth and studies her ice water for a long time before lifting her gaze to mine. "You're not the only one who needed to get away from your hometown. Jackson Harbor is good for that."

I frown. "Do you want to talk about it?"

"Nope." She pastes on a plastic smile. "But thanks for asking."

"I'll try again when you're drunk," I say.

"Drunk, in private, and in the mood for a good cry," she says.

"Damn." I wince. She must be running from something worse than I thought. "Got it."

"Are you going to talk to Ethan?" she asks, shifting the subject back to me. "Do you think last night changes things?"

"Last night doesn't change anything." I swallow. "I'm actually hoping we can avoid another conversation about our relationship as employer and employee. I don't want to go there. I don't want to have a conversation about how it's probably not appropriate for me to fantasize about him *in his bathtub* and then come to a screaming orgasm when I realize he's watching me."

She tries to bite back her giggle, but that only makes the laughter come out in a snort, which makes her laugh even harder.

"I hate you," I say.

"Too late. You said you love me. No take-backs." She's still holding my hand and gives it another squeeze.

"Are we still on for tomorrow? Ethan isn't on call, so I have the whole night free."

"Yes! Oh my God, your twenty-fifth. I can't wait. What are we gonna do? Wanna go to Grand Rapids? They have better dance clubs there."

I wrinkle my nose. "I'm not sure you know this about me, but I'm not really into the club scene. I thought maybe we could just come here and have a couple of beers and some fried food."

"And maybe run into your sexy employer on your night off?"

I roll my eyes. "Since it is my night off, he'll be with Lilly and not at a bar, so no. That wasn't part of my plan."

"How disappointing. I want big things for you on your birthday, including orgasms that don't require the use of your own hand."

"Yeah, well, maybe next year," I mutter.

"Okay, so Jackson Brews it is. And then maybe we can go shopping on Sunday. Think of all the Christmas sales!"

"I feel like this is just you trying to give me a makeover."

She throws her hand against her chest. "Me? I would never."

I shrug. "Whatever. Maybe I need one."

"To seduce Dr. McBroody Pants?"

"To feel good about myself *without* a Dr. McAnything telling me I'm hot."

"Hashtag *goals*," she says, tapping her water glass to mine.

Chapter TWENTY

NICOLE

"You need to come home."

"Nicole," Kathleen says, "I know you're not the type to be comfortable with a lie, but—"

"This isn't about me." I sink into the couch and press my warm mug of coffee against my cheek with one hand and hold my phone to my ear with the other. Lilly's at school and Ethan's at work. I'm alone in this house with the ghost of Ethan's wife, but it's my lies that are haunting me. "It's about love."

"What does that mean?" She sounds weaker every time I speak to her—which isn't often. After that first week, her calls have become the exception rather than the rule.

"Lilly loves you, possibly more than she loves anyone else, and the love you show her in return will lay the foundation for all the great loves of her life." I swallow hard. As sappy as my words sound, I know they're true. I've been thinking about this since the night Lilly got sick. She was so upset after getting off the phone with her grandmother that night, and I realized what Kathleen isn't around to see for herself—that her absence is its own kind of drawn-out goodbye.

"I love her too. That's why I'm doing this." Her words are crisp, almost angry. "I'm protecting her."

"But you're not. You can't protect her from pain. I know they say love shouldn't hurt, but that's impossible. Love—the good kind—fills us so completely that when we feel it pulling away, it's like having our guts cut out."

"Why would I want to do that to an innocent child?"

"But that's just it. You *are* doing it. You're pulling away because you're afraid of what might happen. You need to come home."

Silence fills the line, and I close my eyes. I don't like to say anything that might make someone angry with me, but here I am, saying the last thing she wants to hear.

"Is that all?" she asks. Her voice is softer now. "You've said what you need to say?"

I swallow. "Yes. That's all."

"Then I'll go. But . . ." She hesitates a beat. "Thank you for saying your piece. I will think about it."

I smile, hope blossoming in my chest. "Good. That's all I ask."

ETHAN

"There's nothing wrong with them." My administrative assistant folds her arms and glares at me.

"They're not good enough." I shove the stack of applicants to the side and shake my head. The agency sent me another list of candidates for the position, and I had Dreya go through them for me. I told her to give me the five she thought were the best, and she gave me five applicants who aren't half as good as Nic is on paper—and Nic is even better in person.

Dreya looks to the ceiling for a few beats—the way she does when someone is trying her nerves and she's searching for patience—then takes a deep breath and looks at me again. "No one is good enough for our children. You're looking for someone competent and caring, not someone who's perfect. It's simple."

It's not. I look at the stack again. "Maybe I'll give a couple of phone interviews."

"Why don't you just ask the girl you have to stay? It sounds like she's perfect. Who cares if you bumped uglies? You're adults."

I snap my gaze to hers. "What?"

She rolls her eyes. "This is Jackson Harbor, Dr. Jackson. There are no secrets—especially not about things that happen at your brother's bar."

I try to scowl, but Dreya has worked for me for too long to be intimidated and stares right back.

"If the problem is that no one measures up to her, ask her to stay."

I look into her kind but stern eyes. Dreya's my mom's age, and she's worked for me from the beginning. She's the only one who has the courage to put me in my place when I'm being a prick, and the only one I let get away with it. "What happens when she leaves, Dreya?"

She steps forward and squeezes my wrist in a rare gesture of affection. "People leave. Sometimes because they want to. Sometimes because they have to. That's life, Ethan, but think how much we'd miss if we never let anyone close because we were afraid it might hurt when they leave."

I shake my head. "Lilly isn't afraid."

She releases my wrist and steps back. "I know. I wasn't talking about her."

NICOLE

"What do you think?" Ethan asks as I scan the résumé for the retired preschool teacher. "Isn't she perfect?"

I hand it back to him and manage a smile around the tightness in my throat, reminding myself that I *want* him to find the right candidate for this job, reminding myself that no matter how much I love and adore Ethan Jackson's daughter, I can't stay here and continue to pretend to be someone I'm not. "She's exactly what you're looking for."

He looks down at the paper and then back to me, his Adam's apple bobbing as he swallows. "Should I set up the interview?"

"That's up to you, Ethan. She looks great on paper. Now it's just down to whether or not your personalities are a good fit."

He squeezes the back of his neck. "When you got your degree, did you plan on being a nanny, or was this just a temporary move for you?"

God, I hate the lie. I should have finished my degree. I never should have let love pull me away from my dreams. "I never intended to be a nanny long-term. I wanted to open my own preschool someday, but it hasn't worked out."

"My mom's pushing me to find a long-term live-in nanny for Lilly. I was so opposed to bringing anyone in at all at first, but I wanted her to be able to travel, so I agreed. But now that I see you with Lilly . . ." He looks away. "You're really amazing with my daughter."

My face warms. "She's a really amazing girl."

"I don't want to arrange this interview if I already have the perfect candidate for a long-term position." His eyes meet mine, and I wish I were better at reading people. I see worry and sadness there, but there's more. It's as if he's searching my eyes for answers. "I need to make this decision based on what's best for my daughter, not based on what I want."

Does that mean he wants me to stay or that he wants me to go? "I don't know what you're asking me."

"Your original contract was for three months. What if I don't want to call any of these candidates? What if I want you to continue on until February?"

I draw in a ragged breath. "If you need me, I will."

"And what about after that? Do you have plans?"

"I like Jackson Harbor. I mean, minus the bone-chilling cold. I might like to find a job around here." I freeze. If I stay, he'll eventually learn that I'm not Veronica. If I leave, he'll never have to find out. But where would I go? One thing I've learned about having no roots is that every storm knocks me over. I'm ready for roots, and the longer I'm in Jackson Harbor, the more I want to put them down here. Would I be willing to give that up? To leave in February if it meant Ethan would never discover my lie?

He searches my face. "Would you consider staying on with me longer? When my mother returns, I want her to have the freedom to travel more frequently. I mean, we'd take another look at your contract, of course. Increase your pay or give you some long-term benefits."

Damn you, Kathleen. If we'd been honest with Ethan from the beginning, I could say yes right now. Because I so badly want to stay. Sure, my feelings for Ethan are complicated, but his family is amazing, and I love this little town. Most importantly, I love the time with Lilly.

"Nic? Will you say something?"

I lift my eyes to meet his and shake my head. "I wish I could, but I can't. I'll stay until February, but you'll need someone new then." And I'll need to find a new place to start over.

He studies the résumé in his hands. "Right. Of course. You were never planning for this to be permanent. You have plans and places to be."

My heart squeezes, and the truth sits heavy on my tongue. *I can't stay because I can't continue to lie to you.* "I'm sorry."

He shakes his head. "No. It's not a big deal. Mom will be back in February anyway, so even if this woman isn't a good fit, we'll be fine."

I try to smile, but I can't help but think about how awful Kathleen sounded on the phone this morning. Will she be back in February? If her treatments need to continue beyond that point, what will she tell her family?

"It's worse than I expected," she said when Lilly gave the phone back to me. "Since I was by my husband's side through his treatments, I thought I was prepared for what was coming, but I wasn't. I have some good moments, but not many."

"Interview the preschool teacher," I tell Ethan now. "I bet she'll be perfect." My phone buzzes on the counter, and I grab it without thinking and take the call. "Hello?"

"Ronnie? Is that you?"

I draw in a ragged breath at that nickname for my twin and the voice speaking it. I haven't heard either since high school. "Mom?"

"Happy birthday, baby. How are you? How was your sister's wedding?"

My eyes fill with tears. I haven't talked to my mother in years, but she knew I was getting married. She never calls me, but she knows Veronica's phone number and called to wish her a happy birthday. "This is Nic."

She's silent for a dozen beats of my aching heart. "Nicky?"

I swallow around the lump in my throat and look at the floor. I know Ethan is staring at me. "Yeah. How are you?"

"Oh, you know, pretty good. Where's Ronnie?"

"She's not here right now, Mom. Do you . . ." What am I supposed to say? *Why don't you ever call* me? *Hey, why don't you pretend you care, since you have me on the phone?* "Can I give her a message for you?"

"I just called to tell her happy birthday. She always loved me most. Just wanted her to know her mama still cares."

I close my eyes. *She always loved me most.* Mom never forgave me for trying to make the best of our lives when they took us away again. "I'll tell her."

"You okay, Nicky? That rich boy being good to you?" I don't know if she's drunk or high or if she's spent so much of her life under the influence of something that she just naturally slurs her words together now.

"We broke up," I whisper. "But I'm fine."

"Of course you are. Nicky, my fixer. You never needed anyone. Not like your sister. Ronnie needs someone to take care of her."

"I have to go, Mom."

"Bye, baby. Don't forget to tell Ronnie I called."

I nod even though I know she can't see me. "Okay."

When I hang up, Ethan's still looking at me. "Is everything okay?"

I force a smile. "Everything's fine."

But it's not, and some days, camouflaging my broken heart gets exhausting.

Chapter TWENTY-ONE

NICOLE

I don't find the courage to call my twin until I'm in a booth at the back of Jake's bar waiting to meet up with Teagan. Honestly, only the possibility of Teagan telling Veronica off in the background is making me call my sister now instead of later.

She answers on the first ring. "Hello?"

"Happy birthday, sis." I cringe at the sound of my voice. I sound way too hopeful, too desperate to please. *Too much like the girl I want to stop being.*

"Nic, hi. Happy birthday." Veronica clears her throat, and I close my eyes and imagine her. Typical Veronica would spend her birthday at a bar with as many friends as she could fit in the room. She'd get sloppy drunk and dance on the bar, probably lose a few friends when she was lit enough to tell them what she really thought of them, and go home with her pick of the single men.

Or maybe being single was never a requirement for her.

But this year, Veronica is pregnant, so I guess there will be no drunken escapades.

"What are you doing tonight?" I wince. It kind of sounds like I'm looking for an invitation.

"Marcus and I are just hanging out at home."

Marcus and I. I wait for the jealousy to hit, the longing for that word *home.* But I don't feel heartache over Marcus anymore. The ache in my chest is entirely about losing my sister. "How was the trip?"

"It was good, I guess. I mean, not being able to drink kind of takes the fun out of an all-inclusive vacation, but the beach was pretty."

"Yeah, the pictures looked pretty incredible." I swallow around the lump in my throat.

"Did you end up taking the job in Jackson Harbor?"

"I did." I stare at my water and wish it were something much stronger. But with the one exception of my wedding night, my rule has been not to drink when I feel like I *need* to drink. I've got Mom's genes and don't want to end up like her. "I met with Kathleen, and she asked me to step in for you."

"Wait a sec, okay, Nic?" I imagine her sliding her hand over the mic as her voice goes muffled for a few beats. "Nic, I need to go."

"Oh. Sure. No problem. We'll catch up later. Maybe I'll call tomorrow."

"Actually, don't." She draws in a long breath. "It's just that Marcus and I need to focus on us right now. We're not ready to let you back into our lives yet."

That ache in my chest turns to a dull gnawing. I grasp at anger—I'd be right to be pissed right now—but I can't get a handle on it. Instead, all I feel is *lonely.* So fucking lonely. "You make it sound like I'm the one who betrayed you two and not the other way around."

"I . . . One sec—I heard you, Marcus. Just give me a minute." She huffs, and I can practically hear her rolling her eyes. "It's complicated. I'm glad you took the job. Have a happy birthday."

"Happy birthday," I whisper. But she's already hung up.

I close my eyes and force myself to breathe, to fight the instinct to call her back and beg her to talk to me. I could shovel forgiveness at them they don't deserve in a vain attempt to maintain some sort of relationship with my sister.

I don't want to be the doormat anymore. If our relationship is going to be salvaged, she's going to have to own up to her mistakes.

I wrap my arms around myself and trace the tattoo on my side through my sweater, willing the words inked there to give me the strength I don't feel.

ETHAN

I have a Saturday night off and nothing to do with it. I'm not on call tonight, so it's Nic's night off and Lilly and I were going to have some quality daddy-daughter time, but Shay insisted that she and Lilly both needed a girls' night.

The house is empty, and I can't stop thinking about Nic in my tub, her back arched, her lips parted, and her eyes on me for that brief moment before she fucking disintegrated into pleasure.

When she opened her eyes, I just stood there staring at her while my heart raced. Every move I wanted to make was the wrong one—crossing the bathroom and kneeling to take her face in my hands so I could kiss her with all the hunger I felt, dragging her to my bed so I could make her come again, begging her to let me touch her.

Eventually, I got my wits about me and said, "I'm sorry. I shouldn't . . ." Then I turned on my heel and left the room.

Real fucking smooth.

I'd like to blame that moment in the bathroom for all my inappropriate thoughts, but where this woman is concerned, my thoughts have never been innocent. And now that I know for sure she won't stay on as Lilly's nanny, I can't get my mind off bringing her into my bed.

Rather than stay home and make myself crazy with thoughts of what I can't have, I head to Jake's bar. Jackson Brews has become the Jackson family living room of sorts. On any given night, I can count on running into one or more of my siblings there, in addition to Jake.

But when I head to our typical booth, I don't spot any of my brothers. I see Nic. She's shrunk into the far back of one of the semicircular booths, and a man stands on the opposite side of the table, leaning in as if he's trying to tell her a secret.

"Hey, John." I walk straight to the table and smack the guy between the shoulder blades. "Is there a reason you're talking to my girl again?"

Nic's tense shoulders visibly relax as John straightens, and she flashes me a grateful smile.

"I wasn't bugging her," John says. "I was just keeping her company. There some law against that?" But he can't manage to speak the excuse without running his gaze over Nic again, stalling for too long on the swell of cleavage in the V of her black sweater. *Creep.* When he turns to me, his expression is belligerent. "Anyway, don't feed me your bullshit about her being your girlfriend. I know she's your nanny, and she's here waiting for a date, not for you."

I don't respond. I'm too distracted by his word choice. *Date.* She has a date. *Of course she does, you idiot. Women like Nic don't stay single forever.*

John must take my silence as doubling down on my warning because he walks away in a huff.

"You didn't have to do that," Nic says.

"I think I did. He's got his eye on you, and I think he's figured out that you're more likely to take his shit than make a scene. Let me know if he bothers you again. Jake can't stand that guy anyway. He'll throw him out on his ass."

She snorts. "Good to know." She pats the bench beside her. "Why don't you sit here and keep me company?"

I hesitate. On the one hand, I can't stop thinking about Nic, and every instinct I have wants to take advantage of the opportunity to be near her. On the other hand, I'm not sure I can act like some big-brother figure when her date strolls in to take my spot.

"Come on," she says. And it's the smile that gets me—all her sweetness shows on her face, and I find myself sliding into the booth, the magnet pulled to its mate.

I settle on the edge of the seat. I tell myself I don't scoot farther in because I want to see her face when we talk, but the truth is probably more about resisting the temptation to touch what isn't mine. "You look amazing."

She tucks her chin and reaches for her drink, and I notice she's drinking water. I don't think I've seen her drink alcohol since the night we met. "Thank you."

"Who's the lucky guy?" I want to snatch the words back the second they're out of my mouth.

"What?"

"John said you're waiting on a date." I'm butting in where I don't belong, but I don't care. "I didn't realize you'd had the time to meet anyone."

"I haven't." Her phone buzzes, and she digs in her purse for it. "Do you mind if I get this?" Her gaze flicks to the screen and then back to me. "I hate to be rude, but this is the friend who's meeting me tonight."

"Not a problem." *Friend.* So, not date? I can't decide if this is good news or evidence that I should get up and leave now. I care too damn much. Her love life is none of my business.

She swipes across the screen of her phone and puts it to her ear. "Hey, girl! I'm in a booth at the back of the bar." Her smile falls away. "No, no. Don't worry about it. It's totally understandable. We'll just meet up later." She listens and swallows. "No, it's fine. Please, don't worry about it. It's just another day . . . I know you will. Please don't feel bad. I'm sitting here with Ethan, so it's not like I'm alone." She nods, listening again. "Sounds amazing. Perfect. See? It's fine . . . Thank you. You too. Bye."

She hangs up her phone and slides it into her purse before staring down into her water. Her lips twist as she fights a frown. Anytime she does that, I get the impression she doesn't have much experience frowning. She's one of those perpetually cheerful people who sees the good in every day and lives her life with complete enthusiasm—in other words, she's everything I'm not.

"What's wrong?" I ask.

She shakes her head. "It's no big deal. My friend Teagan and I had plans for my . . . We had plans, and she can't get away from work. The stomach flu is going around the nurses and they don't have enough staff. She feels bad, but it's not a problem at all. We're going to have a do-over at brunch tomorrow, and then go shopping."

"Is it your birthday?"

"It is," she admits with a nod. "I'm a quarter of a century old today, and can I just tell you my life is so much different than I imagined?"

"Different better or different worse?"

She drags her bottom lip between her teeth. "Just different-different."

"It would help if your boss weren't such an asshole."

She gives a sardonic chuckle but doesn't meet my eyes. "You're not an asshole." She shakes her head. "Not at all."

"What else did you think would be different?"

"I'm supposed to be married. I was engaged before I came here."

Wow. "Really?" I feel like an ass. That day I caught her looking in Elena's closet, she told me she wanted to run away, and I was so damn busy looking at her and seeing the faults of my dead wife that I didn't ask what she was running from.

She nods and studies the condensation on the side of her water glass. "I was supposed to be Mrs. Marcus Fitzroy. I was finally going to have a family of my own. He said he wanted kids right away." A tear rolls down her cheek, but she wipes it away quickly.

She seems too young to have already been almost-married. Then again, by the time I was twenty-five, Elena and I had been married three years. Most days, it feels like our wedding was in a different lifetime. "What happened?"

"He fell for my sister?" The words come out like a question, as if she still isn't convinced that's what happened, but then she nods and her chest expands with her deep inhale. "While I was planning our wedding, they were messing around." She lifts her eyes to meet mine for the first time since I guessed it was her birthday. The sadness there pulls at me. I want to take her into my arms. To make her feel cherished. To make her forget the asshole who hurt her. "I found out on my wedding day."

I draw in a shaky breath. I don't know who I'd be angrier with—the sister or the fiancé. "Shit. I'm so sorry."

"I think she helped me dodge a bullet, you know what I mean? But yeah. I've never felt so alone in my life. Then I came here and . . ."

"At least the timing just worked out, right? This job gave you an excuse to get away." She was still upset about him the night I met her, so her wedding couldn't have been too long before Mom posted the position.

She drops her gaze to the table and runs her fingers along

the wood grain. "Sometimes we need an excuse to do something crazy."

"Is your sister still with the guy?"

"Apparently so." She draws in a deep breath and replaces her frown with a smile, but this one is less believable than her usual cheerful grin. "I called to wish her a happy birthday, and he was there with her."

"Today is her birthday too?"

"Yes." She meets my eyes. "We're twins."

This asshole cheated on her with her *twin*? That seems even worse somehow, though I'm not sure my opinion of him could sink any lower. "The night we met, when you got a text and went to the bathroom all upset . . . was that because of him?"

"Yeah." She shrugs. "I don't know. Maybe it was more because of her, ya know? What he said to me just reinforced all those childhood insecurities."

I lean forward on the table. This is more than she's ever opened up about herself, and I want everything she's willing to give. "Like what?"

"I grew up feeling redundant. My identical twin wasn't just like me. She was better. More vibrant, more fashionable, more fun."

"I doubt anyone sees you that way. You're an amazing person, Nic. Always thinking of everyone else."

"That's what makes my sister so exciting. She doesn't give a damn about anyone else. She's the one who gets in trouble but also the one who lives life in a big way. She's like fireworks, and I'm boring. Like a photocopy—a match that doesn't retain the gleam of the original."

"I can't imagine anyone believing that about you. You shine. If your sister is fireworks, then you're the sun. She might flash and dazzle, but you keep everyone warm."

She bites her bottom lip and studies me. "Thank you for saying that."

"It's true."

She breaks eye contact, and it's like I'm released from a spell. "And again, thanks for being such a good sport about all that. I can definitively say you're the only guy who's rescued me from a bathroom stall."

I grunt. "I'm a regular knight in shining armor."

She shakes her head, and her smile is genuine this time. "Lilly thinks you walk on water." Her brow creases. "By the way, I thought she was with you tonight. Where is she?"

"What? I thought you had her."

Panic flashes in her eyes for a beat before she realizes I'm joking. "Touché. You *can* crack a joke. I guess I owe Teagan ten dollars."

I shrug. "Sometimes."

"A sense of humor looks good on you." She narrows her eyes and cocks her head to the side. "You're too stingy with those dimples."

I grin, flashing the dimples she's referring to. "Now that I know you like them, I'll have to use them to my advantage."

She arches a brow. "What do you mean by *that*?"

"That bread you left on the counter?" I rub my stomach. "If dimples will get me that again, I'm not ashamed to use them."

She laughs. "Food prep is in my job description. You don't have to bribe me with smiles, but they're always welcome.

Childcare is *also* in my job description, if you recall, so if you needed a sitter tonight, I wish you would have told me."

"You would have worked on your birthday?" She shrugs, and I know without a doubt that she would have—even if Teagan hadn't canceled their plans. "Don't worry. It was unplanned, but Lilly's having a girls' night with Aunt Shay. Which means I'm free to entertain the birthday girl. So, tell me what we're going to do to celebrate."

Her cheeks flush. "It's just another day. Not a big deal." She scoots around to the side of the booth opposite me and stands. "How's Jake's coffee?"

I make a face and look at my watch. "At this hour, you'd better ask him to make a fresh pot. It's probably been on there since lunch."

"Thanks for the tip." She heads to the bar, and I take a minute to appreciate the sight of her. She's wearing a skirt and the cowboy boots she had on the night we met. An image of her in those boots and nothing else flashes through my mind, and I follow her to the bar like a man on a leash.

I lean against it and study her as she waits for a drink. "You can't spend your birthday alone. Let me take you out. Pick your poison—dinner, dancing, trivia night?" I look outside. If it weren't already dark, I'd offer to take her out to the lighthouse. I bet she'd love climbing to the top and looking out over the harbor.

"Where's trivia night?" Nic asks.

Jake appears on the opposite side of the bar. "Trivia night at Howell's? Why the fuck you gonna turn on me like that, bro?"

I shrug. "It's her birthday. If she's into trivia, you'll just have to deal with us drinking another man's beer."

Jake's scowl falls away as he grins at Nic, his gaze skimming down to her breasts before returning to her face. I want to drag him out back and tell him to keep his eyes off her. Then again, he's human and she's fucking . . . *stunning.*

There's that word again.

"Your birthday, huh?" Jake says.

Nic scowls at me. "You don't need to tell everyone."

"Tell everyone what?" Ava asks, sidling up to Jake.

Jake turns to Ava, and the tension I felt about the way he just looked at Nic fades away when his eyes land on his best friend. Ava might be oblivious, since she's been Jake's BFF since grade school, but he's got it bad for her. If there was heat in his eyes when he looked at Nic, there's an inferno when he looks at Ava. "It's Nic's birthday."

"Happy birthday," Ava says. She leans on the bar and grins at Nic. "By the way, I'm Ava. It's nice to officially meet you. Jake tells me you're in education too."

Nic's eyes go wide. "What?"

"Early childhood, right?" Ava asks. "I teach tenth-grade English. Always good to meet another teacher."

"I don't . . ." Nic looks at me and then back to Ava. "I don't actually have any experience in a real classroom, unless you count preschoolers."

"Hell, girl. That counts. In fact, it counts for everything. As far as I can tell, it's practically a done deal by the time they get to me. You set the foundation for their future."

Nic blinks at her. "Thank you. That's probably the nicest thing anyone's ever said about my work experience."

"Well, I mean it. And I'm sorry about the way I treated you

the first night you were here. When young things come in here set on taking shots, it always makes me a little nervous." She looks at Nic's empty water. "Jake said I'm probably the reason you're afraid to drink when you come in now."

"Don't worry about it. You were right, and I'm glad you slowed me down."

"I knew you'd like each other," Jake says, smiling at Ava.

Ava rolls her eyes. "Jake thinks I need more girlfriends. He seems to think all work and no play makes Ava a dull girl."

"You should hang out with me and Teagan sometime," Nic says. "If you can handle slightly inappropriate conversation and Teagan's general lack of boundaries, that is."

"Sounds perfect." She grins, and she and Jake move to the other end of the bar.

I smile at Nic. I like the idea of her hanging out with Ava and Teagan. I like the idea of anything that roots her to Jackson Harbor. *To me.*

"Why are you looking at me like that?" Nic asks me.

"I'm still waiting for you to tell me how you want to spend your birthday."

She studies me for a beat. "What happened to boss and employee, no blurred lines?"

I stifle a grimace. When I said that, I was trying to deliver a message to myself, not to her. Shrugging, I say, "You're off the clock. Not my employee again until"—I make a show of looking at my watch—"six p.m. tomorrow, I believe."

"You're serious?"

"If you don't want to go out with me, just tell me."

"I didn't say that. I just don't want you to think I expect you to entertain me."

"No, it's cool. I mean, I'd understand if you'd rather spend your evening doing something more stimulating . . ." I look down at my beer before flashing my gaze back up to meet hers. "I would completely understand if you were more interested, say, in a nice, private bath."

Chapter TWENTY-TWO

NICOLE

My jaw drops. Ethan's face is so damn serious. "You didn't just go there." His lips quirk, and my cheeks are so hot that I'm pretty sure they're cherry red. "I can't believe you just said that."

"Sorry. Was I supposed to pretend that didn't happen?"

"You were supposed to *forget* it happened."

He leans forward so his mouth is by my ear. "Nic, there are some things I won't ever forget, and the image of you in my tub with your hand between your legs is high on the list."

A thrill shoots through me. What happened to the broody employer who insisted we keep our relationship professional? The man who was horrified he'd hooked up with the girl he'd hired to be his nanny?

I swallow hard. "I'm still pretty mortified I did that."

His gaze drops to my mouth. "Which part mortifies you?

The part where you were touching yourself in my tub, or the part where you got off because I was watching?"

"Both," I whisper. My cheeks are still hot, but I'm not mortified now, not with the way he's looking at me. I'm turned on, and that's one hell of a welcome change after how I've been feeling. Today was tough, with the call from my mom and then my attempted conversation with my sister.

But in this moment, none of that matters. It's just me and Ethan and his dark eyes telling me he means every word he's saying. I squeeze my thighs together and focus on that feeling.

"I'm starving," I say. Right now, with the way Ethan's looking at me and the words he's whispering in my ear, if we stay here, we'll end up locked in Jake's restroom again. "Maybe we could start with dinner?"

"Perfect." He leads me to the door, and we grab our coats off the rack.

"Don't go to Howell's!" Jake calls from behind the bar. "His IPA tastes like a pine tree pissed in a barrel. That man has no appreciation for the fine art of brewing."

"I wouldn't dream of it," I call back.

"And be easy on my brother," he says, his tone gentler. "He's a little rusty, but I'm sure with enough patience, he can loosen up."

Next to me, Ethan grunts then whispers, "I promise I'm not nearly as rusty as he says."

I grin at Jake. "Understood."

"Do you mind walking?" Ethan asks when we're outside.

I shiver as the cold wind hits my cheeks, but shake my head. "A walk would be good."

"There's a great steakhouse a couple of blocks over. I've

known the chef since grade school, and she owes me a favor. I bet she'll give us a table even if they're booked for the night."

"You don't have to call in favors for me."

"Maybe I want to. Maybe I'm realizing I only get you for a short time and I want to make the most of it. And maybe I'm hungry." The way he rakes his eyes over me when he says *hungry* makes that warmth blossom in my belly. *Oh, yeah. I'm hungry too.*

He leads me to a restaurant on Lakeshore Drive. It's the kind of place with white linen tablecloths and candles on the tables. We're given a table in the back corner of the restaurant, and Ethan orders us a bottle of red wine. I don't usually like dry reds, but this wine is so smooth and delicious that I think I've been having the wrong kind. In addition to my personal rule about not using alcohol as a crutch, I can't drink much because of the medication I take, but I sip on the glass he pours me and let myself enjoy the way it heats my chest and the zip it sends through my blood.

"I'll be right back," he says after we order our dinner. He pushes back from the table and grabs the waitress as he stands. "I have to run out for a minute, but don't let her leave, okay?"

I laugh. "I'm not allowed to leave?"

He grins. "That's right." His eyes slowly sweep down my body. "For tonight, you're mine." He turns to the waitress. "Give her anything she wants. I'll be back as soon as I can."

"You've got it," she says. She smiles at Ethan as he rushes out the front. "Where on earth is he going? The snow's really starting to come down out there."

I turn up my palms and shake my head. "I have no idea."

She studies me for a beat. "You're the nanny?" The question

doesn't bother me this time because her eyes are kind.

"I am for now. I leave in February." *And it's going to be the hardest thing I've ever done in my life.*

"He lights up around you. It's nice to see life in his eyes again."

Jake said something similar the day I had lunch in his bar, and I'm not sure how to respond. "I think he's a good guy. He's definitely an amazing dad."

She beams at me, then gives a slow shake of her head. "The Lord works in mysterious ways." She winks and then walks away.

It feels like forever before Ethan returns, but when he takes his seat across from me, his cheeks are pink and he's smiling. He pulls a box out of his pocket and puts it in front of me. "Happy birthday."

"What's this?"

His dark hair is sprinkled with fresh snow, and he drags a hand through it. "It's your birthday present. Open it."

"Okay, but you really didn't have to do that."

"I wanted to."

I open the small box, and the necklace inside makes my throat go too thick for words. It's a tiny lighthouse on a chain with diamond accents. I'm afraid to look at him because he'll see the tears in my eyes, but the joy blossoming in my chest insists on my turning to him like a flower to the sun.

"I can't take total credit for it," he says softly. "Lilly told me how much you like the lighthouse and that sometimes you drive the long way home from school just to look at it. So, consider it a gift from her, too."

I run my finger over the charm. "I love it."

ETHAN

As we walk back to our cars after dinner, Nic looks up at the sky and sighs. "Is it always this beautiful here?"

I follow her gaze to the dark sky and the cloud-obscured moon. How long has it been since I looked at the sky without Lilly by my side? "Yes." I swallow. Tonight's been bittersweet. On one hand, I've gotten to be close to Nic, and I wouldn't have let myself if she was staying on as my employee for the long-term. On the other hand, I don't like thinking about her leaving. "Jackson Harbor is always beautiful."

"Thank you."

"For what?"

"For saving the day. This birthday could have been a total bust, but you swooped in with your good looks and excellent taste in restaurants and made it one worth remembering." She shakes her head. "I always do this. I build up my birthday in my mind. I expect it to be full of all these incredibly special moments where everything is perfect, and then when it's not, I'm disappointed. I need to stop doing that."

"I'm hurt." I press a hand to my chest. "This night isn't perfect for you?"

She laughs. "Are you saying it's perfect for you?"

It's pretty damn close, but I don't want to reveal how much her company means to me.

I step forward because I want to be closer. Her gaze moves to my mouth and mine goes to hers. Her lips are pink and swollen from being tortured by her teeth. My gut knots. The night is silent around us, as if winter is holding everything still so we won't be disturbed in this moment.

"Ride home with me," I say. "We can get your car in the morning. I'm not ready to let you leave my sight just yet."

If she thinks it's an odd request, she doesn't say so. She nods and lets me open her door and help her into my SUV. I climb in my side and start the car. When I pull onto the main road and reach for her hand, she laces her fingers through mine.

I can't decide if I want the ride to go quickly or slowly. I'm afraid the spell will be broken when we walk in the door. She'll go back to being the dutiful employee, and I won't get to find out how my favorite wine tastes on her lips. I consider pulling over so we can neck in the car like a couple of teenagers, but I want more than frenzied kisses and greedy hands. She deserves more.

After I park in the garage, we walk inside, the silence tense between us. We shed our coats, turn, and stare at each other.

"Thank you again for tonight," she says.

I tuck a lock of hair behind her ear. "The pleasure was mine, Nic." I take a breath. "I'm pretty sure this is where a gentleman kisses his date goodnight so she'll spend the rest of her night thinking about him."

"But you're not going to do that?" she asks.

My gaze drops to her mouth. "I want to, but a gentleman would kiss you and walk away, and I already know a kiss won't be nearly enough." Before she can reply, I cup her face in both hands and lower my mouth to hers.

I don't intend for this to be a soft, sweet kiss. I need for her to feel all the longing I've had bottled in my chest since the day she showed up on my porch. I pass my lips across hers and sweep my tongue over her plump bottom lip. When she opens her mouth beneath mine, I slide my hands into her hair and pull her against me.

"What are we doing?" she whispers against my mouth.

"We're taking advantage of an empty house."

She puts her hand against my chest and looks up at me. "Is this some sort of test, Ethan? Are you going to be disappointed in me tomorrow if I don't stop you?"

"Do you want me to stop?"

She studies my face, and I swear I can't breathe until she shakes her head. "I don't. But I don't want you to be angry with me. Or with yourself."

"The only way I'm going to be angry with myself tomorrow is if I let you walk away without touching you again."

She slides a hand behind my neck and lifts onto her toes to press her lips to mine. "You're sure?"

I answer by pulling her shirt off over her head and unzipping her skirt. When it falls from her hips, she steps out of it. Then she's in front of me in the cowboy boots she was wearing the first night we met, light pink panties, and a bra. "It's like you walked out of my fantasies."

She unbuckles my belt and unzips my pants. "What else do I do in your fantasies?"

I still her hands with mine. "Not tonight," I say, my voice low and husky. "You deserve to be worshipped on your birthday. Don't make this about me."

"Can't I have what I want? Since it's my birthday?"

Her hand slides under my waistband and I draw in a breath through my teeth. "*Anything* you want."

"What if I want this?" She drops to her knees in front of me—like a fucking *dream*—and drags my pants down my hips until my cock springs free. She slides her tongue down the length of me before opening her mouth and taking me deep.

I fist a hand in her hair, trying not to jut my hips, trying not to fuck her mouth, but *Christ*, her mouth is good.

She pulls back, releasing me, and looks up at me through her lashes.

"It's *your* birthday. Not mine." I'm shaking. I want her mouth on me, and I want my hands on her. I want to feel her and make her moan, and I want to take everything she offers.

"And this is exactly what I want." She puts her mouth on me again, stroking me with her tongue as one hand cups my balls and the other grabs my ass.

I lean my head back and grit my teeth. I'm trying not to blow my load like a teenage boy getting his first blowjob, but it feels too damn good. Every time she moans, a vibration ricochets through me, sending pleasure in a hot bolt down my spine.

When I can't take it anymore, I guide her off me. Her lips are swollen, her eyes hazy with need. I want to spin her around and fuck her against the wall. I want to hear those noises she makes when she's turned on, want to get inside her as fast as possible.

Instead, I strip her bare—unhooking her bra and sliding it off her arms and peeling her lacy panties from her hips. She grins at me as she toes out of her boots, and I take her to the couch, sit, and guide her to straddle me. Her breasts are full, her nipples hard, and I lick each one. She rocks against me, her slick heat right against my bare cock.

"We need a condom," I say. I'm a simple shift of my hips away from sliding inside her without one, and as much as I want that, I know it's a bad idea. "I have some in my—" I squeeze my eyes shut. "Shit."

She rocks against me again, and I have to grit my teeth to resist the urge to take this further. I grab her hips roughly and still her movements. If she keeps doing that, I'm going to make a bad fucking decision about what happens next.

"Nic, I don't have any condoms."

Chapter TWENTY-THREE

NICOLE

I lean my forehead against his and make myself slow down. Breathe. Catch my breath. No condoms?

I wish I was the kind of girl who kept them in her purse, but the last time I bought condoms was for my honeymoon, and . . .

I smile. "I have some." I climb off Ethan and offer my hand. "Upstairs."

He takes my hand in his, and I lead him up the stairs. Maybe I should feel awkward or nervous about us giving in to this, about finally doing what we've both wanted to do since that first night, but I don't. My whole body is humming. I want more of him. All of him. We both know this can't last, that it's just tonight—an exception for my birthday. Once again, Ethan's swooping in when I need him the most.

We go into my room, and he shuts the door behind us before

spinning me around and pressing me against it. He kisses me hard, his hands searching my body as if he's lost something and is desperate to find it. He grazes over my breasts, my hips, my ass. Up my thighs and between my legs and finally into my hair as he kisses me harder, longer, and deeper.

I whimper against him. I need more. I'm greedy for it, feeling like if I don't get him inside me soon, it might not happen at all, and if it doesn't, I might fall apart.

"The condoms are in my dresser." I point to the top drawer with all my lingerie.

He pulls it open and blinks at the contents, looking at me and then back to it. He grabs a condom and shoves the drawer closed. "Get on the bed."

I obey, loving the rough command and the simmering desperation in his husky voice. I climb onto my bed, prop myself on my elbow, and watch him roll the condom on his shaft.

"I want to see you do it again." His eyes sweep down my body and then back up, greedy, all over me. "I want to see you touch yourself again."

I drop back onto the pillow, keeping my eyes on him as I trail my hand over my breasts, across my stomach, and then cup myself between my legs. I'm wet, slick with heat and need like I've never been before. My body's ready for him. *Just him. Only him.*

I rub my clit, and his eyes go darker, his nostrils flaring as he takes a step forward.

"Do you know how much I've thought about that night? Do you know how badly I wanted to come in there even before I saw you touching yourself? I couldn't stop thinking about you naked on the other side of that door. I wanted to get in the water with you and fuck you with my hand, wanted to hear you moan the way you did when I put my mouth on you." He grips his dick at the base, stroking himself over the condom. "I wanted to get you off in the water and then play with your tits while you rode me."

I gasp, put more pressure on my clit, moving my fingers faster, because his words are so hot.

"Is that what you were thinking about too?" He takes another step closer. "When you put your hands on yourself that night, were you imagining they were mine?"

"Yes." I hold his gaze and stroke my clit again. My hips buck off the bed, and it's like he feels it too. His lips part and he takes another step. "I haven't stopped thinking about you since the day we met."

"Not touching you has been making me crazy." He joins me on the bed. The weight of him is delicious, and I moan as he settles between my thighs. He trails one hand down my body until he grips my hip. The other stays by my face, skimming my jaw, my lips.

I lift my hips, and he holds my gaze as his cock presses against my entrance and he slowly slides into me.

"You're so beautiful," he says.

I rise to meet him, relaxing my hips and opening my body to take him all the way in. We both gasp, and he buries his face in my neck. "Christ. You feel so good. So fucking good. I knew you'd feel like this."

He kisses my neck. Sucks. The hand at my hip curls into my flesh, guiding me as he moves inside me. He starts slow. I try to urge him on with my hips—because it's amazing and I want more. I want everything he can give me. But he holds me still.

"I'm trying to make this last," he whispers in my ear. "I promise next time I'll fuck you as hard and fast as you want, but if you keep moving like that under me, this is going to be over too soon. I've been waiting for this too long to rush it."

The words shoot pleasure through me as sure as his touch, and with it a heady sense of power. Because he's wanted me as much as I've wanted him. Because this is good for him too.

He sweeps his lips down the side of my neck, and that hand at my hip slides under my knee. He draws up my leg and opens me wider. His long, slow strokes go deeper, and our moans echo off the walls, the sound of our pleasure tangling like our bodies.

"Just so beautiful," he says against my neck, again and again. Every time, he sinks deeper, pressing into me and coiling the pleasure tighter and tighter.

"That's it," he whispers. "Just like that, sweetness. Let me feel you come."

Those words and the feel of his breath on my neck are my undoing. His urging hand grabs my ass as he finally thrusts hard and deep and fast. I arch under him, my whole body tensing against pleasure that is nearly too much, emotion filling my chest that I can't deny. Then I come apart, squeezing around him as my body unravels.

He thrusts again, and pleasure rolls through me a second time, right on the heels of the last wave. I gasp and curl my nails into his shoulder blades as he repeats the motion over and over, drawing out my orgasm. His tenderness washes me away—my fear, my anxiety, and my insecurities gone in this moment in his arms. He kisses me hard, his whole body tense as he holds back.

"So beautiful. Like a fucking miracle in my arms."

I love you, Ethan. I don't say it. I keep the words locked in my chest where they can't hurt us, and I give him my body instead. I grip his shoulders, arch my back, squeeze around him, and urge him to take his own release.

His strokes turn hard and fast and demanding, and when he shudders over me, I wait for the moment of loneliness that always comes at this part—when the man rolls away and disposes of the condom—but it doesn't come, because Ethan doesn't move off me. Not at first.

"Are you okay?" he asks.

"I'm good."

He nuzzles the crook of my neck and trails kisses across my collarbone, and when he does climb off the bed, his eyes meet mine, and I don't feel lonely at all.

ETHAN

"Would you call this a great birthday or the best birthday ever?"

She laughs. "You don't think much of yourself, do you?"

I lift my head and nip at her shoulder, then kiss the spot. We're naked in her bed, a tangle of limbs as we stare at each other. The alarm clock says it's after one, and I'd break the damn thing against the wall if it would slow down time. We've gone through three condoms, and just looking at her gets me hard all over again. Sometime between the second and third round, I turned on the bedside lamp, unsatisfied with my limited view of her body in the moonlight. It's on still, casting a soft glow across the bed. She doesn't seem any more interested in turning it off to sleep than I am, and I'm glad. I'm not ready for our stolen night to end.

"I kind of feel like it's *my* birthday," I whisper before planting another kiss on her soft lips. "You're so fucking sweet." I slide a hand down her body and cup her between her legs. "Are you sore?"

She shrugs. "A little. But I don't mind."

I pull my hand from between her legs before my dick decides we should start all over again. I find her hand, threading our fingers together. "Tell me about your mom."

She blinks at me. "What? Why would you ask about her?"

I sweep her hair from her face. "She called you earlier. When we were in the kitchen? You were upset."

"The woman who called is my mother but not much of a mom." She searches my eyes, and I feel like she's trying to decide if I understand what that means, so I nod, and she continues. "Mom was an addict. *Is* an addict. My sister and I grew up in and out of foster care. For the first few years, Mom would fight to get us back. She'd clean up and get her act together so she could bring her girls home. The courts would let her have custody again, but she'd never *stay* clean, and before long we were shipped off to another family. They always kept . . ." She meets my eyes again and slowly shakes her head. "They always kept me and my sister together. I was grateful for that, but where my natural inclination was to do whatever was necessary to make our new family want to keep us, my sister's was to do whatever was necessary to push them away. She didn't want a new family. She wanted Mom. I think, on some level, she thought if she was bad enough they wouldn't bother taking us away anymore. Or maybe she was just angry that the world had dealt us a shit hand from the beginning." She shrugs. "My mother never forgave me for trying to make the best out of our new families. Why couldn't I be loyal like my sister? Why did I want them to take me away again?"

"Jesus." I slide my hand behind her back and pull her body against mine, then I roll to my back, taking her with me. She curls into me, her hands between our bodies, the side of her face against my chest. I told myself I didn't miss this. Told myself I didn't need it or want it. But maybe that's because I'd never imagined someone like Nic. "Did she take any responsibility for her role in your situation?"

"She didn't see it that way. Not when my twin was so actively trying to ruin our chances for a new family. Mom didn't understand that I just needed to be accepted *somewhere.*"

"What did your sister do?"

"Every time we got placed in a new home, she was a terror. I constantly covered for her. If she broke things on purpose, I'd tell our family I'd done it by accident. I worked hard to make them like me, and I knew they'd be able to forgive me easier than her, the sullen twin. I did my chores and hers. I did extra. We fell into this sick routine where my sister would sabotage and I would repair. Sabotage and repair. When we were in seventh grade, she hated her teacher and wanted to switch places at school. I agreed to do it because she'd been in trouble so many times that I was afraid they'd send her away if she kept it up."

"You could really pull that off?"

"We're identical. No one ever suspected."

"Didn't you get sick of covering for her?"

"It wasn't all bad. She was my best friend. She was all I had, the only constant in my life. And as crazy and destructive as she could be, she applied that same ferocity to her love for me. If kids were mean to me at school, they'd have to face her. If a foster brother bullied me or tried to convince me to do something I didn't want to do, she'd raise hell to protect me."

"I bet that's why you're so amazing with children. You know what it's like to need an adult to *see* you." I tense as an awful thought comes to me. "Were you . . . safe?"

"Mostly." She flattens her palm against my chest and traces my tattoos with her fingers. "I've heard horror stories about foster homes and the things that happen to little girls, so believe me when I say we were lucky. The people who cared for us didn't abuse us. Not sexually or physically, at least. But fighting to be loved takes its own sort of toll on you. Trying to prove that you're worth someone's love wears on you."

"Is that why you have your tattoo?"

Her fingers still where they've been tracing my phoenix, and she sits up and looks down at the ink beneath her breast. I graze it with my knuckles.

I noticed it the night we met. I saw the word *love* and didn't give much thought to whether there was more. But tonight, when I was memorizing her body in the glow of the bedside lamp, I saw that I underestimated her ink that night nearly as much as I underestimated her the next day.

I skim my fingers over the words inked on her skin and read

them again.

My love is enough.

My fingers freeze, and I realize the "i" of the "is" is a semicolon. It's not until I'm tracing it with my fingers that I realize my hands are shaking. "It has a semicolon." Elena had a semicolon too. Hers was on her wrist. A lot of fucking good it did her.

Elena told me the meaning of the semicolon the day she came home with it. "It means I could end it, but I'm continuing to go on anyway." She was so proud of it—so hopeful that inking some punctuation on her wrist could save her. I pretended to be happy too, but inside, I was devastated that she needed it.

I flick my eyes to Nic's, needing to ask but not wanting to. I've pushed my worry about her depression from my mind since the day I saw her prescription, but now it's back and heavier than before. How do you ask someone if they have their depression under control? How do you admit you're not strong enough to carry them if they don't? "Why did you decide to get the semicolon?"

"I like the sentiment of it. It brought me comfort when I needed it." She bites down on her lip, and when she forces a smile, I know it's for my benefit, and my heart aches. I don't want her faking any smiles for me. "Despite what my mother thinks, I loved her so much. I desperately wanted to save her from the darkness, but I couldn't. I tried to be the perfect daughter, to never show my own disappointment, sadness, or fear. I truly believed that if we could just be good enough, the darkness wouldn't swallow her up again, but it always came back. Eventually I had to accept that there was nothing I could do, and of course, since I'm really crappy at relationships, it has other meanings too."

I stroke my thumb over the words. "Like what?"

"Since my sister and I were labeled 'difficult,' we never got a permanent placement. We were moved from one family to another, and when we were teenagers, we were placed in a group home. That was when I decided I'd have to make my own family. I've been in one serious romantic relationship after another since I was sixteen. Afterward, I'd beat myself up for any moment I wasn't supportive and happy and sexy . . ."

I shake my head. "But you're all those things."

"I'm some of those things sometimes, but no one can be all of them all the time." She places her hand over mine, and our fingers skim over the words together. *My love is enough.* "It's a reminder that what I have to offer is enough. When the darkness came back for my mom and when my relationships inevitably failed, I needed to remember my love was enough. That even when I fall short, I'm worthy of love and happiness. I cling to that when the darkness comes for me."

I lift my gaze to hers and hold my breath, as if I'm waiting for her to take it back. I don't want her to struggle with the darkness. Not when I failed Elena. Not when I know what it can do to a family.

"I'm okay, Ethan," she says softly. "I was telling you the truth when we talked about this before. I'm stable. But there were times that I felt like I was being sucked under. I'm okay now, but staying okay isn't always as simple for me as it is for other people."

"You're so damn happy." I grimace the second the words leave my tongue. I, of all people, know mental health isn't something that can be easily observed. We all show the world the faces we think we must.

"Most of the time. But sometimes cheerfulness is just a defense mechanism." She licks her lips. "We all cope in different ways. I'm over-the-top enthusiastic. But I'm okay, and I'm long past feeling ashamed of the moments I'm not." She chuckles softly. "So, there are the bazillion reasons behind my silly tattoo."

"It's not silly." My chest feels tight, and emotions sit on my tongue in a jumble I desperately want to translate to words but can't. So, I wrap my arms around her and bring her back down to the bed, rolling until she's under me. Then I dip my head, lift her arm to have better access to the ink on her skin, and lower my open mouth to kiss her tattoo. And when I lift my lips, I hover there for long, tormented moments, trying to breathe in the words I needed for myself in the hardest years before Elena's death. The words I needed after.

My love is enough.

But my love wasn't. It wasn't for Elena, and I'm terrified it won't be for Nic.

Chapter TWENTY-FOUR

NICOLE

I wake to the sound of pounding feet and little-girl giggles.

Ethan springs up beside me. "Fuck." He jumps out of bed, drags a hand through his hair, and looks wildly around my bedroom. "Where are my clothes?"

"The living room."

"Fuck, fuck, fuck. Can you distract them?" His voice is still husky with sleep. "If you get them into the kitchen, I'll sneak downstairs to my bedroom. Shit. I didn't expect them back so early."

It's not that I expected him to announce to the world that we slept together, or even that I'd want Lilly to know, but I could have gone without starting today with the harsh reminder that last night was a one-time thing he doesn't want his family to know about. It stings even though I don't want it to, hurts even though I agree.

"Sure. No problem." I pull on some yoga pants, a sports bra, and a T-shirt—lazy Sunday attire—and finger-comb my hair before heading downstairs.

Perhaps Ethan's eagerness to get away from me this morning is for the best. Last night, alone in the lamplight, the connection between us was so powerful that it was easy to forget he still thinks I'm my sister. This morning, with the sunlight pouring in the windows and the sound of his daughter's laughter filling the house, I'm all too aware of my lie.

I don't have to lure Shay and Lilly into the kitchen because they're already there, Shay working over the coffee pot while Lilly pours herself a bowl of cereal.

"You two are back early," I say.

Shay presses the button to brew and turns to smile at me. "I only had wholegrain, no-sugar-added cereals at my house, and Lilly insisted on having Cinnamon Toast Crunch for breakfast."

Lilly grins shamelessly and shrugs. "I know what I like."

Shay looks me over. "You're tousled."

"I just got out of bed."

"Hmm."

The steps creak, and Shay peeks around me before I can stop her. I have no doubt she's spotting Ethan. I imagine him racing down the stairs with a towel around his hips.

"That's interesting," she says. "What was Ethan doing upstairs without his pants?"

"Would you shut up?" I growl.

"Can I eat my cereal in front of the TV?" Lilly asks.

"Why don't you go to the basement?" Shay says. She's

grinning, but I suspect Lilly isn't the source of her amusement. "Just promise you won't spill on the sofa, or your daddy will make me pay to have it cleaned."

"Yes!" Lilly says. "I promise!"

My eyes go wide as I remember why the child shouldn't eat her breakfast in the living room.

Shay winks at me. "I told Lilly you must have been doing laundry, and that's why there were clothes everywhere."

My face is on fire and I put my hand over it. "Oh my God . . ."

She laughs and shakes her head before holding up her hands. "I'm not judging. As far as I'm concerned, you're the best thing that ever happened to that grumpy man. If it would make him happy, I'd take her once a week so you two could do your thing."

I shake my head. "There's no thing. We don't have a thing."

"I'm sorry to hear that." She pours herself a cup of coffee. "We've been worried about him for a long time. Even before Elena died."

"Don't worry about Ethan. He wouldn't want you to. He's a good dad."

"I don't doubt that for a minute," she says. "But he's been different. The whole thing with Elena changed him. I think it would change anybody, but . . ." She puts down her coffee and gives me a sad smile. "I thought he'd buried part of himself with Elena, but I was wrong. I see that part again when he's with you."

If that were true, would he have been so panicked waking up beside me this morning? I shake my head. "Don't do that. Don't see things that aren't there just because it makes a good story."

"I already told you, I'm not a writer. I just report on what I observe."

I rub the back of my neck. "We're attracted to each other."

"No kidding." She fills a mug with coffee and pushes it into my hands. "Everyone who shares a room with you two knows that. But what's between you isn't just attraction. He's been attracted to women since Elena died. You're different. You bring him to life again."

I swallow hard and stare at my coffee. It's not that I don't like what she's saying. It's that I like it too much. "I didn't come to Jackson Harbor looking for love, Shay. The opposite is true, in fact. I've been in one toxic relationship after another since I was sixteen. I've cut myself off."

"What if this one's not toxic?" Shay asks, but I don't get the chance to answer, because Ethan comes into the kitchen.

"What if what's not toxic?"

"Nothing," I blurt, and I beg Shay with my eyes to stay quiet. I don't need her playing matchmaker. Not when this is such a mess.

"I think I'll take my coffee to the basement and see what Lilly's watching," Shay says. She winks at me and hustles out of the room.

"Your sister knows we slept together last night."

"Okay." He crosses the kitchen. When he stops in front of me, he folds his arms and scans my face. "And why do I feel like you're about to tell me it was a mistake?"

I swallow hard. "Wasn't it?"

He shakes his head slowly. "It wasn't for me, but maybe it was for you."

You're my boss. The excuse sits useless on my tongue, and I don't insult him by using it. We both know that if that really mattered to me or to him, last night wouldn't have happened. "You're still in love with your wife," I finally say. When pain slashes across his face, I almost wish I could take the words back.

"She was my wife. She gave me my daughter. I'll always love her for that, but I . . ." He cups my face in his big hand. "Fuck, Nic, I've been suffocating with grief for three years, and when I touch you, I can breathe again."

But I can't breathe when I know I've lied to you.

"But maybe this isn't about me. Are you still in love with your ex-fiancé?"

Am I in love with Marcus? How can I be in love with a man I don't even know? The man I thought I knew wouldn't have betrayed me like that. I'm still hurt, but in hindsight, my love for Marcus looks just like my love for every other man I've devoted my life to since I was a teenager desperate for something resembling family. Unhealthy and one-sided. *The wrong kind of love.*

"Is he the reason you're pulling away from me this morning?"

My eyes go wide. "*I'm* pulling away? What about you? You're the one who freaked out when you thought Shay and Lilly were going to find us in bed together."

He grins slowly. "I woke up with a beautiful naked woman in my arms. I had an erection and no clothes. Did you want me to invite them up?"

"Oh." My cheeks heat. I read that *all* wrong. "Not exactly. I just thought . . ." I shrug. "Last night was a one-time thing, right?"

His grin falls away. "I don't know. I guess that depends on you." He touches his thumb to my bottom lip. "I'm not sure I've had enough of you yet."

My heart feels too big for my chest at the idea of spending another night in his arms, but I know I shouldn't. Not with this lie between us. Not when I need to leave in February. "I just got out of a serious relationship. I think rushing into anything else would be a bad idea."

He drops his hand and nods. "Right. I understand."

I'm hurting him, and he doesn't even flinch. Instead, he's shifted back into his default state of sadness. "Ethan, it's not you. *You* are amazing, and I . . ."

He shakes his head and steps back. "Let's not do this, Nic. You don't owe me an explanation. We were just a couple of adults enjoying each other, right?" His eyes skim over me. "And I'd say we succeeded."

Then he leaves me alone in the kitchen, and all I want to do is rush after him and beg him to talk to me. But I don't. Because all I want to say is my real name.

"You know what I'd like to do?" I ask Teagan.

"Model all that for Dr. McBroody Pants?"

I shake my head, pull out the drawer, and dump the lacy contents on the middle of the bed. After I pushed Ethan away with our kitchen conversation this morning, Teagan showed up to take me birthday shopping. When I told her I wasn't in the mood, she insisted on hanging out. Now we're in my room upstairs and she's sitting on the bed where Ethan made love to me last night.

Not that I've told her that.

I've very deliberately *not* shared that little piece of information. I know if I did, I'd also share our conversation in the kitchen and how desperately I want to tell him the truth.

It would feel good to talk that out with someone, but I'm also afraid to. Afraid it'll make me take a long, hard look at the mess I've made, and afraid I'll have to admit that in my desperate attempt to escape yet another bad relationship, I've fallen in love.

"No. I'm not interested in modeling for anyone," I say. "I'd like to have a bonfire with this stuff. I'm never going to wear it and feel sexy. These were all gifts from my bridal shower, and it's always going to remind me of Marcus and the honeymoon that wasn't."

"That is a *lot* of lingerie." Teagan and I turn to see Ethan's youngest brother, Levi, in the doorway to my bedroom, his shoulder against the doorjamb and his eyes wide as he stares at the items cluttering the center of my bed.

"Nic wants to burn it," Teagan says.

Levi winces like we just threw a punch to his gut. "Why?"

"I was supposed to wear it on my honeymoon," I say. "Since my husband-to-be got my sister pregnant and went on that honeymoon with her instead, I don't really want it anymore."

He lets out a long, low whistle. "Ouch. Understood. But still, it seems kind of wasteful to just burn it." He turns to Teagan and points a thumb at me. "She can't feel sexy in it, but there's no reason *you* couldn't wear it."

She rolls her eyes. "Girls don't share lingerie."

"Shh! Shh!" He shakes his head.

"And we don't have pillow fights in our underwear."

"Why do you have to do that? What did I ever do to you?"

Teagan grabs a pillow off my bed and throws it at him.

He catches it. "I'm just saying there's a lot of sexy in that pile, and it's wasteful to destroy it. I want to live in a world where no lingerie goes to waste."

"What are you guys talking about?" Jake joins Levi in the doorway.

I sit on the edge of the bed and bury my face in my hands. "What are you even doing here?"

"Brayden's getting the kitchen painted, so this is where we're doing Jackson Sunday brunch." Jake looks at the bed. "But I think the more important question is, what's going on in here?"

"Nic is going to burn all that lingerie, and it's never been worn," Levi says.

I'm too busy waiting for the earth to swallow me whole to see Jake's expression, but I hear him walking into the room, and when I peek at him through my fingers, he's leaning over the bed surveying the contents of my pile. Why did I even bring this stuff? I could have left it with Teagan the day after I arrived in town. Or deposited it into the nearest trashcan. It's not as if I ever intended to wear it.

"Sweet baby Jesus," Jake whispers.

"Could you two leave or something?" I mutter.

"I . . ." Jake makes a fist and bites his knuckles. "I don't really want to."

"We can't leave until you promise not to burn it," Levi says. "It's a little-known fact, but every time a piece of lingerie is stripped off a woman, a Victoria's Secret angel gets her wings."

"Fashion show?" Jake suggests.

"You're both pigs," Teagan says, but she's grinning.

Levi shakes his head. "If loving beautiful women is wrong, I don't wanna be right."

"What's going on up here?" Ethan says, coming up behind Levi. "Brunch is on the table." His gaze drops to the bed then he lifts it to meet mine, and my cheeks blaze even hotter. His Adam's apple bobs as he swallows, but he doesn't say anything before turning to his brothers. "Nic has the morning off. Give her some fucking privacy."

Ethan turns to leave and the boys bite back their grins, bow their heads, and leave my room, but Levi throws me a wink over his shoulder as he goes.

My phone rings and Teagan grabs it off the bed before I can. "Nic," she says, her eyes going wide. "Oh, shit, Nic."

"What?" I reach out for my phone. "Who is it?"

She places it in my hand. "It's Marcus."

I snatch the phone from her hand, immediately panicked that something terrible has happened to Veronica. "Hello?"

"Nic, thank you so much for taking my call," he said. "Christ, I've missed you more than you can believe."

"Marcus? Is Veronica okay?"

"She not here right now. She's down at the clinic . . ." He clears his throat. "Um, prenatal stuff?"

I meet Teagan's eyes. She folds her arms and shakes her head. "Don't let him sweet-talk you," she says in a stage whisper.

"Why are you calling me?" I ask Marcus.

"Because I miss you. I made a terrible mistake. You and me, we were good together, weren't we?"

I blink. *What a fucking douchebag.* "Were we?" I ask. "You

had me give up everything I loved so I could take care of you. You never touched me but screwed around with my sister."

"But I *loved* you. I still do." He sounds weak, like a whiny little boy. Did he always sound like that, or have I become so used to Ethan's deep, self-assured voice that Marcus doesn't sound like a man anymore?

"You loved that I idolized you. That I cooked for you and picked up after you. You didn't love *me*."

"That's not fair," he says.

"Really? What's my favorite TV show? How do I like my coffee? What's my dream job?"

Teagan grins and gives me a double thumbs-up from the bed.

"None of that matters. All that matters is you and me." He lowers his voice. "You miss me too, don't you? Just admit it. Admit it and I'll get on the first plane to come get you. Bring you home where you belong."

"Goodbye, Marcus. Don't call me again."

Chapter TWENTY-FIVE

NICOLE

"Do you expect me to believe you?" Veronica asks softly.

It's taken me all day to work up the courage to call my sister. I had to process Marcus's phone call enough to know my next move.

"I don't expect anything, Ronnie." I swallow hard when her old nickname slips out. I didn't mean to use it. That was the name I whispered in the dark when we were kids placed in a new home. The name I called out when I was lonely and needed to reach for the only person I could count on to be there. "I just wanted you to know the truth."

"So . . ." She draws in a ragged breath. "Are you going to take him back?"

"What?" I squeeze my eyes shut and shake my head. Is she insane?

"Because, in case you've forgotten, I'm *pregnant* over here." She sounds like she's crying, and the sound tugs at my heart, even though I don't want it to. I want to be cold toward my sister. *She betrayed me.*

But she's my sister.

"I called to tell you that you can't trust him, not to tell you I'm taking him back. Marcus and I are never getting back together. Never."

"And you don't want me to be with him either?"

"I didn't say that. I just wanted you to know he called me, and if he called me while he's supposed to be with you, and you when he was supposed to be with me, who knows who else he's going to call?" I take a breath and contemplate whether I'm going to say more. I told myself this was a fact-giving call—no interpretation, no analysis, no persuasion—and yet here I am, trying to make her see him for the lying cheat he is. "I don't want you to tie yourself to someone you can't trust."

"You're coming home, then? *You're* going to help me raise this baby?"

"I'm not coming back to Jeffe." I've already decided that. I don't know where I'll land, but it won't be there.

She gives a dark chuckle. "Of course you're not. And who would blame you after what I did to you?"

I want to defend her and help ease her guilty conscience, but I swallow back the instinct. I'm not going to gloss over Veronica's flaws anymore. I'm not going to cover for her with anyone, including herself. "You broke my heart," I whisper.

"I wish I hadn't." She sounds so sincere. I want to believe her.

"I applied for a bunch of preschool assistant jobs this week.

Places all over the country. I applied anywhere there was a good opportunity to do the kind of work I've always dreamed about. I never thought I'd have the courage to leave home for a job, but being here has made me realize I can do it. I thought I'd start over somewhere and maybe eventually go back to school. Get the degree I always wanted." I take a breath, making myself pause before my offer. "I'm not coming home, but maybe you could join me wherever I land?"

"Shit. Marcus is home. He doesn't like me talking to you. Shit, shit. I have to go."

She hangs up, and I close my eyes against the sharp pain of feeling her yanked away from me.

Ever since I shut Ethan down on Sunday, Dr. McBroody Pants is back. He's avoided me as much as possible and barely spoken to me the few times we were in the same room. This afternoon, he picked up Lilly from school and left for the cabin.

I think I'm still welcome there for Thanksgiving. *I think.*

I'm exhausted because I've barely slept. I am so conflicted about my relationship with Ethan and the lies that mean I can't let it be more than it is. I have to set clear boundaries. Even if I don't want to. Even if those boundaries make him cold and distant when I want him hot and close.

Because I bake for people when I feel insecure, I go to the grocery store for everything I need to wow his whole family. If I think Ethan might not want me there, I'm going to show up with a few desserts and the freshly baked bread he raved about on my birthday. I add lasagna ingredients to my cart at the last minute, too. They're staying there all weekend, and at some point, they're going to want something other than turkey.

I head to the checkout with my ingredients and pile them onto the belt.

"Hey there," the cashier says. "Did ya find everything you need okay?"

Should I make pumpkin cheesecake too? I bite my bottom lip. I'm definitely overdoing it. "I think so."

"You look familiar," she says, studying me. Then she snaps her fingers. "You're Dr. Jackson's nanny."

"I . . ." I shake my head. "Y'all sure know each other around here."

She nods and beams at me like this is high praise. "Of course we do. So glad to meet you."

"Um . . . you too." I force a smile.

"You know, I'm not surprised he brought someone from out of town to care for Lilly. His wife wasn't a local either. She moved here in high school from California and never really fit in."

I pull my wallet from my purse and nod. "Is that so?" I don't feel comfortable having a conversation about Elena with this stranger when I can't even have one with Ethan.

She drops her voice to a stage whisper. "That woman cheated on him, you know that? Everybody knows that."

I can only stare at her. What am I supposed to say? I want to point out that talking about it now doesn't serve any purpose, but even that seems like its own kind of affirmation of the gossip I don't want to be a part of.

"And then when he found out, she just left him and that sweet girl behind."

"Left him?" But Ethan's wife *died*. Did she leave him before she had her heart attack? Is that part of the secrecy around her death? Are they trying to hide that from Lilly?

"Selfish, if you ask me. So selfish."

"She had a heart attack." My voice comes out weak, but I feel like I should say something and not just let this woman talk trash about Ethan's wife.

"Mmm-hmm, a heart attack. That's what they told everybody."

I load the last of my items onto the belt and head to the other side of the register to help her load them into bags as she starts chattering on about all the *nice* women who would have loved to marry Dr. Jackson.

When I get home, I put away my purchases and put the meat in a skillet to brown. I've always loved the meal preparation part of this job. Maybe because it makes me feel like I have a home of my own.

I try to focus on the task at hand, but as I brown the meat, I keep thinking about the way the cashier talked about Ethan's wife's death as "selfish." I can't say the rumor of the affair took me by surprise after the note I found in her bookcase. Did she leave for her lover? Surely that's what the cashier meant. Elena left and she died after she made that choice.

That's what it has to be. Why would anyone say a woman was selfish for *dying*?

The only other explanation leaves a nasty knot in my stomach, and I push it away as I finish preparing the lasagna.

Once everything's cooked for the sauce and together in the

pan, I step away from the stove to let it simmer. I'll throw it in the Crock-Pot soon, and then after I'm done making the desserts, I'll cook the noodles and layer in the sauce and cheese. I'll take it like that to the Jackson cabin so it'll be ready to slide into the oven whenever they want it.

I stare at the chocolate cake ingredients on the counter. Maybe I should make chocolate truffle layer cake instead. Something with more flare would definitely be better.

I turn to the built-in kitchen shelves and scan the cookbooks. I pull out an old classic and pause when I see a piece of paper peeking out the top. I open it up and read the note.

Ethan,
Love you with all my heart. Need you with all my soul. Thank you for being mine.
Elena

How long has that been here? Three years? Four? And how did it get here? Did one of them use it as a bookmark, days after the note had been exchanged?

I think of the notes she wrote in her book in the bedroom.

Tell Ethan you love him every time you see him!!!

Love born in a lie is THE WRONG KIND OF LOVE!

Was Ethan's love born in a lie? Or was it the love of "M," the man who wrote the note she'd hidden in one of her books?

After returning the note to where I found it, I carefully slide the cookbook back into place and choose another.

I know I think I need to cook and bake to prove myself worthy. I've done this since I was a child.

If you make yourself useful and don't cause any trouble, they won't send you away.

I know what I'm doing even as I find a recipe for chocolate truffle cake. I know what I'm doing, and now I do it while thinking of Elena, Ethan's dead wife, who wrote love notes instead of baking. Who thought if she could express her love to Ethan enough times, it might make up for her mistakes.

A woman I never met but feel like I understand all too well.

A woman I'm beginning to believe took her own life.

Chapter TWENTY-SIX

ETHAN

Four days ago, Nic pushed me away with her little speech about not wanting a relationship. She drew a line in the sand, and it's been hell trying to respect that line. And today it's as if she's trying to make the rest of my family fall in love with her. It's working. And I'm jealous as hell.

She showed up after breakfast with a carful of food. Desserts, fresh-baked bread, and even a lasagna she said she wanted us to have for when we were sick of Thanksgiving leftovers. Levi already had the hots for her, but when he saw the spread she brought, I think he was ready to propose marriage.

Then, when everyone was bundling up to go sledding with Lilly, Jake and Carter insisted that Nic join us. She declined, saying she didn't even know how, but of course they couldn't leave her behind when she'd never gone sledding before.

She didn't disappoint, either. She loved it—screaming as she raced down the sleeping hill behind our cabin and running as fast as she could to the top to do it all over again. The only person I've ever met who was more enthusiastic about sledding is Lilly, and only barely.

I couldn't wait until it was over and we could go back to the house. Every minute I had to watch her with my family was miserable. Because she fits effortlessly. Because she's like a piece I didn't even realize we were missing.

It hurts to know she's put boundaries on what we can and can't be. It sucks to know that I'm finally willing to try a relationship, but the woman I want it with doesn't want me. It is frustrating as hell to watch her fit with my family so damn perfectly and know she has no intention of staying in our lives.

"I had fun this morning," Lilly says as I tuck her into a bed in the bunk room. "And when I wake up, we'll have Thanksgiving dinner and a video chat with Nana, right?"

I nod and smooth her hair back. "That's the plan, kiddo."

"And if we have time, we'll go look for Mr. Wiggles?"

I grimace. She wasn't supposed to take her stuffed rabbit in the snow, but she did anyway, and he got lost while we were sledding. "We'll look, but I don't know if we'll be able to find him."

"We will," she says, closing her eyes. "Mr. Wiggles won't hide."

Lilly rarely naps anymore, but there are exceptions for summer days at the beach and sledding days at the cabin. She was so exhausted after her big morning in the snow that she didn't even argue when I suggested a nap.

I kiss her forehead and quietly close the door behind me

before heading downstairs.

Carter and Levi are in the rec room playing *Destiny* on the PlayStation—the game Jake got them hooked on. They wave me over when I poke my head in, but I decline and head to the kitchen. Shay's at the coffee pot, flipping through a magazine as she waits for it to fill.

"Where is everyone?" I ask.

"Carter and Levi are in the rec room, Brayden is in the office doing a couple of bids, because a day without work sends him into withdrawal, and Jake—" She looks around and frowns. "Where is Jake?" She shrugs. "Jake's probably jacking off somewhere."

"Or he wooed the neighbor girl and is banging her in the barn," Carter calls from the rec room.

Shay snorts. "That's highly probable." She looks at me, then narrows her eyes. "Oh, but you weren't looking for *everyone*, were you? You were looking for the hot nanny."

"Don't call her that."

"She is hot." Levi steps into the kitchen and grabs the pot of coffee Shay's patiently been waiting on. "And she's too young for the rest of you, so if you'd kindly back off, I do believe I'll make my move."

"Don't you fucking dare." My words come out low, and there's far more threat in my tone than I meant to expose.

Levi's eyes go wide and he turns to me. "Is there a reason my celibate brother wants me to keep my hands off the hot nanny?"

"Maybe because she's my employee."

Now Carter steps into the kitchen. Apparently everyone needs to be up in my business. "Or maybe because he already hooked up with her."

Levi draws back to look me over. "Seriously? Didn't she just start, like, three weeks ago? I'm impressed, big brother. Didn't know you still had it in you."

"Why did you tell him?" I ask Shay.

"I didn't," she says. "But you just did."

"Nah, one of the guys at the fire station was talking about it. His sister-in-law was washing her hands when Ethan kicked everyone out of the ladies' room and locked the door." He grabs an apple out of the basket on the island and takes a bite. "And I work out with the girl who was your waitress on Nic's birthday. She said you two had a very romantic evening."

"Why can't anyone mind their own business?" I sound like a defensive little bitch. "There's nothing between me and Nic."

"So, if there's nothing between you, then I'm free to . . ." Levi waits, as if I'm going to give him my blessing.

"Hell no."

"You're a fucking hypocrite. Either step up or step aside."

"She just got out of a bad relationship," I say. "If she's going to give any Jackson a chance after having her heart broken, it's going to be me." The words come out before I can stop them, but once they're said, I don't want to take them back.

The whole room goes quiet as everyone stares at me.

"You're in love with her," Levi says. He sounds spooked.

"Seriously," Carter says. "I had no idea. I just thought you two were fucking around."

I shake my head and stuff my hands in my pockets. "She's not ready. But she will be, and I'll be there."

Shay's conspicuously silent and studying me, her expression pinched.

"Unless Jake beat you to it." Carter nods to the picture windows behind the kitchen table, and I follow his gaze to see Jake and Nic walking up the snowy hill together. They're laughing. Clumps of snow cling to her hair, and her cheeks and nose are bright red. They both look like they've been rolling around on the ground.

I stare for too long, my stomach tight as I wait for him to take her hand or put his arm around her.

Levi clears his throat and nudges my side with his elbow. "I'm sure Jake was as clueless as I was. I'll make sure he gets the message."

"Levi, don't . . ."

He arches a brow.

I shake my head. There's no use asking him not to bring it up with Jake. I fucking meant what I said. "Just be discreet."

I hear them come in the back door and shed their coats in the mudroom. It's all I can do to keep my feet rooted in the kitchen. I want to go after them and make sure he's not touching her. I want to stop her from throwing that gorgeous smile his way. Smiles like hers shouldn't be wasted on the likes of my scoundrel brother. But I don't. I stay in the kitchen, pour myself a cup of coffee from Shay's pot, and wait for Nic to join us.

When they come into the kitchen, they're still laughing. The tops of Nic's ears are bright red, and she's pulled her snow-dampened hair into a sloppy bun on top of her head. She looks gorgeous. *Stunning.*

"You two have a good time out there?" Levi asks, and Carter kicks him in the shin. "Ow. Fuck you, Carter."

Nic is oblivious to Levi's double meaning, and beams. "Jake

took me out on the four-wheeler. I've ridden those through the mud before, but never through the snow. And then I refused to go down the sledding hill on it, so I jumped off, lost my footing, and totally rolled all the way down. I'm soaked."

Jake meets my eyes. My annoyance is probably all over my face. "You were upstairs with Lilly, and I saw her heading back out there. Considering how clueless she is about snow, I didn't think she should be alone."

Nic pulls something soggy and fuzzy from the pocket of her sweatpants. "But it was worth it. Look what I found."

"You found Mr. Wiggles?" I step forward to take the stuffed rabbit from her.

"Girl," Shay says, "you're going to be Lilly's hero."

"I couldn't just leave him out there to freeze. No one gets left behind, right?"

Lifting my eyes to meet hers, I swallow hard. I was half right about her that first night. I was wrong thinking she'd be after a long-term relationship, but I was right in thinking she's too sweet for me. Sweeter than I deserve. How ironic that now I want to give her all the things I was scared a girl like her would want—the family, the home, the promises.

"Thank you," I say.

"You're welcome." She shivers, and her whole body shakes.

I look her over. "Nic, you're soaked through." Her long-sleeved T-shirt clings to her breasts and stomach, and her sweatpants sag off her hips.

"See what I mean?" Jake says. "Clueless about snow. Thinks cotton's gonna keep her warm."

"You need to get into some dry clothes."

She shivers again. "I didn't bring any," she says, still smiling.

"She can borrow something of mine," Shay says. She's been oddly silent since Nic came in, no doubt because I more or less confessed my unrequited affection for Nic to my whole damn family.

"Come on. I'll find you something to wear while I throw your stuff in the dryer." I head toward Shay's bedroom to raid her closet, but as we leave the kitchen, I hear Jake say in an extra-deep voice, "Let's get you out of these wet clothes," and Shay giggles.

I ignore them.

Assholes.

"As soon as we get back home, we're shopping for some winter clothes for you."

"I thought these *were* winter clothes." Nic's shivers are nonstop now.

"Not for rolling around in the snow." I shake my head. "And not if you don't want my brothers ogling your breasts."

NICOLE

I gape at Ethan as he digs through the old dresser. Was the thing about his brothers and my breasts a dig at me or at them?

He comes up with a pair of Shay's black leggings, and motions to the closet. "There are probably shirts hanging in there." He hands me the pants, but instead of leaving or even moving to the closet, he stays where he is, his eyes roaming over me. His gaze pauses at my curves. I never thought much of my body before Ethan, but when he looks at me, I'm conscious of the round of my breasts, the dip in my waist, and the hips he gripped so tightly when we made love. My clothes are soaked from the snow, and if I'd realized before now how much they cling to my breasts and thighs, I probably would have been embarrassed in the kitchen. But I didn't. And now, in this very moment, I'm not embarrassed. I'm half turned on and half angry.

I relish Ethan's greedy gaze on me, and I've missed this the last few days. He's made every effort to avoid it. But the thing about his brothers ogling my breasts kind of implied I *wanted* them to.

"Thank you for finding the rabbit." His voice is gravelly as he lifts his gaze to mine.

I'm definitely overreacting. He's already moved on, and I should too. "You're welcome."

"I was going to search for it later with Lilly. I've told her again and again she needs to leave him behind during outdoor activities, but she's pretty attached."

"I saw there was more snow coming, and I was worried he'd be buried until spring." I smile, because suddenly having him close is making me nervous about keeping all the promises I've made to myself, and smiling is what I do when I'm nervous. "I'm glad I found him."

"Me too." He rubs the back of his neck. "It was nice of Jake to help you."

"It was. I'd probably be even more drenched if he hadn't."

"Did he . . . I mean, do you . . ." He looks away. "You're really beautiful, Nic, and my brothers aren't blind. But if you're going to work for me, I'm going to have to ask that you don't get involved with my family members."

I step back. I guess I wasn't overreacting. My cheeks heat with anger, and I cling to that feeling. If there's one thing I've been proud of since I came to Jackson Harbor, it's that I've been standing up for myself. After years of being a professional doormat for the men I fell for, I love that I've refused to take Ethan's shit. I'm not going to start now. "What is that supposed to mean?"

"I saw the way you and Jake were laughing together when you came up from the pole barn. You didn't do anything wrong, but it wouldn't be fair if I didn't make it clear up-front that—"

"You think I'm going to screw your brothers? What, like, I spread my legs for you, so it only makes sense that I'll line them up and give them each their turn now?"

"Fuck." He drags a hand through his hair. "That's not what I meant. But you two were both covered in snow like you'd been rolling around together. It occurred to me that you might not understand that I wouldn't be okay with you starting something with him. Or any of them."

"You thought I'd been *rolling around in the snow* with Jake?"

A red flush creeps up his neck, but he holds my gaze. "We hadn't talked about it. I needed to make the boundaries clear." He steps forward and looks down at me. His nostrils flare as his gaze dips to my mouth.

Is he going to kiss me? He's looking at me like he wants to. Do I want him to?

Hell yes.

No. I hold tight to my anger. Asshole Ethan is back. No more assholes. "I don't understand you."

"Really?" He brushes his knuckles over my cheek. I step away from his touch, and he drops his hand. "You don't understand why the possibility of one of my brothers touching you would upset me?"

"Why did you invite me here if you just think I'm some slut?"

"I don't think you're a slut." He looks up to the ceiling. "I don't know what you want, Nic. I just know that you came to my house with a bag full of sexy lingerie and a giant box of condoms."

I gape at him. I swallow hard. Once. Then again. I feel like he just eviscerated me. As if my guts are on the floor between us and he doesn't understand why that should bother me. "And you think I want those condoms for your *brothers*?"

"No, that's not what I mean. When I tried to get closer, you pushed me away, and I just . . . *Fuck it.*" He steps forward until he's so close that I have to step back. But he keeps coming, and soon enough, my back is against the wall and Ethan is pressed against me, his hand on my jaw, his mouth hovering over mine. "I can't blame them for wanting you." His breath sweeps across my lips as he speaks. "But I'm asking you not to let anything happen."

"Because I'm your employee?"

"Yeah."

I don't know how long we stand like that—my heart hammering madly, and anger and frustration filling the air between us—but when he finally brings his mouth to mine, I don't stop him. I kiss him with all the desperation and fear I feel when I think about walking away in February. When I think about never touching him again, when I imagine mornings that don't start with Lilly's bright smile, my chest aches. And there's not a single thing I can do about it.

He breaks the kiss and backs away from me, his chest heaving.

I shiver again. I'm suddenly freezing. I'm scared and lonely. I'm exhausted from carrying these emotions I'm not supposed to feel.

I'm missing a man who's standing right in front of me.

"Thanks for clarifying, *boss*." I look to the bathroom. "I'm going to take my shower now." I walk away from him and shut myself in the bathroom by Shay's room. I run the shower hot and strip out of my wet clothes. I step under the spray and swallow back my tears.

When I came here, I thought I'd hit rock bottom, so how on earth did I fall in love?

I press my palm to my chest and force myself to take slow, measured breaths. In, two, three, four. Out, two, three, four. *Breathe, Nic. Don't panic. Just breathe.*

I shampoo my hair, massaging the suds into my scalp and closing my eyes as I rinse it out. I'm reaching for the conditioner when I hear a knock on the bathroom door that makes me jump. I pull aside the shower curtain and stick out my head. "Hello?"

The bathroom door cracks, and Ethan steps in. "Everyone's watching a movie in the basement, and I . . ." He runs his gaze over the shower curtain, and I don't know if he can see my silhouette, but a shiver runs through me, turning hot and pooling low in my stomach.

He closes the door and locks it behind him. In one swift step, he's in the shower fully clothed, his chest pressed against me, my back to the tile, his hand in my hair as his mouth lowers to mine.

Chapter TWENTY-SEVEN

NICOLE

"I was an ass, and you didn't deserve that." He kisses down my neck as his hands slip over my wet skin. "I don't want you with my brothers because I want you for myself. It has nothing to do with you working for me or the fucking condoms. I just know they see what I see. I know they're smart enough to fight for you too, and it would kill me." He pulls back and looks into my eyes, water rolling down his face. "It would fucking *destroy me* to have to see you with any of them when I want you with me."

I swallow hard and try to keep myself in check, but my chest is tight—full of hope and optimism and everything else I'm too afraid to label. I trace the line of his jaw, following the path of the spray as it rolls down his neck. "I have secrets, Ethan." I shake my head. "There are reasons I can't stay."

"We all have secrets, and I know you're not ready. I know he broke your heart and you want to leave in February, but let me have you until then. I don't need promises, Nic. But I want you too much. I will take anything you're willing to give me."

I close my eyes and lift my face to the spray. "I want you too," I admit. "More than you know."

He kisses me hard, and his hand finds my breast. His thumb strokes against my nipple while the other hand strokes down the side of my body. He positions one of his muscular legs between mine, giving me the pressure of his hard thigh right where he touched me on Saturday night. His mouth on my neck, the hot water, the cool tile, his greedy hands sliding over every inch of my skin—the combination leaves me breathless and whimpering for more. I rock against his thigh, and he grips my hips roughly, guiding me to rub over him again and again. Pleasure spirals through me, and I arch my neck and moan.

"Jesus. I can't stop thinking about you," he murmurs against my lips. "About this. You make me insane."

I fumble with the button on his jeans, and he tries to help. We're both too anxious, and our hands get in each other's way as we fight to remove his wet clothes and toss them outside the shower. When he steps back against the opposite wall to finish the job, his eyes are hot on my body, skimming down and back up, pausing at my breasts, my thighs, and every dip and curve between. His lips part, and time seems to move in slow motion as he sheds his briefs. Only then can I exhale. Only when he's stepping toward me naked with those hungry eyes can I breathe again.

He presses against me, and the cold tile is a sharp contrast to his impossible heat. He trails a hand down one thigh and under my knee and then the other, until I'm pinned between his body and the wall, my legs wrapped around his waist and his cock nestled along my slit.

"Fuck me," I whisper. I know he doesn't have a condom, and I don't care. I'm on birth control, and desperate to feel him inside me. "Fuck me like this."

He slides into me a fraction of the way, his eyes floating closed. When he opens them, he kisses me and slides fully in. He feels so good. So close and deep. My body instantly tightens around him, coiling in pleasure I've never found so quickly.

He sucks at my neck between whispered words in my ear. *"I love the way you move." "I can't stop thinking about how you taste." "You're so beautiful when you come."*

The shower rains down on us as he loves me with his body and his words, and when I come in his arms, my fears in that moment disintegrate and are washed down the drain right along with my well-intended boundaries.

NICOLE

I'm pretty sure every time one of the Jackson siblings looks at me, they can tell Ethan and I just had shower sex. As if it's written on my skin or something. But no one says anything, even when Ethan throws me looks at the dinner table that seem to say he can't wait to do it again.

Jackson family dinner is a boisterous affair. The kitchen

counters are overflowing with food, and the dining room table barely fits everyone. There are half a dozen conversations going on at any given moment, and Lilly is so full of energy she's bouncing in her seat. But I'm nearly oblivious to it all, because I'm so focused on the hot tension between me and Ethan, the charge in the air that promises there's more to come. When he takes the seat next to me at the dining room table, I can't think about anything else.

"Is Ava joining us, Jake?" Brayden asks. "I thought she'd be here by now."

Jake shakes his head and points out at the snow. "The snow hasn't slowed all day. She doesn't want to get stuck here, so she decided she'd better not drive out."

Carter gives Jake a pointed look. "Damn shame. Maybe if you were snowed in together, you'd finally find your balls where she's concerned."

Jake's jaw hardens and he avoids his brother's eyes. "I don't know what you're talking about."

"Nothing worse than wasting attraction by refusing to acknowledge it," Levi says.

Carter grunts. "Hey, pot, meet kettle."

Levi flashes him a warning glare. "Don't."

I shoot a questioning glance to Ethan, and his lips quirk uncharacteristically. He dips his head to whisper in my ear, "Jake's been in love with his best friend, Ava, most of his life, but he won't admit it. Honestly, we all had to pretend he wasn't for a long time because she was married to an asshole, but that's over now. If you see him making eyes at her, do like the rest of us do and pretend you don't notice." He shakes his head. "One of these days, she'll come around. She's practically a sister to us already. They might as well make it legal."

I grin. I'm learning there are a lot of sides to Ethan, and I like this side—family Ethan, brother Ethan, *these are my people* Ethan. *Fuck the nanny in the shower* Ethan. "And what about Levi? The whole pot-and-kettle thing?"

The humor falls from his face. "That one's more complicated."

I fold my arms and arch a brow, waiting.

Ethan sighs. "He has a thing for his best friend's girl, who happens to be Ava's best friend." His jaw is hard when he says it. Clearly, Ethan isn't as supportive of Levi's secret love as he is of Jake's. "Obviously he's not going to do anything about it. So, they're just friends."

"Oh." My gaze drifts across the table. I wonder if Ava has any idea about Jake. I totally missed that vibe between them, but I've never been great at picking up on stuff like that. I look back to Ethan, who's helping Lilly cut her turkey. I can't imagine any girl would want to be *just friends* with any of the Jackson boys.

I know I don't.

"You probably need to plan on staying the night yourself, Nic," Carter says, gesturing toward me with his fork. "The roads are getting pretty nasty out there. If you wait until tomorrow, it will be a lot safer."

Ethan smirks. "Yeah. Definitely safer if you stay." He winks at me, and my insides shimmy.

The truth is, driving in the snow is still new to me, and I'm not great at it. I don't like the idea of driving home on slick roads in the dark. "Is there room for me?"

"Plenty of room," Jake says. "There's room for everyone at the

Jackson cabin."

"You can sleep in the bunk room with me," Lilly says, clapping her hands.

"I'm not sure how your dad's gonna feel about that, kid," Levi says, and Carter gives him an elbow to the ribs.

Our attention is pulled from our plates at the sound of a phone ringing—a normal phone ring, not a ringtone on someone's cell.

Ethan pushes away from the table and grabs a handset from the kitchen. "Hello?" When he walks back into the dining room, his expression is grim. "Don't worry about it, Mom. She'll understand. . . Of course you did, but it's not a big deal. Let me put her on." He holds his hand over the receiver and looks at Lilly. "Nana can't video-chat today. She can't get her internet to work right. But she wants to talk to you."

My chest feels tight. The treatments must be taking a greater toll on Kathleen than she expected. She's sounded so tired lately, and I imagine it's easier to hide that on the phone than on camera.

"I wanted to see her face," Lilly says. Her little chin wobbles.

"I know, baby, but we're going to have to try another time." He holds out the phone. "You can at least hear her voice."

She nods and takes the receiver. "Hi, Nana. I miss you *so much*." A tear slides down her cheek, but she keeps her chin high and her voice even. *What an amazing kid.* "Tell me what you saw today."

"I still think she's hooking up with a secret lover over there," Jake says.

Brayden groans. "Don't talk about Mom like that."

"The whole thing happened too fast, if you ask me. One second, we're planning a typical Thanksgiving, and the next, she's got this trip," Carter says. "It's not like Mom to miss the holidays."

"Because she's never gotten the chance to do a damn thing for herself," Brayden says. "Europe is crawling with tourists over the summer. A winter trip makes perfect sense."

I stare at my plate. It's piled with delicious home-cooked foods, but suddenly I don't have any appetite at all. I'm not only lying about my name. I'm holding Kathleen's secret, and if she never comes home, I'm not sure any of her children will forgive me for failing to tell them they needed to say their goodbyes.

Worse than knowing they all might hate me is feeling like they'd be right.

"You really didn't have to help me," Shay says. "We rotate which sibling does the dishes at family dinners, and it's my turn."

I shrug. "I don't mind. I'm not a big football person anyway."

"Shh! Don't say that around here." She gives a conspicuous glance over each shoulder before turning back to me with a grin. She reaches up to the cabinet over her head to slide in a big serving bowl.

It's just the two of us in the kitchen. The boys have all gone to the basement to watch the football game. When I left them down there, Lilly was curled up on Ethan's lap, still pretty upset about not getting to do her video chat.

I'm washing the dishes that didn't fit in the dishwasher, and Shay is drying them and putting them away.

"Nicole?" Shay says quietly. "Can we talk for a minute while everyone is downstairs?"

"Sure."

She grabs the bowl I just rinsed, and when she cuts her eyes to me, I feel like she's waiting for me to say more. "It's about your sister, Veronica."

That's the moment I realize she just called me *Nicole* and not *Nic.* The blood drains from my face. "What? I'm sorry, what did you call me?"

"*Nic* isn't short for Veronica, is it? It would be strange for a girl to use that as her nickname when her sister's name is *Nicole.*"

I stare at the sudsy water. "Very strange."

"I thought something was off when you moved in, but then Ethan said something about your meds the other day."

I frown. I thought the issue of my antidepressants had already been resolved.

She slides the bowl onto a shelf, turns back to me, and folds her arms. "When Mom was still picking between applicants, she told me she asked Veronica about mental illness and medication. It was the one thing Ethan insisted on. Your sister told her about you, and Mom told me. She thought it would be good for Ethan to have someone living with him who understood what it was like to love someone who struggles with depression the way Elena did."

I look around the kitchen to make sure we're still alone. Even when I confirm there's no one close enough to hear us, I keep my voice low. "Why didn't you say anything when you realized who I was?"

"I wasn't entirely sure at first, but Mom confirmed."

"Really?" Half the reason I've kept this secret was for her.

Shay's face twists. "I know Mom's sick. I noticed the postmarks on all the postcards were from Germany, and I started to get suspicious. Why would Mom be in Germany and pretend she's traveling Europe? I guessed cancer. She's been run-down, getting tired too quickly. My brothers think it's old age, but I knew it was worse than that. I wish I'd been wrong." She stares into space, and I can see the devastation in the set of her jaw and the circles under her eyes. She's been carrying this alone.

"I wish you'd been wrong too," I whisper.

"I called her earlier this week and told her I knew she was sick. She didn't deny it. I think maybe she was even a little relieved to talk to me about what was happening."

"I'm sorry I couldn't tell you. I tried to convince her to stay."

"I was so pissed at you at first. *So pissed.*" She shakes her head and sighs. "But then I realized it wasn't your secret to tell."

"I know. Can you convince her to come home?"

"I want her to. This is where she should be, but she's scared we're all going to have to watch her die." She looks away. "And I understand why she wouldn't want Lilly and Ethan to see her dying at Christmas. So . . ." She swipes at her cheeks and shrugs. "I decided to let her be until January. I want you to do the same."

I blink at her. "You want me not to ask your mom to come home until January?"

"I want us both to keep our secrets until then."

Only when my stomach sinks do I realize I've half planned to tell Ethan the truth. I have to find a way to try, don't I? "I hate the lie, Shay. I want to tell Ethan."

She nods. "You should. But not until after Christmas. Christmas is hard enough for him, and I'm afraid . . ."

"Jake told me Elena had a heart attack, but that's not true, is it?"

Her big brown eyes are filled with tears. "That's what Ethan tells everyone. We love him too much to call him on the lie. Besides, technically, I guess it's true. She had a heart attack . . . even if she made it happen."

I squeeze my eyes shut. Poor Ethan, losing his wife to suicide and then finding himself with a lover who struggles with depression. I'm not suicidal, and I'm so hyper-conscious of not abusing drugs to cope that I rarely even drink, but I understand why seeing me with those pills would have upset him. "I planned on leaving in February. I've applied for all these jobs so he would never have to find out the truth."

Her face wilts. "You can't leave, Nic. Please don't. I think he's in love with you."

"I know I'm in love with him. Which is why I can't keep lying."

She squeezes my hand. "Just one month. For my family. Please? And then I'll help you tell him, and we'll work together to get Mom home."

Chapter TWENTY-EIGHT

NICOLE

"What'd we miss?" Shay asks when we make our way down to the basement to join the rest of the family.

I feel eyes on me from across the room, and turn to see Ethan. He's seated in one of the dark leather recliners with his feet up and Lilly sleeping in his lap. His eyes don't leave mine when I look at him, and my stomach flutters as I wonder if he's thinking about where I'll sleep tonight.

I rush to action rather than give that question any thought of my own. I cross the room and crouch next to his chair. "I'll get her to bed."

He's still studying me. "It's fine. I've got her."

"I'll help." I reach out to bring Lilly to her feet. She's a sleepwalker, and I know from experience that I can guide her to the bedroom without having to wake her completely.

Ethan ignores me, keeping her in his arms as he stands. I suppose her fifty-five pounds is nothing for him, but my heart squeezes a little at the sight of this big man carrying his growing baby girl.

I follow him up the stairs and down the hall. When he opens the door to the bunk room I've heard so much about, I smile. "Wow."

The little room was clearly decorated for Lilly and Lilly alone. There are mermaids all over the walls, and the bunk beds are draped with blue and green tulle.

He carries Lilly to a bed and tucks her in. We leave the room, and he closes the door behind him. When I turn to head back downstairs to join the others, he takes my wrist and tugs me back. "I'm glad you're staying tonight," he says softly. "I don't like the idea of you driving on those roads."

That squeeze in my heart releases, sending a thousand butterflies to go wild in my stomach. "I just don't want to be in the way."

"You'd never be in the way, Nic."

I need to figure this out. I'm so off balance trying to navigate these feelings for him and keep my lies straight at the same time. I want to believe Shay's right and I can keep the secret through Christmas without losing Ethan.

"Would you come on a walk with me?" he asks. "I need some fresh air."

It's stopped snowing, and the clouds have cleared out of the night sky. The moon reflects off the freshly fallen snow and lights up the night. I bundled up in my coat, gloves, hat, and scarf and followed Ethan out back, and now we're walking the path to the pole barn that sits on the backside of the property, snow crunching under our boots.

"I keep thinking about your tattoo," he says after long minutes of silence. "I can't stop thinking about it, actually."

He leaves the words to hang on their own in the air, and I don't know what to say. Now that I've had confirmation about Elena's suicide, I'm terrified he's going to look at me and see the wife he couldn't save. But as much as I don't want him to worry about me or to think I'm in a bad place, I also don't want to sugarcoat who I am or the struggles I face. That's what I do every day when the smile everyone expects from me is pasted on my face.

I don't want to do that here, in the moonlight, with Ethan. I want him to see me. "Just because I had the words tattooed on me doesn't mean I believe them all the time." I swallow. "Or even most of the time. The truth is, if I believed them, I wouldn't need them there."

"I like that you found a way to remind yourself. You found a strength in yourself that my wife always looked for in me." We stop in front of the barn, and Ethan tucks his hands into his pockets. "Elena killed herself on Christmas Eve three years ago."

My breath catches—not because the confession comes as a

surprise but because he's telling me at all. "I'm so sorry, Ethan."

"When I married her, I knew she struggled with depression. But it didn't matter. We loved each other, and we were stronger together." He tilts his face up to the sky. "But it only got worse after she had Lilly. The darkness swallowed her, and *I* didn't handle it well. I resented her sadness. I'm a doctor. I know it wasn't a choice for her. I know depression isn't something you can shake off or snap out of. But that didn't change the fact that when she was low, it was like she was punishing all of us. The whole house seemed darker, and everything she did was with this spirit of anger. I felt like I couldn't do anything right."

I step forward and reach for his hand. There's nothing I can say, so I weave my gloved fingers through his and squeeze.

"When she was up, we were unstoppable. We were good together and so damn happy. When she was up, I felt like every failed marriage in the world should just look at us and see how to do it right." He swallows, and in the moonlight, I can see the pain wash over his face. "But when she was down . . . when she was down, I felt like my marriage was a prison, and I resented her for locking me in it."

I swallow and study his face. I understand that he needs to tell this story the way he feels it, but it's killing me to have him present the struggles of their marriage as his own shortcomings, as if he was entirely at fault, when I know that's not true. "How long was she having an affair?"

His gaze drops to mine, and I see the shock in his eyes. "I honestly don't know. Things hadn't been good for us for a long time when a colleague told me about Elena and Mike." His jaw goes hard. "I found out about him on Christmas Eve, and I fucking lost my mind. Here I was, living with her, day in and day out, trying to save her from the darkness, feeling . . ." He snaps his mouth shut, and I squeeze his hand again. "On some level, I felt like her depression was my fault. I was ready to turn our lives upside down to save her from it. She missed California—even though she hadn't lived there since she was a teenager—but I was going to leave my practice, leave my *family*, and move us out there. I was going to let go of everything to save a woman I wasn't even sure loved me anymore. Meanwhile, she was fucking my best friend."

I gasp. I suspected the affair, but I never had any clue it was with someone close to Ethan. I put my hand on his chest, search for the reassuring thrum of his heart under my fingertips. "Ethan . . ."

"I told her I wanted her to leave. I didn't want her in my life anymore. She begged me to reconsider. She told me what was between her and Mike had been a mistake—a horrible mistake. And that she'd only been with him because it made her feel closer to me when I was being so distant." He closes his eyes, and when he opens them again, he returns his gaze to the sky, as if he might find answers floating around somewhere up there. Or maybe he's just ashamed that he responded to heartbreak and betrayal like any human would. "I told her to get out and that I didn't want to look at her. I watched her drive away from me and Lilly on Christmas Eve."

"I'm so sorry. That must have been awful."

"But it wasn't. That's the worst part. It wasn't awful at all." His voice cracks—shame making the confession brittle. "All I could think when she drove away was that I was grateful to be free of her—free of the constant guilt and pain of watching her suffer from her own demons. I went to bed *relieved* that my marriage was over." He places a hand on top of the one I have on his chest and closes his eyes. "Then, sometime in the middle of the night, she came back and finished off all the pills she had in the house. She knew I was done. That I couldn't save her from the darkness anymore."

Reaching up, I put my hand against his face and wait until he meets my eyes. "It wasn't your job to save her."

"Maybe not. But I'm responsible for pushing her over the edge."

"No," I whisper. "You're not, Ethan. She would have been just as crushed had you not cared about her affair. You didn't push her into the darkness; she surrendered herself to it."

"I've gone over that night a thousand times in my mind. If I hadn't let my temper get the best of me, Lilly would still have her mom." He slides a hand behind my back and pulls me into his chest. "My marriage was over the second she got into Mike's bed, but when you have children, your marriage becomes about more than just two people. We could have gotten a divorce. I could have made sure she was comfortable. Maybe she would have married Mike. I don't know." He brings my hand to his mouth and kisses my knuckles. "I just don't know."

"It's not your fault." I pull out of his embrace enough to meet his eyes. "Just like my mom's drug abuse wasn't my fault." I want to wrap my arms around him, but I feel like he needs to look into my eyes while I say this. He needs to know I'm not just trying to appease his guilty conscience.

He might be standing firm, with every muscle tense and his

jaw so hard that it looks like he's been chewing glass, but under all that is the man who kissed my tattoo with tears in his eyes. A man who's spent the last three years wrapped up in the kind of grief that's weighed down so heavily by guilt that it never lets you take a full breath. My mom is still alive, but I know what that kind of grief feels like. Loss comes in many forms.

"I used to think it was my job to make my mom happy. When she started using again because real life was too hard, I thought it was my fault. It wasn't. What happened to your wife isn't your fault. And it's not hers, either. It's a disease, Ethan. You lost her to a terrible disease."

"I don't ever talk about her because I'm ashamed. I failed her, Nic."

"No." I shake my head. "You're the reason she held on as long as she did. I've found those little notes she left you around the house, and I see a woman who wanted to get better for her husband. She just didn't know how."

He closes his eyes and wraps his arms around me. "I thought I was broken forever, and then you showed up. Now I want things I didn't think I'd ever want again."

If my chest didn't already ache from his heartbreaking confession, it would now. When he finds out about my lie, will he still want those things from me? I pull off my glove and reach up to skim my fingers over his jaw. He hasn't shaved today, and the thick layer of stubble scratches my fingers. I have to swallow back my own confession, to remember my promises and save it for another time. "You're not broken, Ethan. You just needed to heal."

He turns his head and presses a kiss against the middle of my open palm. "I just needed you."

Chapter TWENTY-NINE

ETHAN

I. *Want. That.*

It's all I can think when I spot Nic sitting on the couch in the basement. When we got back from our walk, I didn't kiss her goodnight—even though I was dying to. I just squeezed her hand and told her to let me know if she needed anything.

I wanted her to process what I told her. I needed her to know my darkest secret before I touched her again.

Now the whole house is asleep except the two of us, and she's sitting with a bowl of popcorn in her lap and her gaze on the television in front of her. I want to sweep away the popcorn, turn off the TV, and lose myself looking at her. *Feeling her. Touching her.*

She perks up when she sees me, grabs the remote off the end table, and presses pause. "Can't sleep?"

I shrug. "I can't turn off my brain."

"Do you want to talk?"

I shake my head and give a small smile. "I think I've done enough talking for a year."

"Do you want the TV?" She stands, and I hold out a hand, stopping her.

"Please don't. I'll watch whatever you're watching."

"Are you sure?" She bites her lip. "It's *Outlander*. Kind of a chick show."

"Yeah, I'm sure. I want your company."

She settles back onto the couch, still looking skeptical, and I take the seat next to her and steal a handful of her popcorn. "Can I get you a beer or something?" she asks.

"I'm good." I can so clearly see my life like this. I'd come home after a long day to beautiful Nic sitting on the couch. *Just be patient.* I steal another handful of popcorn. "Tell me about this show."

"Okay, well, she accidentally traveled back in time."

"How do you accidentally travel back in time?"

"I think it has something to do with some druids, but . . ." She shakes her head. "Not important. Anyway, she has a husband back home, but in this time she had to marry this man, Jamie, and she's falling for him."

I only half listen as she continues her recap of the show. I get the impression she's watched it a few times. Her face lights up when she talks about it, and I'm relieved to be discussing something other than my moonlight confession.

I couldn't believe how the words poured out of me tonight. I never talk about Elena or what happened. I told my family it was a heart attack to spare them the grief, and if they suspect I was lying, they've never said so. But when I started telling Nic, it was like the story was sitting inside me, waiting for her.

"Are you ready?" she asks, waving to the TV.

"Whenever you are."

She presses play, but after a few minutes, she throws her hand over her mouth then grabs the remote. "I forgot what happens in this episode."

"Don't change it. Now I'm invested." I'm not, but I do want to know what she's so embarrassed to have me see. My fingers brush hers as I take the remote from her hands and put it on my end table.

It turns out this show's pretty hot, but even the characters undressing each other is nothing compared to how sweet Nic looks with those bright pink cheeks. As the characters on the television touch, she keeps her gaze fixed on the screen, as if she's afraid to look at me. I want to know if she's just embarrassed or if part of that flush is arousal.

"This is awkward," she says, cutting her gaze to me.

"What's awkward about it? We're just a couple of people watching a TV show. Totally normal." The woman on the screen drops to her knees. "Unless you're turned on. I guess that might be a little awkward."

"You couldn't prove it if I was," she says.

My gaze drops to her mouth. "I bet if I asked real nice, you'd let me find out for myself."

"What's that supposed to mean?"

"It means you let me fuck you in the shower and then listened to me pour out my heart. I think you might have a soft spot where I'm concerned."

She bites her bottom lip. "Maybe."

Groaning, I shift so I'm sitting the long way on the sofa, one of my legs stretched out behind her, the other on the floor. I wrap a hand around her wrist and tug her toward me, guiding her to sit between my legs, her back to my front. "You can't expect me to go to bed thinking about you being turned on and wanting something I know damn well I can give you myself."

I sweep my hand down the front of her body, and her eyes float closed. I trail between her breasts, over her stomach, across the waistband of her sleep pants. My mind floods with images from our night together. Maybe I could resist if I didn't know how good she tasted. Probably not.

I sweep her hair to one side and lower my face to her neck. "You smell so damn good. Do you know that? I go to bed at night, and your smell is everywhere. It's gotta be in my head because I get to work and I still smell you on me."

I graze my knuckles between her legs. She licks her lips before reaching above her head to thread a hand through my hair. I flatten my palm against her belly. "I was inside you without a condom in the shower."

She gasps as I slide my hand into her sleep pants. "But we can be more careful."

I was lost in the moment at the time, but I have no regrets. "I don't need it if you don't."

Her eyes meet mine and she draws in a ragged breath. "I liked the way it felt."

Those words send a bolt of pleasure down my spine, and I groan. Slowly, I lower my mouth to hers and start what I intend on being a long, slow seduction.

NICOLE

"Stay," he says against my neck.

I roll over in Ethan's arms, tilting my face up so I can see his. He brought me to his bedroom at the cabin, and we fell asleep in each other's arms. This morning, he woke me with his mouth and hands before the sun came up. We made love before saying a word to each other, and now the morning light is slipping through the curtains. "What?"

"Stay," he says again. A hesitant smile hitches one corner of his mouth. "Lilly, she . . . *I* think you should stay. Don't leave in February. Lilly's already attached to you." He props himself up on one hand and traces my jaw with the other. "And she's not the only one. It turns out I'm pretty attached to you too."

My stomach goes into freefall for a minute, but I can't decide if it's joy or panic that has me feeling this way. Maybe both.

He dips his head and kisses me. "Stay," he says again.

"I want to," I whisper. "But when the time comes, you might not want me to."

"I find that very unlikely," he says, his voice husky. He kisses down my neck and rolls me to my back. He holds himself on his elbows so he's hovering over me again. The hard length of his cock settles between my legs as he puts a finger to my mouth. "I'm not just going to stop wanting you. It doesn't work like that."

But it has so many times before with so much less reason. I swallow my fear and meet his eyes. "There are things you don't know about me. Things that might change the way you feel."

He cups my face in his hands. "Let me be your family. You fit here. With us. With *me*."

God, I want him to be my family. I want to stay. I want him to love me despite the lie. Hell, I want him to love me *because* of the lie. I want him to understand why I did it and know that trying to fix people I care about is part of who I am.

"Why are you still hiding your secrets from me, Nic? When will you see I'm not *him*?" He strokes the side of my face with his thumb. "And I'm not your mom, either. I'm not going to push you away. You can trust me."

"I do." I draw in a breath. "I promise I do."

"You've brought so much goodness into my life. You're changing the way I feel about everything, and I'm realizing that even if I remain this stubborn asshole who won't admit he's in love with you, it's not going to spare Lilly when you walk away. And it's not going to spare me, either."

He shifts his hips so he's positioned at my center, poised to enter me again. I hold my breath. Because he's saying everything I want to hear, but I've been here before—in the arms of a man who I think I need to be happy—and I'm wrong every time. I ruin it every time. A tear slides down my cheek, hot and as lonely as this heart I've kept caged. "I love you too," I say, but I can't follow my words with promises, and that breaks my heart.

I shift my hips, guiding him to slide into me. "I love you," I repeat. My voice sounds shaky and desperate.

He lowers his head and brushes his lips against mine. There's no fire in the kiss. No demand. *This* kiss is a question. *This* kiss is asking me to stay.

Chapter THIRTY

NICOLE

I can barely keep my eyes open while I'm getting Lilly ready for school on Monday. I use the espresso machine to add a couple of shots of extra caffeine to my usual morning coffee. By the time I have her buckled into her booster seat and am driving the ten blocks to school, I'm wide awake but no less distracted.

"So, you'll get me after school?" Lilly asks from the back as I pull into the car line that wraps around the school's parking lot.

"That's right," I say as I pull up to the doors. "Go ahead and unbuckle, sweetie." They don't like the adults to get out of the car at the drop-off line because it slows down the traffic, so I wait and let the teacher on morning duty open the door and help Lilly out. "I'll see you later, alligator!"

She throws her backpack over her shoulder. "After a while, crocodile!" she responds with her big grin, showing off her missing front-bottom teeth.

The teacher shuts the back door behind her, and I wave before I drive away.

I didn't sleep much last night, or the three nights before. Once Lilly has been in bed for the night, Ethan hasn't been able to keep his hands off me. And I haven't wanted him to.

And after Ethan falls asleep, I can't turn off my thoughts. I keep trying to think of a way I can tell Ethan the truth without losing his trust or exposing his mother's secret. I keep trying to think of a reason that diving straight into another relationship wouldn't be a total disaster when that's exactly what I promised myself I wouldn't do.

I haven't figured it out, and I know I'm playing a dangerous game. Maybe I'm lying to myself, but when we're together, I believe in our love. Ethan needs to touch me as much as I ache for him to, and that connection makes me believe we'll be okay once the storm hits. Even if I haven't figured out how.

Teagan is waiting for me on Ethan's front porch when I get back from my school run. She just shows up sometimes—like family would. That thought makes me smile.

"Well, aren't you smiley this morning?" she says as she follows me into the house.

I shed my coat and take hers. "I'm always in a good mood in the morning." Nevertheless, I try to hide the evidence by biting back my smile. "That's why they call me a morning person."

She folds her arms and narrows her gaze. She's in yoga pants and a long-sleeved T, her mascara is smeared under her eyes, and her hair is half in and half out of her sloppy bun. She looks more like she just woke from a bender in Vegas than like a nurse who worked a double. "I know this about you, but it's worse this morning." She wrinkles her nose as if there's something truly offensive about a person being perky before nine a.m. "This is something more." Her eyes go wide, and her jaw drops. "You're sleeping with Dr. McBroody Pants!"

My cheeks flash hot. "Where did you get that idea?"

"You ho! I've lived here for two years, and the only guy who's put a smile like that on my face was the one who was giving out free donuts at the mammogram clinic. God, I'm so *jealous* of you right now."

Snorting, I beeline to the coffee pot, where I fill the biggest mug in the cabinet with the nectar of the gods. I take a long drink and smile before meeting my friend's eyes. "I tried to resist him, but he's pretty irresistible."

The self-righteous grin falls from her face, and she shakes her head. "No."

"Yeah. Sorry. He is."

"You're *falling* for him. You're not supposed to fall for the rebound guy, Nic. You're supposed to use him for sex."

"I know! But he's . . ." I bite my lip and think of his mouth on mine, the way his hand feels when it slides over my jaw and into my hair, the pressure of his fingers at the back of my neck. "He makes me melt, Teagan. Like, toe-curling, stomach-fluttering, ice-in-the-hot-sun *melt*. And he *sees* me." I stare into my coffee. "I don't think I've ever let myself be so real with a man before. But I don't have to try to be anyone but myself to win his approval. He just wants me as I am."

"You mean he wants *Veronica*," she says softly. "Because that's still who he thinks you are, right? Unless you've told him?"

My stomach knots in shame, and I glare at her. "Aren't you the one who kept telling me to hook up with him?"

"Hook up. Not fall in love." Her shoulders sag and she shakes her head. "I don't want you getting hurt again, and sweetie, I'm sorry, but this has disaster written all over it."

"I'm going to tell him. Just not yet. I promised his sister I wouldn't say anything until after Christmas."

"And what happens then, Nic? What happens after he spends Christmas with you and you tell the man you've fallen so hard for that you've been lying?"

Love born in a lie is THE WRONG KIND OF LOVE! I wish I'd never seen that note in Elena's book. It haunts me. "I don't know, Teagan."

ETHAN

"Is everything okay, Dr. Jackson?" the postpartum nurse asks, her tone hesitant.

"Fine. Everything's fine." But it's not.

I went home at lunch, and when I checked the mail, I found five letters addressed to Nic Maddox. All with preschool names on the return address label. The preschool addresses were from all over the country—from Seattle to Miami, with the closest in Indianapolis.

She's looking for a job. She's really going to leave.

I felt like I'd been flying high for four days, but when I pulled those letters from my mailbox, I crashed down hard.

"Good," the nurse says, smiling. "I think someone wants to talk to you." She points behind me.

"Dr. Jackson, may I speak with you privately for a moment?"

I slide the chart I was looking at back into the nurse's station and turn to Dr. Weir. She nods to an empty patient room, then steps into it without waiting for my response. *Fuck.* My shit day is about to get shittier.

The nurse who's sitting at the computer by me bites her lip and averts her eyes. That's a small community hospital for you. Dr. Weir and I were sleeping together six months ago, and now the whole staff titters when we so much as speak to each other. They're going to love it if we go in that room together.

Not only do I not want to speak with Kyrstie alone about anything other than our patients, I also don't want to fire up the hospital rumor mill about what is or isn't between us. Especially not while I'm getting closer to Nic. *Who might be leaving. Who might have a job offer waiting for her.*

I follow Kyrstie into the room. She'll just make a scene if I decline.

She closes the door behind me, folds her arms, and leans against it, narrowing in on me with those cold blue eyes. "I heard your new nanny didn't waste much time working her way into your bed."

Anger rushes through my blood. "Jesus, Kyrstie. You just cut right to the gossip, don't you?"

Her lips twist into a smirk. "I'm not gossiping. I'm looking out for a friend."

She isn't looking out for me. She's looking for an angle.

We used to be friends, but we started sleeping together as two lonely adults who both had reasons why we didn't want romantic relationships—or at least I thought we were on the same page, until she tried to remove my wife's belongings from my house without my permission. I ended it that day, and she still hasn't forgiven me. "My relationship with Nic is none of your business."

"Hmm." She twirls a lock of hair around her finger. "It's your family's business, though. She sure found her place with them quickly. I wouldn't imagine just any nanny would be welcome for holidays at the cabin. Unless she's sucking your dick, that is."

I glare at her. She was so pissed that she wasn't invited to Memorial Day weekend at the family cabin. That should have been my first hint that she was looking for more than she said she was. "Back off, Kyrstie. My family's affairs have nothing to do with you."

"Well, maybe I'm wrong about her. I just saw something I thought you might want to know."

My gut pitches. Last time Kyrstie "saw something," I found out my wife was cheating on me with my best friend. Hell, maybe even then she was just trying to carve out a place in my life.

Don't think about that shit.

"It's your call," she says. "I'll walk out of this room right now if you want me to."

I don't want to ask, but knowing she has information about Nic will make me crazy if I don't get it now. Kyrstie's manipulative and cold, but she's not a liar. "What?"

She doesn't try to hold back her smile. She fucking *beams* at me. "Turns out little Miss Veronica Maddox has an appointment with my office next week."

I frown. "What the fuck do I care where she gets her yearly pap?"

Kyrstie wags a finger at me. "Not a pap visit. A *prenatal* visit."

I grunt. "That's ridiculous."

She arches a brow. "Is it? Don't you think it's convenient that she"—she makes air quotes—"'didn't know' who you were and fucked you the night before she moved in with you?"

We didn't sleep together that night, but I know everyone who was at the bar thinks we did. We were locked in the bathroom together, went home together. But we didn't sleep together until a week ago. Even if that first time had resulted in a pregnancy, it would be too soon for her to know. But that doesn't mean she couldn't have been pregnant when she came to town.

"I like the way you look at me. You make me feel sexy and wanted."

"Who made you feel like you weren't?"

"A mistake."

Was her fiancé a mistake because he got her sister pregnant? Or was he a mistake because she was pregnant too?

She was drinking that night though—drinking *a lot.* Sure, there are some young women who don't care enough to abstain when they're expecting, but Nic is far too conscientious for that.

"See?" Kyrstie says. "She's not who you think. Are you ready to play daddy to another man's baby?"

Other than a few sips of wine on her birthday, Nic hasn't had a drink since the night we met. Could it be she didn't know she was pregnant when she came to town? Maybe she recently found out and that's why she's so determined to leave in February—because she *doesn't* want me to feel trapped. "When did she make the appointment?"

Kyrstie rolls her eyes. "You think I'm answering phones now? Who cares? She's pregnant and she's already made her way into your bed and your house. Somebody's looking for a baby daddy, and she's got her eye on you."

God. It makes sense. And I'm fucking relieved, because I can handle this, and now that I know her secret, I can tell her and she can stay. She doesn't have to move across the country to take a new job.

It would be just like Nic to keep this from me just so I wouldn't feel obligated to care for her child.

"I have secrets, Ethan. There are reasons I can't stay."

"There are things you don't know about me. Things that might change the way you feel."

I cover my mouth, but Kyrstie must see my smile, because she gasps. "No. Please tell me you're not falling for this and thinking the baby's yours."

I shake my head. "It's not mine. But it doesn't matter." I'm grinning outright now. "When you love someone, it doesn't matter."

I look at my watch. I'm late to meet Lilly, Teagan, and Nic at the ice festival. *My Nic. Pregnant Nic.* I can't wait to see her. I can't wait to tell her she doesn't need to leave, and that a baby doesn't change anything.

Chapter THIRTY-ONE

ETHAN

I'm late, and the ice festival is packed. I only left the hospital a few minutes later than I expected, but parking was a nightmare, and by the time I found a spot three blocks away, I had a text from Nic asking if I was going to be able to make it. I'm grateful that she understands the reality of my job, but I hate that she thought I might bail on her—tonight or after I found out about the baby.

I can't wait to tell her I know. I can't wait to prove she can count on me to stand by her. But first, I want her to experience a Jackson Harbor tradition—the ice festival. I grew up seeing ice sculptures every winter, so I probably take them for granted. I'm already smiling as I imagine watching Lilly and Nic take in the different pieces of art.

I see Nic across the square. Her hair's down her back in the big curls she puts it in sometimes, and she's standing in front of an ice sculpture of Olaf from *Frozen*. I don't see Teagan or Lilly, so they must be somewhere else together.

Nic's turned away from me, and I slide my arms around her from behind and nuzzle her neck.

She stiffens, and I immediately drop my arms and step back. "Shit. I'm sorry. I thought you were—"

The woman turns to me, her brow wrinkled in confusion, her lips twisted in a tense smile. Her shoulders drop when she meets my eyes. "Ethan Jackson?"

I can only blink at her. She looks exactly like Nic, but she's not. I know she's not. She felt wrong in my arms. She smelled different. And even though her face looks just like Nic's, there's something about her that's just . . . *not Nic.*

She offers a hand. "It's so good to meet you! I recognize you from your picture. I'm Nic's twin sister."

My breath leaves me in a rush. Of course. She said she had an identical twin sister—the one who's pregnant with the ex's baby. I guess I wasn't prepared for how identical . . . or how *different*, oddly. I take her hand. "Ethan Jackson." I shake my head. "Sorry about that. From back there, I thought you were Nic."

She laughs. "It happens all the time. And I mean *all* the time. Mom can't even tell us apart. Gosh, it's great to finally meet you. I'm just so sorry about what happened, but I appreciate you working with Nic."

What happened? Is she talking about the wedding? Why is she apologizing to me for stealing Nic's fiancé? Fuck, if anything, *I* should thank *her*. "I'm sorry. What do you mean?"

Her cheeks flush a brighter pink. Just like Nic's do when she's embarrassed. But the pink in this woman's cheeks isn't nearly as pretty. "I didn't mean to leave you in the lurch. I'm just glad Nic could fill in while your mom took her trip."

She's not making sense, but given her history with Nic, I'm not interested in sitting down for a heart-to-heart anyway, so I don't question her nonsense. "Yeah, it's been great having Nic. She's . . ." Over the woman's shoulder, I spot Nic in line at the Ooh La La! concession stand with Lilly at her side. She's bundled up properly for once, a hat covering her head and a scarf wrapped around her neck. Lilly reaches up to take her hand, and they smile at each other.

My heart squeezes, but I force my attention back to the sister. "I'm sorry. Remind me of your name again?"

She shakes her head in amusement. "I'm Veronica."

"You're not Veronica." Is this woman crazy? She already stole Nic's fiancé but is she trying to steal Nic's identity now, too?

"I'm Veronica Maddox, Nicole's sister. The one who was originally supposed to be your nanny?"

"When we were in seventh grade, she hated her teacher and wanted to switch places at school. I agreed to do it because she'd been in trouble so many times I was afraid they'd send her away if she kept it up."

"You could really pull that off?"

"We're identical. No one ever suspected."

She tilts her head to the side. "Ethan? Are you okay?"

NICOLE

"Three peppermint hot chocolates." The barista hands our cups over the counter.

"Come to me, you sugary goodness," Teagan says, taking them from her hands while I pay. She gives Lilly hers, and Lilly squeals happily and takes her first sip. I dump my change in the tip jar and snag my drink from Teagan before she can get any ideas and double-fist it.

I take a sip, and Teagan says, "I thought that was for Ethan."

"He's running late, and he won't mind sharing with me."

"You two are ridiculously cute." She lowers her voice. "You need to tell him."

I nod. After I talked to Teagan this morning, I decided she was right. No good will come of keeping this secret longer than necessary. I just want to talk to Kathleen and let her know why I have to come forward. "I haven't been able to reach Kathleen, and I feel like she should know before I do it."

"But you're going to." My friend looks worried. "Soon?"

I nod. "I'm in love with him, Teag. And I can't do anything about it until he knows the truth." I just have to tell it without telling the truth about Kathleen's trip and why I agreed to lie in the first place. Unfortunately, with only half of the story, my lie doesn't seem noble in any way.

We weave our way through the crowd, and I spot Ethan near the Olaf sculpture, his hands in his pockets.

Lilly spots him too and rushes forward. "Daddy!" She wraps one arm around him and holds on tight to her hot chocolate with her other hand. "Nic bought me peppermint hot chocolate. She told me a story about the peppermint fairy and the ice goblin she taught to be nice and then they became friends!"

"Did she?" He turns, and his face is etched with anger. About the hot chocolate? No, he wouldn't be upset about that. But he is angry about something. His jaw is hard, and he nods a greeting to Teagan then locks his cold eyes on mine. "Nic seems to be full of stories. This afternoon, I even believed she was pregnant."

"What?" I shake my head. Is that why he's angry? Did he think I was hiding a pregnancy from him? "No, Ethan. I'm not pregnant."

"I know. Your *sister* is the one who's pregnant." He drops to his haunches to kiss Lilly's forehead.

That's when I see Veronica.

"Hi, Nic," she says, her eyes bouncing between me and Ethan. "Surprise!"

Ethan stands and points his thumb at Veronica. "I just met your sister, *Veronica*." His eyes glitter with anger as he says her name. "She was thanking me for letting her sister *Nicole* fill in for her when she couldn't be here."

"Oh, fuck," Teagan whispers beside me.

I swallow hard and step toward him. "Can we talk in private?"

His nostrils flare. "Your sister and I already talked. I don't think I have anything left to say." He takes his daughter's hand. "Lilly, baby, we have to leave. Say goodbye to Nic."

I can only stare at Veronica. It wasn't supposed to happen like this. I was supposed to tell him myself.

"Why don't you catch up with your sister?" Ethan says. "Do whatever you need to do. You can pick up your stuff after Lilly goes to bed."

"What?" Lilly looks up at me with wide eyes. "Why are you picking up your stuff, Nic?"

"It's okay, baby."

Ethan closes his eyes, pain sweeping across his face for a beat before he looks at his daughter again. "She's not leaving forever, baby. She just isn't going to sleep at our house anymore."

I look at Ethan and shake my head. "Talk to me."

"I can't," he says, but this time his voice is so low that I can barely hear him. "I don't know who you are."

"You do." My vision goes blurry, and I realize I've grabbed his hand. I'm desperate for him to listen. I feel like if he walks away, I'm going to unravel completely.

Lilly drops her cup and wraps herself around one of my legs. "You promise you won't leave, Nic?"

"You'll see Nic tomorrow," Ethan promises, his angry eyes on me. *Do you see what you've done? Do you understand what this is going to do to her?*

"We're drawing a crowd," Teagan says softly behind me.

"You lied about who you are," Ethan says. "How am I supposed to believe anything else you tell me?" He shakes his head, but when his gaze drops to Lilly, the anger falls away. He looks back at me, and my heart skips as I realize his anger was replaced with sadness. "Damn you, Nic."

Chapter THIRTY-TWO

NICOLE

"What the hell just happened?" Veronica frowns and watches Ethan walk away. "He came up to me and hugged me when he thought I was you. He *hugged* me, Nic. That isn't a typical employer-employee thing to do."

"They're in love, you idiot," Teagan says.

Veronica shakes her head. "Not again, Nicky. Come on, you were going to start a life for *yourself* in February, remember? You applied for all those jobs."

"I fell in love with him," I say helplessly.

"You always fall in love. You throw away everything for the guy and then he screws you over." Her eyes fill with tears. "You said I could come with you. You said you were going to start anew somewhere."

"It's real this time," Teagan says. "Different."

"If it's so different, can you explain why he thought you were me?"

"She had to pretend to be you to keep the job," Teagan says.

I stare at my sister. My twin. My only family and my own personal saboteur. "I was going to tell him the truth, but he needed to hear it from me. And now . . ." Now he's walked away. Now he's been betrayed. *Now I've lost him.*

"You should have told her you were coming," Teagan says to Veronica.

"What, so I could play along and pretend to be Nicole?" She shakes her head, and she doesn't look apologetic or regretful. She looks angry. "You weren't going to tell him. You're too afraid to be alone to really be yourself. And I should have known you'd be too afraid to really go after your dreams."

Teagan's chest puffs out and she steps forward. I hold my arm out. "Don't. I've got this."

"She's the fucking evil twin," Teagan mutters.

"Why are you even here?" I ask Veronica. "Shouldn't you be in Alabama, living my life?"

"Look who's talking," Veronica says.

"I'm here because of *you.* Because you slept with my fiancé and got pregnant with his baby."

"You're welcome." Veronica throws up her hands. "I've been living with Marcus for a month, and I can tell you without a doubt in my mind that ruining your wedding is the best thing I've ever done for you. He's bossy and controlling. He thinks he can tell me where to go and who to talk to. He wouldn't even let me talk to my own fucking *sister.*" Her voice cracks and a tear slides down her cheek. "I walked away. I came here because I didn't have anywhere else to go. You told me I could come with you, but you're doing it again. Throwing your life and plans away for a guy. Again."

Teagan shakes her head. "You're a real trip, girl."

"I can't talk to you right now," I tell Veronica. I wrap my arms around myself and walk away. "I need to figure out how to clean up the mess you just made of my life."

"*My life,*" she shouts after me.

ETHAN

"Nana! You're home!" Lilly rushes into the living room. There's a single light on by the recliner where my mom is sitting with her feet up.

I'm still registering the shock of Nic's twin, so I'm not as quick as my daughter to register the surprise of Mom's presence.

I follow Lilly into the living room. "What are you doing here? I thought you were supposed to be—" I stop speaking when I see her. She has a knit cap on her head, and her face is haggard. "Mom? Are you okay?"

Lilly climbs into her lap and puts a hand on either side of her nana's face. "Nana's sick, Daddy."

My mom nods. "It's true, sweetie. Nana is sick, but I'm getting better. I'm determined."

"When did you get sick? Why didn't you call?"

"I've been sick for a long while, Ethan." She lifts her eyes to mine and shakes her head. “I was wrong. Nic was right. I shouldn’t have left.”

I tense at the mention of Nic’s name. “What does Nic have to do with any of this? What’s going on?”

She puts her hand behind Lilly’s head and brings her forehead to her for a kiss. Lilly snuggles into her chest, and my mom strokes her back. “I’ve missed my grandbaby.”

“I missed you too, Nana.”

“Did you draw me those pictures?”

Lilly pulls back and nods enthusiastically. “I did!”

“Will you go get them for me?”

She jumps off her nana’s lap and rushes from the living room, her little feet moving as fast as they can up the stairs.

“I wasn’t exploring Europe,” Mom says. “I was in Germany getting cancer treatments.”

“Cancer?” My heart sinks to the floor, and it feels like I’m on one of those rides at the fair that throws you into the air far too quickly. And just like on those rides, I’m sure I’m going to crash to the ground at any moment. My dad had cancer. And then, after he fought for *months*, cancer had him. I never let myself imagine my mother falling to the same fate. “Why didn’t you tell us? Why did you leave?”

“Because I didn’t want my family to watch me die. I didn’t want my children to say goodbye to their mother again and again like they did with their father. I didn’t want you to see me slipping away one day at a time like you did with Elena.”

I feel like someone’s squeezing my throat, and the grip goes tighter with each word.

“I was trying to be noble,” she says. “I wanted to spare

everyone that, but especially you and Lilly."

"If you're sick, you should be at home."

She nods. "Yes. Nic convinced me of that. Eventually."

"Nic *knew*?" Anger shoots through my blood, and I welcome it. Anger is so much easier to cope with than this fucking awful helplessness. "You told *her*?"

"Out of necessity, yes. I did."

"What else was she keeping from me? Did she lie about everything?" I tear my hands through my hair and pace the living room. I've already had my guts ripped out today and now this.

"Don't be so dramatic, Ethan."

"She's not who we think, Mom."

"I know very well that Nic isn't Veronica," she says. "But she only lied because I asked her to." She shakes her head. "I begged her, actually. She didn't want to pretend to be her sister, but a sick old lady asked her a favor, and she couldn't refuse."

I shake my head, but she doesn't take back the words, and my denial does nothing to ease the clawing panic in my throat. What the hell is happening? "You asked her to lie? Why would you do that? Why would you lie to *me*?"

"Her sister didn't show—too busy running off with Nic's fiancé. I did what I thought I had to do at the time."

"That's ridiculous." The whole day's been too much. The letters from prospective employers, the bombshell from Kyrstie, meeting Nic's twin, and now Mom's cancer? This has to be some sort of nightmare. "You should have told us the truth. And Nic should have too."

When Mom brings her eyes to mine, they're hard. "We all do what we think we need to in order to protect those we love more than ourselves. Like you with Lilly and the story you tell everyone about Elena's heart attack. Lies aren't always evil. Sometimes they're necessary."

I stare at her, my eyes cloudy with tears as I try to process everything. *My mother is dying. Nic only lied because she had to. My mother knows Elena committed suicide.*

"I've got them, Nana!" Lilly shouts, racing back down the stairs.

Mom gives me one last pointed look before she pastes on a smile for Lilly. "I want to look at them one at a time, and I want you to tell me everything I missed."

Chapter THIRTY-THREE

NICOLE

I do as he asked and wait until after Lilly's bedtime before going to the house, but when I go to the front door, I'm not sure if I'm supposed to knock or use my key. Ethan pulls it open before I can decide.

I step inside. My duffel bag is sitting in the foyer, bursting at the seams, and Ethan is walking away from me.

I follow him into his office, where he's going through a stack of papers. Résumés for my replacement?

"Ethan," I say softly.

His gaze flicks up to mine before dropping back to the stack of papers. "I know this is the part where we're supposed to have the big blowout fight, but I think I'll pass." He keeps his head down. "Just take your bag and go. But try to do it quietly. Mom's home and she's sleeping in the living room."

My heart lifts and I actually smile—something I would have believed impossible seconds ago. "Your mom's home?"

"She returned tonight." His nostrils flare. "She's very sick, but apparently you already know that."

His anger feels like a knife in the gut. "Ethan, I couldn't tell you. I'm sorry. It was her secret."

His gaze snaps to mine. "And what about your name? What was keeping you from telling me that?"

"I—"

He holds up a hand and shakes his head. "Don't. Please. Forget I asked."

All this time, I've been clinging to the idea of him understanding my lie if he just knew *why* I did it. But he knows and he's still so angry.

"If you can still do afternoons with Lilly, that would be great. She would—" He swallows, and his jaw hardens. "It would make this transition easier for her."

"Of course I will. Anything for her."

He nods sharply. "Great. Shay's agreed to move in temporarily to do overnights and mornings until I figure out a long-term solution. Obviously, Mom can't do it."

"Ethan, I'm sorry. I didn't want to lie, but . . ."

"But you did." He doesn't lift his head to meet my eyes. "You lied about who you are, and you lied about why you were here. And when you knew I might never see my own mother again, you lied and pretended she was traveling Europe."

His words feel like the cruelest insult, and I'm disgusted with myself because they're nothing but the truth.

He drops the stack of papers onto his desk and turns to me.

He looks so damn tired. Back are the sad eyes of the stranger I met at the bar. *I did that.*

"I'm not sorry that I lied to you," I say, "because without that lie, you wouldn't have let me in the door. Living here and loving you and Lilly has been the best month of my life. I'm only sorry I didn't tell you the truth sooner." I reach out and press my palm to his chest, half expecting him to sweep it away. When he doesn't, I close my eyes and take a moment to memorize the feel of his pounding heart under my hand. "And I'm sorry Elena hurt you so badly that you don't believe love is worth fighting for."

"That's just it, Nic. She did hurt me. She hurt me every fucking day that she pretended our marriage was great just to hide from the fact that it wasn't, and she hurt me every fucking day that she hated me for accepting that lie. I've lived a life of half-truths before. I can't go there again. I can't let my house be a prison again. I've fought for honesty and believed love could overcome anything."

I squeeze my eyes shut, as if not looking at him could make this hurt less. "I still believe it can."

"Did love overcome when your sister fucked a guy you were supposed to marry?"

My eyes fly open. I'm ready to defend myself. To lash out and fight for this.

But there's no fight in his eyes. Only sadness and defeat, and I know it's over. It doesn't matter how much I love him or how much I want to make this work. He thinks I'm a stranger now.

"You weren't going to tell him. You're too afraid to be alone to really be yourself."

Veronica's words stung, because she spoke my biggest fear.

Because I'm terrified she's right. Every single relationship, I've tried to be someone I'm not. I didn't think *Nicole* was enough. I told myself this time was different, but was it? I could have told him the truth that first day or a million times after, and I didn't. I was afraid he'd push me away. I wasn't afraid of the lie but of the truth. I was afraid that I wasn't enough. I never have been before.

"Goodbye, Ethan."

He looks away. "Goodbye, Nicole."

ETHAN

"You're the biggest idiot I ever met," my loving sister tells me.

I take a sip of my bourbon, but I'm so low that even the idea of drowning my misery doesn't appeal to me.

Nic took her things and walked out of my house two days ago. I thought I'd feel better when she was gone. I thought the burden of her lies would be lifted and I could start moving on. Instead, I feel worse. Instead, I feel like I made the biggest fucking mistake of my life.

"You're probably right," I mutter.

"Mom told you that Nic lied as a favor to her, right?" Shay says. She walks across the living room and stands in front of me. She folds her arms and gives me her best teacher glare. "She told you Nic didn't want to lie?"

I close my eyes, uninterested in taking in my sister's judgmental glare or in having this conversation *again*. "She told me."

"And *I'm* telling you that I asked her to wait until after Christmas before telling you the truth."

"I heard you the first three times."

"And you're still not going after her? What the hell is wrong with you?"

I press my head into the back of the couch and try to figure out how to answer Shay's question. It shouldn't be so hard, since it's the same question I've been asking myself for the last forty-eight hours. "It's not that she lied. It's that she didn't admit to the lie."

She sinks onto the cushion next to me and takes a deep breath. "I'm trying to be patient, but you're going to have to explain what the hell that means."

"It means that when I found out she wasn't Veronica, I realized she always planned to leave, and I panicked." I roll my head to the side to look at my sister. Pity is etched all over her face. "The months after Elena died are just a blur to me. I was always focused on the next thing that needed doing. One foot in front of the other until the hole in my chest wasn't so raw."

"I know, Eth. But you did it. And you *can* love again. I wasn't sure you could, but I saw it with my own eyes with Nic. We all saw it."

"I don't think I could survive it again, so I made her leave before she could do it herself."

Shay sighs. "Now that's just dumb."

I huff—an empty attempt at humor I don't feel. "Yeah. I know."

"Does your wimpy little heart hurt any less since you did it yourself?"

I close my eyes. "You're a bitch."

"I know." She grabs my hand and squeezes it. "You're an idiot."

"I know."

Chapter THIRTY-FOUR

NICOLE

I'm sleeping on Teagan's couch, and wake to a knock on the door.

"Nic? It's Ethan. Please open the door."

I push aside my blankets and climb off the couch, rubbing my eyes as I head to the door. Through the peephole, I spot Ethan standing in the soft glow of the corridor lights. I pull open the door, but not all the way. "Is everything okay?"

He rakes his gaze over me, and I wonder what he sees. My puffy eyes? My mismatched pajamas? The wine stain on my shirt? "No," he whispers. "Nothing's okay. Can we talk?"

I shake my head. "I don't think we should."

He winces. "I'm sorry."

"For what? For being angry that I lied about who I was?" I fold my arms and fight back a shiver. "I'm pretty sure I deserved that."

"No, for pushing you away before you had the chance to explain. I panicked, Nic. I was hurt and scared and I panicked, but I want you to come home."

Home. The word makes my eyes prick with tears, but I swallow them back. "Maybe you were doing the right thing then and you're panicking now." I shake my head. "Maybe we're both afraid to be alone."

"I've never been afraid to be alone before."

"Really? Is that why you've kept your dead wife in your house for three years?" When he winces, I want to touch him, but I don't let myself. "Your wife has a book on her bedside table. I opened it my first day there and saw a note scribbled in the margins that said that love born of lies is the wrong kind of love. She was right."

"Don't say that."

I stare over his shoulder. It hurts too much to look him in the eye. He sent me away two days ago. I've had two days to dwell on my heartache and think about everything that went wrong. I've had two days to realize that I'm less afraid to be alone now than I've ever been in my life. Jackson Harbor gave me that. *Ethan* gave me that.

"Your name has nothing to do with how we feel about each other," he says.

"But it had a lot to do with how I felt about myself. If I was Veronica, I had her education, her confidence. Nicole would never have told you off about calling her an easy screw, but Veronica wouldn't have hesitated. I've been in relationship after relationship where I'm not quite myself. I'm pretending to be someone better. Someone who has more to offer. I don't even know who I am, and I came here looking and fell into another lie."

"You don't need to find yourself. I can see exactly who you are."

"I'm not sure that's true."

"Nic?" When I shift my gaze to meet his, he steps forward and brushes his lips over mine. I want to throw myself into his arms, to make the kiss longer, but I don't allow myself. "The preschool letters . . ." He swallows and draws in a ragged breath. "Are you leaving? Did you find a job?"

"I haven't accepted anything."

"You don't have to leave. Tell me what you need from me."

I shrug and shake my head. "Space. Time. And then I don't know."

"Okay." He closes his eyes and leans his forehead against mine. "It's yours."

Then he pulls away and leaves. I have to bite back a sob at the gnawing ache of him taking my heart with him. Like I told Kathleen on the phone when I begged her to come home, when love is real, it *hurts* to lose.

I stumble back to the couch and collapse into a heap of tears.

"What the hell was that?" Veronica asks from the hallway.

I tense and swipe at my cheeks. The sound of my sister's voice still makes me angry. We're both staying at Teagan's, but I haven't managed a civil conversation with her. "What was *what*?"

She sinks onto the couch beside me and rubs my back. "What was that bullshit about you wanting space? You're in love with him."

I grab a tissue off the end table and wipe away my tears. "You're the last person I want to talk to about my love life, V."

"Because I slept with Marcus?"

"For starters."

"I'm the one you *should* listen to. You already hate me, so I don't have anything to lose."

I turn to her but I can't make out her features in the darkness. "I don't hate you."

"Well, you should. What I did was *loathsome.* I had excuses. So many I made myself sick with them. But none of them matter. They're all bullshit. I'm so sorry."

I close my eyes. I'm so tired of *everything.* "I'm glad I didn't marry Marcus. It wasn't about losing him. It was about losing you."

"You didn't lose me," she whispers. "You can't. I love you too much. Nicky and Ronnie against the world, remember?"

"But you gave me up for him." The words don't even sound pained. Just flat and matter-of-fact.

"I was an idiot. Marcus . . . he told me I made him believe in miracles. He told me I filled a hole he never thought could be filled."

I sigh. Marcus used those lines on me too. I could tell Veronica that, but it would only add to her embarrassment. I don't want to be cruel, and I'm too tired for more drama.

"You know what's ridiculous?" When she speaks again, her voice is quieter. "He told me he only went through with the wedding because *I* didn't want you to be hurt. He really made me believe he was marrying you *for me.*"

"He's a world-class douchebag, Ronnie."

She chuckles. "God. He really is. But Ethan isn't. He's the real deal, isn't he?"

"I think so." I grab my blanket and hold it to my chest, releasing a long breath. "I just wish I believed I was enough for him."

"You are, you silly, silly girl. You're more than enough. I'm sorry about what I said when I got here—about you pretending to be me because you were too afraid to be yourself."

"Maybe it was true."

"I doubt it. That was uncalled for. I know you, though, Nic, and when I saw that you'd thrown yourself into another relationship, I figured it was the same old thing. But I can see it's different with him. He's the one."

"If that's true, then why did I just send him away?"

She leans her head against my shoulder, and my heart swells at the simple contact. I missed my sister. "You sent him away because you don't need him. You want him. The difference is how I know he's the one."

ETHAN

"I thought Veronica Maddox was *your* patient." I glare at the chart in my hand as I hold the phone to my ear. Any day that requires me to call Kyrstie is not what I would consider a good day, but I'm at my office and was just handed a chart for Veronica Maddox and told she's waiting in room two.

"She called and requested to be switched to you," Kyrstie says with an irritated sigh. "Did you want my staff to argue with her?"

I set my jaw and take a deep breath. "Of course not. Never mind."

"Ethan, wait," she says when I'm about to hang up. "Hear me out for a minute?"

I lean back in my office chair and close my eyes. "Sure. Why not?"

"Veronica is the sister of your nanny, right? She's the sister of the girl you're in love with?"

I pinch the bridge of my nose. "Do I want to know how you know any of this?"

"You know how information spreads in this town." I can hear her clicking her pen—a typical Kyrstie nervous habit. *Click-click. Click.* "If the sister wants you to be her doctor, see if she can help you. Maybe there's still hope for you and Nic."

"And now I'm supposed to believe you care about my happiness with another woman?"

Click-click. Click. "Well, it's true whether you believe it or not. Just because I didn't want to see you trapped by some girl looking for a meal ticket doesn't mean I don't want to see you *happy.* I always had your best intentions at heart, whether you believe that or not."

I blink and straighten in my chair. There's a good chance I underestimated Kyrstie. "I appreciate that, but listen, I have a patient waiting for me."

"Go get her, Ethan."

I hang up the phone, grab my chart, and go into exam room two.

"Good afternoon, Ms. Maddox. How are you today?" I look up from my clipboard and do a double take when I realize Veronica isn't here alone and I recognize her companion. "What are you doing here, Teagan?"

"She needed a doctor's opinion on something," Veronica says.

I fold my arms. "What's that?"

"You're a fucking troll who needs to get over himself and go after the girl," Teagan says.

"For which part of that did you need my opinion?"

"None of that. Those are the facts. The *symptoms*, if you will. The question is, should I sit here and try to talk some sense into you, or should I just kick you in the nuts?"

I lean back against the counter and study Nic's friend.

"The latter probably wouldn't change the facts at all," Veronica chimes in, "but it would feel amazing."

My gaze shifts between the two women, and I shrug. "I probably deserve the kick in the nuts, but you don't need to talk sense into me. I already know I'm an idiot who threw away the best thing that ever happened to him."

Veronica's shoulders sag. "Does that mean I don't get to give my big speech about how you will never—and I mean *never*—find another woman half as good as my sister?"

"I fucked up. She never wanted a relationship, and she really doesn't want me. I'm trying to respect that." *Even if every second I don't go after her hurts like hell.*

"Respect . . . what?" Teagan sputters. "Oh my God, I thought you had some balls in those pants."

I sigh. "Fine. You two want to help? I'm working on something and I could use some extra hands."

Veronica smiles slowly. "That's more like it. What do you have in mind?"

"I'm cleaning out some closets at home. You two up for it?"

Chapter THIRTY-FIVE

NICOLE

"Did you know Marcus calls his penis *Henry*?" Veronica asks.

Teagan coughs on her wine, and I snort. "Don't remind me."

We're all in Teagan's living room. Teagan and I are drinking wine, and Veronica's drinking sparkling apple juice. Honestly, Veronica's lucky Teagan even let her in the door that first day, but she managed to plead her case, and the three of us having been living here together for the last week.

"How desperate was I to have a family that I was willing to marry him?" I ask. "Seriously, every time I fall in love, I think it's the real thing, and I'm always wrong." But I still don't think I was wrong about Ethan. It *felt* different. But I can't deny I fell into the same old patterns. Always searching for love. Always willing to sacrifice anything to have a family.

"I'll be single forever before I marry a guy who names his dick," Teagan says. "Please hold me to that."

My phone buzzes, and I look at it. Shay's texting about some plans for this weekend and who's getting Lilly when.

"You know what I miss about having your cell phone instead of mine?" Veronica asks when I put my phone down. "I miss the ego strokes. Getting random texts from all your adoring fans made me feel warm and fuzzy inside."

I roll my eyes. "What do you mean, my adoring fans?"

"You know, all the people you've bent over backward for over the years. Everyone loves Nicole and her big heart."

"Okay, Grinch," Teagan says. "Can you blame them?"

"Of course not. It was legit *nice* to see what it was like. But I'm back to being me, and that's kind of nice too." She rubs her belly. "Not sure what I'm doing about this, though."

"You'll be fine," I say. "We'll find you a job and an apartment, and I'll help with the baby as much as I can."

"I'll help too," Teagan says. "You just can't live here and cramp my style."

Veronica's eyes water. "I don't deserve you two."

"Those are the truest words that have ever passed your lips," Teagan says.

I take my sister's hand and squeeze. "Even the Grinch needs a family."

"Let's get that homework out, Lil," I call from the kitchen. "We need to get it done if you want to watch the Christmas special at seven."

"Okay," she calls from upstairs. "I'm on my way."

I dig through the pantry to find a snack. I find some crackers and grab the cheese from the fridge. Shay's been staying here since I moved out, and she's awesome, but not the cook or baker I am.

When Ethan first asked if I'd be willing to do afternoons at the house with Lilly, I agreed but wasn't sure I wanted to. I mean, I definitely wanted to see Lilly, but I thought being in Ethan's house might just be too hard. It turns out that girl makes even a little heartache totally worthwhile, and it's been working. I'm grateful for that. It was bad enough to deal with my own broken heart; I didn't want to be responsible for Lilly's, too.

"I have to show you something *so special*," Lilly says. She races into the kitchen.

"I thought we were doing homework?"

"We are, but first I want you to see . . ." She reaches into her pocket and pulls out a necklace. "My beautiful necklace." The chain has a silver charm that looks like a mother carrying a baby. "Isn't it pretty?" she asks. "It was my mommy's."

"Yeah, baby. It's gorgeous."

"I have a whole box now of stuff that was Mommy's." She tugs on her scarf. "This was hers too. And the blanket on my bed. Daddy let me go through her stuff and choose what I wanted to keep. Since she isn't here anymore, he's donating the rest, but he wanted me to have some keepsakes first. This is one of them."

"I'm so glad you have those things," I tell her. And I truly am. My heart swells with love for Lilly and pride for the man I love. I know it wasn't easy for him to take this step. "You treat them with care, okay?"

"I will. But Nicky, I need to ask you a favor before we do homework."

I laugh. It's always *one more thing* before homework. "What's that?"

"Can you take me to the ice-skating rink at the lighthouse tomorrow night? Daddy usually takes me, but he has a date."

I open my mouth to reply, but I can't for a minute. It feels like someone has their fist in my gut. *He has a date. And he's finally getting rid of his wife's things.* "Of course I'll take you, Lil."

"Really? Oh, you're gonna love it so much. They turn the street where *cars drive* into a skating rink, and they have music and there are Christmas lights. It's really the best."

"I can't wait." I mean it. I love my time with Lilly, and I love Jackson Harbor. Instead of accepting a job hundreds of miles away, I've put in applications at all the preschools in the area. This is where I want to stay.

I'm sure tomorrow night will be amazing, but right now, I'm trying to get around Ethan having a date and clearing out his wife's things.

It's not that I wanted the traces of Ethan's wife to be washed out of the house, but I thought he might better be able to move on if he didn't keep her things right where she'd need them if she suddenly came back from the dead.

Maybe that means he's ready to move on now. Maybe I at least did that for him.

Chapter THIRTY-SIX

ETHAN

The weekend before Christmas every year, Jackson Harbor closes part of Lakeshore Drive and turns the street in front of the lighthouse into an ice-skating rink. Lilly likes to go after dark. The big houses along the water are decorated for Christmas and the lights sparkle on the ice. She says she feels like a fairy princess skating in the moonlight.

This year, when I suggested Nic could take her, she squealed with delight. I knew Nic wouldn't deny her when she asked. So that brings me here, to the edge of the skating rink, watching the two girls who own me, heart and soul, skate hand in hand.

It's not long before Lilly spots me and drags Nic in my direction. "Daddy!" she says, launching herself at me across the ice. "How was your day?"

I stoop to my haunches and wrap her in a hug. "It was a good day, Lillypad. How was yours?"

Her eyes go big, and she grins. "It's about to get better," she whispers.

I pinch her nose and swallow hard. "I hope so." I stand up to greet Nic. "How are you?"

She dodges my gaze and pastes on one of her obligatory smiles. "Fine. I hope I'm not ruining your plans. Lilly said you had a date, but I didn't realize you'd be here."

I shrug. "It's not like you're in my way."

She swallows. "Right."

"I saw your sister at the clinic again today." I tuck my hands into my pockets. "So, you two made up?"

She shrugs and turns to watch Lilly, who's returned to skating circles on the ice. "She's the only family I have."

"That's not true." My voice is husky. "You have my mom and Lilly; you have my brothers and Shay." *You have me.* "They might not be your blood, Nic, but they are your family. They will be regardless of what's between you and me." I swallow hard. "And regardless of where you live."

She still doesn't meet my eyes as she speaks. "You have no idea how lucky you are to have your family. I know it's a cliché to say, but they're amazing."

My brothers and Shay and I have had our own issues, but there's a reason we've all settled down in Jackson Harbor when jobs could have pulled us all over the country. "I don't take them for granted."

"Good." She closes her eyes for a beat, and then finally looks at me. "Thank you, Ethan. I mean it. I think it's good that you let Lilly go through her mother's things. I'm sure it wasn't easy to let go of the rest either."

"It was time. Past time, really."

She nods then looks back to the ice, desperate to get away from me, as always. "Have a good time tonight."

After she skates away, my sister comes to stand by my side. "Are you ready to do this thing?" she asks me.

I nod. "I'm ready."

"You look like you want to throw up."

"That's because I'm afraid she's going to reject me. Again."

"She won't." She smacks me on the back. "You've got this, brother."

"Thanks, sis." I take a breath and walk out to the lighthouse, where I slowly climb up to the top.

NICOLE

"Nicky!" Lilly shouts, wrapping her arms around my legs. "Will you climb to the top of the lighthouse with me?"

I turn in that direction and frown. "I don't know, sweetie. It's late. Are we allowed up there after dark?"

"Sure we are! Daddy takes me every year so I can see the Christmas lights. And all the people ice skating look like miniature dolls." She tugs on my hand, a movement that makes us both wobble in our ice skates. "Please, please, please?"

"Of course. That sounds great." I really don't know that I'm capable of telling that sweet face no.

We change out of our ice skates and head to the lighthouse. As I slowly start to climb the stairs, Lilly races past me. "Come on! Don't be a slowpoke now!"

"Looks like I'll get my workout in today after all," I say with a laugh, picking up the pace.

Her enthusiasm is contagious, and I chase her up the spiral staircase. There's a door at the top, and Lilly stops in front of it. "I need to tell you something important."

"I thought we were going to look out the windows at the Christmas lights," I remind her.

She nods and holds up a finger. "Whatever happens in there, you and me are always gonna love each other. Daddy promised. Me and Nic, to the moon and back."

My heart fills so completely that it shoves all the tension from my limbs. "Of course, Lil. You'll always be my girl."

She grins. "To the moon and back?"

"To the moon and back." *This. Girl.* "Can we go in now?"

"Sure thing," she says. She swings the door open, and Ethan's standing inside. He's not staring out the windows at the lights or out across the water. He's looking right at us, as if he's been waiting the whole time.

I bite my bottom lip. "What are you doing up here? I thought you had a date."

He shrugs. "It might have been a little premature to call it a date. I haven't asked the girl yet, and between you and me, she's *way* out of my league."

Behind me, Lilly giggles, and I hear Shay call her name from below. She must have followed us at least partway up the stairs. "Come on, Lil. Leave your daddy and Nicole to talk."

Lilly waves to us and scurries away, pulling the door shut behind her.

"Do you remember the night we met?" Ethan asks.

"Yes," I manage. "Of course."

"You didn't want to exchange names at all. And when I pointed out that I already had your name, you quoted *Romeo and Juliet.*"

I swallow the emotion building in my throat. I can't get ahead of myself and assume this is something it isn't. "I was pretty tipsy."

"I liked it," he says. "I feel like fate planted us there that night. As if we were destined to meet in that moment—when you needed to feel beautiful because Marcus had broken your heart, and when I didn't know enough about you to realize you could so easily steal mine." He reaches into his pockets and pulls out a stack of papers. "I've been cleaning the house and finding all these notes Elena left behind. She liked her notes and she liked her platitudes. When she was having a bad time and was especially angry with me for . . . whatever . . . she used love notes like Band-Aids. She left them for me everywhere, and sometimes they were her words and sometimes they were quotes."

"I found some while I was staying there," I admit. "I never knew what I should do with them."

He smiles. "I guess that makes two of us. I always left them where I found them. After all, you shouldn't pull off the bandage when the wound hasn't healed." He takes a step toward me, and I stiffen—not because I don't want him close, but because I do. So badly. I've missed him. I've thought of a thousand ways to throw myself at him—crawling into his bed, showing up at his office, joining his gym, anything that would put us in the same room again. "After you left, I realized I was done grieving for my wife and it was time to gather up the notes, time to take off the bandages. As I did, I realized something."

"What's that?"

"I like to think fate got us in Jake's bar together that night. That was your wedding night, right?"

I nod. "Yeah."

"You could have been with Marcus or even crying in your bed at home, but instead you followed an unlikely path that brought you to me. Forgive me for saying so, but I'm fucking *grateful* your sister screwed around with your fiancé. Because if she hadn't, you wouldn't have changed my whole world. You came here and taught me joy. You freed me from grief I didn't believe I'd ever escape."

I hold my breath and wrap my arms around myself so I don't go to him. He's clearly planned this out, and I don't want to miss anything he has to say. Not a single word.

"So many stars had to align to bring you to me. More had to align to get a stubborn-ass grump to open his heart. But they did." He hands me three slips of paper. "I think maybe my wife played a part in that."

"What are these?"

"Notes I found in Elena's bedside table."

I read them in order, immediately recognizing the loopy script as Elena's.

Call me but love and I'll be new baptized.
–Romeo

I look up at Ethan. "That's what I said to you, isn't it?"

He nods, and I tuck the note on the bottom of the stack and read the next one.

Have courage to trust love one more time and always one more time.
-Maya Angelou

My eyes fill with tears as I slide it to the back and read the final note.

Ethan, never doubt your love is enough for me.
- Elena

I blink at him through my tears. "What are the chances?"

"It's like she's trying to tell me something." He draws in a big breath. "I've been spending a lot of time with your sister." When I gape at him in surprise, he laughs. "Crazy thing, though? I'm not in love with her."

I blink. "What are you talking about?"

He tucks his hands in his pockets and tilts his head to the side. "If I only fell for you because you were pretending to be her, she should be my dream girl, right?"

"Ethan—"

"No. I get it." He holds up both hands. "She's hot, I won't deny that. And she's been an amazing help getting Elena's things sorted for me." He lowers his voice. "But her blush isn't as pretty and her smile doesn't make her eyes dance. The smell of her doesn't get my gut in knots and turn me on."

I draw in a breath and it comes in shaky, as if the air itself has jagged edges. "Ethan."

"I *know* you, Nic—maybe better than you know yourself. I know how to make you laugh and how to turn you on. I know you like the same sappy books Elena did and that you take in coffee like it's oxygen." He steps forward and cups my face in his hand, wiping away a tear with his thumb. "I know that you warm up every room you're in and you love taking care of the people around you." He swallows hard. "And I know how you feel about Lilly."

"To the moon and back," I say on a ragged exhale.

"Exactly. And I know you're the kind of person who wouldn't let Lilly's asshole father keep you from doing right by her." He pauses a beat. Maybe he's waiting for me to reply, but I can't. My throat is too thick with tears. He wipes the tears from my cheeks. "I don't regret my years with Elena. I loved her, even when I did it badly. And she gave me Lilly." He shakes his head, still holding my face in his hands. "I only regret that the guilt and fear her death left in me almost made me lose you."

"You never lost me," I say, looking into his eyes. "A love like this is too big to lose."

He lowers his mouth to mine and kisses me, and I wrap my arms around him and trust love. One more time.

Epilogue

NICOLE

"It's a turkey baster," Ava says. She frowns at Teagan, who laughs so hard she nearly falls out of the booth.

Ava waves the turkey baster in the air and tries to scowl at Teagan, but her disapproval isn't very believable since she can't stop smiling. "You're a bitch."

We're sitting at the back of Jackson Brews for our biweekly girls' night out.

"I guess I should make an announcement," Ava says. She's the guest of honor tonight as the birthday girl, and her words slur just a little bit.

Tonight, it's Ava, Teagan, Veronica with her newly popped baby bump, and me. Sometimes Shay comes, and those nights are always extra special, but she couldn't make it tonight. She and Kathleen spent the day in Grand Rapids on the last of this round of chemo treatments. The woman is exhausted, but she's a fighter, and if anyone can kick cancer into submission, it's Kathleen.

"I want to hear your announcement," I say. "Spill."

"Since it's my birthday, I decided to get myself a present."

"You deserve it," Teagan says. Her words are a little slurred too. What can I say? We've been having a good time tonight.

Girls' night is the best night.

Well, next to date night. And Nic and Lilly night. And just every freaking night of my life right now. I'm in a sweet spot, and I know it. I'm enrolled in classes at the community college, falling in love with a cute little town and all its gossipy residents, slowly repairing my relationship with my sister, and believing for the first time in a long time that happiness is something I can feel rather than a mask I need to wear.

"What kind of present?" Veronica asks.

"A baby." We stare at her. "I decided I'm going to have one," she says, as if that explains everything.

"Like, immaculate conception or . . ." Veronica says.

Ava scowls at my sister. "Okay, bitch. I'm fully aware of the missing piece of this puzzle, but I'm thirty years old, and that doesn't seem to be changing anytime soon. But I couldn't conceive the entire time I was married—"

"A blessing in disguise," Teagan says.

"—so I feel like I should start trying now," Ava finishes.

"Trying . . . to get pregnant?" I bite my lip. I don't want to be a bitch, but Ava was still single last I checked.

"Yeah, 'cause who needs a dude to do that?" Veronica says.

Ava shakes her head. "Listen. I swear I'm not crazy. I've already been married and that didn't work. As nice as it would be to find a guy to spend my life with, it's not necessary. But pregnancy and a baby? That's something I want to experience." She smacks the table and grins. "I want a family, and I'm not getting any younger, so I'm making one myself."

"Good for you," Veronica says, raising her glass of water.

"I think that's great," I say. "Really, really damn brave, but great."

"So . . ." Teagan scans the bar. "Do we get to just pick from the guys at the bar or what?"

Ava rolls her eyes. "I've already talked to some sperm banks. I'm looking through donors now, but here's the deal—what if these men are crazy? There's no checkbox for that on the questionnaire. How do you know you're not putting crazy-man semen up in your business? I want to love my child, not wonder if maybe his dad had some weird rubber-glove fetish."

Teagan nods. "This seems like a reasonable concern. Because genetics."

"I'm confused," Veronica says. "You're using the sperm bank, or you're not?"

Ava sighs. "I haven't decided. Obviously, that's the easiest way to get a baby in a position like mine, but . . ." She groans. "But ever since I got this crazy-guy thought in my head, none of the profiles are good enough. I'm nervous."

Teagan shrugs. "Why not just ask for some sperm from a friend? The turkey baster works the same way if the sperm is free, you know."

Ava arches a brow. "That's a thing?"

"Sure," Teagan says. "My cousin did it. She was like you—wanted a baby, didn't want to wait—so she just asked her best friend for some sperm, and he filled a cup for her. Nine months later, *voila!* A baby of her own who she knows has no rubber-glove fetish gene."

"That would definitely be ideal, but how do you even decide who to ask?"

"Well," Veronica says, "not that I get to choose, since I already made my bad decision, but if I were you, I'd definitely go after some Jackson genes."

"They do make some good-looking boys," I say. "And they're all brains, too."

"I've been friends with the Jacksons all my life," Ava says. "Levi's probably the hottest, and he's easygoing and stuff, but I'm pretty sure that conversation would be awkward even with him." She lowers her voice. "And I think he might secretly have a thing for my friend Ellie."

"And he'd want to actually fuck you," Veronica says. She's only met Levi a couple times, but I'd say her assessment is accurate. "No turkey baster."

"Jake's your best friend, isn't he?" Teagan says. "What about him? I bet he'd do it for you."

Ava wrinkles her nose. "It's kind of weird, isn't it?"

Teagan nudges Ava's glass closer to Ava's hand. "Finish this and ask him to fill a cup for you."

"I guess it is my birthday. It can't hurt to ask, right?" She swallows hard. "Here goes nothing."

That's the moment I realize Ava is way more drunk than I realized. She doesn't hesitate. She climbs out of the booth and goes *right* up to Jake, turkey baster in one hand, empty glass in the other. He leans forward as she whispers something in his ear.

He frowns, looks at us, then back to her, and nods, then they leave the bar.

"Well, damn," Veronica says. "That was easy."

I spin on Teagan. "You know Jake has a thing for her, right?"

Teagan's eyes go wide. "He does?"

"Yes, and has his whole life. As in, he's madly in love with the woman you just sent up there to ask for his sperm."

Teagan chuckles and claps her hands. "Well, this is going to be fun, isn't it?"

I drag a hand over my face. "Girl."

"What's going on over here?"

I was so busy being mortified on Ava's behalf that I didn't even notice my insanely hot boyfriend walk into the bar.

Ethan puts his hands on the table and scans the array of mostly empty glasses in front of us. "You ladies have been busy."

"Just water for me," Veronica says.

"That was mostly Teagan and Ava," I tell him. "Though I did have one glass of Jake's new watermelon sour."

He grins. "Wild thing." He takes my hand and gives it a light tug. "We have a babysitter for another hour. Any chance I can steal you away from the girls?"

I slide out of the booth and wave to Teagan and Veronica. "Goodnight, ladies."

"You're gonna get laid, aren't you?" Veronica says.

Teagan scowls. "God, I hate you right now."

I blow them both kisses and head across the bar with Ethan, only he doesn't go to the front door. He grabs something from under the bar and leads me down the hallway to the bathroom.

"This is the ladies' room now," he announces to the line of

women, smacking the magnetic sign on the men's room. He tugs me into the other restroom and has me pinned against the wall before the occupants even have a chance to leave.

"Get a room," a girl mutters behind us.

Ethan grins at her over his shoulder, then pulls open the door to facilitate her exit. "Just did."

When the rest of the women file out of the bathroom, he closes the door and turns the bolt.

"Hi, Dr. Jackson." I grab his tie. "Did you need something from me?"

He steps back so he can look me over—from my cowboy boots to my skirt, up to my red knit sweater. "You're fucking right I do."

I release the button on his pants then slowly lower the zipper. "And do you need it *stat*?"

"How could you tell?" he asks, grinning against my mouth.

"Oh, you know, lots of experience." I take him in my palm, and he lets out a low groan.

"But not nearly enough." He kisses me harder, grinning the whole time, and I agree. I'll never get enough of this man or tire of his smiling kisses. And maybe, just maybe, I needed all the *wrongs* to find the right kind of love.

The End

Thank you for reading *The Wrong Kind of Love,* book one in The Boys of Jackson Harbor series. If you'd like to receive an email when I release a new book, please sign up for my newsletter on my website.

I hope you enjoyed this book and will consider leaving a review. Thank you for reading. It's an honor!

Author's Note

Dear Reader:

Depression is a bitch. It's a liar—telling us we're not enough, whispering insidious untruths that make us want to hide from everyone, to retreat from life itself. And it's a thief—stealing the joy from our days, and the confidence from our hearts.

I've wanted to write a book about depression for a long time, but I was worried no one would want to read it. People read romance to *escape*, not to feel sad. Then, as I wrote Nic and Ethan's story and learned more about my characters, I realized that I'd been writing my passion project without realizing it. And I'm so very glad I did.

Everyone experiences depression differently and to varying degrees. Nic's experience isn't representative of anyone's experience but her own. For some of us, it's manageable. For some, debilitating. I have a sister and a niece who have been hospitalized at different times on suicide watch, and I will *forever* be grateful they were able to admit they needed help.

I love that Nic isn't ashamed of her depression. She treats it like any other diagnosis—something she must tend to and deal with diligently, but nothing to be ashamed of. I watch my niece grow into a young woman and hope she'll be able to do the same.

If you struggle with depression or have suicidal thoughts, please know that there is help. The suicide hotline is available twenty-four hours a day at 1-800-273-8255. You are enough. You deserve all the goodness life has to offer without darkness pulling you under.

Acknowledgments

First, a big thanks to my family. Brian, thank you for believing in me and my stories and for understanding when they (inevitably) take more time to finish than I expect. I love having you by my side for this journey. To my kids, Jack and Mary, thank you for making me laugh and helping remember that there is a world outside the book. I'm so proud of you two! To my mom, dad, brothers, sisters, in-laws, aunts, uncles, various cousins and cousins-in-law, thank you for cheering me on—each in your own way.

This book is dedicated to my four brothers. They tormented me, protected me, challenged me, and entertained me. Growing up, I thought that I was the coolest kid around because I could claim those four. Still do.

I'm lucky enough to have a life full of amazing friends, too. Thanks also to my workout friends and the entire CrossFit Terre Haute crew, especially Robin, who checks up on me when I disappear too long into the writing cave and likes to remind me that taking care of myself is important too, and my coaches, Matt and Chaz. A huge thanks to Mira Lyn Kelly, who gets me like no other. I've gotten a lot of amazing things from this career, but her friendship tops the list.

To everyone who provided me feedback on this story along the way—especially Heather Carver, Samantha Leighton, Dina Littner, and Janice Owen—you're all awesome. Rhonda Edits and Lauren Clarke, thank you for the insightful line and content edits. You both push me to be a better writer and make my stories the best they can be. Thanks to Arran McNicol at Editing720 for proofreading. Clearly, it takes a village.

Thank you to the team that helped me package this book and promote it. Sarah Eirew took the gorgeous cover photo and did the design. A shout-out to my assistant Lisa Kuhne for trying to keep me in line. (It's a losing battle, but she gives it her all.) Thank you to Nina and Social Butterfly PR for organizing the release. To all of the bloggers, bookstagrammers, readers, and reviewers who help spread the word about my books, I am humbled by the time you take out of your busy lives for my stories. I can't thank you enough. You're the best.

To my agent, Dan Mandel, for believing in me and staying by my side. Thanks to you and Stefanie Diaz for getting my books into the hands of readers all over the world. Thank you for being part of my team.

Finally, a big thank-you to my fans. My biggest dream was to make a career with my writing, and I still can't believe I'm living that dream. I couldn't do it without you. You're the coolest, smartest, best readers in the world. I appreciate each and every one of you!

~Lexi

The Wrong Kind of LOVE
Playlist

"Bad at Love" by Halsey
"Use Me" by The Goo Goo Dolls
"New Rules" by Dua Lipa
"Something I Can Never Have" by Nine Inch Nails
"Stay" by Zedd feat. Alessia Cara
"1-800-273-8255" by Logic, Alessia Cara, and Khalid
"I Like Me Better" by Lauv
"One More Light" by Linkin Park
"Let You Down" by NF
"Perfect" by Ed Sheeran

Contact

I love hearing from readers. Find me on my Facebook page at www.facebook.com/lexiryanauthor, follow me on Twitter and Instagram @writerlexiryan, shoot me an email at writerlexiryan@gmail.com, or find me on my website: www.lexiryan.com